Stones Corner

Turmoil

ORLA
KELLY
PUBLISHING

Jane Buckley

This book is intended for your personal use only and is a work of fiction, but the storyline is loosely based on actual events during 'The Troubles' in the North of Ireland. The views expressed in this book 'are seen' through the eyes of the author, and while the characters are entirely fictitious, the author uses interweaving storylines to highlight how it is right for us all to try to move on from 'The Troubles' but in doing so, it's important to understand how and why they occurred taking into account the lessons, hardships and sorrows that affected our country and others.

In memory of Daddy, Charles and Brian,
sorely missed and much loved.

And to the 3,500 people who died and 50,000 who were injured as a
result of the North of Ireland's Troubles from the
1960s to the present day.

This book is dedicated to my best friend and husband, John – thank
you for your tolerance and support – and to my beautiful girls,
Mammy, Maggie, Cassie and Grandson and Granddaughter,
Charlie and Alba.

With special thanks to Lynn Curtis for her guidance and advice.

Truth, Justice, Healing, Reconciliation

Contents

Prologue

Stories were told in the barracks of the first tour of Londonderry in 1969: Operation Banner. The initial arrival of 300 troops from the 1st Battalion, Prince of Wales's Own Regiment of Yorkshire, was at first welcomed and cheered by the Catholic Nationalists. The Regiment had been brought in to relieve the fatigued Royal Ulster Constabulary (RUC), which had fought a bitter three-day battle in the Bogside area of the city following a Protestant Apprentice Boys' march that resulted in serious rioting. The RUC had resorted to using CS gas, water cannons and eventually guns but could not quell the rioting.

The Nationalist Bogsiders were jubilant and believed they'd broken the morale of the much-hated police and their auxiliary force the B Specials (known as the Protestant Army). Within an hour of the Regiment's arrival, the predominantly Protestant RUC left the chaotic scene and, naively, the British Army replaced them. Most Catholics believed the "Brits" had arrived to protect them and would be unbiased peacekeepers. Women even offered tea and biscuits to the young soldiers as they patrolled the streets in those first few peaceful weeks known as "the honeymoon period".

Operation Banner was meant to be a "limited" operation, and at first, the army was guileless and ill-prepared. They looked almost comical in riot gear previously used in Aden, complete with Arabic warnings written on the shields. Many senior Aden and Cyprus veterans treated Northern Ireland just like any other British colony. But soon they realised this "war" was different. Here it was impossible to physically identify the enemy – here everyone looked the same.

In a short space of time, the atmosphere grew more tense and dangerous. People were terrified. Nationalists, Loyalists, the RUC and the British Army, were shooting or bombing in retaliation for the many atrocities carried out by all sides. Their escalating thirst for revenge could not be sated. Each group was angry and determined to attain total victory.

A few prominent Loyalists were furious about the intrusion of the British Army. They were critical of the British Government and felt Westminster was interfering with "their" Province. The army was seen as being too "soft" on the Nationalists, making very little effort to stop them creating their no-go areas.

In time, these disillusioned views changed as the army began to escort and act as protector to the many Loyalist Orange marches and protests. The honeymoon period was over.

In February 1971, a young gunner was the first British Army fatality of the "Troubles", and in retaliation, the army introduced Operation Demetrius – or Internment Without Trial. On the first of many raids, over 300 suspected Republicans were arrested. So shoddy and out-of-date was the army's intelligence, however, that some of those listed as Republican sympathisers had, over time, died! Not one Protestant Loyalist was arrested until a year or so later. Internment proved to be a catalyst for a tidal wave of violence and protests by the furious Republicans.

In January 1972, what soon became known as "Bloody Sunday", the shooting dead by the British Army of 13 unarmed Catholic civilians (and the wounding of another 14 people, one of whom later died) took place during a Civil Rights march in Derry.

Chaos and violence continued throughout the Province, leading to Operation Motorman where the no-go Republican areas were finally dismantled by the British Army after 11 months.

The Northern Ireland Parliament was suspended, and Direct Rule was imposed by Westminster. In all, 500 people, just over half of them civilians, lost their lives in 1972. That year saw the greatest loss of life throughout the entire conflict. However, at that time, no one ever thought the bloody murders and bombings would spiral out of control and continue for decades.

Chapter One

SEPTEMBER 1972
DERRY/LONDONDERRY

They were hyper… almost manic. All day they'd sat through briefing after briefing. Finally, it was time. They agreed, enough was enough. A few secret vodka shots added to their exhilaration as they prepared to leave the barracks, all with their faces disguised by camouflage paint. Some of the men climbed into Saracens or Centurions while others went on foot, fighting to hold onto their berets as they filtered past three lit-up stationary RAF Wessex helicopters. The ear-splitting din of their whirling blades sounding as impatient for action as the men themselves. The promise of air cover was reassuring. Tonight was likely to get messy and the soldiers welcomed any backup they were offered. After Bloody Sunday and Operation Carcan – the largest British military initiative since Suez in 1956 – they'd taken shit from every direction. Tonight was payback. They were ready. Fuck, were they ever. For Queen and Country!

Warning shouts were heard as the illuminated giants – resembling monstrous dragonflies – eagerly took off, one after the other, powering through squalls of rain towards the west of the city. The remaining men and vehicles followed in haste.

Within minutes, the line of flying predators reached their destination and hovered menacingly for a moment before descending, lower and lower, upon the streets of back-to-back terraced houses. The downdraught from the whirling blades rattled doors and windows in their frames. The few working streetlights struggled to stay intact against the battering they received. Steel rubbish bins clattered and scraped over tarmac as they and their contents were blown about the pathways. Almost immediately as the racket started, the street's occupants began to wake in terror, struggling from sleep one after the other to lurch out of bed and switch on the lights.

Nineteen-year-old Caitlin McLaughlin was luckier than most, not snatched from sleep but already lying restless and awake in her single bed. Against the bitter chill in the barely heated house, she lay with her legs bent up against her chest and her arms clasped around them, shivering beneath the doubled-over blanket. She couldn't sleep for worrying about her brother Martin, wondering where he was and, more importantly, if he was safe. He'd been arrested recently and the family had heard nothing.

At first, she wasn't quite sure what was causing the commotion overhead, but quickly recognised the sound – a helicopter – and it was right above the house. The noise and the buffeting sensation became overwhelming as the roof tiles and windows shook and banged in protest. Caitlin clapped her hands over her ears against the relentless assault. Feeling dazed and disoriented, she sat up and pulled back the thin floral-print curtains to look down upon the chaotic scene in the street.

A probing searchlight shone menacingly through her window. Its beam quickly scanned up and down her bedroom walls, over her bed, and stopped when it reached her. She defiantly tightened the cardigan she wore over her nightdress as she glared challengingly at it. The light remained fixed on her for a few short moments until – as if disappointed in its find – it mercifully moved on. Caitlin could hear the frantic voices of terrified women and children screaming from the houses that backed onto their street and the sickening squeal of tyres along with male voices raised intimidatingly. Her heart hammered with fear as she watched the dimly lit road swarm with soldiers and police. Army Saracens and jeeps, lit up with powerful spotlights, sped erratically along the narrow road, stopping at random to park halfway across the pavements. Several armed men clambered out of the vehicles – some running to take cover and observe, whilst others filed purposefully towards the pebble-dashed houses. A large number of police struggled to hang on to their overexcited German Shepherd dogs, frustrated at being held back and salivating at the end of their leashes. Urgent hand signals passed back and forth between the raiders as they cautiously assessed their surroundings.

In pairs, soldiers strode up garden paths towards front doors. The street dogs barked ferociously and snapped at the heels of the darkly dressed shadows, who impatiently kicked them away, cursing. Fists hammered against unanswered doors, no sooner followed by the sounds of splintering wood and smashing glass. Loud, confident English voices cried out names from lists brandished in gauntleted hands.

Protective mothers frantically tried to bundle small children under the stairs, for fear of them being trampled underfoot or callously brushed aside by the soldiers forcefully entering their homes. They searched living rooms, kitchens and bedrooms for the men on their lists, leaving a trail of destruction in their wake. Furniture was needlessly shoved over, drawers were shaken out and cupboards emptied with the sweep of an arm or the kick of a boot. In their hallways, shocked and shaking, the women stood in nightclothes and bare feet watching the brutal violation of their homes. Some tried to soothe crying, half-asleep children or wordlessly clutched their babies to them, only to be pushed aside as the gun-wielding troopers continued their onslaught.

In house after house along the street, every light began to blaze as more and more front doors were rammed open and dazed men and women were hauled pitilessly and harshly from their beds. Many of the screaming wives attempted to snatch their men back from the aggressors but were struck aside mercilessly by batons.

By now, Caitlin was shaking with terror. This was the worst she'd ever seen. She jumped as her younger sister Tina erupted into the room, her fiery red hair bristling and freckled face tight with indignation.

"Jesus, Caitlin, you've got to come," she said indistinctly, struggling to remove the braces she wore on her teeth. "The Brits are at it again. It's another raid…there's going to be murder!"

She yanked her braces free and shoved them in the pocket of an old school blazer she'd pulled on over her pyjamas.

"The bastards are lifting loads of boys. I've just seen them grab wee Joe by the hair. They hammered him and threw him in the back of a Pig. Caitlin, Mammy's going crazy. You'd better come, she's off on one. Daddy's in bed – sure he can't get up."

"Aw, Tina, not again!" Caitlin cried – remembering the night of her brother Martin's arrest. She rubbed her eyes, still dazzled by the brilliant light, and looked around the room for something warmer to wear against the bitter cold. Seeing her father's heavy Aran jumper lying on the floor – she'd been wearing it earlier that evening – she quickly pulled her cardigan off and yanked the thick woollen jumper over her head. It reached down to her knees. Without pausing to find any shoes, she pushed Tina out of the door ahead of her.

On the landing they were met by the sight of their wide-eyed, defiant mother, who stood at the top of the staircase, supporting herself against the wall with one hand and the bannister with the other. It was clear Majella McLaughlin had been drinking again as she let go of the bannister to fumble nervously with the silver crucifix that hung around her neck. She swayed dizzily.

The women simultaneously jumped in fright at the furious knocking below, followed by a rending, smashing sound as their front door was broken down. Within seconds, two soldiers in battledress appeared at the bottom of the stairs, looking up at them from features smeared and semi-obliterated with dark paint. They started to climb the staircase as Majella screamed abuse. In the background, Caitlin could hear her father's voice raised in panic, demanding to be told what was going on. She froze.

With his leering blackened face and huge lumping boots, the lead soldier was a figure from a nightmare. The sleeves of his camouflaged

4

combat jacket were rolled up slightly, and Caitlin glimpsed a flash of red on his forearm – some sort of tattoo. He was clutching the wooden stock of his rifle close to his chest; she could see its white hand-written issue number. Below it, a baton slung ready for use on a tight green webbed belt.

Unlike his partner behind, who was tall and gangling, he was short and compact, his neck bull-like and bulging with muscle beneath a thin mesh scarf. His naturally protuberant eyes swelled with excitement. Instinctively she sensed danger and a hatred that emanated from his whole being.

Her mother stopped her abusive rant and leaned closer as he approached. With her face just inches from his, she hissed almost triumphantly: "You stupid bastard, our Martin's not here. You've already got him!"

She lashed out with the full force of her ringed hand and struck him hard on the cheek: "Get the fuck out of my house, you English bastard. Leave us alone. Fuck away off back to wherever you crawled from!"

The soldier didn't bother replying. Using his free arm, he thrust her aside, sending her spinning against the wall where she knocked her head hard. Blood gushed from the wound and streamed down the side of her face. Caitlin rushed to her and examined the injury. It was small but deep; Majella's eyes fluttered shut for a moment, and when they reopened, she had trouble focusing them as she slid down onto the floor. Caitlin knelt down and looked up to see the soldier touch his face to assess any damage. The rings had cut his cheek, and it was bleeding. He stared at the frightened women with his cruel eyes as a malicious smile crossed his face. He said nothing but shook his head in silent reproof. Immediately Caitlin knew things were going to get worse, much worse.

Her father continued to cry out as the soldiers quickly nodded to each other and removed their batons for the ready. The bleeding soldier began to search the upstairs bedrooms while the other stood waiting and watching the women carefully.

"Clear!" came a call from Caitlin's room.

Downstairs the women heard other soldiers joking and laughing. The noise was overwhelming as they worked their way through the McLaughlins' home – intentionally causing as much damage as possible. Caitlin held her mother's hand and watched the soldier continue to search and walk towards a closed door. Cautiously, he opened it and found a walk-in linen cupboard. With his back to them, he roughly searched the shelves, violently throwing the beautifully ironed linen and towels onto the floor. He then deliberately stepped on the pristine laundry, grinding his wet, muddy boots onto it. He looked at Majella and growled.

"By the way, you mad bitch, we're not here for your fucking Martin. We're here for that husband of yours, Patrick."

Caitlin stood still in amazement. He was Irish, not English! He saw her confusion and nodded his head smirking. Next, he strode into Martin's open bedroom and found its walls adorned with IRA and 1916 Irish Rising posters.

He sniggered. "Nice décor." Furiously he tore some the posters off the wall, spat on them and left the room.

Finally, he reached her parents' room, with Patrick McLaughlin inside. He'd been there since his son's arrest and could barely get out of bed without help. According to the family doctor, his heart was very weak, and his son's detention had, without doubt, worsened his condition.

The pair of soldiers made eye contact again, and this time they both entered the room. Caitlin frantically looked at her mother, who had pulled herself up from the floor to slump back against the landing wall. She was shoeless and wearing a short, well-worn nightdress that had become a little rucked up around her hips. Oblivious to her lack of underwear, she rubbed her throbbing head then stared in surprise at the blood coating her hand.

Caitlin put her hand on her mother's arm as she stared through the open bedroom door and told her reassuringly, "It's okay Mammy. I'm here. Let's get you up."

The older woman hung her head dejectedly and began to weep. Her frail body rocked back and forth. Caitlin delicately adjusted her mother's nightdress to cover her nakedness.

Loud cries and thuds began to emanate from the bedroom as Caitlin's heart beat wildly. What were they doing! She had to help daddy, but she couldn't leave her mother alone. She looked pleadingly at her sister.

"Tina! Help me quick. Help me get Mammy up!"

No chance. Tina was useless and in shock. Her head shook manically from side to side as she grasped the door frame of Martin's room as if holding on for dear life.

The loud thuds and screams continued from the bedroom until Majella grabbed Caitlin's arm, squeezed it and wailed.

"Do something, Caitlin, please! They can't hurt him, love. They can't take him too!"

Caitlin stepped into the bedroom nervously, horrified by the sight that met her eyes. Her father stood, naked and spread-eagled, against the far wall. His hands were raised high above his head, each finger separated and stretched out. He could barely stand as his fragile body shook and spasmed uncontrollably. Under normal circumstances she'd have been mortified to see his nakedness, but not now. To see him so vulnerable and degraded was truly heart-breaking. With pity and terror overwhelming her, she ran to him. However, she was violently thrown aside by the Irish soldier who, with a face like thunder, cried out angrily:

"Stand back, you stupid cunt. Don't you fucking go near him!"

He screamed at her again, holding his snarling face only inches from hers. Hatred and disgust coloured his every word.

"We'll take you too! So back off. NOW!"

Her father wailed at his captors, "Jesus Christ, get her out of here, will you!? Get her out! I don't want her to see her own father like this!" She could see tears of shame on his drawn face.

Suddenly the soldier raised his baton at Patrick and struck out at his lower back, producing a sickening crunch. He struck again, but this time on his legs. Patrick McLaughlin cried out and fell to his knees. Caitlin ran to him but was cruelly stopped as a huge hand wound itself around a hank of her hair. The pain from her torn roots was excruciating until the hand released her. She screeched in agony and fell down alongside her father. Patrick weakly reached out to comfort her in vain.

Speaking for the first time, the tall, gangly soldier pulled his partner back by one arm and cried out: "Fuck that, man! That ain't on, leave her be! We've got what we need!"

His restraining hand was pushed away as the Irishman stooped down low next to Caitlin and, holding his baton in readiness, commanded: "*Tell me*, you fucking Fenian bitch – before I give you something to cry about – who else is in the house?"

Caitlin only glowered back and said nothing.

About to strike again, his arm was stopped and held midway by his furious companion.

"I said enough, Morris! We're out of here. **NOW!**"

For a moment, it could have gone either way. Morris finally grunted before lowering his baton grudgingly.

"Okay, okay. I hear you. Fucking wimp!" He got to his feet to leave, but before he did, he stood over Caitlin and told her pointedly, "I'll find you again, sweetheart. You can count on it."

With that, he stuck his bloodied fingers in his mouth and sucked them provocatively.

Caitlin shuddered and shrank away but never took her eyes off him. She saw him removing something from a pouch and shake it open; it became a black sack-like hood that he began to place roughly over her father's head. Once more, his furious partner screeched and fought to take the hood away.

"You're going too far with this, mate. This is just too fucking far!"

Morris wasn't going to be stopped. He'd wanted to use this for ages and loved the idea of scaring the shit out of the old man.

"Like hell, it is. He fucking deserves it! Get the fuck out of my way and move. It stays on!"

Grabbing his naked prisoner, he forcefully pushed Caitlin aside and prepared to leave. Hooded and naked, Patrick could barely walk and within seconds hit his face sickeningly hard against the edge of the door. She gasped and screamed in horror.

"Dear God, he can't see where he's going. At least let him get dressed, give him some dignity! He's sick. Please!" She was attempting to free her father when suddenly she felt a searing pain in her head and fell into darkness.

Chapter Two

Private Robert Sallis of the 2nd Battalion, Royal Regiment of Fusiliers climbed onto his upper bunk and rested his head on a thin, hard pillow, stretching his long wiry body as he did so. He took a deep breath and exhaled as he reflected on his day.

Fuck, it rained here all the time! He'd been in Londonderry for six weeks and could count on one hand the number of times the sun had been fucken out. He was continually cold and miserable, and today he'd been particularly fed up.

He'd stood for hours working the checkpoint on Craigavon Bridge. Not only was he saturated and frozen, but he'd also become more and more depressed as he stopped the cars and vans only to encounter blatant hatred and loathing from most, if not all, the drivers. It dismayed him.

Lately, Robert had watched the News and read the papers more, in a vain attempt to understand what was going on here. He'd begun to recognise that the British media was in it with the Government by not clearly or even-handedly reporting events in this forgotten part of the UK. They certainly hadn't explained the depths of despair and bigotry shown by the people here. Experiencing it first-hand was a very different matter from reading about it or seeing it on the box. At first, like many others on the mainland, he'd heard the reports but had paid little or no attention to what was going on in Northern Ireland and the IRA. He hadn't given a fuck. But now the streets of Britain had become a war zone, and Rob and the lads just weren't prepared for it. They couldn't understand the bombardment of vicious hatred they continually encountered. After all, they were still in the UK, weren't they? And, for Christ's sake, they were just doing their jobs. Before leaving for Ireland, their short briefing had consisted of: "*The situation is an*

internal security matter between the Roman Catholics and Protestants."
That was it!

At first, Robert couldn't understand why the city had two names, but soon learned the reason. The Catholics call it Derry (*Doire* in Irish, meaning "oak grove") and the Protestants Londonderry (after the Protestant London merchants who'd helped pay for and build the walled city). This discrepancy was especially important when the soldiers were questioning suspects. If they answered "Londonderry", you should be okay, likely a Loyalist or Unionist, though you still had to be cautious. If they answered "Derry", be mega careful – they were more likely to be the enemy, a Nationalist or Republican.

They stopped, questioned and searched people constantly in their cars or on foot. Robert had been told to find out as much as possible about them for background intelligence – name, address, age, occupation, where they were going, where they were coming from, even to note their dress sense and general demeanour – everyone was a suspect, especially young men and women.

The Sallis family back home in Newcastle was continually worried. He sensed their fear and concern by their frequent letters. When he wrote he tried his best to sound good-humoured, telling them they'd nothing to worry about – it was a doddle. But deep down he was, he admitted to himself, afraid. He hated the overt loathing from the members of the Catholic Nationalist community he encountered. Ironically, Robert had himself been raised a Catholic. Both his mother's parents were Irish, from Kinsale in the Republic of Ireland.

Tracey, his fiancée, was just as concerned as his parents. He'd encouraged her to keep in touch with them and asked that she involve his mam as much as possible in the planning of their forthcoming wedding the following summer. Robert was an only child, and his mam had taken to Tracey the moment she'd met her. He'd known she would. He was desperately looking forward to the big event, especially their Spanish honeymoon. He could almost feel the heat of the sun – lovely!

It was just under three months until his next leave and his twenty-first birthday, which should make it even more special. He secretly hoped he wouldn't have to do another tour here, but it was highly likely. As luck had it, the majority of the lads were glad they were stationed in Londonderry and not in the merciless South Armagh region – aka "Bandit Country". South Armagh was a Provisional IRA rural stronghold bordered on one side by the Republic of Ireland. Gun battles, ambushes and sectarian murders were rife on its never-ending maze of country roads. In time, he'd been told, it had become so dangerous the lads were primarily transported around the area by air!

At last, his body began to warm up, and Robert, with a veiled smile, silently appreciated the thermals his mam had sent. When he'd first opened her package, he'd thought them ridiculous, and the other lads had taken the piss – big time. But now having worn them, he didn't give a shit; they were a godsend. The cold dampness of the make-shift barracks was lethal. Several of the guys no longer laughed – instead, they got some too!

"What a bliddy awful day," someone groaned from the lower bunk.

Robert smiled as he leaned over to look at its occupant: Val Holmes, his best marra. They were inseparable at school in Byker and had signed up for the army together on the same day, having failed to be taken on the apprenticeship scheme at Swan Hunter in the Toon. Robert shivered and replied to his friend.

"Too right. Thought I'd nivver get off that bridge. At least you were on patrol and could keep moving. I've never been so fucken cold and wet in my life."

"Wimp!" Val retorted, laughing.

He had a laugh that could make the dead smile. It was hard to describe. At first, it was loud and deep, but the harder he laughed, the higher the pitch of it rose. It was a bloody awful laugh, but this in itself made it more amusing.

"Howay, man," he continued. "Foot patrol is no joke. I can feel hundreds of eyes on me back the minute we hit the streets. I'm waiting all the bliddy time for that fucken pop and *whoosh!*"

He mimed a gun firing at the side of his head.

"Little kids an' all, shouting fucken bad language I don't even understand and throwing bricks and bottles. I swear, I thought I saw a bairn in nappies hurling stuff at me. I'm not jokin' you!"

Robert leaned back and imagined the scene. Humour was crucial in the job and being close to Val was a howl. His mate was popular throughout the unit for his stock of jokes and ridiculous stories. Salt of the earth, Val was. He kept them all sane.

The bunk suddenly shook followed by a loud thud as Private Billy Morris struck its metal bed frame with a hardback book. Mocking an upper-class English accent, he asked them both: "*Well, Gentlemen, any shots fired today? Can we report there's one less Fenian fucker to tick off our list?*"

Neither Robert nor Val had any time for Morris. He was a Northern Ireland Protestant, born in Coleraine – a fiercely Unionist small town in County Londonderry not far from the city.

None of the lads wanted to be anywhere near him. His hatred for Catholics, Republicans, Fenians, or whatever noun Morris used, was unpalatable. All the lads knew that one day he'd overstep the mark. They didn't want to be implicated when he did, and every other squaddie avoided him like the plague. No one would cover his back, that was for sure.

Robert barely raised his head to look at him. Morris was an ugly git and built like a brick shithouse. His cruel rodent-like eyes above a hook nose and thin-lipped mouth didn't help. Added to that today, Robert noticed a long red cut freshly sliced into his cheek. His square head was almost bald from continual shaving. He wore a pair of baggy black tracksuit bottoms together with a short-sleeved white tee shirt that showed off a massive over-exercised torso. On his lower forearm

– visible to all – was a large illustrated red and white tattoo of the "Red Hand of Ulster" with "No surrender" written above.

Robert was surprised Morris had even gotten into the army; much less been posted to Northern Ireland. From what he'd seen and heard, it was obvious that he was a racist who continually looked for ways to pick on and irritate the Nationalists.

At the lack of any response from Robert and Val, Morris hit the bed frame again and in his hard-grating accent shouted impatiently: "Sooooooooo, *did* you two shit bags get up to anything?"

"None of your business," Robert replied sourly.

Morris got the hint. Thick as thieves, those two Geordies. Like a couple of tarts. Fucking useless. He muttered crossly, "Ah, screw ye then, Sallis!"

"Piss off!" Robert snapped.

From the lower bunk, Val yelled, "Divven't give him the satisfaction, Rob. Away to fuck, Morris!"

The Irishman stood and sneered nastily at them.

"You know what? You two are a pair of useless twats. I'm still high from raiding this mornin'. Got a load off me chest, hit a few Fenian bitches a right smack! Landed a beaut on a wee darlin' of a Pope-loving virgin. Knocked the cunt right out cold! Happy days!"

His fingers touched his lips as he suggestively blew a kiss and strode off towards the door, singing at the top of his voice.

"I feel good, I knew that I would now, I feeeel good..."

As Morris's bulk retreated Val and Robert lay silent for a moment until almost simultaneously, both cried out after him: "Wanker!" The two friends laughed at the coincidence and howled wildly like wolves.

Chapter Three

He'd been looking for someone like her for a while and had noticed her months ago as she stood talking to a small group of friends in town. She wasn't a great looker, but he saw her potential. He'd kept close, watching her all the time and soon concluded she'd be perfect for his needs. She was the girl for him.

He knew he'd surprised her when he'd first walked over and introduced himself. He'd bowed slowly, taken her hand and gently kissed it and in a deliberate deep velvety voice, said, "Good morning, Princess. I'm Kieran."

She'd laughed quietly and replied simply, "Hi."

It hadn't been difficult to spot him before, and a few times she'd even caught him staring at her as she'd hung around the street or in town. He was probably around eighteen, and he reminded her of one of those flirtatious Spaniards or foreigner ones with his heavy fringe, long, jet black curly hair and swarthy skin that only showed a set of delicious chocolate brown eyes with long lashes she'd kill for. He was tall and slimly built, perfectly dressed in spotless flared blue jeans, a mega expensive-looking corduroy jacket and a pure white open-collared shirt. As he talked to her, his hand would continually sweep his heavy fringe to the side and away from his face. He was absolutely gorgeous...

"Fancy a cup of tea sometime?" he'd asked her. She was so nervous she didn't know how to respond.

"Ah, right, me... um, really, yes. Aye, that'd be nice!"

Kieran had smiled approvingly and began to walk back to his friends. Perfect. He'd looked back and cried out as he'd crossed the noisy road.

"Great! I'll see you. Alana Café, five o'clock tomorrow?"

She'd heard the jeering and whistling of his friends as they'd patted him on the back and laughed. She wasn't sure he'd heard her reply.

"Great. See ya."

But he had heard and bowed comically again before he turned and walked off towards the city centre, leading the small group of boys.

At first, she'd seen him almost every day. He was a kind, clever and funny boy and talked all the time about Ireland and its history.

Kieran was especially pleased when she became more and more interested in what he was saying. He saw cold anger rise in her against the British, the more they talked about the once-great Empire and its global domination.

He found her a first-class pupil and took delight in her progress towards becoming a committed Republican just like him!

Sometimes they'd walk down a street and should a speeding RUC jeep or army vehicle go by, with his fist high in the air, Kieran would shout excitedly: "End repression, end Internment NOW!" Over the weeks she was worried that one day they'd be stopped and he'd be taken from her. It never occurred to her that she was likely to be arrested too. Instead, he'd laugh and reassure her. Sure he was invincible!

She loved being with him even though at times she didn't fully understand what he was going on about, especially when he used big fancy words. But It didn't matter. She'd do anything for him – anything. She had it bad...

Chapter Four

Caitlin woke up feeling violently ill. Her head was spinning uncontrollably. She was nauseous and could taste blood at the back of her throat. Disorientated, she tried to rise, but a gentle pair of hands pushed her back onto the pillow, and a soft, soothing voice whispered, "Shush, love, shush, you're okay."

She tried hard to remember what had happened and looked around her bedroom. Her mother was sitting on the side of the bed, wearing her daddy's black dressing gown over her blood-splattered nightie. Brown congealed stains covered one side of her face and neck. Caitlin noticed Tina, standing still and pale-faced, at the foot of the bed.

Shaking her head in denial, Caitlin began to remember. She attempted to throw back her bedclothes and screamed, "Where's Daddy, Mammy? Where's Daddy!"

She was shushed again, and her head pushed gently back down onto the pillow. She looked up sadly at her mother, realising what she was about to hear.

"The Brits took him, love. He's gone."

"Ah, Mammy, no… I think I'm going to be sick!"

Caitlin ran for the toilet. She fell to her knees on the cold tiles, just remembering to bundle back her tangled, torn hair. With the reek of bleach stinging her nostrils, she vomited into the bowl. Her head pounded, and she shuddered as painful spasms ripped through her tummy.

After a few minutes, she'd finished and allowed her hair to fall back and cover her drawn face. She sighed wearily, got up and held her taut stomach. She looked down to see fresh bloodstains on her father's Aran. He'd murder her; this was his favourite jumper, and he wouldn't let anyone else but her wear it. These stains would never come out.

She flushed the toilet and opened the door to find her mother and Tina waiting patiently outside. Caitlin could see that the strewn contents of the linen cupboard had been tidied up. Tina was barefoot, still dressed in her favourite girlie pink broderie anglaise pyjamas. She'd put her braces back in and looked younger than her seventeen years and more vulnerable than usual as she bit what was left of her fingernails.

Majella asked with concern: "You okay, love? Believe it or not, you'll feel better after that."

Caitlin wasn't sure but answered anyway.

"I know, hope so. My throat is burning, though, and my head is killing me. Are *you* all right?"

"I'm grand, love. It doesn't help to have a friggin hangover on top. But then, that's me own fault… Tina's been next door already and phoned your Uncle Tommy. He'll be here in no time. He'll know what to do."

Tommy was their mother's brother and loved by all the family. He was well known locally as a "fixer".

"What time is it?" Caitlin asked, looking at Tina.

"Half-five."

Attempting to dismiss the pain in her head, Caitlin tried to take off her father's stained jumper but found she couldn't bring herself to do it. She'd wait a minute or two. In a light voice, she suggested to Tina: "Listen, you've got to get to college. Go to bed for a wee while and try to get some sleep – at least for a couple of hours. Go on. I'll stay here with Mammy and get the rest of the house sorted. And don't worry, we'll get Daddy back."

Tina refused to budge and shook her head in response.

"I don't want to go to bed; I want to stay here with you two. There's no chance I'll sleep after all this!"

Caitlin understood and looked at her sister whose thick red curly hair was dishevelled and loose but hung long and proud to her shoulders. It seemed when they'd both hit their teens their bodies had chosen to go in different directions. Caitlin had become tall, willowy and flat-chested, and stood just under six feet. This greatly annoyed Tina, who at a disappointing five foot four was apple-shaped with full breasts. She was a bit of a tomboy who paid very little attention to the latest fashions or indeed boys – whereas Caitlin loved to keep up to date with the latest trends, spending any free time she had looking at the magazines the office girls shared at the factory where she worked. She particularly loved *Jackie* and *Company*. At times, poor Tina's body would break out in nasty eczema rashes, and although she dosed herself with whatever remedies she could find, none of them ever seemed to work. Puberty had not been kind to her so far.

Fortunately for Caitlin, she possessed clear porcelain skin with bright blue eyes and a mass of long, thick black hair. She was envied for her beauty by most of her peers and subsequently had just a handful of close friends.

"You've got to trust us, Tina. Now please go to bed," she encouraged her sister.

Tina recognised Caitlin's stern tone and nodded whilst admitting to herself she did feel tired. Normally the sisters shared a room, but with Martin gone, Tina was sleeping in his bed.

"I suppose so. G'night then," she said reluctantly.

"Night, love," they both replied.

The door closed quietly, and Caitlin looked at her mother. She shivered again. Rubbing at the dried bloodstained jumper, she said, "I need to get this off. It'll be ruined if we don't soak it. Go you on down and put the kettle on for Tommy. I'll be two minutes."

Majella nodded and pulled her husband's over-large dressing gown more tightly around her. She took care as she walked down the staircase, leaning heavily on its wooden bannister. Her head ached and Christ she was dying for a drink. She didn't know how she'd get through the day and dreaded it already. Most probably she'd have to try and get some more tablets off the doctor. There wasn't any money for a cure although, my God she had a thirst on her!

Back in her room, Caitlin opened her wardrobe. She grabbed a black ribbed jumper and blue jeans and quickly put them on before walking into her parents' bedroom. Sighing, she made her way to the window and looked down. They'd gone and left behind a quiet street with rubbish strewn across the road and half-emptied dustbins and lids everywhere. She could just make out a few people walking in and out of each other's houses – no doubt trying to work out who'd been lifted.

Even indoors she could smell the pungent odour of petrol bombs and burning rubber tyres from a hijacked car that glowed brightly at the end of the street.

She sat down on the small stool before her mother's dressing table and picked up a tarnished silver hairbrush and began to carefully brush her sticky, bloodied hair. Once finished, she tied it neatly up into a ponytail, knowing she'd have to wash it later for work. The mirror showed her a swollen face and, even worse, a black eye. With a deep breath to steady herself, she got up and made her way downstairs, to be confronted by the chaos left after the raid.

She checked the living room over and made a futile attempt to tidy up. It was a mess, with broken glass from picture frames lying scattered amongst the debris of torn, damaged books and newspapers. They hadn't had much in this room to begin with so it could have been worse, she supposed.

Her mother called loudly from the kitchen.

Caitlin made her way in but stood by the kitchen door and watched her mother frantically dabbing at the smeared worktops with a damp cloth – a clear sign she was stressed. Their home was usually spotlessly clean, and her mother was proud of it. A large round wooden table stood in the middle of the kitchen surrounded by six chairs. Over the years, they'd shared secrets, laughed and talked around its cheap pine frame. Each chair was "owned" by a different member of the family, with the sixth being nabbed by Uncle Tommy who spent more time here than in his own house. The kitchen had become the heart of their home. Right in the centre of the kitchen wall hung a large, crooked portrait of Pope Paul VI complemented with a set of broken rosary beads draped over it and literally hanging on by a thread.

Her mother passed a cup of tea to Caitlin who asked wearily, "So where do we go from here, Mammy?"

Before answering, the older woman removed a cigarette from the pack lying on the windowsill. Noticing it was her last one, she shook the pack in frustration and threw it angrily on the table. She lit it up, intent on making it last, and drew on it deeply before releasing the smoke. The acrid fumes surrounded Caitlin who, unusually for her, didn't pay any heed. Ordinarily, she hated smoking.

"I don't know, love. I'm at a loss," Majella sighed, looking crushed by sadness and worry. "Martin was lifted over a week ago, and there's been nothing from him since. Now, this! Your Daddy won't survive, love. Not in his condition. And this is my last fag too... Fuck it!"

She took another slow draw before telling her daughter, "I ran after them, you know, with your Daddy's tablets, but that turncoat soldier wouldn't take them!"

Pointing to the dressing gown she wore, she continued to spit out her words angrily.

"Bastard wouldn't even let him put on his dressing gown! Fucking twat!"

Caitlin nodded in agreement.

" Jesus, Mammy, what was he all about? And him Irish too!"

"Irish my arse! Sure, didn't you notice the tattoo? Red Hand of Ulster. He's an Orange bastard, that's what he is!"

That explained it. Caitlin could now understand his behaviour. Un-be-fucking-lieveable!

She drank her tea as her mother relished the remains of her cigarette and ranted on wildly.

"Anyway, what goes around comes around... he'll get his comeuppance that one, don't you worry! One way or the other!"

Caitlin took her mother's hand and gently squeezed it.

"Listen, I'm sure they'll let him see a doctor if anything goes wrong. He'll be okay."

"I wonder…" her mother sighed in response. Her cigarette was finished. God, she needed a drink, badly.

In solemn silence, they waited at the table until the back door was thrown open and a man swept into the kitchen on a gust of cold wind and rain. Not overly tall but solid, with a massive chest topped with a thick, freckled neck that sat on broad shoulders, Tommy O'Reilly made quite an entrance. He was wearing a dark green and khaki fur-hooded parka jacket and jeans. His face was flushed, and Caitlin noticed a few spidery red burst veins around his flat, broken nose and upper cheeks. His long red hair and thick moustache were drenched, with rainwater running down his forehead and face. Within minutes, the thick, black-framed glasses covering his blue eyes began to steam up from the heat of the gas rings they'd left on to warm up the cold kitchen. He took them off and looked around the kitchen in vain for something to wipe them on, finally resorting to using the bottom of his jumper. He glanced at the seated women.

"Grab us a cloth, Caitlin love."

She got up to find a clean cloth as Tommy hugged his only sibling.

"There now," he said. Silent tears ran down her cheeks as she struggled to tell him what had happened. He looked at the cut on her head and swore viciously as the beginnings of her story unfolded.

Caitlin waited for her mother to pause before passing Tommy a cloth. She talked loudly over the sound of her mother, who'd started to cry again.

"Jesus, Tommy, they took Daddy away with a hood over his head! They wouldn't even let him get dressed, and beat him with a baton, loads of times! He couldn't walk straight or see where he was going. Mammy said they wouldn't let her give him his dressing gown or tablets. And they've friggin' bashed the front door through! Have you heard anything?" Before answering, Tommy wiped his face and head quickly in an attempt to stop more water dripping onto the floor. His voice was muffled and angry under the cloth, and the women strained to understand.

"It's a fucking mess, is what it is! They've wrecked the streets and lifted something like forty youngsters and men, including your da. They won't tell us anything. Fucking nothing! God forgive me for cursing." He blessed himself.

Tommy was a Sinn Féin "Community Worker" and well-liked and respected within the Catholic population. He was charismatic, clever and trustworthy, renowned locally for his patience and letter-writing skills. For those who couldn't read or write, Tommy would wage a letter-writing campaign in an effort to solve all sorts of unfair issues and decisions, mostly around housing. His success rate was high, and his natural ability to communicate had, surprisingly, gained him a certain respect even within the Unionist community. He was heavily involved in the Civil Rights Movement and helped organise many of its key events.

He exhaled and ran his hand along his moustache in an attempt to tidy it before gulping down some tea from a Liverpool FC mug placed before him. Caitlin had never seen him so upset. He looked so worried. It unnerved her to see her usually calm and competent uncle in such a state.

"Things are going to get worse," he sighed. "It's really bad this time. The Brits are arresting boys everywhere. Do ya know there wasn't one Proddy lifted last night!? Not one! There's Catholics lying dead in Belfast because of this!"

He gulped his tea and looked longingly at his sister's cigarette pack lying abandoned on the table.

"Jesus, I'm frozen. Do you have any fags, Majella? I need a smoke."

"None, Tommy, sorry. That was my last. Maybe you'll find some ends in there."

Majella offered her brother the half-filled ashtray, but he refused.

"You're all right, thanks. I'll get some in a bit. There're rumours of beatings at that camp the Brits just opened in Magilligan. It looks like they've taken the hardliners there. Eight or ten huts for prisoners right in the middle of an army camp – what about that? They say they're setting the dogs on them and starving the poor critters. Worse still, they won't let them sleep! It's like the feckin' Gestapo."

Caitlin was horrified. She looked at her uncle and cried, "There must be something we can do, for Christ's sake, Tommy! Isn't there someone we can talk to?"

She stood up and walked to the kitchen window that overlooked their wild back garden. Tommy answered her in a deflated tone of voice.

"I don't know, love. I'm at a loss for once. Mind you; there is *one* bit of good news… Well, sort of good. I've found out about Martin. He's in the Kesh. They've said I can see him. He'll be in a bad way, mind. I'll get the solicitor to come with me to check it out."

"Jesus Christ, if he's in the Kesh, they'll never let him out!" Majella shouted back at her brother. She'd heard about the awful conditions at the Kesh prison. She blessed herself and asked to join her brother on his visit.

"You can't come, love; they won't allow women visiting… not yet anyway. Listen, forget about that for a minute, I'm going to find out where Patrick is. Sure, I'll try and see Martin the 'marra. I'll need to sort out a lift." Tommy didn't have a car of his own. Finishing his tea, he stood and looked at his sister.

"Come to think of it, Majella, you'd better put some clothes and things in a bag for Martin. Throw in some food too – if you can."

Patting down his trouser pockets, he announced, "God, I really need a fag! You sure you haven't *any* left?"

"I'm sure. Sorry, love. I'll go and get that stuff for Martin."

Majella left the kitchen wearily. As soon as she'd gone, Tommy made his way to the hallway and searched under the staircase for Patrick's half-empty toolbox.

"Let me grab this and see what I can do to fix this front door."

He spent ten or so minutes in an attempt to mend the door as much as he could. In the meantime, Caitlin tried to tidy the downstairs of the house as Majella searched upstairs for some of Martin's things.

Tommy sighed and stood back to admire his handiwork – it'd have to do. He returned to the kitchen and Caitlin gestured for him to sit.

"I'm so worried about Mammy," she whispered to him. "I don't think she can take much more. She's up to her eyes on those pills Tommy, and she's drinking like a fish. You know Daddy won't survive being locked up. What will it do to her if anything happens to him? What will it do to all of us!?"

Tommy shook his head and moaned deeply. His head was spinning. He was up to his neck with so many requests for help. Caitlin and many like her hadn't a clue what was really going on, and he certainly didn't want to have this conversation with such a youngster. Taking extra care not to drip any more water, he began to put on his sodden parka and quietly spoke to his niece.

"Caitlin, I know. Your mother's breaking down in front of us. I'll sort your Dad out first. Just do me a favour, love, try and keep a close eye on her for me."

Tommy was extremely fond of his sister and always had been. He watched as she returned to the kitchen holding a white plastic Spar bag containing some clothes and toiletries. She passed it over and walked to the larder to get some food. There wasn't much to give, but she did her best, adding just a few items. As ever, there was little or no money and, to make matters worse, Patrick's Giro had been delayed because of rioting. Most of the postmen were too scared to deliver here anymore. It was a dangerous job at the best of times, and many of the postbags and vans had been robbed time and time again.

Patrick hadn't worked for years. He'd wanted to, but unemployment amongst Catholic men was widespread, especially for men in their mid-forties. Any decent jobs advertised unambiguously stated,

"Protestants only need apply". Patrick and many other Catholic men had no chance of finding well-paid work. Most of the young men and women left to work in England or beyond and sent money back.

Tommy thanked them for the tea, and cautiously opened the back door against the elements: "I'll phone next door as soon as I've news, I promise." Cursing the weather as he walked down the back yard, he battled against the howling wind and rain.

Her mother wearily placed the empty teacups in the sink.

"I have to put my head down, love." Caitlin didn't blame her.

"'Course you do. Go ahead. I'll finish up here."

Her mother kissed her on the cheek and disappeared. Caitlin started to wash up the red and white mugs. Her body ached, and the pounding in her head was worse. She took a glass from a shelf above the sink, added some water and stirred in two soluble aspirin. She watched them slowly dissolve as she sat in her chair at the table. She felt sick, lonely, sad and fearful – dreading what the new day would bring. She had a bad feeling – *a very bad feeling*.

Chapter Five

After just a couple of hours of restless sleep, the new day arrived. Caitlin tried hard to eat some of the toast her mother placed in front of her. She could just about sup the tea. Tina sat next to her, looking tired, but for once not complaining about having to eat her breakfast cereal mixed with Marvel. She hated the dried milk, but it was all they could afford. For college – locally called "the Tech" – she could wear what she pleased and had been pleased to leave her school uniform behind. Today she was dressed in a bizarre mixture of colours consisting of a torn short black skirt with grey tights, a pink blouse and purple-braided cardigan. Her wild hair was loose against her tired face, which appeared swollen and red from weeping.

Majella – damp cloth in hand – wiped down the sink and units in silence. Attempting to reassure her, Caitlin said, "Don't worry. We'll hear something this morning I'm sure. Tommy'll sort it. You know how good he is. He'll call as soon as he has news… and, remember, he's going to see Martin later."

Tina looked up excitedly. She adored her brother. In her eyes, he could do nothing wrong.

"Martin? You've heard about Martin?"

"Ah, Tina, sorry, we should have told you. They've agreed Tommy can see him. He's in the Kesh."

Tina's face dropped, and she cried, "The Kesh? Why the feckin' Kesh? He hasn't done anything. Our Martin wouldn't hurt a fly!"

Tina was in denial. Everyone knew Martin was somehow involved with the Provisional IRA (PIRA) and wasn't the innocent his younger sister believed him to be, but Caitlin knew it wasn't the right time to confront her.

"I know, Tina, but they're lifting all over the place. The Brits are paranoid. They think everyone's involved – every Catholic, that is. Tommy says not one Proddy has been arrested so far – not one!"

"Enough now!" Majella snapped, putting an end to the conversation. She looked at Tina angrily. Her stomach was cramping, and her head thumped, she needed peace and quiet.

"Tina, finish your cereal and get your bag; you're going to be late! Keep your head down and if you see ANY sign of trouble you get straight home – do you hear me? The barricades are likely to go up again today, so stay close to Emmett; he'll keep an eye on you."

Tina threw her spoon into her half-empty bowl and hurried to her room. She hated how her mother was always angry these days. Life was shit, and now she was going to be stuck with Emmett.

Emmett was Tina's "friend" and one of the McFadden children, who lived next door. He was two years younger than her, and they'd grown up together. They were an unlikely pair with Tina's red-headed temperament and Emmett's tranquil and love-struck behaviour. Sadly for him, Caitlin could see he was beginning to get on Tina's nerves. He was crazy about her, but she'd outgrown him.

As if on cue, there was a knock at the back door, and Majella got up to open it, saying, "That'll be him now."

And there he stood, waiting devotedly on the back step. He was turned out in his St Peter's school uniform consisting of a black food-stained blazer with a torn school crest on the top pocket, along with a black V-neck jumper, white shirt and black trousers. A school tie dangled from a brown leather school bag that was hoisted over one scrawny shoulder. His flared, hand-me-down trousers were held up by a thin plastic belt. Too long, they completely hid his shoes.

Tina returned to the kitchen, ready to leave. She looked unhappy as she stood impatiently waiting to go. She hated travelling to college with Emmett now. He was pathetic. However, her mother insisted they still get the bus together every day.

"How you doing, Emmett?" Majella asked.

"Not too good, Mrs McLaughlin. Me Mammy's in an awful state. They've lifted our Joe. She says I'm lucky I look so young otherwise they'd have taken me too! She's thinking of sending me to me Auntie Trish in Greencastle over the border. But I've told her I can't miss school; we're not even back a couple of weeks, and I've got me exams coming up. Have you heard the Brits are parking some of their Saracens and Pigs in our school car park!? It's really cool, but they keep trying to talk to us and all, and it's really bad, 'cos we can't talk back to them, can we? They've even asked us to play footie!" he gabbled.

With her hands on her hips, Majella answered: "I've heard, love. Don't you go getting involved with them now. You keep your head down and out of all that business. Do you hear me? You're a good lad, thinking of your exams. Good for you!"

Emmett nodded eagerly at his neighbour. He knew what he needed to do all right! He'd get out of this hellhole, go to university and get some real money in. He was tired of watching his mother work every hour God sent whilst his big eejit of a father sat on his arse all day, smoking and watching the racing. There was still some paid work out there, but you had to go and find it. Sure hadn't Emmett himself got a job delivering the newspapers – that was work, wasn't it? He hated having no money so he'd get a degree, a good job with a fancy car, a big flash house somewhere, maybe America or Australia, and sure Tina and his mammy would come with him. They were his world. He had it all worked out.

Looking at Tina and patting Emmett fondly on the back, Majella smiled at him as she pushed them both towards the door.

"Anyway, off you go now with "laugh a minute" there! Keep close and come straight home, the two of you, as soon as you're out."

Tina remained silent and shoved Emmett roughly through the door ahead of her. She didn't say goodbye. She hated it when her mother made fun of her.

"Bye then! Missing you already!" Caitlin shouted at the slamming door.

Caitlin thought about Tina. God, she could be miserable at times! She was lucky she could still go to College. At sixteen, Caitlin herself had no choice but to leave school – she didn't want to, but they needed the money. She'd started as a runner, or message girl at a local shirt factory and was now working in the payroll department. Mrs Mugan, her favourite teacher at school, had encouraged her not to leave without some qualifications, so she'd taken a number of secretarial and administrative courses and passed with flying colours.

University had never been mentioned in their house. It wasn't even an option. Most of Derry's sixteen-year-old girls left school and became hemmers, cuffers, or worked on the buttonholes in the city's last few shirt factories. It was mundane work, boring and depressing. However, for many, the prospect of payday, getting dressed up and boogying on a Friday or Saturday night, made the work tolerable. The factory buzzed every Friday in expectation of the weekend.

Caitlin gathered her things to leave. "I have to go now, Mammy. I'll come straight home after work."

Majella sat at the table and looked at its neatly positioned empty chairs. She yawned. She was exhausted and rubbed at her temples to try and distract herself. She was seriously gasping for a cigarette and a drink. She looked at her elder daughter and told her sadly, "Your sandwich is there for you, love, only bread and sugar, sorry. There isn't anything else. I'm going to go to the Sorting Office today to see if Daddy's Giro is there. Maybe they'll give it to me early. If not, I'll have to go and see Granny."

Caitlin was stunned.

"Really? Good luck there then. Remember, I get paid soon so we should be okay. Why don't you go and lie down again? I'll see you after."

Majella rose from her chair and kissed Caitlin on the cheek.

"Bye, love. See you later."

Caitlin didn't particularly like her grandmother. Granny O'Reilly had always hated Patrick and felt he was not good enough for her only daughter. She was a snob. When Caitlin's parents had first met, he'd worked on the docks along the River Foyle. But the work dwindled when the shipping lines started to use container ships, and for many thousands of men, there was nothing left but a life on benefits. Most men either fell into deep depression or drank. At first, alcohol was a friend, but soon it became their greatest enemy, leaving a trail of destruction and pain in its wake.

The words of the posters displayed on billboards everywhere throughout the city didn't help either. They couldn't have been any more blatant or hurtful. *"The Dole Destroys the Soul"*. It was depressing to watch a discarded generation of proud men search for work that barely existed.

Granny O'Reilly had wanted her daughter to marry a "professional". She'd indulged Majella with singing and piano lessons. Granda died in World War II, so a lucrative marriage for her daughter became granny's sole purpose in life. She was a cold soul and especially showed very little interest in or feeling for Tommy, her youngest. Granny had grown into a bitter, crabbit old woman, who now kept her distance from both her children. Neither Majella nor Tommy cared particularly. They had each other.

Caitlin and her siblings visited her as little as possible, and when they did, it was purely out of duty and always at Christmas. Caitlin hoped her mother wouldn't have to ask the old bat for money – she knew they'd never hear the end of it.

Taking a gigantic deep breath, she quickly buttoned up her three-quarter-length black-and-white checked coat and tied her red headscarf tightly under her chin. She grimaced as the scarf brushed against her tender head. She'd washed her face and hair earlier and at first, had tried to cover her bruises with makeup, but it didn't help. If anything, it made her injuries look worse, so she had taken it off.

It was time to go. Tommy was right, she thought, as she stood on the front doorstep overlooking their semi-fenced, neglected garden. The weather was shite, and she couldn't remember the last time the sun had shone. They'd had a lousy summer – typical Ireland. The rain had been unremitting. The kind of rain that soaked you to the bone. She struggled on the doorstep with her old umbrella as she fought to open it. Other front doors opened and shut noisily along the street as girls and women left home to walk to the factories.

The carefree days of the vibrant, buzzing shirt factories were long gone. As a child she remembered watching large groups of women linking arms and making their way, laughing and giggling, to the factories scattered around the city. In the 1920s, the city had been home to forty-four shirt factories employing over 8,000 women out of Derry's 45,000 population. So streamlined was the manufacturing process that it was said a shirt could be produced from scratch in just sixteen or so minutes.

Sadly, a downturn arrived when the factory owners started to send their work to the Far East, where they could pay their workers as little as £2.50 a week – much less than the Derry women expected. The boom was over, and the majority of the factories had no choice but to close.

Fortunately, Rocola, where Caitlin worked, was the largest factory in the city and still in business, although – according to rumour – only just.

She tightened her coat and began the walk to work. Within a matter of minutes, she was seized from behind by Anne, her best friend.

"Mornin', missus!" she cried as she hugged Caitlin and from habit linked her arm. Their umbrellas bumped, and they laughed until Anne took a second look at Caitlin and stopped short in horror.

"Jesus Christ, woman, look at your face! What happened?"

Caitlin gingerly touched her cheek.

"Sure, we were raided this morning, and a friggin' Brit smacked me one. Well, not exactly a Brit, an Orangeman dressed as a Brit – it's a long story! It's killing me though – it's really tender and sore – and they've lifted Daddy too! Took him away with no clothes on, Anne, nothing. We don't know where he is, and he's got no medicine or anything…"

They began to walk towards the factory again as Anne asked for more details. Caitlin told her everything.

"Ah, Jesus, love, what a mess. Are you sure you want to come to work?"

She had to; she couldn't miss it, especially now.

"I must, Anne; we need the money. Do you think Mrs Parkes will notice?" Caitlin asked, carefully touching her puffy face and black eye.

"Feck Mrs Parkes! She wouldn't notice if her hubby's dick was in her mouth – or, come to think of it, any dick!"

"God, Anne, you're awful! Don't make me laugh; it hurts! I can't believe you said that; that's terrible! If Father McGuire could hear you…"

Anne laughed heartily at her friend. Caitlin never ceased to amaze her.

"You're such a prude, Caitlin McLaughlin, you really are!"

Caitlin looked at her and felt relieved to think that she had such a ray of sunshine in her life – what a tonic Anne was, and such a dear friend. Caitlin wouldn't have believed she'd be capable of laughing today, but already Anne had made her feel better. Anne had an idea and gently reached out to touch Caitlin's eye.

"You didn't get a number or name for that Proddy soldier so you can report him? That's going to be a beaut, Caitlin."

"Ouch! Get real, Anne! Me report a soldier. It'd be a waste of time. They wouldn't do anything. He'd just deny it, and it'd be his word against mine. My face is minor compared to some of the stuff that went on. Tommy says there's been awful beatings and loads of houses have been wrecked."

"And you don't know where your Da is?"

"Not a word. Tommy is on it, though." Caitlin couldn't help but touch her swollen face again as she thought about the morning's events. She was worried sick about her mother also but too ashamed to tell Anne about her recent drinking. Her friend tried to comfort her.

33

"It'll be fine, love, don't worry. Your Da will be fine."

They continued to talk, barely noticing the numerous houses and gabled walls daubed with angry graffiti and slogans as they passed: "*Don't ball-lick the British – fight them! IRA(P)*" or "*They can kill a revolutionary, but not a revolution!*" Plus many similar sentiments.

Arm-in-arm the two girls walked down the steeply sloping Blighs Lane to Rocola, stepping around the pulled up and broken paving stones and other debris left recently by rioters. The wide road was burned and scorched from numerous petrol bombs. Children were scouring for discarded rubber bullets amongst the debris of glass, wood and burned-out cars, to keep as mementoes and show off later. Rubble from demolished houses lay in piles, interspersed with a few remaining condemned but inhabited homes.

Housing was a cause of major resentment and anger towards the Unionists and Government since Protestants were always given priority allocation by the Unionist-controlled council. First built in 1947, the adjoining Creggan housing estate, at its height, contained 15,000 homes all of them Catholic-occupied. It was purposely built in one area to keep the Nationalists together, suiting the Unionist-led Government – which was then able to manage the voting boundaries, allowing the Protestants to stay in power.

"Let's change the subject!" Anne cried out merrily. "Have you heard from that gorgeous Seamus of yours?"

Seamus was Caitlin's ex-boyfriend. He'd asked her to marry him the previous Christmas. They'd been seeing each other on and off for several years. She didn't love him and had never succumbed to his many advances. She'd wanted to wait and keep her virginity, knowing deep down it wouldn't be lost to him. He was a nice boy, but as his love for Caitlin grew, it had outstripped hers for him. She'd refused his marriage proposal so, heartbroken and bitter, he'd left Derry and emigrated to New York. Majella was annoyed with Caitlin for weeks afterwards. She'd loved Seamus and saw him as another son. Fortunately for

Caitlin, her father understood and quietly supported her. She'd heard nothing from Seamus since his move to America.

The rain was getting heavier as they drew closer to the factory. Caitlin smiled and told her friend, "No, I've heard nothing, not a word. But then I don't expect to, bless him."

They started to run and cried out as the heavens opened, and the rain poured down relentlessly. Finally, they reached the factory gates and walked through along with hundreds of others. They clocked in, and soon Anne set off to the left of the site, to start her day in the stock and dispatch room. She yelled to Caitlin across the din of the machining room.

"See you after, missus. Don't worry; your Da will be fine! Try and get something from First Aid for that face!"

Caitlin acknowledged this by raising her hands in the air whilst opening and closing her fingers, "Nag, nag, nag!"

Anne laughed back and soon disappeared from sight.

Walking to the administrative block alone, Caitlin missed her friend already as a wave of tiredness in reaction to the night's events came over her. The lift was being serviced and was out of order. Just great, she thought as she dragged her sore body up each step to the office on the fifth and top floor. She couldn't get her father out of her head and prayed on the way up that he'd be home by the end of the day.

Finally, reaching her destination, Caitlin walked down a narrow corridor that led to the main offices set on either side. The names of the managers were neatly etched on each glazed door: Mr Henderson, General Manager, Mr McScott, Accountant, and so on. She walked to the end of the corridor and opened the last remaining door. This office accommodated the Office Manager, Mrs Parkes, her two junior payroll assistants and Caitlin. She noted she was the first to arrive as she entered the cold room.

She removed her coat along with her scarf and hung them neatly on a corner coat stand. She knelt to switch on an old-fashioned gas heater. After many futile attempts, it finally ignited, and she moved the dial to the lowest setting. Mrs Parkes, renowned for keeping costs down, refused to allow them to set the heat high. She was so careful with money she didn't seem to recognise that sick days among the office girls increased significantly in the winter, primarily due to their working in such cold conditions.

It wasn't long before Mrs Parkes herself walked in. She rarely smiled; her face was held in a constant frown. She was not a handsome woman and tiny at just under five feet. Her face was long and thin, as was the salt-and-pepper hair scraped back neatly in a bun. The rest of her was slim to the point of being scrawny. She had married a local man she now loathed and longed to return to her hometown of Bangor on the east coast – a commuter town near Belfast and predominantly Loyalist.

In her broad Bangor accent, she announced, "Morning, Caitlin."

The woman removed her coat and shook out her wet umbrella but stopped as she waited for Caitlin's response. The girl hadn't said a word, which was unusual, so Mrs Parkes looked up and noticed her bruised eye and face. Unsurprisingly she didn't comment. Most likely a crack from the father. It wasn't uncommon for Londonderry women to get a smack from their angry, unemployed, useless men, especially after a few Guinness.

Eventually, Caitlin acknowledged her and answered shyly, "Mornin', Mrs Parkes."

The office manager sniffed noisily, said nothing and left the room, seeking the kettle to make her morning cup of tea. She never offered any of the girls a hot drink, nor would they dare ask.

Caitlin sat down at her desk and unlocked the drawer that held her paperwork. She placed it neatly in front of her and started her working day.

Within minutes Sinead and Moira – the two junior girls – arrived together. They were loud and giggled as they entered the office until they saw Mrs Parkes. They quickly stopped chattering and wished her good morning. In return she acknowledged them with a grunt and watched them as they removed their wet coats and umbrellas, placing them on a coat stand. Like schoolgirls, they sat at their respective wooden desks in preparation for work. Trying desperately hard not to giggle, they caught each other's eye and then smiled, silently mouthing "Mornin" to Caitlin. They immediately noticed her injuries and looked at her with concern. Caitlin made a face back, silently entreating them not to say anything.

The office was quiet for the next few hours as the girls worked diligently in silence. Mrs Parkes watched them like a hawk.

Near lunchtime, their work was interrupted by an unexpected visitor. There was a sharp knock on their door before an elderly man in a classic black three-piece suit, white shirt and red tie walked into the office. This was Roger Henderson, the factory's general manager and owner. He was normally a fine, impressive-looking man with well-trimmed, neatly combed salt n' pepper hair. However, today he looked pale with noticeable dark rings under his eyes. Caitlin hadn't met him often, but when she did, he was always sweet to her. She thought he was a decent man. A young man she didn't recognise followed Mr Henderson into the office.

The factory owner acknowledged Mrs Parkes with a nod and smiled at the girls.

"Mrs Parkes. Ladies."

The office manager quickly stood up and smoothed down her heavy serge skirt. It was most unusual for Mr Henderson to visit her office. She hated surprises and stuttered when she returned his greeting.

"Wh-Wh-Why, Mr Henderson, good morning! What a surprise!"

In a beautiful soft Irish lilt, he replied, "A quick visit is all, Mrs Parkes. I simply wanted to introduce my nephew James... James Henderson. He's recently arrived from Scotland and will be working with us here at the factory – I hope for some time."

He smiled encouragingly at his nephew. Caitlin peeked at the young man, who smiled and greeted Mrs Parkes. His eyes moved to take in the group of girls. As he came into full view, Caitlin was pleasantly surprised. At over six foot he towered above Mrs Parkes, his head topped with thick auburn hair. Caitlin couldn't help but notice his eyes. They were intensely green. He was unquestionably attractive and beautifully dressed. A musky scent of aftershave filled the room.

"Good morning, ladies," he greeted them in a soft Scottish accent.

"Morning, sir," they chorused in return.

In a brusque but humorous tone, Roger Henderson – undoubtedly aware of the effect his handsome nephew was having on the young women – rushed on.

"Right. Good, that's done! Mrs Parkes, I'll talk to you later to confirm what young James here will need, including secretarial support."

At this, Sinead and Moira began to giggle until Mrs Parkes gave them her killing look. In fear, they stopped immediately.

Roger Henderson turned to leave the office. His nephew stepped back, allowing him to pass. James waited until his uncle had left the office before he took a last look back into the room where his eyes met Caitlin's. He frowned as he studied her. She self-consciously raised her hand to hide her injuries and turned away from his all-encompassing stare. She heard him say, "Thank you, ladies. I shall look forward to meeting you again. Good morning."

Cheekily, he winked at the two young sniggering girls and smiled as he closed the door behind.

Sinead and Moira couldn't help but laugh and talk excitedly about offering their secretarial assistance *any time*! Once again miserable Mrs Parkes barked angrily, "That's enough, ladies, now back to work, **NOW!**"

For Caitlin, the day dragged on until she heard the horn blow at five o'clock. She felt rotten and hadn't been able to eat. Her poorly filled sandwich lay unopened on her desk. Mrs Parkes and the girls had been in some sort of training all afternoon, and she'd welcomed the time alone. Gathering her papers, she returned them to the drawer, locking it. She stood up tall, stretched out her arms and groaned. She double-checked that everything was stowed away and in its place, until finally, she snatched her coat, umbrella and scarf from the coat stand ready to leave.

Outside it was still raining. Anne stood loyally waiting for her by the entrance to the administration building. She leaned against the wall under her umbrella, smoking. Anne was a pretty girl – a typical Irish colleen. Beautiful pale strawberry-red spiral curls swathed her head. Any attempt to straighten her temperamental mane failed, and her stubborn curls returned time after time.

Anne's beautiful face, much to Caitlin's annoyance, was only marred by the nasty cigarette that hung from her otherwise perfectly shaped rosebud lips. Caitlin had tried time and time again to get both her mother and Anne to stop smoking but to no avail.

"Aaaagggggghhhh, will you for feck's sake throw away those cigarettes? You know I hate them. They'll kill you! You stink!" Caitlin informed her friend.

Anne jumped in fright. She screwed up her face playfully and removed the half-smoked cigarette from her mouth. She gently flipped the end of it with her fingers until it was extinguished and placed the remainder back into a half-empty pack. Saying nothing, she offered Caitlin her umbrella to hold as she removed her boring flat pumps and exchanged them for a pair of red stiletto heels. Throwing the pumps into her bag, she smiled.

"Now isn't that better?"

She took back her umbrella, and the young women linked arms. It was the same routine every night after work. Anne was passionate about her stilettos. She was a 1950s style fan and follower of vintage rock and roll addict. Her bedroom was covered with posters of glamorous 1950s movie stars and singers. It was filled to the brim with wide-petticoated full swing skirts that hung alongside snug pencil skirts and tight tops. She believed her stilettos were sexy and definite man-catchers as they added height to her tiny five-foot-two frame. Her dearest wish was to have a pair in every colour of the rainbow. Caitlin didn't know how she managed to walk in them, especially in the rain, but Anne did, displaying her beautiful legs proudly.

Caitlin had adored her from the first day they met at the age of five in the playground of Nazareth House Primary School. Without Anne, Caitlin's world would be a very dull and lonely place.

They spent the journey home talking about their day, especially Caitlin who told Anne about James Henderson. Their umbrellas barely protected them from the cold rain, but they were used to it. After saying goodnight, Anne sauntered towards her family's small condemned terraced house, which was inhabited by Anne herself, her numerous siblings and permanently weary mother. For as long as Caitlin could remember, Anne's mother was pregnant or had just given birth. The family were terribly poor. Anne's father was rarely seen at the house, and when he was there, it was obviously for one thing only and then was off again. He was an IRA man, on the run, and spent most of his time in the Irish Republic.

It was common knowledge he had another woman set up there, but no one would dare tell his wife. Anne suspected she knew already, but the subject had never been raised. She shared a bedroom with three of her five sisters. They all worked at Rocola as well. Her older brothers had already gone away whilst the others were too young to work, so the family depended on its women.

Over the past few years, Caitlin had listened for many hours as Anne fantasised about meeting a rich, blond, tanned Yank, who would sweep her off her feet, marry her and take her to America – where her great-aunt Rose and many like-minded Derry girls had gone during and after World War II. Caitlin knew Anne wasn't joking. She'd always dreamed of living in the States.

Drenched and cold, Caitlin arrived home, cursing as she feverishly searched for the door key in her large handbag, trying desperately to hold onto her umbrella at the same time. Finally, she found the key and quickly opened the partially repaired door, shook her umbrella on the doorstep and placed it – still dripping – in a corner of the tiled hallway.

She called out but was greeted by silence. She felt bitterly cold as she hastily removed her wet coat and hung it in the cupboard underneath the stairs. She cried out again.

"Mammy, are you in? Tina? Anyone?"

Nothing. Caitlin walked up the stairs and across the landing to the bathroom. She sat on the edge of the white enamelled tub and turned on the hot tap only. She desperately hoped the water would be hot and waited patiently with her hand held under the tap as the cold water started to flow. She didn't feel well at all.

It was almost dark outside. The wind howled, and heavy rain slapped against the small, frosted window. She sensed the water warming up. Thank God! Sighing, she placed the stopper in the plughole and waited as hot water flowed over her hand. Steam formed in the cold air of the bathroom. As if sensing her need for heat, the hot water cruelly receded and was replaced by a freezing flow. Certainly not enough for a bath. Caitlin swore quietly. Adding to her woes, the bathroom light suddenly went off, and she was left sitting in the dark. Agitated, she tried the switch, but when there was no response, she realised the electric must have run out of money.

Tears welled up. Her mother obviously didn't get the Giro. She quickly wondered if there was any money anywhere in the house. She ran into the bedrooms, searching trouser pockets, cupboards and drawers, but found nothing. As a last resort, she wondered if Tina had cashed in all the lemonade bottles, she and Emmett had collected from adjacent building sites early in the summer. The workmen were forever leaving empty Maine bottles lying around for the children to find and return to the local shop for a financial reward.

In the darkness, she carefully sought her way to her bedroom, got on her knees and pulled up the bedcovers to search underneath their bed. At first, she couldn't find anything but stretched her arms as far as she could until she eventually felt and pulled out a plastic bag. She looked inside and was relieved to find a few empty bottles. Just a few, but it was a start. She dragged the bag after her and gasped with the effort as she got up from the floor. Next, she heard the front door open, and her mother call out, "Caitlin!"

Thank God! she thought, and quickly descended the stairs.

"I'm here! Did you have any luck with Daddy's Giro?"

She watched her mother remove her wet coat and place it next to Caitlin's. Talking to her from inside the small cupboard, Majella said, "They promised it'd be out tomorrow. That'll do. And to be honest, I couldn't face your Granny. Not today."

She walked into the hallway and looked around questioningly.

"Why's it so dark in here?"

"Electric's run out. Do we have *any* money?"

Her mother frowned, picked up the two shopping bags and showed them to Caitlin. She walked through to the kitchen before she answered.

"I've got about 40p. For fuck sake, I thought we'd at least had enough in the meter to get us through 'til tomorrow."

Caitlin followed her into the darkened kitchen.

"Doesn't look like it. Where's Tina?"

Majella placed the bags carefully on the table and looked at her daughter properly for the first time. She reached out and touched her cheek.

"Tina? Ah, she's next door helping Mrs McFadden with something. I've just knocked, she'll be here in a minute. God, Caitlin, even in this poor light, I can see how bad your face is. That eye's going to be a beaut."

Caitlin laughed quietly recalling Anne using the same words earlier that day.

"You're not the first to say that."

Her mother didn't look too well and once again appeared unsteady on her feet. Caitlin wondered whether she'd been drinking. Majella noticed the plastic bag in her daughter's hand and asked, "What's that then?"

"Some empties I found under our bed. Tina's going to have to take them to the shop. Hopefully, there's enough with your change and these to feed the meter 'til the morning. Mind you; I think she's been saving them for a while."

"Ah, that's okay. Thank God! Don't worry, leave Tina to me, I'll sort it. I'm sure I've got some old candles around here somewhere in the meantime, to light this place up. Put those gas rings on to get some heat in here."

The women walked carefully around the kitchen in the darkness until Caitlin had turned on all four rings of the hooded gas cooker. She sat and watched her mother reach into a kitchen drawer in search of candles. Success! She looked at Caitlin with a tired smile.

"There you go. We'll be sorted in a minute."

She removed a lighter from her pocket and awkwardly lit two of the candles, placing them in saucers taken from the draining board. The bright candles were placed carefully on the windowsill, and in seconds, the room looked almost magical as it lit up softly.

"Any news about Daddy?" Caitlin asked her mother gently.

"Nothing, love. Haven't heard a word."

Majella opened the shopping bags and removed a bag of potatoes, a large onion and two packets of Irish special mince. Stew for dinner. Next, she placed a pint of milk on the table. She talked as she put the food away.

"I've been here all day and heard nothing, so I just ran out to get this stuff."

Their next-door neighbours the McFaddens' had a secure pay phone in a garden shed for their neighbours to use. They kept it locked, and to use it, you had to ask for the key. It was a community initiative, allowing those who couldn't afford a phone of their own the chance to call the many sons, daughters, brothers and sisters who had left Derry to find work in England, America or even as far away as Australia and New Zealand. Most, if not all, of the red public phone boxes in the area had been vandalised.

The front door soon opened, and a moment later, Tina walked into the kitchen. Her face and hair were wringing wet. She'd made no effort to protect herself from the rain. Water dripped onto the floor from her plastic mac as she took it off and asked her mother in a worried tone, "Any news?"

"Nothing, love. Jesus, Tina, hurry up and get that coat off before you die of cold. The electric's gone. Dry up for a minute, will you, and then stick my coat on. I want you to take these bottles to the shop so we can top up the meter. We need a fifty pence coin so take this too."

Tina took the few coins from the palm of her mother's hand. Caitlin watched the anger rise in her sister's face and her lips tighten, knowing where the bottles had come from. Ready to object to the request, but thinking better of it, Tina bit her lip and mumbled, "Right. I'll be back in a minute."

She picked up the bag of bottles and left the kitchen to find Majella's coat. Moments later, the women heard the broken front door slam closed. Caitlin felt for her sister. Tina was an odd one, a deep thinker, always keeping things to herself. Sadly, they didn't have a good relationship, and at times it hurt Caitlin when she'd attempt to talk to her sibling but would get very little back in return. She wished they were closer.

Chapter Six

An hour later, the mince was cooked, and the brightened house had finally warmed up. All three women sat at the kitchen table. Majella had let the candles continue to burn, and a soft and cosy atmosphere permeated the kitchen. Caitlin questioned Tina about her day at the Tech and whether there was any more fighting amongst the students (it was one of the very few places where Catholics and Protestants mixed). Apparently, there'd been no trouble, but she'd seen Mrs McFadden who still hadn't heard anything about her son Joe, and she too was worried sick. Turns out the Brits had kicked the Dohertys' poor dog so badly when it went for them that the loyal old thing had died. They'd also arrested a thirteen-year-old boy, believing him to be someone else. Under pressure from a furious Father McGuire, who turned up at the Strand Road barracks, they'd reluctantly let him go. A thirteen-year-old – imagine that! Mrs McFadden was right to think about sending Emmett over the border, and the women agreed they had a lot to thank Father McGuire for.

As they talked, the house suddenly shuddered and shook as it rocked in response to an almighty boom. It had to be a bomb. There'd been nearly fifty so far that year and they'd all grown used to the regular blasts. This one wasn't close, but it was near enough to give them a shock and a big one at that.

The boom was immediately followed by a loud, frantic knocking at the front door. Caitlin ran to open it and found Mrs McFadden standing on their doorstep in the rain. She was desperately trying to protect her bleached blonde hair, which was coiled around numerous coloured rollers. She was coatless and wore a flowered apron tied tightly across the front of her large bust, which only served to highlight its size. She jumped into the hallway as soon as the door opened.

Caitlin was very fond of Mrs McFadden. She was a kind woman who obviously adored her role as wife and mother. She worshipped young Emmett and looked after herself and her home so well considering she worked full-time as a catering supervisor at a large city hotel. She'd held numerous Tupperware parties in her house as a means of bringing in extra cash and was well known around the street.

In her rasping smoker's voice, she delivered a message.

"Hello, love. Tommy is on the phone looking for your Mammy. I think he's been trying to ring before, but sorry, I didn't hear the phone. I was upstairs with the hoover on. He sounds worried. You'd better get her now." She quickly turned and ran as fast as she could back towards her own house, shouting.

"Bye, love. Tell her to hurry!"

"Right, okay, I'll get her! Thanks, Mrs McFadden. Thank you!"

Caitlin rushed to the kitchen, crying, "Mammy, quickly, Tommy is on the phone at the McFaddens'!"

At this, Majella jumped up and ran full pelt to her neighbour's house. The impact of the slammed door behind her made a piece of door panel fall onto the tiled floor.

The sisters looked at each other. In an effort to keep moving and not have to think the worst, Caitlin suggested, "Let's set the table."

They placed the plates, knives and forks alongside tumblers of water and cheap paper napkins. Majella insisted they had napkins at every meal, including breakfast – even if it was just a piece of kitchen roll. Caitlin continued to talk as she placed the last glass down.

"I know you could have thrown a real fit about us taking your empties, Tina, but I'll make it up to you on payday."

Shaking her head, she replied, "It's okay. It's just we've been saving them, and half the money was Emmett's. Mind you; he's driving me crazy. He keeps asking me to go to the pictures to see *The Godfather* even though he's seen it twice! I wish he'd leave me alone."

Caitlin laughed. Poor Emmett.

The table was soon set, and the girls sat in awkward silence, waiting for their mother to return. Tina stared at her sister, feeling sad. She'd always found Caitlin hard to talk to. They were so different, and even though she knew her sister tried hard to get close to her, Tina found her difficult. Martin was the only one who understood her, and she missed him. She was lost when he wasn't around and sometimes felt alone in this house even when she was surrounded by the rest of her family.

She wished her life were different. She'd love to leave Derry but wouldn't go without Martin. When she'd suggested it, he'd only laughed and teased her. She hated these awkward feelings and wondered whether there was something wrong with her. At times she felt she didn't belong anywhere.

She found the continued silence uncomfortable so, making an effort, spoke quietly: "Mammy's taking her time, isn't she? Something must have happened."

As if to answer her a frantic knocking on the door began, and they both rushed to open it, bumping into each other as they ran down the hallway. Tina got there first to reveal a dishevelled Mrs McFadden standing next to their mother. Her hair had lost several of its rollers. She pushed her way into the hallway, literally holding Majella up.

Her mother's eyes were filled with raw pain as she gazed at Caitlin. In a short time, she seemed to have aged years. The sisters were really scared now.

"What is it?" Caitlin cried as she helped their neighbour hold up the distraught woman. "What's happened!"

Majella remained quiet, and Caitlin looked to Mrs McFadden for an answer.

Unusually for her, their neighbour hesitated before she spoke.

"God, Caitlin, your father's had a major heart attack. They're taking him to the hospital. Emmett's gone to get our Charlie to drive you over. It's not looking good. Your Mammy was on the floor when I went looking for her. Poor Tommy was still hanging on the other end of the phone, shouting! He's in a desperate state but says he'll meet you at A&E."

"I don't believe this is happening!" Caitlin cried. The small group of women remained fixed in the hallway, unsure of what to do.

Caitlin placed her hand on her sister's arm and in a calm tone told her, "Let's get Mammy out of the hall and into the living room."

They all agreed, and Majella was led slowly into the room and helped onto their brown corduroy buttoned sofa. Her body shuddered as she mumbled to herself incoherently. Caitlin couldn't even offer her a drink to help calm her – there wasn't anything left. She looked desperately at Tina, and in an authoritative voice, ordered her to put on the kettle.

"Make a strong tea for Mammy with two sugars, quick as you can."

Tina nodded and left the room, relieved to get out of the way.

Mrs McFadden and Caitlin sat with Majella for the next few minutes and talked until Tina returned with the tea. No one seemed to know what to say.

The minutes passed slowly as they waited for Charlie. The only sound was the relentless ticking of the old-fashioned wooden mantel clock that annoyingly appeared to get louder and louder as time went by.

Mrs McFadden couldn't sit still any longer and got up to go to the kitchen to make another pot of tea. Her nerves were wrecked, and she needed to do something to keep her occupied. Majella was in a bad way. Mrs McFadden herself was worried sick about Joe. Her only consolation was that, unlike his brother Emmett, Joe was a tough one and could handle himself. He'd been in and out of trouble so many times now she'd lost count, but she still worried about him – constantly. Tonight she felt old and tired. *What was happening to their world?* She thought as she returned to the living room with fresh tea.

Eventually, another loud thump on the door made them jump. Tina ran to answer it. "Big" Charlie McFadden stood there in the rain looking extremely worried. He brusquely rushed past Tina and called out his wife's name.

"In here!" Mrs McFadden replied.

He followed her voice and entered the living room where he looked suspiciously at his wife and then at Majella's shocked face.

"What the hell's going on, love? Our Emmett just gave me feckin' heart failure, grabbing me out of Mailey's bar like that! Stupid git's been talking gibberish the whole way here. What is it?"

Mrs McFadden quickly answered him.

"Sure, it's Patrick, Charlie; he's had a heart attack in custody. Have you had a lot to drink? Do you think you can drive them to the hospital?" indicating Caitlin and Majella.

"Ah, shit. Poor Patrick? Aye, no problem, I'll go and get me keys. I'm fine; I've only had a pint. It'll be some journey, though. Did you not hear it? A bomb's gone off in some shops next to the barracks."

Without saying more Charlie hastily disappeared to retrieve his keys from next door.

Caitlin knew the journey would be difficult, especially now. After any incident, there was always a chain reaction in an attempt to catch the perpetrators. Security would be heightened with more army and police checkpoints. Since the bomb had gone off on the west bank of the city, it meant all the ambulances would have to cross the city's only bridge, Craigavon. The general hospital was quite a way over on the east bank of the Waterside. A permanent checkpoint had been set up on the bridge and on any given day caused mayhem with local traffic. After a bomb, it was anyone's guess how long the journey would take.

Caitlin snatched their coats from under the stairs and offered to help her mother put hers on. The sugared tea seemed to have helped a little as Majella now appeared more settled, though still visibly upset.

She pushed Caitlin away as she attempted to put on the coat for her.

"I'm okay, love. I'm okay. I'll do it." She glanced at Tina and saw how unhappy her younger girl looked.

"Tina, shush now; don't worry. You stay here with Emmett and keep an eye on the house. We'll phone as soon as we know what's happened."

Majella looked at Mrs McFadden, who nodded back in agreement with an encouraging smile. She was very fond of Tina and hoped that maybe, someday, she and Emmett would get together. They'd make a lovely couple, and she knew how much Emmett adored the girl.

Charlie returned to the room and impatiently jingled his car keys, keen to get moving.

"Right. Let's go before they start another riot."

Tina's tear-filled eyes looked weary as she kissed her mother. She moved closer to Caitlin and whispered urgently, "Promise you'll call me as soon as you know anything. Find out about our Martin too, will you?" Caitlin nodded and hugged her tightly. Tina hugged her back uneasily.

The trio left the house quickly and made their way to the waiting car.

Charlie's pride and joy was his beloved red Ford Zephyr. It was his "baby", and he was regularly seen polishing and shining its immaculate bodywork.

Once inside the car, cosy in its fleece-covered seats, they set off. As the Ford inched its way through the battle-worn streets, Caitlin looked around.

They seemed relatively quiet tonight. Since it was teatime and pouring with rain, the rioters wouldn't likely be out until they'd eaten, and the rain had stopped or eased up a little.

Small groups of older men gathered on intermittent street corners and warmed their hands by the flames burning in cut-down oil drums. Others attempted to play football with discarded Coca-Cola cans. They nodded in recognition and approval as the car drove by.

The Ford slowly made its way down Abercorn Road, which led to the upper deck of the bridge. Predictably there was a long traffic queue, and the vehicle was stopped. As if sensing the urgency of its journey and in frustration at having to crawl, loud noises came from the car's powerful engine. Caitlin moaned.

"It's going to take forever to get through this, Charlie. Do you think if I go and tell them we're trying to get to the hospital, they'll let us straight through?"

Charlie exhaled and leaned back against his headrest. He was so massive he almost touched the roof of the car. He tutted at the question.

"Sure it won't make any difference… they'd probably slow us down even more just for badness. We'll have to wait, love. Don't worry; we'll get there soon enough."

By now it was pitch dark, and the rain poured down, drumming against the roof and sides of the car. Majella hadn't spoken a word since they'd left the house. Lost in thought, Caitlin reflected on the changes in their lives in just a few short months. Their mother had started to take antidepressants a year or so ago. She'd known Martin was deeply involved with the PIRA and had started drinking heavily too. Before all this, she'd been fine, but now even with a handful of antidepressants to mellow her, she was unmistakably on edge. Suddenly, it was all too much, and Caitlin just felt like crying.

The car edged past the red-and-white signs that warned oncoming drivers to dim their lights as they approached. While they queued to be inspected, ambulances sped past with their human cargo. The Ford inched forward for twenty long minutes until they were next in line. Charlie rolled down the driver's window and held out his driver's licence, ready to present it to the soldier.

Caitlin instinctively tucked herself back into the rear seat and stared straight ahead to avoid looking at the soldier who checked them, but she listened to his conversation with Charlie.

"Where you off to, mate?" the soldier asked.

"Altnagelvin, this woman's husband's had a heart attack."

The soldier bent down and shone his torch into the back of the car. He looked at Caitlin then moved the narrow beam across to Majella. The light lingered as he attempted to get a better look. He saw her distress and awkwardly looked back at Caitlin whose stare remained fixed and directed straight ahead. He stood back up and with the aid of his torch, scanned Charlie's licence. He handed it back and nodded.

"Move on but be quick. You can see there's been a major incident and the hospital is expecting casualties. Good luck."

Charlie quickly rolled his window back up and whispered under his breath,

"Jesus, some of them *are* human, after all."

The three-mile drive to the hospital took nearly forty minutes and felt like an eternity as the Zephyr's wipers screamed and fought against the downpour. Charlie kept to the main roads – it was wise to avoid the many Protestant areas of the Waterside where the kerbs were painted red, white and blue – accompanied by limp Union Jacks hanging from the same red, white and blue painted streetlights.

The Waterside was home to the many Protestants/Unionists of Derry. Over the years, the majority of Protestants had left the west bank of the city to move across the river. Unlike the slum terraces and hordes of unemployed on Derry's west bank, there was an air of prosperity here. Most of the men had jobs either in the Civil Service, the police, or were self-employed, and the majority of the houses were privately owned. A large number of Protestants had moved from the Fountain – a small Protestant enclave close to the city walls on the Derry side – whilst it was being redeveloped; very few of them moved back. They were the minority there and didn't feel safe so close to the Bogside where they were constantly threatened and came under daily attack. In their anger at this, many of the Orange Order Apprentice Boys became vigilantes, to protect the homes lying just metres outside the walled city.

The traffic remained heavy as they approached another checkpoint at the main entrance to the hospital. Four or five cars queued ahead. Charlie slammed his hand hard on the steering wheel, and Caitlin felt her mother give a start in response. She placed her hand on Majella's arm for reassurance as Charlie, in a deep blue rage by now, growled, "Fucking nightmare, this is! Fucking nightmare!"

Caitlin knew if the soldiers saw him angry, they'd only make it more difficult to get through or, worse, arrest him. Calmly, she told him to relax.

"Charlie, we're here now; take it easy. Whatever you do, don't let them see you're angry. They'll wind you up even worse. Careful now."

He knew the young girl was right, but they'd wound him up so much already, and there was only so much a man could take. It was the same everywhere: stop, search, go; stop, search, go. He was majorly pissed off. He couldn't understand how it was going so wrong! Everywhere you looked, there were soldiers and policemen. He'd never imagined that one day 22,000 soldiers would be living on their shores and, after Bloody Sunday, would likely be here for a long time. He was filled with dread and anger.

He repeated his earlier actions, rolling down the driver's window and preparing to present his licence once more. The camouflaged, caped soldier took it and studied it. His face half-hidden by a large hood, he asked tersely, "Where have you come from, sir?"

"Creggan," Charlie replied.

"What's your business here, sir?"

"Woman's husband's been brought into the hospital with a heart attack." Charlie impatiently pointed in the direction of the back seat.

"When, sir?"

"When what?"

"When was he admitted … sir?"

"I don't know. Last I heard he was in an ambulance!"

Charlie couldn't believe this! What was this twat up to?

"Can I ask you to get out of the car and open your boot, please, sir?"

Charlie hit the steering wheel again and exclaimed in exasperation: "You've got to be joking! We have to get to A&E! Jesus, the man might be dead by now!"

Ignoring Charlie's outburst, the soldier repeated his request but this time in a harsh, impatient tone. He was pissed off too; he'd been standing in this shitty rain for hours.

"*Sir*, for the final time, get out of the car and open your boot."

Charlie sighed heavily and climbed out. Rain poured down on him with a vengeance. Using his keys, he quickly opened the boot and lifted it up. He stood holding on to it. The soldier lazily leaned forward to search and check its contents, using his flashlight to illuminate them. He slowly and deliberately removed the lids of boxes and threw them aside, patently in an attempt to antagonise Charlie. Once satisfied, he nodded, and Charlie slammed down the boot in frustration. The soldier then shone his torch on the body of the car and checked underneath it as he made his way unhurriedly around to the bonnet. He smiled as he saw that he was annoying the driver and asked him to open the bonnet.

Caitlin watched as Charlie held his breath and attempted to calm himself. Reluctantly he opened the bonnet of the car, and the soldier, using his flashlight, peered inside. Nothing of interest there. He nodded. Charlie slammed the bonnet closed too and stood waiting. He was soaked, rigid and furious.

Taking his time re-reading Charlie's licence, the soldier then pointed the flashlight directly into Charlie's face. He smirked, and with obvious sarcasm quipped, "Move on quickly now, sirs. You're causing a queue." With that, he walked towards the next car.

Charlie couldn't speak. He simply shook his head, closed his eyes and groaned. He climbed back into the driver's seat and turned on the engine. As the Ford made its way into the hospital car park, Charlie mockingly repeated the soldier's words: *"What's your business here? What the fuck does he think we're doing here – out fucking shopping? It's a fucking hospital for Christ's sake!"*

The women said very little else but allowed their neighbour to rant until he calmed down and stopped talking. Eventually, they found a parking space, left the car and quickly made their way to the entrance of the Accident and Emergency department.

Chapter Seven

Not far away, in a fine residence in Prehen, James Henderson finished off a beautifully cooked dinner of partridge served at the long linen-draped table in his uncle's candle-lit, opulent dining room. James loved this room. His uncle had taken great pride in keeping to its original design, which had included the restoration of the Adam fireplace in which flames danced, casting a warm red glow over the room's lavish Chinese hand-painted wallpaper.

Outside, the rain continued to pummel against the sash windows. James looked towards the gathering of men dressed in black ties sitting around the table with him. His father, James Snr, sat proudly at one end of the table whilst Roger, James's Uncle, faced him from the other end. Father and son stared at each other for a moment as James thought about how alike the two brothers were. They were both tall and well-built with salt-and-pepper hair. They could easily be twins, but their temperaments couldn't be any more different.

His moustached father was ex-army, a former Captain who had served bravely in World War II and numerous other smaller campaigns until his retirement a few years ago. He was a severe man, a devout Presbyterian, and James found him difficult and argumentative most of the time. He suspected his father was jealous of the success of his elder sibling, who in return offered James Snr nothing but support and generosity.

To their left and right, along with James, sat a number of Ulster's most prominent businessmen, politicians, Churchmen, members of the City Council and security personnel as well as various senior employees from Rocola.

James was bored as inevitably "The Troubles" issue had once again raised its ugly head. The guests heatedly discussed their fears about the changing political climate.

James's mind wandered as he thought about his day. He'd been restless all afternoon and now found himself reflecting on Mrs Parkes and the admin staff. Several times since meeting her, his thoughts had drifted to the girl with the bruised face and black eye. He'd looked at her for only a few seconds, yet he'd sensed the fragility and the spirit in her and experienced a brief wave of protectiveness. Even with her injuries, she was stunning.

His feelings confused and irritated him. To calm himself, he sipped more fine red wine from a heavy Londonderry crystal glass. His career came first – it always had. He had plans, great plans, and little time for women, whether stunning or not. He'd made it clear to the very many he'd encountered that he wasn't interested in love or commitment – just sex. Most had walked away from his coldness, and that suited him. It made things easier. If any suitable woman was prepared to meet him on his terms, he was happy to oblige. Given the availability of liberal-minded women at Oxford, he'd become very experienced in the bedroom and enjoyed flitting from one sexual encounter to the next. Even so, he found himself rattled by his earlier meeting. His instant attraction to the young woman took him into unfamiliar territory, and he didn't like it.

His attention returned to the dinner as he looked across the table to a fat, bearded, red-faced individual sitting opposite him, who was clearly intoxicated. James had been introduced to him earlier that evening by his father, who appeared to know the man particularly well, it seemed.

Mr Charles Jones was a retired businessman from Belfast and reputed to be very wealthy, with major interests in the city's shipyards. He was also known to be a colossal contributor to and powerbroker within the Ulster Unionist Party. Almost immediately, James had taken a great dislike to the ugly, arrogant little man. He listened expressionless as Jones rudely proclaimed to the assembled diners:

"We are a divided party! This talk of a *Sunningdale Agreement*, why, it's poppycock! Those Westminster bastards are betraying us! The very thought of Papists being near – let alone inside – Stormont… Over my dead body!"

"Calm now, Charles, please," Roger replied firmly, and nodded to his nephew.

"James, kindly top up Mr Jones's glass, will you?"

The young man reluctantly leaned across the table and deliberately added just a tiny amount of claret to the empty glass. Roger had visibly been made uncomfortable by his guest's hectoring tone as he commented: "There isn't anyone round this table who doesn't agree with some of what you say, Charles. However, I think we need to consider the future. You've seen the news, so many dead this year, and I'm afraid this whole Shankill murders business is very unsettling too."

Jones shook his head and struck one fist against the fine mahogany table. The shining cutlery and glasses jumped under its impact.

"The vermin deserve it! We can't and will not lose control of our country. **Our** country, gentlemen! Many of us fought for and died for it, didn't we? What about the Somme? Ulster is ours! It's not for those Fenian fuckers in the South to tell us what to do with it!"

His words spewed out angrily through a spray of finest Médoc. Roger shivered at this barrage of hatred and James knew he needed somehow to help him by changing the subject. He was incredibly fond of his Uncle and didn't like to see him so upset.

Roger was a fair-minded man and vehemently loyal to his monarch, having also fought in World War II. Like many, he never talked about his service to King and Country. He hosted such dinners only because he was passionate about Rocola and the city. It was important to him to forge alliances within Londonderry's business community and to stay abreast of any changes in the political climate and local economy. He was one of the biggest employers in the area and bitterly torn by the barbaric events and escalation in violence across the Province. He loved Ireland, but lately, laughter and good humour were in short supply, and Roger suffered accordingly.

James was about to interject and end Jones's rant when a large, balding and distinguished-looking man, who sat next to him, spoke up in a loud commanding tone of voice.

"Charles, we have to try and find a way to stop all this violence. We need a middle ground and comments such as yours are certainly not going to help."

The speaker was George Shalham, Chief Constable of the RUC and son of a retired Westminster Member of Parliament. He knew the city well and was known for his impartiality, though the Nationalists were outraged that the son of an English MP should head a police force of which ninety-three per cent were Protestant.

Shalham was a modest and practical man who lacked any airs and graces. Against strong advice, his telephone number and home address were listed in the Phone Directory, thereby exposing him and his family to potential assassination. But he wasn't deterred.

Jones – not pleased about being interrupted – rudely reached across and grabbed the bottled wine that stood before James. Jones re-filled his glass to the brim, causing some of the blood-red wine to spill onto the pristine white tablecloth. Ignoring it, he hollered back: "Fuck the middle ground, George! Hang them all, including their numerous offspring. That Glenanne gang are doing us a favour. They're doing exactly what we want, only no one has the balls to say so. They're getting rid of the Papists for us!"

Loud gasps were heard around the table, and some of the shocked guests put down their cutlery or glasses.

Roger had pre-warned James that Jones – while under the influence – could likely cause trouble. It was time to stop him, so James decided to take charge. He looked at the guest seated to his other side, Albert Brown, a local solicitor, and asked him in a voice loud enough for the whole table to hear,

"So, Albert, do you think Mary Peters has done the right thing by ignoring the threats to her life and returning home?"

Relieved by the change of subject, Albert replied confidently.

"All credit to her, James. She's a tough cookie. Many women would have given up the ghost, but I suppose that's why she's an Olympian. We should all be proud of her."

Albert was right: it shouldn't matter what the athlete's background was. James nodded in response, but their conversation was rudely interrupted by an angry Jones, who cried out: "Bloody disgrace, I call it. The woman is brilliant! I mean, to win a medal for her country, return to Ulster and be warned she can't go back into her *own* home! A fucking disgrace! She's made of steel that one. A toast to her!"

He drained his glass oblivious to other guests, who sat by in silent embarrassment, looking at each other with eyebrows raised.

"Enough now, gentlemen," Roger exclaimed anxiously. He looked at his nephew again, imploring him for assistance. Christ, James thought. Will this night ever end!

"Uncle, I had a good look around the factory floor this afternoon. I'd forgotten how enormous it was. I mean, it's amazing and so streamlined. This time-and-motion study process is very clever too! I'd like to talk to you about it some more?"

"Of course, James, we can do it tomorrow," Roger replied.

James raised his voice and joked, "I don't think I've ever seen so many women in one place. I felt quite intimidated!"

The other guests chuckled in agreement as the atmosphere relaxed.

"Too true, James, too true. I've often felt the same way myself. Bloody terrifying! Regrettably, however, competition is growing, and our costs are increasing – particularly when compared with the Far East. The unions are putting us under real pressure too. There's talk of more strikes planned in protest against internment. Eight thousand workers across the City walked out last month alone! In the long term, our industry is not sustainable. We need to think to the future – and fast."

Roger appeared saddened by his own words and quickly drained his glass.

"I have some ideas, Uncle," James told him. "Perhaps we can talk tomorrow about those as well?"

"Certainly. A young man's ideas are always welcome. Very welcome indeed!"

The conversation lightened and continued late into the evening until the candles dimmed. In a drunken stupor by now, Jones quickly grew bored by the small talk and rudely removed himself from the table, to sit alone by the fire. His eyes were closed, and he appeared to be sleeping.

James got up, tossed his napkin down and glanced at the guests remaining around the table.

"Gentlemen, please excuse me. I've got a long day tomorrow. Now that my Uncle is looking for inspiration, I have to prepare. I will say good night." After exchanging pleasantries, he left.

At James's departure, Alfie McScott, the factory's bachelor accountant, stood up too. He was a nervous and self-conscious man, who wore thick bottle-bottom glasses that appeared to be too big for his long, thin face. Roger regarded him highly. He was a first-class accountant and totally dedicated to his job and Rocola's success. He just managed to save his glass of water from spilling over as he stood up from his chair. In his unassuming voice, he told the group, "Yes, yes, it's time I headed off as well. I didn't appreciate it was so late." He semi-bowed to Roger, thanked him for a wonderful evening and bade goodnight to the other guests. Jones also woke and left the house, grunting his thanks to Roger. He'd accepted George Shalham's offer to share his waiting police escort home.

Within a matter of minutes, the candle-lit room was empty of its guests, leaving just the two brothers, Roger and James Snr, who sat together by the fire. Hypnotised by its flames and enjoying the heat, James Snr talked quietly.

"I'm worried, Roger. These are serious times. I believe the Province is in real danger of collapsing. I've never seen anything like this before.

Think of Motorman… Such a giant operation! The Republicans aren't going to give up. Jones is right to be concerned. This is going to be a long and gory struggle. The PIRA are exploiting Bloody Sunday to recruit volunteers – hundreds of young men *and* women." He looked hard at his brother and waited for him to respond.

Roger thought for a moment. "You're right James. This referendum in the spring will be a farce too as most of the Catholics probably won't even vote – they'll likely be told to abstain. Such tension. It's a disaster, all of it and on top of that – what about the issues we have at the factory! I need another drink. Do you want one?" James Snr refused his offer.

Roger walked unsteadily to the table, refilled his glass and returned to his warm chair. Minutes passed in silence as the two men watched the dying flames. After a while, James Snr spoke.

"Do you think it's safe for my son to be here? He's surprisingly naïve. I don't think he truly understands what's going on."

Roger looked at his brother and knew he was right to be concerned, but also that James would be fine. He was a clever one. He'd pick it up soon enough.

"You're probably right, but James is a smart boy, and I agree, he needs to gain a better understanding of our ways here. You know what he's like, he's your son after all – once he gets something into his head, he won't easily give up on it."

It was late. The brothers talked some more until their glasses were empty. They stood and left the room after blowing out the candles, said their goodnights in the hallway and climbed the wide wrought-iron staircase up to their rooms.

Chapter Eight

Caitlin led the way as they entered the reception area of the A&E department. The screams of the injured and the haunting sounds of claxons reverberated throughout the hospital. As they walked through the double doors, they were hit by an overwhelming stench of sickness and fetid air coupled with the normal oppressive heat of any hospital. All three of them quickly removed their coats and attempted to cover their noses to avoid the searing smell of burned clothing and flesh. The small group stopped and stared in confusion at the turmoil before them in the overcrowded space. It was bedlam.

With no waiting space left, patients and visitors overflowed down the narrow corridors where doctors and nurses scuttled from patient to patient. Orderlies rushed past with laden trolleys and demanded access to cubicles, most of which were already filled with distressed and bloodied bodies.

The Great Hall – regularly used for such emergencies – was currently closed and idly awaiting the return of decorators the following day. The area was covered in tarpaulin and scaffolding with tins of paint tucked neatly into one corner. It couldn't be used. Anxious staff made every effort to find space for the many casualties. In frustration, nurses cried out at worried relatives, who manically pulled back privacy screens and curtains in search of their loved ones. Some even entered and searched the X-ray room oblivious to its many dangers.

Armed soldiers with minor wounds stood huddled in corners as they cautiously watched the scenes of carnage unfold around them. Shocked, white-faced men, women and children leaned against the green two-toned walls, or as a last resort, slumped on the grey vinyl floor. Patients with scorched bodies and torn clothes lay on stretchers, shrouded in a fine, grey-white powder. Heartbreakingly, the blast had claimed some larger items of their clothing and Caitlin could not help but stare as relatives and volunteers tried to modestly cover their partially dressed bodies with green paper-like shrouds. The noxious odour of burning hair and skin became more pronounced the further into the hospital they progressed.

Two middle-aged, uninjured RUC officers attempted to question a young man who could barely stand. His body shook uncontrollably, and the eyes he fixed on them looked glazed. With zero empathy and visibly frustrated by his lack of response, they barked their many questions, one after the other, at the shocked youngster.

"What's your name? Where were you when it happened? What did you see? Your name? What's your name! Did you see anyone or anything suspicious?!"

An attractive young female doctor in a white coat appeared out of nowhere and angrily attempted to push back the tallest policeman. She looked furious as she placed one arm protectively around the traumatised patient.

"For Christ's sake, he's in shock! You'll get nothing out of him! He probably can't even hear you!" She frowned at them both. "Where's your sense of compassion? Look at him. He's away with it!"

The smaller of the men pulled his colleague away and whispered something unintelligible in his ear. As they turned to leave, Caitlin managed to hear him tell the doctor menacingly, "Okay, but we'll be waiting outside; we're not going anywhere. We know one of those fucking bombers is likely to be here!"

He pointed at the shocked boy.

"And it could be him!"

They walked past Caitlin and disappeared through the exit into the night.

She and Charlie looked at each other and shook their heads. Unbelievable. Caitlin peered around the room and spotted the admissions desk. She took hold of her mother's arm tightly, and they pushed their way through a sea of bodies towards the desk. As they approached,

Caitlin took a look at the unsmiling nurse who was staffing it. She was in her fifties, with black-dyed hair, eyes set too close together and a generally miserable-looking face.

Once they got closer, they found themselves in a long queue. Caitlin sighed and sent her mother to wait at the side of the room, where it was a bit less crowded. At the head of the queue, a smoke-blackened woman in her early forties was shrieking at the dour nurse. Tears rolled down her black-dusted face and left two streaky white trails against her dirtied skin. She cried out in frustration at the nurse, who showed very little emotion or interest.

"She's five years old! I had hold of her hand! She was right beside me! I had her hand and then she was gone! Where is she? Is she here?!"

The nurse didn't look up as she answered. Her reply was inaudible. Caitlin stared in horror as the crying woman placed her head closer to the nurse, to try and understand. She couldn't hear her properly.

"What? What! I've told you a hundred times… Rosaleen McGuinness, she's five years old."

Charlie touched Caitlin's arm and whispered, "We aren't going to get anywhere here quick, love. Let's go straight up to Ward Eight; that's the Cardiac Unit."

"Actually, Charlie, I think I'd better stay here with Mammy and find out, just to make sure. You might as well go on up. At least that way we're both on it. Mammy's still too shaky. Look at her; I think she's away off again."

Caitlin jerked her head towards her mother, who was looking confused by her surroundings. Charlie nodded.

"You're right. Okay, I'll be as quick as I can."

He walked purposefully towards the door that led to the lifts and excused himself as he pushed gently through the throng.

Caitlin continued to watch the turmoil around her until, surprisingly, she heard a woman's voice call out her name. Her eyes searched the room until she eventually found its source.

"Caitlin, what the heck are you doing here? Are you all right, love?"

It was her cousin Kathy, Tommy's daughter. She'd just finished her paramedic training and had recently started to work at the hospital. They hugged. Caitlin could feel the sharp bones of Kathy's back jutting through her long hooded black waterproof. She was always amazed that Kathy could do such a job since she was a tiny thing – there wasn't a pick on her. However, her cousin's stubbornness and determination prevailed, and Tommy was proud as punch when she'd joined the ambulance service. They all thought it an unusual career choice for a woman. Caitlin had never been so glad to see her.

"Ock, Kathy, it's grand to see you! It's Daddy… We got a call to say he's had a heart attack, but we're getting nowhere here." Caitlin shook her head towards the sullen nurse on the admissions desk.

Kathy pulled back her hood and wiped her face with her hand.

"He's likely in Ward Eight. But listen, I'm in the middle of all this, I honestly can't stay, I have to go out again. There are more casualties to bring back. It's a messy one, a gigantic bomb. I can't help you now, love, but I'll do what I can when I get back."

Caitlin nodded understandingly and encouraged her to go, but Kathy took a second look at Majella and frowned. She went and took hold of her aunt's arm, coaxing her to move over so she could get in beside her.

"Majella, why don't you sit down? You don't look too good."

She led the older woman towards a row of occupied seats and approached a young boy, who sat swinging his legs back and forth. His head was lowered, and he stared down at the floor. He looked bored, but he was clean and tidy and showed no signs of injury.

Kathy hunkered down to his level and whispered conspiratorially to him.

"You wouldn't do me a favour, wee man? Could you just let this woman sit here for a minute? She's not feeling too well."

"Aye, no problem," he replied as he smiled and with childish energy jumped off the seat. Majella took his place with a tired smile and thanked him.

Kathy returned to touch Caitlin's arm lightly, looking apologetic as she declared,

"I'll try to get back to you as soon as I can. Listen, your Daddy'll be grand; he's in good hands up there. I'll see what I can do when I'm back. Promise!"

Kathy turned to leave, pulled her hood back up as her tiny resolute outline was magically swallowed up in the crowd.

Caitlin eyed the door that led to the lifts and upstairs wards. There was still no sign of Charlie. She spotted the smoke-blackened, sobbing woman from the queue earlier, now grasping on tight to the tiny, bloodied hand of a child on a trolley. It was being pushed at great speed by a frantic nurse and a green-robed doctor. They vanished through the swing doors. That had to be the lost child, Rosaleen.

The queue shuffled forward until, at last, they were next. Caitlin called her mother over to join her. The dour nurse ignored them at first and appeared to be more interested in some files on her desk. Caitlin began to grow angry, remembering this woman's uncaring attitude towards the traumatised mother in search of her child, who had been here all along. But the girl was determined to keep calm and not let the old bag intimidate her.

Taking her time, the nurse looked up and snapped.

"Yes?"

"My father has been brought in with a heart attack. Do you know where he is?"

Caitlin noticed her staff badge: Nurse Elizabeth Blood. Not a local for sure.

"Name?" She asked as she looked down at her papers once more.

"Patrick McLaughlin."

In a terse tone, she responded, "Hmmm.... Date of birth?"

"Twenty-fifth of December, nineteen thirty."

The nurse mechanically fingered through a large red plastic index box and thought to herself that by rights, she shouldn't have been working tonight. She was supposed to be having a quiet night in, just her, Tabby and *Crossroads*. That was until she got the phone call ordering her to report for duty. Why did she have to deal with all this shit! She'd been nursing too long and wanted out. It was only because her ignorant dead husband had screwed up his pension that she still worked. She was resentful enough about everything as it was, and now, she had to deal with this lot as well. God, she was so tired.

She couldn't conceal her resentment as she asked for the patient's address and looked at the young woman for an answer seeing the bruises on her face and evident distress. The older one standing behind looked away with the fairies. Tough titties. It was going to be like this all night, and Nurse Blood had only been on this godforsaken desk for a couple of hours and was already screaming inside.

She found the patient's details on a white card and read it.

In a brusque voice, she told the girl, "He's here, Ward 8. But you can't see him. He's a Category A patient, no visitors."

"But he's my father; we have to see him!" Caitlin cried.

The nurse stared coldly at her, stood up and barked over her head to the next in the queue, using her finger to encourage a woman to jump forward and push Caitlin aside: "Come ahead, will you!"

Caitlin didn't know what to do and stared at her mother, who appeared oblivious. Fuck this, thought Caitlin. She took her mother by the arm again and made her way to the doors leading to the lifts. Ironically, as Caitlin pushed through the double doors, she was met on the other side by Charlie, who was surrounded by a sea of staff, families and patients.

Frustrated and angry, he updated her on developments upstairs while holding his nose against the growing stench. Caitlin had grown used to it.

At any other time, she would have laughed at Charlie, who looked ridiculous as he held his nose and told her in a thick voice, "I was right; Ward 8. The Sister won't tell me anything as I'm not next-of-kin – only that he's not allowed any visitors, not even you, love. And wait 'til you hear this one! An orderly I know tells me your Da's in a private room with two fuckin' RUC men keeping guard outside!"

Caitlin's mother surprised them both when she unexpectedly cried out and grabbed Charlie's arm.

"What's going on? What are we going to do?!"

Caitlin stared at him and thought for a moment. With false bravado, she told him, "Charlie, can you please take Mammy and try and get her a cup of tea? Anything, just keep her going. I'm going to go up there myself and see what I can find out."

Passing Majella's arm to Charlie, she whispered soothingly, "Mammy, go with Charlie and get a hot drink. Leave it to me. I'll find out what's going on with Daddy."

Charlie half-smiled in agreement and led Majella gently back through the double doors to the emergency room.

Caitlin heaved a deep sigh as she watched them disappear and pushed her way to the front to press the call button for the lift. She looked up at the descending numbered lights as they indicated its slow journey to the ground floor. She spotted a cleaner in the hallway washing the bloodied floor with a crimson-headed mop. The woman didn't look up as her mop mechanically moved back and forth, left and right. She was lost in her own world.

Caitlin's heart was hammering. If her father was a Category A patient and in a private room with police guards, something definitely wasn't right. By the time the first lift arrived two trollies with crying, groaning, and obviously distressed patients were pushed in front of her. She looked at the broken, bloodied bodies and stepped away. She'd never seen anything like it.

Moments later, a second lift appeared, and Caitlin quickly squeezed her way inside along with too many others. The smell of vomit, blood and burning was even more nauseating in the confined space. She looked down and could see a blood-stained floor. The cleaner hadn't thought about the lifts, but fortunately, there were no trolleys this time. The lift decided to stop at each level until finally, she found herself alone with just a black-dressed, tiny old woman for company. They smiled at each other but remained quiet. Once they reached the eighth floor, the woman left the lift first and smiled sadly at Caitlin. "Night, love," she said. That was it, and soon she had disappeared down the long corridor. She reminded Caitlin of the old photos of Irishwomen seen outside their cottages a long time ago. There had been something very sad in her eyes as she'd said goodnight. What a day this had been, Caitlin thought as she looked left and right along the corridor, not quite sure where to go.

Other than the fading footsteps of the old woman, there was utter silence – in acknowledgement of the many "Silence Please" signs that decorated the walls. Caitlin decided to walk in the opposite direction until she found a sign to the Ward Sister's office. Soon enough, Caitlin stood outside the door.

With a loud exhalation of breath, she knocked on the door rather too loudly and waited. A few short seconds passed until a petite, pleasant-faced nurse dressed in an immaculate white linen butterfly hat, white-collared navy dress and starched apron, answered. Upon seeing Caitlin, the nurse smiled warmly and immediately, Caitlin felt better. A name tag next to her nurse's fob watch read, *Sister Moira Gallagher*.

"May I help you?" she asked kindly.

"Yes, please. My father was brought in earlier tonight. I've been told he's here. Patrick McLaughlin?"

"Ah, yes. Mr McLaughlin. He's in a private room."

She gestured for Caitlin to enter the small office, which was furnished with a single paper-strewn desk, two red plastic chairs leaning against a wall and a tall grey filing cabinet. Noticeboards hung on every available inch of wall, pinned with rosters, calendars, announcements and an assortment of thank you cards.

"You're his daughter, are you?"

"Yes."

"What's your name, love?"

"Caitlin."

"Well, Caitlin, as I explained to the gentleman who asked before, I can't tell you much – only that Special Branch have instructed us not to let *any* visitors in. On this occasion, we have to agree with them – at least for tonight. Your father is a very ill man. I'm sorry, but he may not even make it through to morning. He's in a bad way."

"Dear God, no! My mother's downstairs. We have to see him! Do you know what happened?" Caitlin was so shocked she fell heavily into one of the chairs lined up along the wall. She couldn't bear to think of losing daddy.

"I don't know what went on, but I noticed he has some bad bruises and cuts on his face. His lower back and the backs of his legs are bad too. Between you and me, they look like baton marks. I've reported them to the doctor, and I've made sure they're written down in his notes."

Caitlin wrung her hands together as she told the sister what happened.

"They nearly killed him when they took him – the Brits. They put a hood over his head. He was naked when they shoved him out in the street. I mean, nothing, no clothes on him at all!"

The Sister placed one hand on Caitlin's arm and patted it sympathetically.

"I'm so sorry, love. I'm so very sorry. There's been some serious trouble with internment."

Caitlin sighed as silent tears flowed down her cut and bruised face. Sister Gallagher continued to talk quietly to her.

"What happened to you, love?"

"I was punched by a soldier. I tried to stop them from taking Daddy."

Sister shook her head and thought, *God love the poor thing*. She considered for a short while and then whispered to Caitlin that she had a plan.

"Tell you what, you stay here, love. Just for a minute. I'll go and see what I can do."

Chapter Nine

Caitlin waited quietly in the nurse's office until she returned, looking excited.

"Right, I've had a quick word with the doctor. I know he's a real pain in the arse at times, but he's fair. You can see your Da quickly, for a few minutes, but only you, Caitlin. No one else, I'm afraid. And only for a few minutes, mind. Follow me."

Caitlin followed her guardian angel out of the office and turned left along the dimly lit corridor with semi-closed ward doors to either side. The half-open doors allowed her to see into shadowed wards where rows of patients in bed either slept or looked out at her. When they arrived at the last door, two burly RUC men were standing vigilantly outside and staring straight ahead.

They deliberately ignored the women until the Sister reached out to open the door. She was abruptly stopped by one of the menacing-looking men who gripped her tiny freckled hand with his. In a forbidding tone, he told her, "No visitors."

Caitlin's ally looked at him, smirked and said forcefully, "Sir, you keep to your job, and I'll keep to mine. I've spoken to Dr McGinley, and he's given permission for this child to visit her *very* sick father for a moment. So kindly move your hand *NOW* and get out of my way." She waited and watched before she spoke again.

"Please."

The man thought for a moment and wisely, but reluctantly, removed his hand. Caitlin was impressed. The nurse shot her a smile, and they closed the door quietly behind them. Caitlin immediately rushed over to the bed and to her father, who appeared to be asleep. The green woven bedspread tucked his lower body in tightly, and only his face, shoulders, and upper chest were exposed. His gaunt face was marked with deep cuts as well as red and purple bruises, particularly around his eyes and mouth. Wires branched from numerous machines, attached to his torso and arms. They bleeped continually and confirmed to Caitlin that he was alive – just.

She talked softly to him at first, leaning closer to his drawn and haggard face but with little effect. The sight of him lying still, helpless and unresponsive was terrifying and, in a panic, she cried.

"Daddy. Daddy, can you hear me?" Her own bruises and cuts stung as tears flowed freely down her cheeks, but she paid no attention. She tried again and pleaded.

"Daddy, it's me, Caitlin. Daddy… Please, just open your eyes for me."

The only response was the incessant pinging of the machines.

Sister Gallagher touched her shoulder and gently attempted to pull Caitlin away from her patient.

"Caitlin, love, he needs to rest. I'll keep a close eye on him tonight. It's getting late now, and you look exhausted. Take your mother home and give the ward a call in the morning." But Caitlin couldn't leave. She just couldn't leave her father here like this on his own.

"But what if something happens to him tonight?" she cried. "He'll be on his own… I can't leave him here! Please, Sister, let me stay with him?"

Caitlin looked at the nurse imploringly. Sister Gallagher's heart almost broke at the pain she was witnessing, but she had no choice. She'd been told to allow a visit of a few minutes only, and this was much harder than she'd thought. The poor girl was in a bad way and couldn't stay much longer, or the two hulks at the door would be in after her.

"You can't, love. We have to go. You don't want to get me into trouble, now do you? Sleep is the best thing for him. Trust me. Please, we have to go."

Caitlin knew she had no choice, and she certainly didn't want to get the kind nurse into trouble. So slowly and reluctantly, she released her father's hand. Before she left, she tried one more time to wake him.

"Daddy, Daddy, wake up! It's me, Caitlin!"

Again, there was no response from the motionless body on the bed. Caitlin stood and wiped her face using the sleeve of her coat. Her nose ran and dripped onto her lips. She hardly noticed. She took one final look, bent down and kissed him tenderly on the forehead, patting one of his torn cheeks. Sister stood beside her and thought enough was enough. She firmly placed her arms around Caitlin and led her out of the room. The guards watched the women – who ignored them – as they left and returned to their positions, watchful and silent.

They walked to the lift together until finally, Caitlin thanked the Sister – who continued to reassure her Patrick was in safe hands. They said goodnight and the nurse, head down and feeling dejected, walked back towards her office.

Caitlin waited an eternity for the lift to arrive. Frustratingly, it stopped at every level again until eventually, she was back on the ground floor. She re-entered A&E and realised that the sullen-faced nurse still remained behind her desk but faced an even longer queue of newly arrived and frightened visitors. The smell had become even worse and was almost suffocating in the overheated atmosphere.

She made her way towards her mother, who sat holding a white polystyrene cup that shook in her hands. Charlie saw Caitlin and rushed to her, asking impatiently,

"Any luck, did you see your Da?"

"I did, Charlie, the Sister in charge let me in. She wasn't allowed to at first, but she was lovely and had a word with the doctor. I managed to see him literally for a few minutes. The policemen were well pissed off. He's really bad! His colour is awful, he's badly cut and bruised, and he's out cold. She reckons he's had a beating – a bad one. She's worried he might not make it through to the morning!"

With this, Caitlin fell into Charlie's wide-open arms and sobbed.

As Majella watched her daughter break down, she cried, "What is it, Caitlin? Is he dead! Jesus, Caitlin, is he dead?"

She pulled herself out of Charlie's arms and ran to her mother.

"No, Mammy, no, he's not dead, but it's not good. We have to phone in the morning to see how he goes. They won't let anyone else see him tonight, not even Tommy. We should get home to Tina."

Charlie quietly swore and added to no one in particular, "British bastards are panicking in case anything happens to your Da because he was in custody when he had the heart attack. There'll be murder done if anything happens to him. You're right, love, let's get home."

Caitlin suddenly remembered her promise to her sister, and exclaimed, "Christ, I forgot! Tina! I need to ring her. Give me two minutes. She'll be worried sick. It could take ages to get home, Charlie. Does anyone have any change?"

He looked in his pocket for coins and gave Caitlin what he found. With a quick smile of gratitude, she rushed to the public phone and called their neighbour. Mrs McFadden answered almost immediately, and Caitlin updated her. She assured Caitlin she would go straight round to Tina and tell her they were on their way back.

Fortunately, as they prepared to leave, they met Tommy. He looked haggard and stressed. Instinctively he placed his fingers over his nose to stem the wretched smell, looked at his sister's tormented state and thought, *Christ, don't tell me I'm too late!*

"He's not dead, is he!" His sister sighed and comforted him.

"No, love; he's alive, but in a sorry state. They won't let me see him." She looked at her daughter. "But Caitlin did. Tell him what the Sister said, love."

Tommy turned and looked questioningly at his niece, who sighed and looked into his tired blue eyes as she told him the news.

"He's not good. They're not sure he'll make it to the morning. He's asleep, I think. I tried to wake him up, but nothing."

Tommy hissed and placed his head in his hands.

"I'm so sorry... Sweet Jesus, if he dies, it'll be a nightmare. The rioting has already started. There'll be murder on the streets! And what the *fuck is that* smell?"

Caitlin looked at the chaos around them as she explained.

"It's the bomb, Tommy. It's the smell of skin and hair. Jesus, it's been shocking... People have had their legs and arms blown off. I've never seen anything like it!"

He was lost for words when Caitlin asked, "Tommy, do you know what happened after Daddy was arrested? Did you hear?"

Before he answered, hairs rose on the back of Tommy's neck. He looked in dismay around the emergency room and took in the broken men, women and children, crying openly at the horror around them. He had to cough to stop his emotions taking over and answered her quietly.

"Not everything, but I spoke to Seamus Kelly, one of the lads who was lifted at the same time as your Da. Sixteen years old he is, only a boy. He says after getting a good hiding from the Brits in the back of the Pig, he and your Da were taken with two others to Strand Road Police Station. They were told to put boiler suits on – bastards wanted Kelly's clothes for forensics – and then a medical. The other two boys wouldn't wear them and refused the medical so were taken away. Kelly didn't see them after that."

Tommy paused and took a little time before continuing.

"Anyway, your Da and Kelly changed and agreed to a medical. Some medical! Apparently that fucker Harris walked in, all matter of fact and asked how they were – even though there was blood trickling down Kelly's nose and big chunks of his hair missing. Kelly tried to tell him your Da wasn't well. Harris ignored him, quickly signed a form stating, *"In his opinion, both men were fit for interrogation"* and left." Bastard didn't give a shite. Your Da and Kelly were split up after that. Jesus, Caitlin, you should see the state of Kelly. Patrick must be as bad or even worse."

Caitlin nodded. "He's had a good battering, no doubt about that. The Sister says it was likely a baton on the back of his back and legs. But we knew that already. It's his face; his face was worse – all cut and bruised. She's put it all in his notes and reported it to the doctor."

Tommy sighed and looked around the waiting room in search of an empty seat. He knew the doctor would do nothing with the notes. There was no point. He needed to sit down. His mind was reeling. There wasn't a chair anywhere so, still standing, he told her what happened next.

"Kelly says they were in interrogation for a couple of hours until he and Patrick were put back in a cell together. He knew Patrick wasn't good 'cos of his colour and 'cos he kept keeling over and jerking. When your Da started to hold his chest, Kelly knew he was in serious trouble and cried out for help. He says he was ringing the bell for ages, but no one came, and he literally ended up screaming and trying to kick the cell door down. When the lazy bastards arrived, they saw what was going on and called Harris back. Apparently, as soon as he saw your Da, he nearly shat himself, and straight away they phoned for an ambulance. Kelly said Harris looked as sick as a dog afterwards. I bet he did! It's a sin to call that man a doctor!"

Tommy felt sick and found it hard to continue, but the women prompted him to go on.

"Kelly reckons they only released him 'cos he saw it all. Apparently, Special Branch warned him if he opened his mouth, they'd make an example of him and his family."

"Dear Jesus!" Majella screamed. "But my Patrick? Sure he's never been involved! Didn't he warn our Martin not to get caught up in all of this? Didn't he? He told him so many times! Interrogation? Patrick knows nothing about nothing!"

Caitlin was solemn as she replied, at first quietly and then angrily when she talked of her brother.

"We know, Mammy, but this has to be because of our Martin. They know he's well involved and probably think Daddy is too. If I had my hands on my brother now, I'd kill him. But we have to go. I can't take this place or that smell any longer. And, Tommy, you don't look too good. You need to go home. There's nothing else we can do here."

The sorry group eventually made their way back to Charlie's car, having said goodnight to Tommy, who promised to visit them first thing the following morning. They made the long journey home in silence as they passed through the same roadblocks and interrogations – some carried out more menacingly than others – by a succession of angry, tired, wet and homesick soldiers.

Chapter Ten

James Henderson woke up the next day, feeling shaky. He'd been up for most of the night writing notes as his mind ran through the many ideas with which he'd hopefully impress his uncle later that day. His double bed was strewn with papers, books, notepads and pens. He yawned loudly and stretched his arched back as he extended his long arms high into the air. He grabbed his watch from the bedside table and saw it was still early.

He jumped out of bed and walked to the tall bay window where he pushed back the shutters to look outside. He was surprised. It was a clear, crisp morning that allowed a swathe of bright sunshine to flow into his room and immediately light it up. James saw the sunshine as a good omen. He murmured to himself as he tidied up his bed. "A quick run? Yep."

He hunted for a set of running gear in a tall dresser and got changed. Once ready, he left his bedroom quietly so as not to wake the household. He tiptoed carefully down the curved staircase to the halfway point and was startled to be greeted by his Uncle, who stood waiting at the bottom. He was already dressed for work and drinking from a porcelain mug. A newspaper was held under his other arm.

"Morning, James. Away for a run, eh? Forecast is for rain, so make it quick!"

"Morning, Uncle. You're up early. Everything all right?"

"Not really. I've a lot on my mind – didn't sleep a wink. Massive bomb last night in the city – surprised we didn't hear it. Major casualties including a five-year-old girl. Heart breaking. There'll be retaliation today, lad, I'm sure of it, so be careful on the way to the factory."

James wasn't worried. He could handle himself.

"Ock, Uncle, I'll be fine. I'm new to all this political stuff, I know, but don't worry. I don't understand it, nor do I intend to get involved." James smiled as he bounded down the stairs. "See you later."

The young man didn't see the look of surprise and hurt on his uncle's face as his eyes followed his nephew's departure.

Roger sighed and walked into the breakfast room, muttering to himself.

"Doesn't understand, does he? You will soon enough, my boy, you will soon enough."

Later over breakfast, after James had returned from his run and showered, the three Henderson men sat reading the local papers. Two were prominent on the table, the Catholic (or Nationalist) *Derry Journal* and the Protestant (or Unionist) *Sentinel*.

Roger was shocked as he summarised a story from the *Derry Journal*.

"Apparently, it was a bloodbath last night. At a tea shop. Can you imagine planting a bomb in a tea shop! Says here there was a Provisional IRA telephone warning, but they only managed to get half the people out. Children too! A poor wee girl pronounced dead late last night."

James Snr threw his paper down on the table and looked across at his brother as he snorted angrily.

"Absolute bastards! They're all thugs. How could they? Something has to be done, I tell you. They should all be taken out and shot! Or else locked up for good!"

Roger was stunned by his brother's rage. He'd never heard him talk like this and wondered whether his budding association with Charles Jones had started to have a negative impact. He'd have to talk to James Snr later, alone. He tried to pacify his younger brother as he answered, in a voice full of sadness.

"The poor mother and father must be heartbroken. Children shouldn't die before their parents. It's against the law of nature, isn't it?"

The table fell silent as his question remained unanswered. James Jr sensed the change of atmosphere and decided it was time for him to go. He didn't want to be caught up in the middle of another debate and so quickly folded his newspaper, drank the remainder of his coffee and announced, "Well, I'm off. Uncle, when you're ready. Would you like me to drive you in?"

Roger shook his head wearily and placed his newspaper back down. He'd read enough for one day.

"Not quite yet for me, lad. I've got a few things to do here at the house this morning. I'll meet you after lunch – in the early afternoon, perhaps?" Secretly James was relieved; he loved his uncle but enjoyed making the drive to the factory by himself. He got up and left the room, adding, "Fine. That'll do. Bye then."

"Bye, James," the two older men answered in unison. Roger was still fretful and cried after him: "Be careful." But James had already gone and hadn't registered his uncle's concern for him.

It was 8.30 when he slowly manoeuvred his sleek Jaguar down the long, tree-lined driveway. He loved his uncle's house, Melrose, with its award-winning rose garden and impressive, white-rendered Victorian façade complemented with beautiful, characteristic sash windows. It was a classic house. His Aunt Jocelyn, before she died, had spent numerous hours and days in its now mature and carefully tended garden. Sometimes, he could still feel her presence – especially in the rose garden. He'd been fond of his aunt and had spent most of his school holidays here alone with just her and Roger, who were childless. He'd never asked why he had no cousins. It was sad really; they would have made amazing parents.

James's own mother disappeared from his life when he was a very young child. He didn't remember her and was to find out years later that she'd run off with a much younger man, to start a new life in South Africa. Ultimately his childless aunt and uncle rescued a very young James and took him under their wing, encouraging him to spend as much time as possible with them in Ireland. His father, by now, had retired from the army, and James grew up knowing never to mention or ask about his mother. He knew his father was still bitter and frustrated at the way his life had turned out and was regularly prone to drink and gambling. He seemed to be in a continual foul mood and would disappear for days or even weeks on end. James knew more about his father's gambling addiction than he let on, having recently discovered it was the reason they'd lost their beautiful home in Ayrshire. James Snr had no choice but to sell it to cover his rising debts and soon turned to his loyal brother Roger, who gave him and his son a roof over their heads whilst keeping Roger's debtors at bay – or as much as he could afford too anyway.

As soon as James graduated from Oxford and before his uncle suggested he work at Rocola, James had worked for a year or more at a large fabric manufacturer near Ardrossan, thirty or so miles from Ayrshire. He'd enjoyed it at first, but soon grew bored and was relieved when Roger asked him to join the family firm in Northern Ireland. It was yet another of his uncle's many acts of kindness.

The drive into the factory in Londonderry, occasionally known as the Maiden City – proudly named as its walls were never breached despite three sieges over the last few hundred years – proved to be an onerous and frustrating journey. James was stopped more times than usual at the army checkpoints. Although he was fairly new to the city, his black Jag was well known and recognised by both the police and army. Normally he would have been waved through quickly. But not today. In the aftermath of the bombing last night, security had undoubtedly been heightened. At the last checkpoint, he'd been stopped by a polite and particularly young English soldier, who looked like he'd just got out of school. James thought about how different their lives were and how lucky he was.

Finally, he reached the factory and entered through the main gate. He parked the Jag in its newly allocated space and made his way, briefcase in hand, to the office building. He was annoyed to find thoughts of the battered-looking young girl re-entering his mind, so he quickly dismissed them. No time for that now. It was a big day today, and he'd some great ideas to propose. Life-changing ideas.

He made his way to his small office and settled down. A while later, there was a hard knock at his door. James didn't respond but looked up as Mrs Parkes briskly entered his office and held out a china cup and saucer to him. God, what a miserable-looking woman, he thought as he accepted the offering graciously. She greeted him sourly. "Mr Henderson. Tea."

He knew he would have to keep in with her. She was ultimately one of those know-alls who could either make life easy or unbearable. He had to tread carefully with her, very carefully.

"Morning, Mrs Parkes. How are you today? I must say; you're looking very smart!"

He noticed her neck slowly break out in red blotches and her face flush as she responded to such an unusual and unexpected compliment. She looked at him and wondered if he was toying with her. He didn't appear to be.

"Thank you, Mr Henderson. Now. Your Uncle called and asked me to put some time in the diary for you to meet him this afternoon. May I suggest two o'clock?"

"Two o'clock is fine. Thank you, Mrs Parkes." She nodded and turned to leave, but James suddenly remembered something and asked as politely as he could, using his most charming voice,

"Actually, Mrs Parkes, there is one small thing you might be able to help me with." She was intrigued.

"Really. What's that then?"

"Well, confidentially, the purpose of my meeting with my uncle this afternoon is to talk about my new role here. As he said yesterday, I will be needing secretarial support, and I wondered whether you could free one of your administrative staff to help me. Someone trustworthy."

James playfully winked at her. She was determined to ignore his flirtatious manner but couldn't help herself and blushed. Annoyed by her reaction, she placed her hands on her cheeks in a bid to hide her blotched face and neck. He was a smart aleck, this one, and she didn't think it would be right for any of her young girls to work with such a man.

"Well, let me think. The office girls are rather young and inexperienced. I think it best I help you myself. I'm sure Mr Henderson would agree. I'll discuss it with him when he comes in."

James panicked at the thought of her suggestion and quickly retorted, "Oh, no, Mrs Parkes, I wouldn't dream of it! The hours will be long, and I certainly wouldn't want to impose. I'm sure my uncle needs you much more but thank you for your kind offer."

The woman normally got her way. "No, Mr Henderson, I insist. Let me talk to him."

James wasn't having any of it. His tone became harder as he stood up and faced the stubborn woman, telling her in a resolute voice, "I don't think so, Mrs Parkes. You are, I have no doubt, much needed elsewhere. Perhaps there's someone else you could suggest?"

From his tone and demeanour, she knew she had no choice and suddenly felt quite nervous; after all, he was the boss's kin. "Ah, well, in that case, I suppose there is someone."

Good, he thought and listened to her suggestion, "There's Caitlin. Caitlin McLaughlin. She's a serious wee thing, but she keeps her head down and works hard. Has good secretarial qualifications too."

She knew that were she to suggest any of the other office girls they'd be useless to this man with their continual school-girl giggling.

James shrewdly asked in an innocent tone, "Caitlin, was she there yesterday when I visited your office?"

Mrs Parkes nodded and softly sighed.

"Aye, she was. Tall, skinny. Too skinny for my liking, but she's a good girl. Professional like."

Suddenly Mrs Parkes remembered something and looked worried. James noticed the change in her expression as she hesitated over something and finally divulged it.

"Mr Henderson… There is one thing I hadn't thought about, and perhaps on second thoughts I should help you after all."

James had no idea what the woman was talking about and queried.

'What is it?"

"Well, it's like this; she's a Papist."

James immediately fell into his chair.

"I'm sorry. You have me confused. She's a what?" He was unnerved by the woman's matter-of-fact prejudice.

Mrs Parkes began to fidget with her hands and looked down at the young man behind the desk. Maybe she should have kept quiet. She tried to explain.

"A *Catholic*, Mr Henderson. She's the only one of them in the office, but she's got a good head on her – a clever girl she is. Is that a problem for you, sir?"

James shook his head in disbelief and glared at her. "Frankly, I couldn't care less if she was the Pope himself."

For the second time that morning, he was oblivious to the impact of his words, though he did notice as an angry frown crossed the woman's face. An awkward silence hung in the room until – in a bid to lure her back on to his side – he concluded their conversation.

"Okay Mrs Parkes, I'd like to meet this Caitlin. Shall we say twelve o'clock, please?"

The woman thought for a moment about the plan for her day.

"I suppose so, yes. Twelve o'clock, it is. I'll bring her in myself."

James had to contain his laughter as the flushed woman almost semi-curtseyed before closing the door and left. He smiled inwardly as he removed his suit jacket and placed it carefully on the back of his chair. So the girl's name was Caitlin. A beautiful name. He felt a stir of excitement but thought no more of it as he returned to his books.

Sometime later, there was a soft knock on the door, and it opened. James watched as Mrs Parkes came through and impatiently waved a young woman into the office. Although the girl was simply dressed, her face still bruised and marked; she was more stunning up close.

"Please… come in, come in. Thank you, Mrs Parkes. If you allow me half an hour with Caitlin, I'll get her straight back to you."

Mrs Parkes wasn't particularly pleased about leaving the girl on her own in a closed office, at least not yet.

"Oh, right. I see. If I must."

She looked at Caitlin and gave her a look that reminded Caitlin of the stark instructions the woman had spat at her as they'd walked here a few short minutes ago.

"Only speak when spoken to. Don't ask too many questions. Listen carefully and make sure you talk slowly; otherwise, he won't understand a word!"

Escorted by James, Mrs Parkes reluctantly left the office, and he quickly closed the door behind her. He circled around his desk and smiled at Caitlin, aware of a slight increase in his heart rate. Surprisingly, he was a little tongue-tied and gestured for her to sit.

Caitlin sat down on one of the low visitors' chairs. She was nervous and still feeling quite ill after the strain of yesterday. She placed her shaking hands neatly on her lap, lifted her head, straightened her back (as her mother continually told her to do at the table) and looked directly at the young man who sat rather formally behind his desk. She could smell his aftershave again. It was strong, prickling her nostrils, but nice.

He was a handsome man, strongly built, with broad shoulders and soft green eyes. She'd noticed his smile when she'd come into the room. His skin was flawless and slightly tanned. She wasn't sure but thought he seemed nervous too. The office remained quiet as she waited for him to speak.

"Caitlin, you've been recommended to me by Mrs Parkes. I believe you are to be trusted, which is extremely important for what I am about to tell you. The simple truth is, Rocola is under serious financial pressure, and I have been tasked to find ways of easing this pressure. I need a secretary. A good one. The hours will be long, and I cannot guarantee extra pay, but I will try. Is this something you might be interested in?"

Caitlin immediately thought his soft Scottish accent sexy, but more importantly, he was offering her a change of job and maybe more money! She'd do anything to get away from Mrs Parkes and that cold dismal office. God, yes! She'd take the job. She fought to control her excitement and answered slowly and clearly – bearing in mind Mrs Parkes warnings.

"It sounds very interesting and, yes, Mr Henderson, I'd like it. I don't mind working long hours. No problem."

James was delighted. "Terrific. Okay, let me tell you more."

They continued to talk about their roles and agreed Caitlin would start the following week. This would allow her to manage her current tasks and hand them over. True to his word, the interview finished thirty minutes later, and he offered to walk her back to the admin office. She refused and thanked him again and self-consciously left, aware that he was watching her closely.

As soon as she'd gone, James let out a huge groan. Had he done the right thing? Whether he liked it or not, the girl had an effect on him, and he found this feeling odd. She wasn't exactly in his league. Her clothes were shabby if neat and her shoes well worn. Very noticeably, he and she were from very different worlds. Another bizarre feeling of protectiveness overcame him as he wondered how she'd been hurt.

He allowed his imagination free rein as he pictured her in designer clothes and shoes. She could be amazing. Rubenesque women didn't do anything for him. Caitlin was tall, slim and waif-like – just his type. He swivelled his chair around to look outside the factory window. Somehow, she had got under his skin. Deep down his instincts warned him of potential dangers, but he ignored them, sat back and enjoyed a lightness in his heart he hadn't felt in a very long time.

Chapter Eleven

It was Robert's turn to go out on foot patrol in "brick" formation alongside Val, two other squaddies and their Lance Corporal, or as they called him: their *Lance Jack*. The smallest patrol unit the army allowed. The brief was to proceed cautiously alongside the multi-coloured brick terraced houses and streets on the Lone Moor Road – a notorious Republican area in the Bogside.

They'd just left the safety of their barracks, running out as fast as they could through a single corrugated door at the back of the tall, iron-grilled barrack wall. As ordered, they'd zig-zagged left to right and back again across the open road, hoping to avoid any snipers and find safe cover. It had been Robert's turn to carry the riot gun, which was heavy and cumbersome.

Even though he'd normally prefer foot patrol, today he was frightened, but couldn't let anyone know. He'd slept badly the night before. It was always difficult knowing they were headed for a five- or six-hour patrol on the open street. They were like fairground ducks: exposed and waiting to be won as a prize by the many gun-wielding Provos of the city. At the briefing, their captain had shown them numerous mugshots of the usual suspects, plus some new faces. He'd drilled them on being vigilant and alert as they'd have to report back any issues, sightings of suspects, or vehicles of interest. They must expect the unexpected, they were told.

The army's experiences in Aden and Cyprus were proving useless in this Irish guerrilla war. At first, the men found it difficult to grasp the dangers of patrolling this city full of hate. It looked very like several other cities on the mainland as day-to-day the people shopped and made their way about their business. Sadly, some of the young soldiers, to their peril, didn't learn fast enough and had fallen victim to a bullet or bomb.

As he walked along the narrow street, Robert checked warily for loose bricks in the walls of the two-tone houses. Small deadly explosives could easily be tucked behind them. The unit also avoided burned-out cars and empty containers that might contain explosives to be remotely detonated as they passed.

He'd carefully studied the litter-strewn street and in particular focused on some burned-out houses adjacent to the demolished remains of others. A perfect hiding place for snipers. He paid even more attention to the movements of the adults and children on the street as he inhaled the air and smelled the burning coal from what seemed like hundreds of chimneys. The air was thick and heavy and caught the back of his throat. He was relieved to see lots of people about. It was much more dangerous when the streets were virtually empty and quiet.

He watched the children playing in the road. Some of the young girls swung on long pieces of rope tied around lampposts, their bottoms cushioned by thin coats, whilst others played hopscotch or skipped using old nylon washing lines or rope. Most of the boys kicked a deflated football around as a few lucky ones played with yo-yos, openly frustrated by their failed attempts to do tricks. The children had nowhere else to play. A few, if not all, of the playgrounds, had been ruined by the frequent riots. Regrettably, the patrols used the children for protection. They'd deliberately stay close to them and hunker down to the children's height. It gave them the chance to rest and take in their surroundings. It was unlikely they'd be shot at with children so close by.

A few of the lads with families of their own often felt guilty about using the kids as shields. Even so, they attempted to talk to the smaller bairns – who were none the wiser – yet. The older ones would ignore or swear at the troops, so they were left alone.

By now Robert had recognised the many "Dickers" from mugshots. Dickers were young men or women who monitored the patrols and anticipated their routes for future reference and potential attacks. They'd gather this information and feed it back to the Provos. It was a game of cat and mouse. At times, he'd acknowledge them with a wave to let them know he was onto them.

As he'd continued to walk along the single-file footpath, he passed many apron-clad women who stood straight-backed and proud, arms folded defiantly, on their recently washed doorsteps. As soon as they spotted the patrol, a few disappeared inside their houses but returned shortly afterwards holding out steel dustbin lids. As the soldiers drew closer, the women kneeled down and struck the bin lids hard against the ground. The noise was deafening.

Within seconds, the children had heard the sound and stopped playing. They rushed for the safety of their homes. The clanging continued as Robert, with a hammering heart, tried his best to ignore the racket. His pulse raced as fear gripped him.

He walked towards the first of the women and met her stare of contempt. She stopped banging the bin lid as he passed and, without warning, spat at him and screamed in his ear.

"Ye British bastards – out now. Brits out now!"

A few other women angrily joined in. Robert felt his heart race even faster.

He didn't understand this hatred and didn't think he ever would. He ignored the taunts and walked on at a much steadier pace. He had to be professional and not react.

He wiped the woman's saliva off his face with the back of his gloved hand as he listened to his Lance Jack, who told him to keep cool. The thunderous racket of the bin lids started again, but this time it was worse as it was accompanied by some of the older outraged children, blowing hard on plastic whistles.

Instinctively, Robert circled and watched them as he stepped backwards. He wouldn't see a sniper shot coming and knew it. He had to keep going and not think about it.

Eventually, he reached the corner of the street. He heard his Lance Jack whisper urgently from behind. Robert turned and watched as the corporal gestured to the riot gun, "Sallis, keep your guard up. Be ready to use that thing. I don't like this."

Robert wasn't sure what he referred to so followed the direction of his gaze and watched closely. At the other side of the street stood a group of forty or so women and children, who jeered and screamed brutally at a young girl. She was tiny, no more than eighteen, with long flowing, dark brown hair. She was dragged along by three black-masked women who all wore black jumpers and A-line skirts. The young girl was dressed in a brown and white smocked blouse with a long brown skirt and flat scuffed shoes. She looked terrified and was sobbing uncontrollably.

Robert gasped as he realised, she was pregnant. Her large bump supported a makeshift sign that sat high on top of it. One sleeve of her blouse was torn and revealed a bare shoulder. Her mouth was covered with tape and her hands crudely tied behind her back with what looked like a clothesline. The women deliberately propelled her towards a lamp post at the end of the street, next to the shocked patrol.

"Take cover, fast!" shouted the Lance Jack.

Robert had found a safe kneeling position. His eyes remained riveted on the scene being played out before him. He'd no idea what the mob was going to do. Suddenly it came to him as the young girl turned and he was able to read the cruel words written on the large home-made placard:

Turncoat Sanger Banger!

Her head hung low in defeat, shrouded by her long hair. Lance Jack told them all gravely, "Don't move, lads, keep alert, mind. We can't get involved in this."

The procession moved closer until it teasingly stopped right in front of the young soldiers. Robert heard the guttural sobs of the girl, who looked up and saw the lamp post for the first time. She understood, and immediately thought of her unborn child. They couldn't! Women wouldn't hurt a baby!

She screamed like an animal caught in a trap as she tried desperately to wrestle herself away from her captors and kicked out wildly through her muffled taped screams. The three masked women drew close to her and began to kick the young mother on her behind and legs, pushing her closer to the lamp post. Next, the ringleader reached into a black sack and pulled out a large pair of steel hair shears. She raised the blades high in the air for the shrilling crowd to see and approve. Slowly and deliberately, she raised long locks of the girl's dark hair and began erratically chopping off thick chunks and casting them randomly into the baying crowd.

The mob roared back in appreciation. Some of them yelled, "You were warned! You're a fuckin' traitor, whore!"

Others laughed as someone else roared out, "Ye wouldn't take your knickers off and stick to your own, could ye? Serves ye right!"

The Lance Jack gasped but repeated his instructions sternly to his men.

"Remember men; don't move. Keep calm and stay put. We can't do anything for her. Stay alert."

The three masked women tied the girl's feet to the lamp post first, in an effort to stop her legs from kicking out. Her beautiful long hair had now been replaced by a mass of jagged tufts. She continued to moan and sob. Tears poured down her face and onto the broken pavement.

Robert wanted so much to go to her, to help her, but he couldn't. Where the fuck was the RUC? He couldn't understand it. He'd heard of several girls being punished for fraternising with soldiers, but to see this happen crushed him. It was organised brutality. For the first time since he'd arrived in Ireland, he was truly angry and could feel a deep hatred rise inside towards these people. He'd never wanted to feel this way. This wasn't what he'd trained for. He had to remain professional and indifferent. But how could he after what he had just seen! He wouldn't survive here if he allowed this stuff to get into his head. How could these people do this – and women too! Fuck, this was like something out of the Middle Ages!

The Lance Jack noticed Robert's dazed look and knew they were in a potentially dangerous situation. He needed to get his lads out, and fast. He shook Sallis's arm and warned him again.

"Alert, Sallis! Listen, all of you. We're going to move back slowly on my count. Be ready when I say the word and follow me, slowly and quietly."

They acknowledged the order and Robert waited. Before he moved away, he took one last look at the wretched girl. By now, the crowd was clapping and cheering as the ringleader poured from a steel bucket a warm, gluey, black liquid all over the young woman's sheared head. The dense fluid slowly oozed down onto her shoulders and arms and pooled thickly on the pavement. She stood eerily, still making no sound. She was humiliated and broken and hoped that by remaining still; she'd somehow protect her baby. Adding to her humiliation, white and brown feathers were thrown over the tar and stuck fast – covering her head and body. Loose feathers fell around her or floated away.

The defiant ringleader stood with her hands on her hips and addressed the patrol. She was deliberately challenging them, and like a circus ringmaster announced,

"Right, everyone, show's over; leave the bitch alone. It's startin' to rain, and I've got to cook me man his dinner!"

The crowd clapped and laughed in response. The ringleader studied their reaction. She'd enjoyed that. She watched as the soldiers slowly rose from their positions as the Lance Jack ordered them to move out.

The disheartened soldiers were even more alert after that and continued the rest of their patrol, which thankfully proved uneventful. Hours later, they'd re-enacted their departure and hastily zig-zagged into the back entrance and safety of the barracks. They hated that last hundred-metre run. They were tired, and it felt like the longest run in the world. Sometimes it felt like the most dangerous part of the day.

They just wanted to get to safety, scoff down their dinner, and if lucky have a shower, a few beers and sleep.

Once inside, the patrol walked to a sandbagged corner where they carefully unloaded their arms, checked their ammo and had a debrief in the operations room. They remained solemn as they talked through what they'd witnessed.

Outside the operations room, Val placed his hand on Robert's shoulder and squeezed.

"You okay, canny lad? Nivver thought you'd see something like that on a British street, eh?"

Robert grunted and in an exasperated voice, responded, "Can you believe it? I mean she was fucken' pregnant, Val, and just a young girl too. This godforsaken country is mad… They did that to her because she was with one of us!"

Val nodded. He couldn't disagree with his friend, who was clearly shaken. He tried hard to cheer him up and chuckled as he put his hand on Rob's shoulder.

"Howay, bonny lad, let's get into our civvies and grab a few beers. It's been a shitty day." Robert was exhausted but knew he wouldn't sleep. Why not have a drink?

The two men quickly got changed and left for the games room. Adding to their woes, they met Billy Morris, who was frantically walking up and down the hallway outside the shower room. He was in a blinding rage as he shouted and swore at the empty corridor. He turned around and saw them, screeching out, "I'll kill them! I swear I'll kill all of them, the dirty Fenian bastards! Do you know what they did to me!"

He pointed at himself as he continued to shriek.

"Some little fucker threw a bucket of piss and shite out the window, right on top of me! They threw crisp packets full of shit at us too! Can you fuckin' believe it? And that dick-head of a corporal wouldn't let me go in after them!" He lifted his shirt and smelled it.

"Fuck, I'm minging!"

Robert and Val daren't look at each other as Morris waited for some sort of supportive response. Poker-faced, Robert answered, "That's a pisser, shitty." Morris was too angry to pick up on Robert's sarcastic innuendo and immediately shouted back, "Too right; believe me, I'll get them. I know the house!"

A young soldier walked out of the shower room, sniffed and looked at Morris who stared back at him with loathing and waited for the lad to comment. However, the youngster was wise enough to quickly recognise the Irishman's mood and half ran down the corridor to the safety of his bunk. Morris snorted as he hauled his putrid-smelling self towards a vacant shower, leaving Val and Robert alone in the corridor. The friends burst into laughter. Val patted his mate on the back.

"Pisser, shitty! Canny, Robbie, real canny! The radgie didn't even get it!"

They continued to snigger and laugh as they made their way to the games room. Their barracks had once been a public library in a beautiful walled parkland, and the games room was impressive with its high-corniced ceiling. The room was barely carpeted and contained six snooker tables. The air was filled with cigarette smoke and at the far end of the room, next to a barred window, stood a long, crude bar that offered cold drinks and light beer.

Randomly placed around the walls were sofas and chairs filled with mostly young men and just a few women, who were either reading or watching a small black-and-white television set. A group in one corner played cards and concentrated on their game. Posters of beautiful semi-nude women were interspersed with Union Jack flags and pictures of the Royal Family that adorned the walls. Rod Stewart's latest hit "You Wear It Well" belted out loudly from a battered old record player.

Val disappeared to the bar as Robert sat down on an empty sofa and watched the nearest snooker game. He sighed as his thoughts took him back to the pregnant woman and wondered how she was and whether she was still there, attached to the lamp post, all on her own.

He felt sick. If these people could do this to their own, what else were they capable of?

As he tried to relax, lost in his own thoughts, a young man came up to the sofa. Robert had seen him before and recognised his unique head of cropped but stark white hair. He was a young guy, short but well-built – the latter obvious from the solid upper body with rippling muscles and arms bursting through his shirt. He smiled as he looked down at Robert.

"Okay, mate? This seat free?" he asked, pointing to the empty spot next to Robert, who nodded and moved across the decrepit sofa.

"Yeah, fine, go ahead."

The man sat down and fell back into the depths of the sofa. He too watched the snooker game but wasn't paying much attention as he spoke.

"Heard about that girl. Suppose you saw it? Just unbelievable. Turns out they shot the father only last week. Seems he was from here and all. Joined up years back and came home on leave. Stupid git. Him a Catholic too."

"Jesus." Robert was shocked by the tragic story. The white-haired man offered his hand. Robert shook it as they introduced themselves.

"Steve North."

"Robert Sallis. Who you with? I've seen you around."

"Oh, I'm with Felix."

"Felix?" Robert asked, perplexed.

"Yeah, Felix like the cat… nine lives and all! You know, bomb disposal!"

"Aaaahhhh. Right." Robert thought likely that explained the white hair. It was some job. He couldn't understand how they did it. Mega-risky. All the lads admired them.

"You guys are legend."

"Nah, not really. I just happened to fall into it. I'm told I have steady hands even though they look like spades!"

As if to prove his words Steve, raised his hands for Robert to inspect. He was right; they were mammoth. Robert couldn't understand how the man could do such a delicate and frightening job with hands that size.

"They do an' all! Want a drink?"

"No, thanks, back on duty tomorrow. But ta anyway."

Val returned to the sofa with two beers in hand. He looked at Robert and raised his eyebrows. Robert quickly familiarised them with each other.

"Steve, Val. Val, Steve. Steve is with Felix."

"Felix?" Val asked.

"Yep, bomb disposal. Felix is our call sign."

Val passed Robert his drink and slowly whistled, impressed, as he wiped the front of his shirt that had somehow managed to attract spilt beer and now bore a long dripping brown stain. He was a slob, but a slob Robert trusted with his life. He smiled as Val, who'd given up on the dark wet stain, asked Steve, "Bomb disposal. How'd ye hack it? Is that what happened to the hair?" Steve laughed at Val's bluntness. He immediately liked him.

"Nah, went white for some reason – almost overnight – just happened. Was like it before I joined up. I've only been here a month. Some of the vets say they've never seen anything like it here. That two-day security brief they gave us doesn't prepare you for this shite. We're up to three bomb scares a day. Three! I've already had enough practice to last me a lifetime!"

He lowered his head and added sorrowfully, "Bad day today. Lost a man. He'd no chance. Report came in of a couple of suspicious-looking milk churns hidden on the side of a country road outside the city. RUC had to cordon the area off and push back the locals. Some of them wouldn't leave and just stood gaping at us. Others gave us aggro and started stoning the crew. Fucking mad! Anyway, device went off before he had a chance. Annihilated him. Twenty-five years old and nothing left, just pulp. Here one minute, gone the next. A good guy too. Just got married. You know what the fucking crowd did? They started singing that Queen song: *"Another one bites the dust."*

Steve's face blanked out as he remembered the scene.

"Jesus wept!" Robert cried. "Are you sure you don't want that drink?"

"Nah, thanks. Just needed to get away from the crew and try to switch off. Not doing a very good job, mind. I have to lock it all in this little black box." He half laughed as he tapped his head with his finger.

Robert and Val looked at each other, neither knowing what to say. It certainly put their day into perspective. Robert had an idea and turned to Steve, challenging him.

"Right, Stevie boy, let's switch ye off for a while."

He looked across the room and searched for a free snooker table. He saw one and cheerfully rumpled the young man's white hair.

"How about I beat your ass with a game and a laugh!?"

Steve smiled back in appreciation of the challenge. He needed a laugh and boldly reached for a snooker cue.

"You're on!"

Chapter Twelve

She smiled to herself as she thought how Kieran had spent a small fortune on her over the months. They'd been to the cinema a few times, sitting at the back cuddling, kissing and giggling as they'd watched the latest films including the Mark of the Devil. She hadn't enjoyed it; it scared the living daylights out of her, but he'd held her close as she watched it through her fingers.

He'd been shopping on his own and bought her loads of clothes and make-up. She was thrilled and told him numerous times how much she appreciated it.

At first, she'd thought it weird when he'd offered to help with her make-up and hair. How could he know anything about it or be interested in such things, but he proved to be a natural.

The time had come to step things up and unveil her new look. She stood in front of the mirror with her eyes closed. Kieran was behind, holding the top of her arms as he whispered excitedly in her ear, "Don't open them yet. Let me just tuck your hair in a bit." He spent a minute or two fixing it tightly into place and held his breath for a second. It felt oddly intimate.

"Okay, done. After three, open up. One, two, three!"

Almost afraid, she'd opened her eyes in amazement. She couldn't believe the change. She looked incredible!

He'd bought simple, but hip, short floral dresses as well as a black cocktail dress, some fake pearls and a pair of black patent shoes. She especially loved the three-quarter-length lace-up boots he'd bought to match the dresses. Together it all looked amazingly sophisticated. Her hair was simple but sexy and her make-up natural with trendy pearlescent eyeshadow.

"Oh my God!" she cried, studying herself. "Kieran, that's amazing. Thank you so much. Can we go out?!"

He'd laughed and agreed – as soon as he'd showered and changed. She waited in his lovely flat. She'd been amazed at the place and couldn't understand how he could afford it, but later he'd confessed it didn't belong to him but to a friend who was travelling.

She was full of excitement and kept looking in the mirror to take in her new look. She sat back on the sofa happily and thought about this amazing man who'd come into her life. He was a private person, refusing to tell her much about himself. However, he did talk about his ex- and her betrayal. They'd been together for a couple of years until one day she'd simply told him she was leaving him for his best friend. He was shocked and devastated, and although it was over a year, he said he wanted to take things slowly before he would make love to another girl. It would take time for him to trust again, and she understood. She had all the time in the world and would wait until he was ready.

Chapter Thirteen

Patrick McLaughlin finally came home. His body had been released by the hospital early that morning. Caitlin stood wearily next to the brass-handled pine coffin that took up the centre of their living room. She looked at his corpse and blessed herself. He was dressed in his best suit and tie with his only pair of cufflinks attached to the cuffs of an especially bought crisp white shirt. The coffin was lined in horrible cheap blue shiny satin. His face was expressionless – the typical look of the dead.

She studied his thick red freckled fingers, intertwined with rosary beads, and remembered the many times she'd held his hand as they'd walked in the city before he was ill. It'd become a joke between them until she reached sixteen and he wouldn't let her hold his hand anymore. He would laugh and tell her: "*People will think you're my girl-friend!*" She didn't think it was funny as she loved clasping his hand while they walked. It had made her feel safe when she was close to him. Passing cars would pump their horns, and Patrick would wave. She'd ask him who it was, and he'd laugh – he didn't have a clue!

Since his return, people had come in and out of their house with its closed curtains. They'd brought food, flowers and sympathy. As the numerous mourners stood over his coffin and prayed, they'd all agreed, "*Sure, he looks grand.*" She thought their words ridiculous. He looked far from *grand*! He was a lifeless shell that – to her – was nothing like him. She was so angry with him for leaving her.

Tommy placed a big hand on her shoulder and gently caressed it. He was wearing a dark suit, black tie and white shirt underneath a long black leather coat. His hair was tousled and evidently hadn't been combed. His eyes were shadowed and pouchy-looking. He moved closer to her as he whispered,

101

"I need you for a minute, Caitlin; can you come into the kitchen, please?"

She nodded and followed him through the strong smell of flowers. As she passed, people nodded and shook her hand as they solemnly murmured, "*Sorry for your trouble*". She hardly recognised any of them.

As she entered the kitchen, she sought out her heartbroken mother, who sat in Patrick's chair. The doctor had strengthened her medication, and it had noticeably worked. She wore a dark dress – not black, she didn't have one – her hair tied loosely in a ponytail away from her pale, tear-stained face. She was drugged to the hilt and sat listless and uninterested in her surroundings. Tommy politely ushered some mourners out of the kitchen and closed the door, leaving his sister, Caitlin, Mrs McFadden and himself alone. He steered his niece towards a chair.

"Sit, Caitlin; I need to talk to you."

She sat down and looked at him across the table. Everyone had been so kind. The table was overloaded with assorted sandwiches, biscuits and hot pies. How ironic there was so much food when just a few short days ago they'd hardly been able to give Tommy anything for Martin.

Tommy sat down opposite her and in a sombre tone voiced his concern about his sister. He gestured towards her.

"Caitlin, look at your Mammy – she isn't fit to lead today. I need you to do it. Also, the Boys have asked – out of respect – if they can escort the funeral and put a Tri-colour on your Da's coffin."

She couldn't believe what he was suggesting.

"Jesus, Tommy! Are you serious? Respect! Daddy didn't want anything to do with them. He warned us to keep our heads down and, God love him, look how he's ended up. He's dead, Tommy. So no, definitely not, they're not going to use him as another martyr!"

Tommy knew she was unlikely to change her mind but tried again.

"Are you sure, love? You don't turn those guys down just like that and most likely if Martin were here, he'd say yes."

Martin hadn't been released, and Caitlin was angry that Tommy was using him against her and his subtle threat of upsetting the Provos. She loved her uncle usually, but now she was furious.

"Well, Martin isn't here, and I'm certainly not worried about the other. I'm the one who's here for Mammy and Tina. He made his choice. Anyway, I blame him for this. He's the real reason Daddy's dead!"

Tommy sighed and looked at Mrs McFadden, who shook her head. It was clear she knew he was right, and Caitlin was wrong. But he knew his niece was close to breaking point.

"Okay, love, if that's what you want, but I still think you should agree. This tragedy is important to them and the Cause."

Caitlin took his hand and answered sadly. "No, Tommy. I can tell them if you want. But if it's better for you to do it, the answer is still no."

Tommy took a deep breath and wearily got up from his chair to leave the kitchen. They wouldn't be happy. As for Martin, he'd be furious too. Feeling frustrated, he quickly left the house of mourning and walked across the street towards a darkly dressed figure, who sat smoking and patiently awaiting an answer. He nodded a greeting as Tommy reached him and said,

"Sorry, it's no. They're well upset, especially the oldest girl. Our Majella is out of her head; she's away with it."

In response, the man grunted and threw his cigarette angrily to the ground as he started to walk away.

"Aye, right. I'll let them know."

Meanwhile, Caitlin remained in the kitchen and watched her mother, who sat frighteningly still. Mrs McFadden worked her way busily around the kitchen and made more tea as the house began to fill up again with a never-ending stream of mourners. Caitlin watched through the kitchen door along the hallway as half bottles of whiskey were discreetly shared and shots added to the hot drinks.

Mrs McFadden wore another of her flowered aprons over a simple black wool dress with thick black tights and flat black well-worn shoes. Her blonde hair was without her infamous rollers and brushed back from her face in a mass of rigid waves, set stiffly with a copious mass of hairspray. Caitlin looked around the small kitchen as she murmured, "Thank you for all your help, Mrs McFadden. I spoke to Granny earlier, but she still refuses to come. I really don't understand that woman."

Mrs McFadden smiled sadly.

"People are strange creatures, Caitlin, and sometimes families are the worst. It's no problem to me, love. I'm just so very sorry Patrick's gone. Your Da was a good man. I was in the same class as him at school; did you know that?" Her eyes filled up as she added, "I'll miss him."

Caitlin had always known Mrs McFadden had a soft spot for her father.

"I know. Daddy told me. He was very fond of you."

A moment passed between the two women until Caitlin took Mrs McFadden's arm and linked hers through it. Despondently she shook her head and gestured around the room.

"I'm not sure I can handle all of this on my own. I'm worried sick. Mammy might as well be a zombie; Tina hardly speaks to me and as for Martin... I'd kill him if I had my hands on him!"

The older woman unlinked their arms and turned to Caitlin to hug. Caitlin took comfort in the familiar scent of their neighbour's Fleurissimo perfume. She was a good soul and had been a solid fixture in Caitlin's life for as long as she could remember. Holding her tight, Mrs McFadden whispered encouragingly, "Listen, I'm with you all the way, love. Sure I love you like me own. And don't worry about Tina, you know what she's like. One step at a time, darlin'. So let's just take it slowly and try and sort your mother out first. Why don't we see if we can get some tea into her and bring her back to Planet Earth, eh?"

Caitlin pulled herself back from the comfort of her neighbour's arms and sighed as she wiped her eyes with her hands. The older woman was right. They had to do something.

"You're right. Sorry. I'll put the kettle on again."

Caitlin picked up the red kettle and placed it under the tap. Mrs McFadden sat next to her friend Majella and, for a few moments, studied her. They needed to do something and fast. She quickly stood up and advised Caitlin that she should get her mother ready for the off.

"Why don't you go on and take your Mammy upstairs and get ready? As soon as the kettle's boiled, I'll bring a pot of tea straight up."

Caitlin nodded and helped her mother from the chair and out of the kitchen. Although the staircase was just a few feet away, they found it difficult to break through the sea of people who appeared to have taken over their home. As they passed, they shook hands and thanked the many mourners who offered their sympathies. Eventually, they reached the top of their staircase and walked into Majella's bedroom.

Inside Caitlin looked at the neatly made double bed, as always adorned with its old threadbare pink candlewick bedspread. There was little furniture in the room. A fabric-topped stool sat opposite a three-drawered dressing table. On this, amongst the makeup and a few toiletries, were proudly displayed a series of black-and-white family photographs.

Majella sat down on the stool as Caitlin kneeled beside her and said lovingly,

"Mammy, listen, we need to perk you up a bit. We're going to be leaving the house soon. The crowd is going to be massive, so let me tidy you up."

Caitlin took her mother's much-loved hairbrush from the dressing table and released her hair from its loose ponytail. She brushed it slowly and carefully and then styled it into a small, neat bun. Finished, she opened the single wardrobe and began to search for a decent pair of shoes for her mother to wear.

As promised, Mrs McFadden soon knocked on the bedroom door and walked through. She placed a large pot of tea and a mug on the dressing table, smiled and left the room. From the treacle colour of the tea – it was obviously strong and most probably dosed with sugar.

A few minutes later, Tina entered the room and sat on the bed. She was wearing a black top and trousers, her fiery red hair tangled and unkempt. Her tear-stained face spoke for itself. Caitlin wanted to hold her but knew she'd likely be pushed away. She sat down next to her sister and spoke to her softly.

"Please don't cry anymore. We have to make Daddy proud and keep our heads high. I'm not sure what to do here and…"

But Caitlin didn't get a chance to finish as Tina jumped up and with a pained grimace on her face, cried, "If our Martin were here, he'd fucking know what to do!"

Caitlin was livid at her sister's outburst – especially in front of their mother. She stood up and pointed her finger angrily in her sister's face.

"Don't you dare use that language with me, young lady! And will you all just forget about big, perfect Martin? All I hear is our Martin this, our Martin that! Well, he's not friggin' here when we really need him! Today is about getting Mammy through this shit, and that's it. Get out of my sight!" Caitlin half-expected a response, but Tina had already gone, slamming the bedroom door hard behind.

As the girl walked into the bathroom, she realised she'd gone too far. She never snapped like that at Caitlin, but today her heart felt broken. She knew her sister had been trying to do her best. Deep down, she couldn't believe her daddy wasn't coming back and that he was gone – for good. She'd briefly seen him in his coffin, and he'd frightened her.

Majella had watched her daughters argue but remained silent. Caitlin returned to the cupboard to look for her shoes until she eventually took out the best she could find.

Slowly the tea began to revive Majella, and she looked at her eldest daughter reflected in the dressing-table mirror. Her voice was slurred.

"Tina's taking it bad. Don't… don't be angry with her, love."

Caitlin didn't comment. Her mother finished the remains of the tea and turned to face her. In her anguish, she asked, "What am I going to do, Caitlin? Your Da was the love of my life. I can't go on without him. He was my world."

Caitlin understood as she took Majella in her arms and whispered, "I know, Mammy, I know, and I'm so sorry. Let's just get today over with, please."

Majella stared at her for a moment, aware that Caitlin looked shattered, and took a deep breath. She had to pull herself together. She'd do it for Patrick and the girls. "You're right. I'll take another cup of that tea. It's well strong. Those tablets have really knocked me. Come on. I'll be okay."

Caitlin gave more tea to her mother, and then dejectedly entered her own bedroom. It was a small room with Holly Hobbit posters half-attached to the walls by yellowing, dried Sellotape. Her single wooden bed was covered with clothes after Tina had sought – unsuccessfully and without permission – to find something to wear for the funeral. Caitlin's only black dress was displayed on a steel clothes hanger that hung over her wardrobe door. She took it, began to dress, and swore as she remembered she didn't have any tights, having put her finger through her last pair. She had no choice but to put her bare feet into her recently polished black shoes. No one would notice and anyway she couldn't care less. She had more important things to think about.

A short time later, the family and just a few close friends gathered in the darkened, candle-lit room to say goodbye to Patrick. Majella cried as she bent over and kissed her husband on the lips, placing a single white rose alongside the rosary beads in his hands. She stepped away and looked at Tina, who remained expressionless as she did the same.

They watched as Caitlin took her turn. Hot tears welled up behind her eyes, but she slowly and deliberately closed them as she attempted to stem the flow. She'd done nothing but cry over the last few days, and she couldn't understand how she could have any tears left. Her throat felt like it was closing, and she found it hard to breathe. She swallowed deeply as she carefully leaned over the casket and kissed him – as always – on the forehead. In a low, shaking voice, she murmured,

"Bye, Daddy, I love you."

God, it hurt so much; she'd never felt pain such as this. She stood back and took a final look around the room. She bit her lip to stop the tears and struggled to contain her sobs. Tommy, who could see she was in trouble, took her hand and tightly squeezed it.

The black-suited undertakers had stood at the doorway, waiting for the family to say goodbye. They'd removed their hats out of respect. But it was time now, and Caitlin watched as with practised skill they gently laid the lid on the coffin. She was the last of the family to leave and so saw the men as they screwed the coffin lid shut. It was final. So very, very final.

Tommy stood in the hallway alongside her mother and Tina. Caitlin could smell whiskey on his breath. She'd never drunk alcohol, but at this moment she'd welcome anything or anyone who could take this awful pain away. She was dying inside and dreaded the next few hours.

In silence, the women put on their coats and walked outside to the waiting black funeral car. Tommy was to be one of the six pallbearers along with Big Charlie and some school friends of her father.

Unsurprisingly it was raining, with a light mist that mixed with the smoke emitted by the endless coal fires from the houses, and the sky was almost dark. Caitlin looked about as she tightened her black lace scarf. The street was heaving with people as far as she could see. In their hands, many held umbrellas, black flags or Ireland's Tri-colour flag raised high above their heads on wooden sticks.

The noise of helicopters was deafening and brought back horrible memories. Caitlin looked up to see two hovering, glass-fronted scouts monitoring the crowd below. The noise was truly ear-splitting – they were so low. The occupants were likely taking photographs and filming, to study the footage later. Around the streets, cordons of heavily armed RUC and army stood and waited. They were fully kitted and prepared for trouble in their hard hats, man-high plastic shields, guns and batons. They stood in grim silence alongside their steel-clad jeeps and APCs.

At the front of the crowd and closest to the house were countless reporters, photographers and camerapeople. As soon as they saw the family, they raced towards them, holding out their many microphones and cameras, barking question after question.

"Mrs McLaughlin, have you asked for an enquiry into the death of your husband? Have you seen an autopsy report yet?"

"Are you angry, Mrs McLaughlin? Do you condone the rioting and deaths last night in Londonderry and Belfast?"

"Mrs McLaughlin, was your husband ever involved in the IRA?"

"We understand you've refused to allow a Tri-colour on your husband's coffin. Is this true?"

The incessant questions continued until the reporters and camerapeople were pushed back by some local men, who roared angrily at them.

"For Christ's sake, leave them alone. Let them be!"

Through the commotion, the women struggled to get to the funeral car. Caitlin was in front and looked back to make sure her mother and Tina were right behind. She reached out to grab their hands and pulled them towards her until all three were safely inside the black Mercedes. The noise outside was deafening, and Majella shook in rage.

"Jesus, Mary and Joseph, what's happening? What *was* that? Did you see those people? Your Daddy would've hated this, Caitlin!"

"I know! Tommy said it would be bad, but I didn't think it'd be anything like this! We just have to wait a few more minutes, and then we'll go."

Caitlin twisted her body around and looked out of the rear-view window of the car. She could see Tommy, Charlie and the pallbearers bring the coffin carefully through the black crêpe-adorned door and place it inside the hearse. They then positioned the family's white roses on top of and to either side of the coffin and closed the rear door.

Through the rain, Tommy ran to the family car and climbed in. His coat was wet, and he shivered and trembled.

"I knew there'd be a crowd, but Jesus, I've never seen one this big! God, I need a drink!"

Caitlin stretched over and placed her hand in his, holding it tightly. It was her turn to reassure Tommy, who was visibly nervous and unsteady. Nothing was said between them, but his eyes acknowledged her gesture. They were okay again. As confidently as she could, Caitlin told them, "As I've said, we have to make Daddy proud so let's keep it together. I know he's here with us, I can feel him. Okay?"

No one answered, but they smiled sorrowfully and silently nodded their agreement.

She was relieved. "Good."

The engine started as two of the undertakers, in sombre black ribboned top hats and long black fitted Crombie coats, began to walk slowly to the front of the hearse to begin the funeral procession. As they walked, reminiscent of the parting of the Red Sea, the crush of people divided to allow the cars through. They murmured and mumbled as the gap closed and followed the cortège to the local church.

During the short drive, Caitlin could see that the crowd hadn't dwindled. If anything, it'd increased. People were everywhere, and some of the younger boys had climbed the black-flagged lamp posts for a better view and held on tight for dear life. Men, women, children, and mothers with prams stood solemnly in the rain and blessed themselves as Patrick's hearse passed. There was very little traffic but any cars they encountered quickly stopped in respect, switched off their engines and waited.

The car drove up the short slope to the entrance to the church and parked alongside the hearse. Tommy, with a nod to the women, climbed out and made his way over to the hearse to continue as a pallbearer. The women looked at each other and Caitlin, with a half-smile, whispered, "Okay, here we go. Deep breath."

Majella got out of the car first and was met by Mrs McFadden, who thankfully turned up from nowhere and offered her hand to her friend. Caitlin and Tina followed behind. Together they watched as the coffin and flowers were removed from the hearse. The six burly men lifted it painstakingly once again onto their shoulders before taking a few moments to find their balance. The undertakers then placed the family flowers carefully on top. The pallbearers were ready and climbed up the few steps to the entrance. Caitlin looked at the granite building. It wasn't a traditional church, far from it. Cruciform in shape, it had been built on a two-acre triangular site in the late '50s. Normally she would have derived comfort from it. She especially enjoyed the magnificent view from its entrance over the city and Foyle Valley. But not today.

Mrs McFadden steered Majella between her two daughters. They took her arms and made sure she was secure and supported. Slowly they followed the coffin.

Inside, the church was vast with arched columns and an elevated two-tiered ornate ceiling. The women walked past the endless rows of packed wooden pews that stood on either side of the long flagstone aisle. Ever since she'd been a little girl, Caitlin had dreamed of walking down this same aisle with her father on her wedding day. Not anymore.

The choir sang gently in the background as the funeral procession made its way to the white marble altar at the far end. Their priest Father McGuire – whom Caitlin had known all her life – waited, accompanied by a young priest who was new to the parish. Father McGuire looked weary in his white robe and purple vestments. The overwhelming smell of incense hung stubbornly in the air as an altar boy swayed a thurible to and fro.

Caitlin watched the undertakers remove the wet flowers from the coffin. The pallbearers carefully eased it from their shoulders and placed it on a stainless-steel gurney. As the choir sang, she recognised the hymn "Here I Am, Lord" – Patrick's favourite.

The church continued to fill up. Later that day, Caitlin was told that the crowd had overflowed through the gates of the church car park and into the nearby streets. Outside, loudspeakers had been set up so as many of the people as possible could hear the Requiem Mass.

At last, it began, and the women held each other tightly. Tina sat upright and rigid until she stood to make her way to the altar. Her voice shook as she started to read the psalm, only to break down halfway through. Old Father McGuire rushed to her and quickly but gently led her back to her mother. He looked at Caitlin, who immediately knew he wanted her to finish. She nodded and rose to the pulpit to complete the words. She looked at the congregation before she began. The church was full. Men stood along the sides and back as the seated women quietly sobbed: the only sound as the congregation listened to her continue the psalm.

At the end of the psalm, both the worshippers and Caitlin finished together. "*The Lord is my shepherd; there is nothing I shall want.*"

In his sermon, Father McGuire told the congregation about Patrick's life and how he had known him well. They had been good friends. The priest assured them that he knew Patrick would not want his death to be the cause of any more violence. In a voice drained by tiredness, he pleaded desperately to the crowds inside and outside the church.

"So every man, woman, boy and girl listening to me here today; go home and find it in your hearts to forgive. Patrick's death is a tragedy, an awful tragedy. But let it be just that. No more of this violence, please."

The church remained silent and respectful. The old priest knew it was too late. The trouble had already started here in the city and Belfast.

The Mass ended, and the pallbearers removed the coffin. The family car and hearse were followed by a giant crowd to the nearby eighteenth-century walled cemetery. It had finally stopped raining, and the sky appeared brighter. On either side of the road, they drove past numerous burned out and overturned cars before they entered the cemetery gate, passing more RUC and army vehicles next to Stones Corner.

Inside, they were driven to a newly dug grave on the far side of the vast graveyard. Caitlin, freezing in her bare legs, walked over the rain-soaked ground towards the yawning pit.

The crowd was silent as Father McGuire started to pray. As he gave his final blessing and the coffin was about to be placed deep into the water-drenched grave, a colour party of four darkly dressed, masked men carrying pistols calmly and determinedly appeared from amongst the crowd. In pairs, they stood to attention on either side of the coffin.

The crowd gasped. One of the armed men carried a folded Irish Tricolour and carefully draped it over Patrick's coffin. Within seconds a volley of gunshots echoed across the vast cemetery and then – as mysteriously as they'd arrived – the gunmen ducked and were absorbed into the throng of people and disappeared. Instantaneously there was a wave of applause and cheers.

The three women could only stare at the coffin now adorned in its green, white and gold shroud. Caitlin could feel Tommy's eyes on her as he watched for her reaction.

Instead, she looked down the hill towards Derry's infamous city walls, over which hung a beautiful vibrant-coloured rainbow. She no longer paid any attention to the draped coffin nor the noise of the cheering crowd nor even the deafening helicopters that searched frantically above her for the vanishing gunmen.

She knew the rainbow was a sign and smiled gently at Tommy, whose face and body immediately relaxed as a huge wave of relief washed over him. She had no fight left and instead sensed a sudden peace surrounding her. Daddy *was* here. She could feel him right beside her.

Chapter Fourteen

He'd kept her sweet for what seemed like ages, but now he had no choice: the pressure was on. They'd just left the picture house and sat in a small café along the street. He'd been withdrawn from her all night, and he knew she was concerned. She took his hand and asked, "What is it, Kieran? You've been so quiet."

He looked at her, and his eyes welled up. She'd rarely seen a man cry. Shocked, she grasped both his hands, leaned closer and asked gravely, "What is it, Kieran? Tell me."

He seemed to find it hard to look at her until she raised his chin with her finger and made him meet her trusting eyes.

"Tell me."

He swallowed and began to speak.

"I'm in trouble, Honey. Big trouble. I need your help."

In their short time together, she'd never seen him so vulnerable and wanted to make things better.

"What sort of help?"

Siobhan, an old waitress everyone knew, brought their drinks and left. Kieran began telling his story in a tone of desperation.

"You mustn't tell anyone. Please. No one."

"I swear."

"I've been doing the odd job for the Provos lately, nothing big, just simple things, low risk. Anyway, they've told me they're giving me a mission, and this time they're not asking; they're telling. I don't know what to do."

He moved closer and whispered,

"They want me to set up a honey trap?"

She was confused. "A honey trap. What do you mean?"

"It's when a woman lures a man into a trap."

"Why? What for?"

"Information. They want me to get a couple of soldiers set up so they can interrogate them."

"But how can you do that? You'd need a woman to do it... Aaaah! I see."

He remained silent as he watched her face change expression as she slowly understood.

She looked at him carefully and thought for a second. He'd been so kind and generous and made her feel like she was the only woman alive. She was convinced he was falling in love with her, and she couldn't imagine her life without him.

She chuckled and shook her head. Kieran couldn't believe it was so easy when she smiled and asked, "What do you want me to do?"

Chapter Fifteen

James had spent the last few days getting organised at home and then at the factory where Caitlin – when allowed by crabbit Mrs Parkes – helped him set up. This was followed by a weekend with friends in the Victorian seaside resort, Portrush. The beaches were incredible, and he particularly loved the long stretch of white sand at Benone, which was continually pounded by enormous, roaring, white-crested waves. He'd also visited the world-famous Giants Causeway, which never ceased to amaze him. He found the whole Antrim coastline overwhelming. Wrapped in warm, waterproof clothing, he'd been prepared for the unceasing rain and so had walked for miles. The rain never bothered him; he loved being outside and laughed when everyone else moaned about the weather. This was Ireland after all!

His friends had commented on his good humour and playfully asked him the reason. He knew a small part of his mood was the prospect of working with Caitlin, but instead told them he was excited about his new job and its opportunities. No more than that.

He'd had a haircut and studied his appearance in the mirror. Subconsciously he'd taken extra care while dressing for work that morning. Sporting a dark grey suit, one of their own Rocola white shirts and his favourite grey and white striped tie, he felt good. To finish, he slipped on a pair of black leather Church's shoes and splashed on his favourite Eau Sauvage aftershave.

Over breakfast, his father warned him to be careful driving to the factory. There'd been a wave of riots whilst he'd been away – something to do with a local man dying in custody that had resulted in several deaths across the Province. A good quantity of RUC men and soldiers had been injured and a substantial number of people arrested. James only half-listened and assured his father once again he'd be fine so, with a hurried good-bye, he left Melrose.

As he arrived at Craigavon Bridge checkpoint, the traffic slowed to a crawl. From his Jaguar he was able to read the giant handwritten blackboard fixed to the bridge's superstructure.

MAKING ULSTER SAFE	
	Since Operation Motorman we have recovered to date:
	18th September at 07.30 a.m.
388	Weapons
57,638	Rounds of Ammunition
20,530	Lbs. of Explosives
Making Ulster a safer place for you and your children to live in If you know of anymore, ring Londonderry 2340 Confidentiality will be respected	

James was fascinated by these statistics and wondered whether anyone ever called the number in the hope or assurance that their one call could "*Make Ulster Safe*". He didn't think so.

James re-read the sign. Lost in thought, he didn't notice that he'd allowed a wide gap to form between his Jaguar and the car ahead. He looked up and swore loudly as he drove hurriedly towards the checkpoint. It was a dangerous thing to do, and now he was driving too fast. Shit!

The young soldier was wary as he watched a black Jaguar accelerate towards him. He raised his hand and ordered his colleagues to keep a close watch as the car approached. New to Londonderry, he'd didn't recognise the vehicle or who was driving. He remained vigilant and positioned himself a few paces back from the vehicle as James wound down the driver's window.

Relieved beyond belief, the soldier heard someone shout to him from behind:

"It's okay, mate. We know him. He's a good 'un!"

The soldier inhaled and made his way towards the car. He carefully glanced past James and around the car's interior. He intended to follow the correct procedure to the letter.

Instinctively James passed his licence to the soldier, who didn't even look at it.

"Morning, sir," he said. "In future, can you keep your eyes on the road? That was a very dangerous thing you just did, speeding up before a checkpoint."

James knew he was right.

Your name, please?" the soldier asked, examining him closely.

"James Henderson."

"Date of birth?"

"7th April 1947."

"Can you tell me where you have come from today?"

"Home."

"And home is…?"

"In Prehen."

"Where are you going now?"

"Work."

"And where do you work?" the soldier asked. He looked down at the licence and tilted his head slightly.

"Rocola Factory, Blighs Lane."

"Blighs Lane, eh? Is that the one near Stones Corner in Creggan?" The soldier appeared newly suspicious and looked again inside the car. A brave – or stupid – driver tooted his car horn impatiently from the queue of cars behind.

"Is there a problem?" James asked in a slightly terse tone. He wasn't used to this type of questioning and didn't like it. He knew he'd messed up, but this guy was just being antagonistic.

"Not so much a problem, sir. You have a Scottish licence and not a Northern Ireland issue. Why's that?

James had no idea what he was on about. A licence was a licence, wasn't it?

"I've lived in Scotland. Moved here with a new job."

"Ah. A Scot."

James didn't like his tone and retorted, "Have *you* just arrived here?"

"Sorry?"

"Are you new here?"

"Yes, sir."

"Like it?"

James's question was ignored as the licence was almost thrown back at him.

"Get yourself a Northern Ireland licence. You can go. Thank you, sir."

He dismissed James with a wave, waited for the next frustrated driver to move forward, and thought of his drunken Scottish stepfather who'd regularly beat the shit out of him as a youngster.

Maddened, James drove on, thinking about the soldier for a moment until he relived the heated conversation, they'd endured over dinner on Saturday night.

One of the guests was an RUC man who worked for Shalham, called something like Bonner. James soon discovered that the man was a pain in the arse, solidly entrenched in his opinions and refusing to listen to reason from any of the other guests. He'd reminded James of Charles Jones. He continued to insist that the British Army had been too soft on the Roman Catholics. It was a disgrace that for eleven months they'd had their own "no-go" areas, giving them the chance to hide terrorists and build up their stocks of guns and bomb-making equipment. Operation Motorman had come far too late, in his opinion. He believed the British Army now "policed" Londonderry with very little or no help from the RUC. He'd told them of the infamous three-day Battle of the Bogside from which he still bore nasty facial scars. He openly despised the Nationalists.

For the first time since he'd arrived in Londonderry, James had been deeply troubled. This man was a policeman, someone who should have acted as a peacekeeper, a protector, yet he was an unashamed bigot. Later, James spoke at length to his uncle and father about the man and his opinions. His father could only suggest that James attend a meeting of the Waterside Apprentice Boys – one of the Protestant Loyal Orders. He'd said it might help James gain a better perspective of the Troubles and the complex history of the city and indeed Ireland. Additionally, it was a good means of meeting other local businessmen. James didn't want to take sides but told him he'd think about it.

The Jaguar had continued to move along the Foyle Road and past the city cemetery. A huge redevelopment programme had begun on the West Bank. Long rows of terraced slums had been recently demolished. The resulting open space had been taken over by gangs of young children, serious-faced and intent on their games. As he drove past, he watched two young boys of nine or ten drag a steel-framed single bed towards a poorly built barricade. Their attempts were futile. It was too heavy, but comical to watch. Most of the schools had been closed to coincide with an ongoing rent and rate strike called in protest against internment.

He passed what looked like a metre-high makeshift memorial that sat forlornly in the middle of the road – another reminder of a civilian fatally shot by the British Army. Similar to a tent frame, white scaffolding posts protected the memorial and were held in place by grey breeze blocks. Someone had placed in the middle of the makeshift structure a framed photograph of the victim along with numerous Mass cards, statues and flowers. On its perimeter, four yellow arrows had been painted, pointing to the exact spot where the victim had fallen. A large black flag had been tied to one of the posts that stood adjacent to a Celtic cross. With their heads hung low in prayer, a man and woman stood next to it. The weeping woman held a handkerchief to her face.

James felt sad at the sight and to divert himself, he switched on the car radio. The announcer informed the audience that it was 9 a.m. and the news report began with an account of the weekend's disturbances. He listened carefully.

"There have been full-scale riots and a number of deaths throughout Londonderry and Belfast over the weekend in response to the death of forty-two-year-old Patrick McLaughlin, said to have been badly beaten whilst being held in custody following Operation Motorman. The SDLP have strongly condemned McLaughlin's death and have called for an independent inquiry, not only into this case but all those where beatings and torture have been reported."

The announcer continued with other updates and finally finished with the sports news.

"Due to the increased security risks for visiting football teams, Derry City FC has withdrawn from senior football in the Irish League..."

The presenter didn't get a chance to finish as James exasperatedly switched off the radio. His good mood had all but evaporated as a sudden feeling of heavy depression descended on him. This place was starting to get to him.

Finally, he arrived at the factory. The last stream of latecomers with lowered heads rushed past him and through the doors, desperate to clock on in time.

The lift had not yet been repaired, so he climbed the stairs and, slightly out of breath, opened his office door. Mrs Parkes stood dutifully to attention in the room with a cup of tea for him waiting on his desk. She smiled as he came through the door.

"Good morning, Mr Henderson. I take it you had a good weekend?"

"Yes, thank you." He removed his coat and shook it before hanging it on a carved oak coat stand that stood half-hidden in the corner. He didn't want the woman hovering over him. He sat down and in an irate voice announced: "Mrs Parkes, Caitlin starts working for me today. I suggest you redistribute her workload. We can't recruit anyone for her old position, given our current financial difficulties."

Mrs Parkes was evidently perturbed by this news. She'd known Caitlin would be moving but was peeved that she wouldn't be able to replace her. It meant more work for her and that useless pair of dim-wits!

She stood and waited for him to continue but was met by silence.

"Right. I see. Well, however, I do need to check with Mr Henderson Snr first..."

James, who wasn't best pleased at finding the old bat lurking in his office, and still recovering from his depressing journey to work, was furious at her suggestion.

"You have my authority to make the necessary changes, Mrs Parkes. No need to involve my uncle!"

He then said, slowly and deliberately, "Has Caitlin arrived yet?"

Bloody cheek of the man, thought Mrs Parkes as she mentally added him to her hate list – she had a habit of evening the score with those who featured on it. In a cool voice, she answered, "Yes. I've sent her to get some stationery. She's setting up outside your office. There is something you need to know. She isn't very..."

James had had enough of the woman's interference.

"What is it this time, Mrs Parkes? What has that Papist, as you cruelly called her, done wrong now?!"

Mortally offended, Mrs Parkes stepped back in horror at the young man's accusation and tone. She was visibly upset, her neck and face turning a painful shade of pink. How dare he reproach her for stating the truth?

James began to realise he might have gone a tad too far as the woman stuttered and stammered and tried to explain.

"Wh-Wh-Why no, M-Mr Henderson, no! My goodness, nothing like that! I just wanted to warn you. You might have heard, but that man who was in police custody and died, Patrick McLaughlin… He's Caitlin's father. I was just trying to warn you, that was all."

James was speechless. He pressed his hands against the desk and bowed his head for a moment. He'd got it completely wrong and badly misjudged this woman. Shit! He definitely owed her an apology. With a big sigh, he looked up at the office manager.

"Mrs Parkes, I am truly sorry for my behaviour. I made assumptions and was inexcusably rude to you. Caitlin's father? My God! How is she? And why is she here at all… Doesn't she need to be at home?"

Mrs Parkes recognised she now had the upper hand. In a formal, controlled manner she told him, "I spoke to her for quite some time when she arrived this morning. I did tell her to go home, but she was determined to get on with her work. She said that keeping busy would be good for her. She won't accept any sympathy from me. None at all."

James thought for a second.

"Oh… I see. Well, okay, good. Good for her. When she's back please send her in. And thank you for telling me, Mrs Parkes, thank you."

She nodded curtly and left without delay. She'd not forget that put-down in a hurry.

Downstairs Caitlin was collecting stationery from the store cupboard. Her stomach felt like stone. Attending the funeral, arranging the food and drinks – on tick at a local bar afterwards – and finally getting her mother home, had left her exhausted. In the end, Tommy had become extremely drunk and continued to apologise to her all night about the colour party. She'd told him time and time again not to worry, but he was so drunk he didn't hear her. It hadn't really mattered. Tommy was so good to them that she didn't want to fall out with him. He was family.

As soon as they'd made it home, her mother vanished to her bedroom along with a glass of whiskey and several sleeping pills. She'd been in bed since. On the rare occasion she woke, she'd refuse to eat or drink. Caitlin was desperately worried about her. Tina had remained quiet and withdrawn and stayed in her bedroom – probably lost in her books. Caitlin had been left alone in the messy kitchen and hated it. She'd spent most of the night cleaning up after the wake.

Earlier that morning, Uncle Tommy had appeared, completely hungover and looking like he should be taking up the next spot in the cemetery. He said he'd called in to check on her. He'd brought some milk, bread, and unbelievably a pair of tights. He'd noticed her bare legs at the funeral and knew she started her new job that morning. After such an act of kindness, she couldn't be angry with him but instead offered him a drink, which he gratefully and whole-heartedly accepted. As the whiskey worked its magic and he began to feel better, he tried to cheer her up by relaying a story about some Republicans who'd recently played a trick on one of the local characters whose stocky body stood just over four feet tall.

The little fella had been asked by the Boys to man a barricade near Little Diamond just off William Street. He was overjoyed to be given such a giant responsibility. They'd also ordered him to keep an eye out for a specific car they were looking for. They said they suspected it was being used by undercover filth so warned him to look out for a particular model and registration and couldn't emphasise enough how important it was that they find it. Eager for the task, the poor lad spent three days diligently checking every single car that passed through his barricade. Finally admitting defeat, he was then told that the car was right in front of him all the time, sitting proudly but burnt out at the top of his very own barricade! Caitlin thought it funny if a little cruel. Tommy assured her the young man had taken it well and the story had already become a legend.

She took what she needed from the stationery cupboard and knew she had to hurry back otherwise Mrs Parkes would be wondering where she was. Caitlin was nervous about the new job, but she had to stay strong; they needed her wage. She was the only one bringing decent money into the house.

James looked up in response to a soft knock on his office door. Caitlin. He called out for her to enter.

He noticed the signs of grief etched onto her pale face. Her eye had yellowed, and her bruises were less noticeable. She looked sad and frail as he held out a chair for her to sit down. He seated himself and leaned across his desk to offer his condolences.

"I'm so sorry, Caitlin, I've just heard about your father. I didn't know."

"You wouldn't, Mr Henderson. But thank you."

"Is there anything you need? Do you want to wait a few days and we can start work when you're ready?"

"No, sir, not at all. Please, I need to keep busy."

Keeping busy was probably the right thing to do, he agreed. Selfishly too he needed her and wanted to get started as there was a lot to do.

"I understand. Well, if it helps, I hope I have a bit of good news. I've managed to persuade my uncle to increase your salary slightly. Not a lot, but something. It appears I'm going to be in Londonderry for quite some time."

Caitlin inwardly winced as she heard him use the name "Londonderry" but answered gratefully.

"That's wonderful, sir. Thank you."

"Caitlin, please don't call me 'sir'. It's too formal. I'm James, just James. Okay?"

"Okay, sir. I mean… James," she answered demurely. He stood up and continued talking.

"If you want me to keep you busy, then I will. First, I need a list of the names and addresses of all the chief representatives from every political party in the city. I also need a list of senior representatives from the British Army, the RUC, and leaders of all the churches. I need to know their background, family history, likes and dislikes, etc. I need to know everything about them. What makes them tick."

He carried on talking to her as she quickly opened her notebook and took some notes.

He stopped and stared at her as his ideas ran through his head.

"Secondly, I need to get to know the local businesses too. My uncle has his own contacts, which should be useful, but you can phone the Chamber of Commerce and ask for a list of their members. There must be other smaller organisations I might have missed. You know, like the independent William Street Traders… That type of thing. They're just as important."

"Of course," Caitlin replied as she listed his requests. There was one particular issue she had on her mind, and so rather hesitantly she said to him,

"James, there is one thing. I'm not sure how I go about contacting the army or RUC?"

You're a dick, Henderson, he realised. "Oh, God, no! Sorry, of course not! My father and uncle will help me with that. That was insensitive of me, Caitlin."

"No, it's fine. Don't worry." She wasn't offended and listened as he tried to explain what they had to do.

"Security is a priority, Caitlin. Rocola must ensure our employees and goods arrive and leave safely. If they can't, we'll lose even more orders and, believe me; we've already lost enough. This continual rioting next door in Stones Corner hasn't helped, with lorries being hijacked left, right and centre. Worst-case scenario we may have to close, which would be a disaster for the city."

He drank some tepid tea and kept going.

"So… my idea is to get everyone together – and I mean everyone who has any influence at all in Londonderry – to sit down and come up with a plan to help save Rocola. We need to find investors too. If we were to close, believe me, one way or another, it would affect every business and family in this town. We can't let that happen."

Caitlin sat in shock. He was right. It would be a catastrophe, not just for her but also for Anne's family and all the hundreds of other families who depended on the factory. It was too awful to contemplate.

When he'd finished explaining his plan, James sighed.

"Given what I've just told you, Caitlin, remember– everything you see and hear in the coming weeks must remain strictly confidential. No one else at all must hear about it."

"Of course, James. It's a frightening thought, that's all."

"I know," he replied.

The pair of them continued to work together until lunchtime when he yawned, stretched, and then asked her, "Do you want something to eat?"

She couldn't believe she was hungry; food had barely entered her mind for days, but now she realised she should eat.

"I'm starving," she admitted. "But I forgot my lunch bag."

James laughed. He was *"starving"* too.

"Don't worry; I'll get Mrs Parkes to go and get something for us."

Caitlin almost choked.

"Are you sure? Really? I don't think she will like that one bit or even us two having lunch in here together."

"Leave Mrs Parkes to me!" James smiled mischievously.

She watched him leave in search of the dragon. She couldn't believe her luck with this job or with James. He was so lovely, and she'd get extra pay too! Yet she was worried sick about what he'd told her, and since she'd promised it would remain confidential, she'd have to carry the burden alone.

As expected, Mrs Parkes was unmistakeably furious with James's request for sandwiches to be brought to his office but fifteen minutes later delivered them with a stern face and in cutting silence.

They ate while they continued to work, and Caitlin began to feel slightly more human. As she finished up for the day, she'd felt guilty for feeling a little better, but knew her father would be proud of her.

Chapter Sixteen

Several weeks passed, and once again, it was payday. James – as Caitlin confidently now called her new boss – had indeed arranged a very welcome increase in her wages and it had made a difference. Around 26,000 Catholic homes in the city were refusing to pay their rates and rents as a protest against internment, which was good news for the McLaughlins'. They wouldn't have to pay rent for the time being, and this allowed them to keep their heads above water. Caitlin was still desperately worried about her father's funeral costs. The bill had arrived promptly and now sat untouched on the kitchen windowsill.

Majella stayed despondently in bed. When she woke, she became frantic and cried hysterically, asking for Patrick. No one could soothe her. She hadn't bathed in days. Tommy was worried about his sister and called in daily. As a last resort, he'd suggested to Caitlin that he should ask his mother to help, but in the end, they'd both baulked at the thought and decided against it. They'd give it a few more days and see if Majella improved without her mother's far from tender nurturing.

Caitlin looked at the kitchen clock. It was still early. She sat across the kitchen table from Tina, who stayed silent while she ate a meagre portion of cereal. She'd been more quiet than usual over the past few days, and Caitlin was worried about her. She no longer wore her braces, but sadly her eczema had returned, and the skin on her neck and face looked angry and sore. Caitlin asked with concern, "Are you all right, Tina? I've hardly seen you."

"I'm fine. Leave it, will you!"

Caitlin was slightly alarmed by her sister's sharp reply.

"I was just asking. I'm sorry, I haven't been here much, but this new job is taking up all my time."

"I'm fine," the girl repeated gloomily.

Caitlin was at a loss and tried again to engage her sister's attention. "How's Tech?"

"Fine."

The conversation was going nowhere, so Caitlin gave up and drank the remainder of her tea in silence.

Tina finished her cereal, muttered something and threw her bowl and spoon noisily into the sink. She then took her bag from the back of her chair and walked out. Caitlin rose and switched on the radio, searching for some music. A loud thumping song she didn't know came on, and in frustration, she quickly turned it back off.

Tina returned to the kitchen, now wearing her coat.

"Bye then," she said, and walked out of the back door without another word.

Caitlin decided she'd had enough. She ran after her sister down the garden path, which was flanked on both sides by a small privet hedge. The gate was still swinging. Caitlin peered down the street and screamed as loudly as she could.

"Tina! I want to talk to you!"

The girl ignored her calls and turned the corner to disappear from sight.

What in God's name was she going to do with her? Caitlin thought as she shuddered and wrapped her arms around herself. It was bitterly cold, and she wore only a light jumper and nothing on her feet. She hurried back towards the warmth of the kitchen.

Halfway up the path, she heard a slight rustle and stood still. She looked around and waited while she listened carefully. But there wasn't a peep. She couldn't see particularly well but intuitively knew someone was there. She wasn't afraid, just pissed off, so cried out angrily, "Who is it? Who's there!"

There was no response, so she boldly walked nearer to the thick waist-high hedge. She used her hands to prod and pull the leaves back. She was right. There was someone in there. She swiftly stepped back and watched in astonishment as a British soldier rose slowly from his hiding place.

His face was painted as black as his badged beret, but she could make out the features – ordinary, unremarkable, except for a pair of warm hazel eyes. They met hers with a pleading expression. He held a rifle in his lowered right hand, and in the other a Leica camera on a strap.

"Please, miss, don't scream," he said softly. "Just walk inside and close the door."

Time stood still as the young man and woman stared at each other. It was a life-changing moment, though neither of them knew it. They stood together as still as statues. Caitlin knew she should call out and within seconds there'd be people converging on them from every direction. Rifle or not, he wouldn't stand a chance. This was a British soldier, and the Brits had just caused the death of her father… She opened her mouth and closed it again. Patrick McLaughlin had not believed that Ulster's problems could be solved by violence. For his sake, and no one else's, she told herself, she would stay silent.

"I think you should go," she told the soldier.

He disentangled himself from the hedge, walked down the path and peered over the gate. At the top of the street, she heard the rumble of a heavy vehicle. The soldier's radio crackled. He murmured into it, and the next moment he was gone, running up the street as if the hounds of hell were on his heels.

"Too much," Caitlin whispered to herself, and shook her head before walking back inside.

As soon as she'd closed the back door, her heart began to race. She should have screamed. Why didn't she scream? Why the fuck should she care what happened to one lousy soldier? It was all too much for her.

She slumped down at the kitchen table and cried uncontrollably.

Eventually, she sensed the presence of someone else in the kitchen and looked up. In the doorway stood her mother, dishevelled and confused. Caitlin got up and seized on to her for dear life. The women held each other close, Majella gently stroking her daughter's hair and offering a few indistinct words of comfort.

A short while later, her mother groaned as she looked around the untidy kitchen. Caitlin had got in late from work the previous night and hadn't had a chance to tidy up Tina's mess.

Majella was feeling awful. However, deep within her, she heard a voice tell her that she needed to sort herself out. Somehow. She looked at her tired and tear-stained elder girl.

"I've really left you both in it, haven't I? I'm sorry, love. I just wanted to disappear for a while. I'll try and sort myself out, I promise."

They hugged. Caitlin loved her mother so much; she would do anything for her. She'd missed her since the funeral.

"I've got tons to tell you, Mammy," she said, the words coming out in a rush. "My new job is brilliant, and I'm getting more money too. I get paid today."

Majella hadn't even been sure what day of the week it was. Friday and payday? Thank God. She might be able to get a wee drink later on. She faked interest and enthusiasm as she told her daughter, "That's great news. How about you tell me all about it over tea tonight?" She looked up at the clock. "Now you'd better hurry; you can't be late – especially now!"

Majella ran one hand distractedly through her greasy hair. She had to clean herself up and get this place sorted. Patrick would want her to try.

On the way to work, Caitlin decided to try and put aside a little of her wages to buy some fabric and make herself a few skirts and blouses on their old sewing machine. Anne, who'd linked arms with her as soon as they'd met, had talked and talked about some new man she'd met. Caitlin hadn't really listened as her own thoughts wandered off. Perhaps now her mother was out of bed, she'd help with the sewing. Majella had been a wonderful seamstress once, having worked in a shirt factory before she'd married. She'd taught her daughter a great deal about dressmaking, but Caitlin wasn't half as good as her.

After saying goodbye to Anne, Caitlin made her way to the fifth floor, where she met James in the corridor. He looked amazing and as always smelled of expensive aftershave. He appeared to have an unending selection of smart suits, ties and shoes. He smiled and held the office door open for her to pass through ahead of him.

Caitlin had managed to cool down her swollen eyes before leaving for work, but he looked questioningly at her pale face and asked if she was okay. She assured him she was fine, just a little tired.

She'd found herself observing him just as closely as the rest of the day passed. She blushed when he caught her, but he simply looked bemused. She loved the job and, oddly, found that she missed him when he was out. She particularly loved it when he'd telephone her, and she'd hear his cut-glass accent.

They were in his office later that day when she heard him say: "Caitlin! Earth to Caitlin!" then laugh aloud at her mortified expression. He'd been talking to her, and she hadn't heard a single word he'd said.

"Oh! I'm sorry, I was away there. What did you say?"

He was worried by how tired she looked. Maybe this job was too much for her with everything else that had happened. He'd have to keep a close eye on her. She was obviously a clever girl, but he couldn't afford the time to babysit. He had too much work to do and repeated himself.

"I was saying; now we've got the list of names we need I'd like to set a date for a one-day meeting at a local hotel."

"Yes. Yes, of course. Any preferences on which hotel and when?"

He watched her closely as he thought.

"City Hotel maybe? It's central and secure. Yes, that'll do. Let's try to organise it for the beginning of next month. Call them. We'll need a private room for forty or so guests, ideally with a round table. I want to be able to look them all in the eye. There are a few more VIPs I want to

132

invite as well, and they'll likely need accommodation if they're coming from out of town."

That was all he needed, and Caitlin had already stood up to leave when she suggested:

"James, I'm just thinking, I'll call the hotel today, but I can easily drop in there and pick up more information myself tomorrow. I have to go into town anyway."

"Perfect. Maybe if they have availability, they could show you the conference rooms too. Thanks, Caitlin."

James was excited by the way his plan was coming together. He'd spent weeks meeting as many businessmen and women in the city as possible. They all seemed keen to be involved in the meeting as they recognised there was too much at stake to pass up the opportunity. If Rocola closed, the economic implications would be felt by them all.

That evening, to Caitlin's delight, her mother sat with her in the kitchen as she proudly displayed her new payslip. A two pounds increase was much more than she'd expected and backdated as well!

"I can't believe it, Mammy. It'll really help, especially now," she said thankfully.

Majella had done as she'd promised herself. She'd taken a bath and washed her hair. She now wore fresh clothes though sadness still hung over her like a cloud. Caitlin guessed she might have taken some pills – when in fact she'd been drinking vodka. However, it was a start, a good start.

Her mother looked lovingly at Caitlin and the payslip and money in her hand.

"I'm thrilled for you, love. You're so good. Why don't you keep some for yourself? As you say, let's get some fabric, and we'll make a few outfits – especially if you're going to be meeting all those fancy VIPs, eh?"

Caitlin had told her very little about the real reason for the meeting but couldn't help mentioning that she'd soon be meeting some prominent people.

"Ah, that'd be great! I've asked Anne to come into town with me tomorrow. I said I'd treat her to tea and cake in Austins."

Majella smiled.

"Good idea; she'll love that! By the way, your Granny phoned next door. She tried to give me excuse after excuse for not going to your Daddy's funeral." It'd been a difficult conversation as Majella had listened to her mother demean Patrick even now when he was dead and in his grave.

Tina joined them then and stood in the kitchen doorway. She smiled at her sister.

"Caitlin, I'm sorry for being so miserable. I miss Daddy, and I've been worried sick about Mammy. You've been really good, looking after things on your own."

Caitlin welcomed this surprising show of remorse. Now they were all together she immediately felt better.

"I was worried about you too, Tina."

She reached for her pay packet, took out some small coins and passed them to her sister.

"Here you go, there's the money I promised you for the bottles."

"Ah, Caitlin, that's great! Thanks."

Tina rushed enthusiastically to the under-stair cupboard, grabbed her coat and ran out the front door shouting goodbye. Majella and Caitlin smiled and spent the remainder of the evening in the kitchen, talking about good times.

Chapter Seventeen

Robert looked up from his book and grimaced with pain as he heard his best friend walking towards their bunk. Val was whistling and looked noticeably happy even with a bandaged hand and cut face – the result of being hit by various missiles while on mobile patrol that day. The two men were shattered. Lately, they'd been working eighteen-hour shifts with very little rest or sleep.

Robert was intrigued by his pal's good humour, though he attempted to appear casual and uninterested. Val knew Robert was dying to know what was up but held back for a moment. He'd been eager to tell him the good news but hadn't had the chance so far. Eventually, Robert couldn't take it any longer. He sat up and stared at his friend.

"Go on then. Spit it out."

Val shrugged his shoulders, pretending he didn't know what his friend was on about.

"Spit what out? Chill, man."

Robert wouldn't be put off. He pointed a finger at Val.

"Just remember that I know you like the back of my hand! You're up to something. So come on, tell me."

Like a scene from a spy movie, Val looked from left to right, ensuring they were alone. He tiptoed closer to the top bunk and in the worst German accent imaginable, whispered into Robert's ear: *"It is like thiz, Agent Sallis. I ave zee information, but 'ow can I be sure zat I can truzz you?"*

The man was clearly mad, and Robert playfully struck him on his bandaged hand with the book. Val jumped back and pretended to be angry and insulted at such a low move. He raised his wounded hand in the air and cried: *"You dare to torture me? I vil tell you nothing. I die first!"*

The two men laughed until Val moved next to Robert. This time the German accent was omitted as he furtively shared his news.

"Actually, Robbie, you're not to take the piss when I tell you this, but *I* have met a member of the female species!"

Robert was shocked. How on earth had Val met someone – and where? He quickly pulled himself upright, only to scowl at the pain that drove through him. He'd been injured too in the rioting, though not as badly as Val.

He lobbed his book to the bottom of his bunk for later. He was ready to listen and utterly intrigued. This wasn't like his friend. Val's fun-loving personality would immediately evaporate as soon as women either acknowledged him or, even worse, spoke to him. His natural banter would be replaced by a shyness that had plagued him for as long as Robert could remember. Poor Val wasn't gifted when it came to chatting up girls. But Robert was delighted by the news and cried out excitedly, "Canny lad! You have my full attention."

Val knew his friend would be pleased and explained what had happened.

"Well, you remember a while back when we were supposed to go to the Lighthouse for a few beers and you were called away?"

Robert remembered only too well. He was still pissed off by the Captain's last-minute request.

"Yep, I had to cover for that gobshite Morris." It seemed their unpopular comrade had got himself into some kind of trouble.

"Yeah, well, since you *sort of* abandoned me, I headed off with a few of the other lads. The place was buzzin', and we were on the Guinness – pure beltas like! Anyway, the next thing this gorgeous blonde comes over to me and starts chatting me up!" Val gestured to himself as if surprised. "I mean, seriously! She starts coming on to *me*! Jesus, Rob, she was something else. The bazooms on her… Never seen anything like it!"

He opened and closed his fists against his own hard chest and rolled his eyes in their sockets comically.

Robert laughed so hard it hurt. Val continued in a more serious tone.

"I've seen her a few times like and I'm plannin' to take her somewhere real special next – like that fancy French place in the Waterside. Christ, I've been dying to tell you for ages. It's bad, man!"

Robert remembered the tarring and feathering of the young girl and the warnings from their officers about getting involved with local girls. When the army first arrived in Northern Ireland, it'd been a cause of massive irritation to the local men that a few of their girls went out with soldiers. Robert tried not to spoil Val's good mood and so asked tactfully, "Is she local, Val?"

His friend knew immediately what Robert was implying and answered quickly.

"Totally get you. I've thought about that already, but she's sailed through all the checks. She's good."

At that, Val threw himself into the bottom bunk and swore as searing pain ran through his bandaged hand.

Robert was relieved. If the girl had been security checked, then Val should be okay. However, reminding himself of the tarred and feathered girl, he added, "Gan canny, mind, Val. Remember that poor lass we saw tarred and feathered?"

"Yes, Mam!" a voice replied from the lower bunk. Val sighed, smiled and closed his eyes to let his imagination run wild.

Above him, Robert stretched out to reach his book and continued to read. But soon he found it too difficult to concentrate, so instead, he lay back and rested his eyes. Good for Val. He looked forward to meeting this girl.

It had been a shitty day. The "aggro" weather hadn't helped. A clear azure sky with warm autumnal sun meant there was more likely to be trouble. Good weather always brought out the troublemakers. In addition to that, Robert had received a phone call from his family the night before. As always, it had taken a lot of energy and concentration for him to stay sounding upbeat. Tracey's voice had sounded flat and sad. She wasn't her usual cheerful self, and that depressed him even more. He'd asked her continually what was up, but she'd insisted she was fine. He knew she wasn't; he could tell from her voice. In the end, he spent most of his allocated ten minutes trying to suss out what was going on with her and came off the phone feeling miserable and none the wiser.

And then this morning they'd been on mobile patrol. They were in the middle of a two-week stint as part of a supply column to Blighs Lane. This was an armoured barracks where 115 officers and soldiers were stationed, in order to protect and maintain the presence of just two RUC men alongside a small number of Royal Military Police. The heavily guarded site stood on a steep hill leading up to the notorious Creggan Estate, where gun law prevailed. To one side of the heavily guarded compound was Stones Corner, scene of many of the worst riots orchestrated by the merciless men, boys and even children who frequently gathered to throw stones or petrol bombs at the barracks. To the right of it stood the main entrance to a local shirt factory, Rocola. The compound had four sangars that acted as the eyes of the army and fed back regular information on what was happening outside. Behind it, and far too close for anyone's liking, were terraced houses offering useful shelter to the Nationalist gunmen, women and bombers. It was a sniper's dream.

The compound was surrounded by triangular concrete blocks and barbed wire. Inside it looked like a scrapyard, jam-packed with rubble, dead trees, burned-out buses, lorries and cars… Anything that could be commandeered to make a barricade. These were regularly cleared away by sappers from the Royal Engineers, using Centurion tanks with their cannons replaced by bulldozer blades. The scrap vehicle was dragged back into the compound so that it couldn't be used again – a continuous depressing cycle of destruction and clearing up.

The Stones Corner rioters were mostly made up of bored youths angry about the recent curfews and, in consequence, relentless in their attacks on the compound. Overnight any cleared barricades would be replaced by fresh obstacles. The locals were determined to block the delivery of supplies to the compound. Rarely did they succeed for long, but they certainly didn't make life any easier.

In their briefing, Robert's unit had been ordered to be extra careful. The schools were closed, and there'd likely be young children out there. A five-year-old Catholic girl had been run over and killed by a mobile patrol unit a few days before. Tensions were running high. On the one hand, the patrol could not speed too quickly through the streets, but on the other hand, they knew the risk would be greater the slower they proceeded.

As the flak-vested unit left the well-protected maintenance base (an old submarine depot alongside the River Foyle), they mentally prepared themselves for the ten-minute journey and inevitable hail of abuse, slogans and stones at the end of it. They couldn't use soft-topped vehicles so instead had loaded the much-needed supplies into armoured ones. One of the lads had painted "*Woodstock*" on the front of one of the Pigs that escorted the convoy, which carried everything from ammunition, riot guns, rubber bullets and CS gas to supplies of food and drink.

The atmosphere inside the Pig was charged, stifling and claustrophobic. The sergeant did a radio check and raised the door visor to look around before he screamed over its roaring engine.

"All clear. Okay, lads, let's get this over with!"

The noise inside had been deafening as, in line, the convoy moved out. Robert and Val sat side by side and held on tight to their fibre-glass shields. Their hard helmets with visors were uncomfortable and strapped tightly under their chins. It was too noisy to hear, so no one spoke. It didn't take long before all hell broke loose as a continual torrent of missiles smashed against the half-inch-thick steel body of the armoured vehicle.

Instinctively, Robert ducked as the impact and noise of the bombardment became unbearable. He squinted through the slit on the side of the Pig and glimpsed the packs of young men and children throwing bricks and petrol bombs and screaming out filthy abuse. The Pig accelerated and sped closer to the compound. Soon the riot guns from the fortified sangar above shot rubber bullets and CS gas into the angry crowd, in an effort to push it back and allow the convoy to enter.

As they'd approached the compound's entrance, cordite fumes stung their eyes and nostrils, and Robert and Val were ordered to jump out and help the men inside open the large, armoured gates.

Their only protection against the smoke and barrage of missiles was their helmets and shields. They got out of the Pig as quickly as they could and ran towards the gates. But soon they'd been spotted by the mob and became a soft target as torrents of missiles were deliberately realigned and thrown at the two struggling soldiers. Robert and Val cried out in fury as their un-gloved hands and bodies were repeatedly hit while they attempted to heave the colossal gates open.

Finally, the gates opened, and the two men stood back to allow the roaring Pigs to enter. Along with the other soldiers, they closed and locked the gates and quickly ran for cover to avoid possible snipers. They gasped for breath after their exertions and waited until they got the "all clear" from the high-level sangars.

They'd spent most of the day unloading and sorting out the supplies until eventually, they'd left under the relative cover of darkness. They'd met some resistance and hostility at the exit, but it'd been nothing like before.

Val, with impeccable timing, had attempted over the noise of the Pig to entertain the lads with impressions and jokes. Weary after the long day, they'd welcomed his antics. Anything to speed up the journey to the safety of their barracks. Tomorrow they'd be on covert ops – quieter, for the most part, deadly if their luck ran out.

Chapter Eighteen

The weeks flew by. It was Saturday again, no work today, and that was good since Caitlin hadn't slept much. Recurring nightmares about her father's arrest and its aftermath had left her shattered. She was relieved when morning finally arrived and finished off a quick prayer before she climbed out of bed. She found it hard to pray these days. She didn't want to be angry with God, but she was.

Anne would cheer her up when they met later. Caitlin always looked forward to going into town with her. She drew back the curtains and was greeted by a bright, blue, sunny morning. What a change! As she looked down at the garden, she remembered the concealed soldier. Suddenly conscious the house could still be under surveillance; she quickly pulled the curtains closed.

That morning the three women cleaned the house thoroughly from top to bottom. It needed it. They grabbed some Campbell's tinned tomato soup for lunch before Tina went out and Caitlin prepared to leave for town.

Just a few "good" shops remained in town along with the city's only department store, Austins. It was a lovely old building with its creaky wide wooden staircase and rasping caged lift – the oldest independent department store in the world. Caitlin loved walking through the main doors and being met by the aroma of expensive perfume that filled the air. The girls behind the counters were all so smart and perfectly made-up. Unlike many, she didn't feel intimidated when she browsed around Austins. She and her friend could spend hours and hours just looking through the items on sale. They were well known in the store and liked by the professional but friendly staff.

Another of their favourite shops was the tiny, dark-red-painted boutique, *She,* at the bottom of Pump Street around the corner from

Austins. It was owned by two cool sisters who visited London regularly to bring back the latest trendy fashions to Derry. It was incredibly popular but far too expensive for Caitlin even with her recent pay rise.

She stood patiently at the top of Shipquay Street, one of the four main highways within the walled City, waiting for Anne. In the sunshine, she appreciated the ancient oak trees that adorned the hill and the small square at the top known as The Diamond. This was home to an impressive WW1 Memorial designed in 1927 by a young English sculptor, Vernon March.

Along the square, several bombed-out shops were boarded up. Others lay in ruins. Anne was always late, so in an effort to pass time, Caitlin watched an army patrol walk cautiously down the hill. Like ghosts in the night, they were ignored by all the passers-by.

She scrutinised the patrol closely and wondered if the young soldier she'd encountered so unexpectedly might be there. He wasn't, but she was stunned when she recognised the tattooed soldier who'd hit her. He caught her eye and nodded, flicked his top lip suggestively with his tongue. He was vile, and she quickly turned her back on him. Jesus, what a creep! Next, a girl's voice called out her name. It was Anne – thank God! She eyed the pedestrians and saw her friend playing the fool, climbing up the hill while holding her hand pressed to her chest and breathing exaggeratedly.

Anne was a funny sight in her red stilettos, full yellow skirt, matching turtleneck jumper and a red scarf tied dashingly at the side of her neck. When she got to Caitlin at the top of the hill, she reached out both her hands in a theatrical gesture and gasped: "Jesus, that hill's going to kill me one day. It doesn't get any easier, does it!"

Accentuating her Derry accent, Caitlin laughed and replied, "*It's the fags, Anne. It's those fags. You're going to have to give them up!*"

Anne knew Caitlin was right. She should give them up, but they helped curb her appetite.

"Sure, I know, Caitlin, but where else do I get *ANY* satisfaction in this world, eh? She winked naughtily at her friend. "Right, missus, since you're in the money, where are you taking me? And, more importantly, I'm dying to hear all about this Adonis you're working for!"

Caitlin, about to answer her friend, was stopped by a colossal flash and a booming noise. A wave of air lifted her off her feet and flung her violently against the boarded-up window of a shop. She lay stunned for a moment until an indescribably strange sensation overcame her as, once again, she was surrounded by darkness.

Chapter Nineteen

James loved his weekends. His uncle was hosting another house party. A few of James's friends from London had arrived late last night after a weary drive through the Sperrin Mountains from Belfast airport sixty or so miles away.

Tonight there was a black-tie dinner, and the house looked stunning with its entrance hall festooned in tiny white fairy lights complemented by extra-large vases of white roses and hydrangeas.

The dining table had been pulled back and was set up, buffet-style, along one wall. The sliding doors had been pulled back, too, thus allowing plenty of room for the beautifully dressed guests to dance on a temporary dance floor or just mingle and catch up with old friends.

A spread of rich food, including lobster, oysters and crab, was beautifully displayed on silver platters laid adjacent to crystal wine glasses that sparkled in the soft light. Ice buckets held numerous bottles of Dom Perignon and white, Burgundy, already cooled and waiting to be served. Carafes of decanted Châteauneuf-du-Pape were laid out around the room, ready for the waiters and waitresses who walked amongst the guests and topped up their glasses.

Just before the party was due to start, James heard a tap on his bedroom door as he finished dressing. He brushed down his trousers and shouted, "Come in!"

His uncle, looking elegant in his timeworn black dinner suit, peeked around the door and walked in. He held a thick cut crystal tumbler of whiskey almost filled to the brim. James gestured for him to take a chair. Roger sat down, took a mouthful of Bushmills and asked, "How are you?"

"I'm fine, Uncle. You?"

"Tired and slowly getting drunk. I don't know why I give these blasted parties. I never enjoy them. We've got fifty or so guests coming so I thought I'd get a few down before they arrive. Dutch courage, I suppose!"

He laughed, saluted and took another slug of his drink. James felt a wave of love for his Uncle. He sat down on the edge of his bed.

"It's been a busy few weeks I'll update you on Monday, but my biggest concerns are the safety of our employees and the location of the factory. We're sitting right between that humungous army compound and Stones Corner! It's not safe for anyone. We need to come up with a security plan."

Roger was aware of the issues and the danger of being caught in the middle of the riots.

"I know, son; I've been thinking the same thing for quite a while."

James was eager to tell him what he thought.

"This curfew around the Bogside and Creggan really worries me too. If we were to change shifts, the workers wouldn't be able to get to or from work. I read today the British Army have closed the cinema for three months. I imagine half the problem in this city is that the youngsters are bored stiff! What else is there for them to do other than riot? I mean if…"

Roger somehow managed to splash the contents of his tumbler over his trousers, interrupting James's concerns.

"Bugger! You're right, James, but mark my words, it's going to get worse, far worse! I don't see an end to it. The RUC don't trust the army and the army don't trust the RUC. There's no pleasing either of them. I've told Shalham something needs to be done!"

Roger's voice rose as his outburst continued. James had never seen him so worked up.

"I love this country, James, but I'm at a loss. Do you know a bomb went off today by the Bank of Ireland on Shipquay Street? The UVF (Ulster Volunteer Force) blame the PIRA, and they blame them back! Turns out it *was* the UVF. They've been deliberately carrying out and blaming the Provos for a number of bombings, just to stir things. One's as bad as the other!"

The whiskey began to take its toll on Roger, who had started to slur his words.

"And listen, wait for this one." He swallowed the last of the drink, looked down into his glass and saw it empty. He rose and was about to leave as he walked unsteadily to the door but gazed back at his nephew.

"You remember that bomb that went off recently where that little girl died? The one in the tea shop. You know how they did it? They put explosives in the frame of a bike! The hollow bit, the bike frame. Amateurish, but deadly. So many innocent people, James. So sad."

James could see his uncle was visibly shaken. He patted his shoulder.

"Please, Uncle, try not to get yourself so upset."

Roger hung his head and murmured dejectedly, "I can't help it. This Darlington conference has been a disaster too. No one seems to have the sense to sit down and talk. There could easily be a civil war."

James thought he was exaggerating. Most likely, it was the whiskey talking.

"It'll be okay, Uncle. I know it's difficult, but it'll be okay."

Roger half-smiled at his nephew.

"I'm going down now, but there's one last thing. I know discussion is inevitable – especially after a few of our friends have a drink tonight – but let's try and keep politics out of the conversation and have a light-hearted evening. I've already depressed myself enough as it is. Can I depend on you to smooth things over?"

"Yes, yes, of course; leave it to me."

Conscious of the time, he attempted to steer his uncle through the door, but Roger wasn't quite finished.

"You're right about the factory too, James. Security is crucial, now more than ever. We've just won that large Glasgow order and can't afford delays of any sort."

James could just about hear him as Roger mumbled, "If we lose that one, we're finished. We're all finished."

He looked at his nephew, pointed a finger at him and shook it as he asked, "How's that young girl working out for you, in the office? You do realise you've upset Mrs Parkes – and that, my boy, *is not a good thing!*"

James knew it already. She'd been a real pain in the arse, watching him and Caitlin with those beady eyes of hers. She'd have to go.

"Yes, I know, Uncle. She doesn't like me very much, does she! The girl? Ah, yes, Caitlin. Actually, she's doing rather well. She's sharp, but she's had a tough time lately. Turns out her father was Patrick McLaughlin – you know, the man who died in custody recently?"

His uncle nodded slowly.

"Ah, yes. I heard. Sad, that. Apparently, a good man. Word is he wasn't involved in any way. Another innocent. His heart gave up on him; it seems. Has a son in Magilligan Camp or somewhere who's said to be very involved and quite a dangerous fellow? Be careful with her, James. I'm all for fair play, but you're still quite naive about the ways of some people."

James was surprised by this piece of news. Caitlin hadn't mentioned a brother, let alone a brother who was in prison.

Oddly he'd missed her today. She'd crept into his thoughts as he took his morning run beside the river in the sunshine and then, sporadically, throughout the day.

Later, James stood in the dining room surrounded by three of his London guests plus, to his dismay, Charles Jones. He listened as they talked about the bomb that afternoon. It sounded horrific. The lovely widow Mrs Kerry Brookes, an old friend of the family, stood to his left. He knew she was in love with his father and had been for years, but James Snr was oblivious to her overtures. James had tried to tell his father on many occasions, but he'd rejected his son's comments and waved him away. He sometimes wondered whether his father still lived in the hope of his mother coming back. He doubted it, but then again, he'd rarely discussed his personal life with James.

To his right stood John King, an ambitious young up-and-coming Westminster politician. Opposite stood the gregarious Marleen Fry whom James adored. She was a year younger than he was and a great friend. He knew his father would welcome her as a daughter-in-law. However, this was not to be. She had, in confidence, told James a few years earlier that "...*You're simply not my type, darling; I much prefer the female form!*"

James loved her forthrightness. Unfortunately for her, she stood next to the odious Jones, who as usual held a wine glass filled to the brim.

James watched Marleen as she talked to Jones in an unapologetically English accent.

"Gosh, I do love coming here to Londonderry and Melrose, Mr Jones. Mind you; it sounds absolutely dreadful what's going on at the moment. I simply can't understand what it's all about. Please can someone explain?"

She looked imploringly around the group first and then deliberately stared at James as she waited for an answer. He remembered his uncle's request.

"Not tonight, my love. It's extremely complicated, Marleen, and I've made Uncle a promise we are *not* to talk politics on such a beautiful evening. I'll try and explain it to you tomorrow, I promise. We'll take a walk on the beach."

But Jones had other ideas and defiantly cried, "No, no, no! Absolutely not, young man!"

He looked at Marleen, boggle-eyed. It was clear he was already well-oiled.

"Young lady, I will tell you what *it's* all about! *It's* all about control and keeping those Fenian bastards in their proper place!"

James attempted to interject and pushed himself in front of Marleen to protect her from Jones.

"Charles, please. Not now. I insist! You are a guest in my Uncle's home, and it is *his* wish that we all enjoy a relaxing evening by avoiding such sensitive subjects!"

Astonishingly, Marleen pulled James away and back from Jones as she pleaded,

"Darling James, please, I *do* **so** want to know. Let Mr Jones speak. I mean, everyone back home reads the papers and watches the news, but half of us really don't get it. Let's be honest, we see these ghastly things happening, and we don't really know why! After all, now that I'm here, I would so like to go home and explain it to everybody. Please, darling, let Mr Jones talk."

Jones looked at him triumphantly. Their eyes locked and the Ulsterman slowly drank more wine, relishing the moment for as long as he could. Marleen continued to encourage him to speak.

"Well, young lady, it's a very long story," he began. "So to make it as simple as I can, I'll explain the basics. By we, I mean us Unionists or Protestants, you and me. Well, we believe the Nationalists, or Catholics, are inherently disloyal to our Queen and Country. They're determined to force us into a United Ireland against our wishes, so they breed more and more brats, like rabbits, in a poor attempt to increase their voting population. I must add that Rome certainly hasn't helped by encouraging them to have so many sprogs. Come to think of it; they should be neutered!" Jones laughed loudly at his own witticism and continued to speak in a tone of disgust.

"For example, some of their women have fourteen or fifteen children… Revolting! *AND a*re any of their men working? No! But they're taking unemployment benefit from the British Government. The Government they hate so much. Not only are they asking us to give them money; they're now asking us to build them free houses so they can fill them up with little Papist buggers!"

Jones finished off his wine oblivious to the reaction of the onlookers, who stood silent and aghast. His hatred for the Catholics was clear and unrestrained as he drunkenly raved on.

"And now… now there's talk of power-sharing. Power-sharing my arse! What they want now is something like a Council of Ireland. I don't *fuck-ing* think so! Why should we share what is already ours with those southern Fenian bastards? Sir Craig was right!" Jones theatrically recited: '*All I boast is that we are a Protestant Parliament in a Protestant state!'* The British Government have failed us. They have betrayed us! They are weak, and they should be ashamed! I say, 'No surrender!'"

At this, Jones's fist flew high in the air in a victory salute and his wine glass slid from his fingers, smashing into myriad pieces on the parquet floor. Slivers of glass and remnants of red wine sprayed onto Marleen's white dress. She quickly grabbed a napkin to wipe them off as conversation in the room came to a complete stop. James was furious with her for persisting with her question when he'd tried to head her off. He was even more furious with Jones for ruining the mood of the evening.

But Jones was suddenly aware of the silence and coyly placed his raised hand back by his side. The other guests remained bewildered and still. Moments passed until some waiters started to pick up the broken glass, and Marleen was offered more napkins to wipe her spoiled dress.

James, like many others in the room, found it extraordinary to hear such open and flagrant hatred. He knew he had little understanding of the Troubles in Ireland. Even though most of his time as a child was spent in Londonderry, he'd simply enjoyed the freedom of the beautiful surrounding countryside during school holidays. Perhaps until now, he admitted to himself, he'd remained selfishly detached from the political realities, none of which had affected him before. Then Jones had brought his contempt and hatred into their home, and slowly James began to understand his uncle's fears. The country was on a precipice. With such hatred amongst the people and more men like Jones and Bonner, then perhaps Roger was right; it could lead to Civil War. To hear someone as educated as Jones talk in such a way was repulsive beyond words.

John King came to the rescue, scathingly remarking to Jones, "Charles, with respect, I find your tirade offensive, not only to Catholics but in particular your damnation of our Government. As a gentleman, I refuse to comment on your defamation of Catholic families and Rome, given the fact that there are ladies present. I will, however, add that I am myself a practising Catholic."

James hadn't known that. What an evening this was turning out to be! He listened as King continued speaking.

"However, you must remember that Direct Rule *had* to be enforced. It was – I admit – intended to be a temporary measure. However, with the failure of Stormont to contain the security situation here and the escalation of violence; the British Government had no choice. As to the Unionists, they weren't prepared to allow the Nationalists to peacefully protest, although, I may add, they are well within their democratic rights to do so."

Chatter in the room built up again as Roger nervously walked around, urging his guests to relax, eat and drink.

Unusually, Jones seemed stumped by John King's revelations. The politician continued to speak, uninterrupted.

"As to the British Government, you *must* remember, it was against internment in the first place, but again the Unionists insisted! How many times has Stormont introduced internment over the years? Four, five times… Maybe even more? And has it ever worked? No! What it has done, my friend, is create a catastrophe for this country, which I believe will take years – decades perhaps – to resolve. By the end of this year alone, it's predicted that nearly five hundred people will die in Northern Ireland. Five hundred! Think about it."

King sighed and closed, "Now, I refuse to continue this line of conversation as we are guests in this beautiful home and young James here is keen that we all have a good evening. So enough said, I think?" King looked to James for approval.

"Well said, sir! Absolutely!" James cried as he slapped the young MP on the back and thought, *That'll show you Jones, you bigoted little bastard!*

Jones remained silent though evidently furious over his chastising by King. His bulging eyes swelled in his fat, drunken red face. He realised he might have gone too far. After all, he wasn't in the Orange Lodge here, in front of his usual adoring audience. But he wasn't finished yet and attempted to respond to King. That upstart young prick Henderson promptly interrupted and cried out merrily to his girlfriend, "Okay, that's enough for tonight, ladies and gentlemen! Time to dance! Marleen, unless you wish to change first, would you care to boogie?"

He offered his hand to his woman friend who ignored the stains on her dress and accompanied him on to the dance floor, where they sniggered together like teenagers. John King and Mrs Brookes quickly moved away from Jones, who stood alone, smouldering with suppressed rage, as he scanned the room for a waiter and more wine.

Chapter Twenty

After a few attempts, Caitlin managed to open her dust-filled eyes. Her head rang as she lay flat on her back, looking up. The air was filled with swirling dust. The din of screaming voices confused her. She couldn't understand what they were saying. She touched her ears and felt sticky blood. With great effort, she pulled herself halfway up against a wall. She looked down at her lower body and found it blanketed with torn leaves and branches from the trees that once lined the street. She strained to brush them off but cringed as the splinters of wood embedded in her legs dug in further. She licked her sore and bloodied lips. She felt like a doll that'd been thrown angrily across a room, smashed and broken, as pain overwhelmed her. Dazed, she studied the scene of the devastation before her. Her throat was smarting, but she didn't have the energy to cry.

A fire raged behind the broken windows of the bank. The scorching flames snaked angrily in and out of the building's shattered windows and doors. White paper flew up in the air like a stream of kites then drifted gracefully to the ground. Bikes that had once been attached to the railings lay further along the street, bent and twisted. A fireball shot out of a shop window followed by a deafening bang. Disorientated people, wandering about or simply observing the scene like Caitlin, shrieked in terror.

It was an apocalyptic sight. Soldiers with scorched hair and charred faces checked the motionless bodies that lay strewn across the square for any signs of life. Ambulance crews and RUC men walked amongst dismembered limbs that lay strewn across the pavement and road amid scattered, deadly, shards of glass.

A small car had smashed into the gilded wooden windows of Austins department store and was jammed halfway into the shop, draped in rails of clothes and mannequins. Two lifeless bodies lay inside the car. She couldn't believe what she was seeing – the body parts, the blood, the carnage. She was in hell. Her hands shook violently, and her teeth were chattering. The street was strewn with everything imaginable from window frames to pieces of office furniture. Curtains flew free and high into the air from wrecked apartments above the shops.

Caitlin tensed. *Anne. Where was her friend!*

She tried to stand but quickly fell back down. Her eyes were dry, sore and burning. In a rasping voice, she cried out, "Anne! Where are you, AAAnne!"

She scanned the debris and the bodies, searching for a glimpse of her friend. Eventually, she spotted something red and familiar. She gritted her teeth and dragged herself towards it, only to pull back in horror when she understood what it was. A lone blood-stained red stiletto – Anne!

Dragging herself up into a semi-sitting position, she croaked, "Anne, Anne! Where are you?"

The continual noise of ambulance bells and the screams of the injured overwhelmed her. She couldn't believe this was happening. It wasn't fair!

She began to feel light-headed and sleepy. She shook her head hard to keep herself awake, but every part of her was in pain. She forced herself to scream loudly,

"Anne, where are you? Anne!"

Her eyes were getting heavier, and her head drooped. She had to sleep. However, by some mere miracle, she heard a faint but weak response coming from her friend.

"Caitlin, is that you? Caitlin, I'm here!"

"Oh, Anne, thank God! Keep talking; keep talking! I'm coming to find you!"

No reply. In frustration, Caitlin screamed at the top of her voice: "Anne, Anne! Talk to me…"

Minutes passed before the voice returned.

"I'm over here, Caitlin. I'm over here."

Anne kept talking. Caitlin concentrated on the direction of her friend's voice until she spotted a yellow bloodied arm under a pile of red bricks and torn-up railings. She had to get to her friend!

Suddenly someone grabbed her arm and in a shocked voice asked, "Jesus Christ, Caitlin, is that you!"

The sight of Kathy was too much for Caitlin, and she broke down. Her cousin held her lovingly.

"I don't believe this! I don't believe it's you, Caitlin! Are you okay, love?"

She couldn't believe the girl had survived so close to the centre of the blast. Her coat and blouse were ripped apart, and her clothing was torn and scorched. Her hair was sticky from the heat, with paper and twigs intertwined in its long locks. It didn't look like she had any major injuries, though. Thank God. She was obviously in shock; her hands shook, and her teeth chattered.

Caitlin looked at her cousin gratefully. She had never seen Kathy so dirty and dust-stained before, but she was a wonderful sight.

Her cousin said encouragingly, "You're going to be okay, love; you're okay. We'll get you sorted, and out of here soon, I promise. I'm just going…"

Caitlin grabbed her cousin's arm and said fiercely, "Kathy, no; wait! Anne's been hurt! She's over there, by that red shoe!"

Caitlin pointed frantically to a pile of rubble and screeched, "Anne, Anne! Kathy's here! She's coming to get you!"

Half-laughing and half-coughing, Anne cried out, "I'm here, Kathy! I need to get this stuff off me legs, please! All I can see is white light… Jesus, is this it? Is this the end?!"

Neither of the women could believe Anne could joke at such a horrific time. But then, that was Anne.

Kathy looked again at the devastation that surrounded them and once again decided Caitlin was a very lucky young woman.

"Someone is definitely looking after you, Caitlin McLaughlin! You're going to be okay."

Caitlin knew exactly who was looking out for her. *Daddy.*

Kathy told her earnestly, "I'll go and check on Anne. Listen, Kevin, my partner, will be here in a sec and he'll take you to an ambulance. You okay?"

"I just feel a bit sick, that's all. Find Anne. Leave me. I'm fine."

Caitlin watched as Kathy carefully scrambled her way through the carnage and towards the bloodied shoe, calling out Anne's name. She heard a weak response and walked away from the shoe and towards the voice. Ten or so metres later, she stopped and stooped down. Anne was almost completely covered, just her face and one arm visible among the rubble. Kathy struggled desperately to remove the debris until a black-suited fireman in a white helmet spotted her. He immediately jumped to her aid over numerous hosepipes that writhed like sea serpents across the sodden streets.

Together they lifted away stone and brick, and both groaned in unison as they revealed the jagged piece of iron railing that had pierced deep into the young girl's right leg. By this time, Anne had passed out and lay on the ground at an awkward angle, half on her side. They looked at each other, shook their heads and sighed. This was bad.

By then, Kevin had arrived to help Caitlin. She placed her arm around his neck as he helped her stand, but she immediately felt dizzy and sick. Pushing him quickly away, she violently retched onto the street. She groaned loudly as she steadied herself against a wall. The man waited patiently for her to finish and wiped her face gently with a handkerchief that he produced from his silver-buttoned tunic. Assuring him she was okay; she leaned heavily on him as he led her to the white ambulance where he placed her carefully on the wet ground against the vehicle's side. She waved him away in protest as he tried to assess her.

"Please go to Kathy. Go and help."

He nodded, picked up a red canvas stretcher and left. Caitlin's eyes followed him until she saw the pair talking for a few moments. Next, they placed Anne tenderly on the stretcher. The embedded railing poked out from her bleeding leg, and Caitlin could see the injury was bad.

Caitlin shook as she looked around the demolished square. The statues on the War Memorial had been shattered. She noticed two soldiers combing the rubble. One of them appeared to have lost some teeth – he held his jaw in his hand as he talked. Even under his grey-dusted face, she knew this was her assailant, the Irish soldier. Apart from a few missing teeth, he appeared uninjured. *Shame.*

She managed to rise as the stretcher party approached. Immediately she knew she was going to vomit again and quickly hobbled out of sight. She retched and retched. God, it hurt so much. After a short time, Kevin came to her aid, covered her with a blanket and helped her step up into the ambulance.

Anne was already on board, her pale face barely visible under a large oxygen mask. Two black straps were fastened over the red blanket that covered her torso and kept her secure but stopped where the railing protruded from her leg. She looked so tiny and helpless. Kevin smiled reassuringly at the women and closed the vehicle's double doors. Soon the sound of ambulance bells reassured them, taking them further and further away from the bloodbath.

Anne remained unconscious for the ten-minute journey. Fortunately, the ambulance was waved speedily through the security checkpoint on the bridge. At the hospital, she was swiftly taken into theatre.

Caitlin was handed to a waiting nurse as Kathy and Kevin said their goodbyes and quickly drove back to the bomb scene.

Caitlin began to feel slightly better, and her nausea settled. Her ears no longer bled, but her hearing hadn't fully returned. The nurse placed her in a chair and told her she'd return for her soon.

Caitlin waited and waited, but no one came. Eventually, she had to go to the toilet and shuffled herself off to the nearest Ladies. Awkwardly, wincing from her heavy bruising, she managed to use the loo and wash her hands. Her throat was still burning, so she drank water greedily from a tap. She looked at herself in the mirror. Her checked coat was torn and shrouded with fine dust along with twigs and leaves that had stubbornly stuck to its fabric. Her trousers were torn, and she could see fragments of glass and bloodied wooden splinters piercing her legs. Her hands continued to shake as she carefully washed her dirty neck and face, ignoring the pain. She entered a cubicle again, placed the toilet seat down and proceeded to pull out as many of the splinters and glass fragments from her legs as she could.

After a while, she returned to the Emergency Department and was met by a flood of injured patients and relatives. She found a seat in a quiet corner as far away from the commotion as she could and made no attempt to be noticed. She'd given up and was too worried about Anne to think about herself – or, for that matter, anyone else! The clock on the wall told her it was 4.30 p.m. It was surreal to think that just an hour or so ago she'd been laughing at Anne as she'd watched her walk breathlessly up Shipquay Street. A lifetime ago. Subconsciously her eyes closed as an inner voice asked: *How could my life change so much for the worse in just a few weeks? Daddy... And now Anne.*

Her leaden eyelids closed and she slept until a loud crashing noise woke her much later. She couldn't remember where she was at first, and then reality hit her like a train. She looked at the clock high on the wall. Jesus! 7.15 p.m. She tried to get up but couldn't. She should have phoned home ages ago.

Instinctively she looked for her handbag only to remember it must have been blown away with the blast. She thought regretfully of the extra pay she'd had in her purse.

In a weakened state, she found the nearest public phone and called the operator, asking her to make a reverse charge call to the McFaddens'. The operator rang through, and Caitlin could hear Mrs MacFadden accept the charges and cry out in frustration.

"Hello! Hello… Is that you, Caitlin?"

"Hello, Mrs McFadden. Yes. It's me. Caitlin. I'm sorry I've had to make a reverse charge call."

"Ock, hen, don't fret yourself about that. Your Mammy's been here with me for ages! We've been worried sick. She hadn't heard from you, and with that friggin bomb an' all, we thought you might have been caught up in it. She's a mess. Are you okay, love? Here, hold on, I'll put you over to her!"

"Caitlin… Caitlin love? Where are you? I've been worried sick. Jesus, Caitlin, why didn't you ring sooner? Where are you!"

"Mammy, I'm so sorry. I'm at Altnagelvin. I'm okay. I fell asleep. I was a bit sick and shaky, but I'm fine now.

"It's Anne, though. She's caught a bit of railing that went into her leg. She's been in surgery for ages. Listen to me, Mammy, I need someone to run to Anne's house and tell them straight away what's happened. Her mother will be in a terrible state if she doesn't know already, and Anne will want her here as soon as she wakes up. Can Emmett run over and tell them? I'll wait until they get over."

As Caitlin turned around, she came face to face with Kathy, who stood right in front of her and pointed at the phone. She mouthed anxiously, "Is that your Mammy? Let me talk to her."

Caitlin passed her the phone reluctantly. She'd wanted to make sure Emmett would tell Anne's mum the news.

"Majella, it's Kathy. I'm here with Caitlin. She's a bit shook up, but she's fine. I'll be finished soon, so I'll bring her back with me – okay?"

She listened for a few seconds and nodded her head.

"Yeah, right; I'll tell her. She'll be fine, I promise. Okay, night-night."

Kathy replaced the phone in its cradle slowly. She looked exhausted and dishevelled, drained of energy.

"You'll have to go straight home as soon as Anne's mum gets here. I'll take you back. I won't be much longer."

Kathy touched Caitlin's forehead with the back of her hand. She looked carefully in her eyes and then took her shaking hands. Her cousin's colour concerned her, and she felt cold and clammy.

"Caitlin. Has anyone looked at you since you got here?"

"Eh? Sorry, no, I fell asleep over there. I didn't want to bother anyone, Kathy. Mind you, I have a cracking headache and feel like I'm going to be sick again." She rubbed her head carefully with one hand.

Kathy thought she probably had a bad concussion but wasn't going to take any chances – not after the day she'd had. Working at the scene with the Fire Service and police, the body parts of up to ten people had been uncovered. It'd been a living nightmare

"You don't look great. Let's get that head checked out."

Much to the objections of the people in the queue, Kathy made her way straight to the Information Desk. Caitlin's details were taken, and Kathy took her back to the main seating area to wait to be called in.

"Can I get you anything?" she asked.

"No, I'm okay, thanks. I'm worried sick about Anne, though. I'll die if anything happens to her."

Kathy sighed wearily but told her cousin, "Tell you what; I'll go see if I can find out what's going on."

Kathy left to get an update. Surprisingly, she returned soon after and sat down next to Caitlin. She didn't want to leave her young cousin alone for too long. More worryingly, she wasn't sure how she could tell her the bad news. Christ, what a day! Kathy exhaled deeply before she began speaking.

"Okay, I've spoken to the lead nurse in Theatre. The good news is Anne's injuries aren't life-threatening. But there's bad news."

"What is it, Kathy? Tell me. Is she going to be all right?"

"She'll be okay, but her leg isn't too good. I had a feeling that injury was close to an artery, and I was right. She's lost an awful lot of blood. I'm sorry, Caitlin, but they couldn't save it. They've had to amputate at the knee. Sorry."

Caitlin sat and stared at her in disbelief. She knew it could be worse, but also that her lovely friend Anne would be devastated. Her beautiful leg. She recalled Anne's innocent joy at wearing her ridiculous but jaunty stilettos. A wave of unbelievable sadness enveloped Caitlin then. Her chest heaved with the effort of not allowing herself to cry. What in God's name had any of them done to deserve this?

Chapter Twenty-one

When she'd first told Kieran she'd help him he'd cried even more. He'd refused the offer at first until she'd told him forcefully that he'd no choice. Ever since then, he'd been more attentive and loving. He'd kissed her tenderly a number of times and continued to spoil her. She grinned uncontrollably as she thought of their precious time together. He'd made her feel alive and needed.

The first time had been much easier than she'd hoped. She'd followed Kieran's instructions to the letter and lured the soldier outside to the car park at the back of the bar. As soon as the dark-clad men grabbed him, she'd completely ignored them and left without looking back.

However, things had gone more slowly for her since then. The next soldier had been incredibly shy at first, but after a few drinks had relaxed. Surprisingly she'd enjoyed his company, though she couldn't get him on his own to begin with. He seemed to be particularly wary. She wasn't going to give up that easily however and had seen him numerous times before he'd issued an invitation. She laughed inwardly and studied herself in the mirror as she thought of the fail-proof plan for tonight!

Kieran had applied her makeup beautifully, and she wore yet another new dress. It was stunning. The soft red fabric felt amazing and flowed as she walked. Kieran had told her he liked her to look classy, so he'd added a pearl necklace and afterwards kissed the nape of her neck until she shuddered with delight.

She adored his apartment and deliberately left behind a few of her personal items in the hope he'd ask her to move in. She especially loved the luxurious queen-sized bed that seemed to take up most of the bedroom. They hadn't slept in it together – yet. She was still being careful not to push him. Above the bed hung a lone black and red poster of Che Guevara to which Kieran had added in bold handwriting at the bottom:

"In my son's veins flowed the blood of Irish Rebels."

She put on her coat and heard the taxi outside beeping its horn impatiently. One final look in the mirror told her that she loved this new sexy, confident image that smiled back. Then she concentrated on the task in hand.

Val sat waiting at the bar. He'd been both nervous and excited at the thought of seeing her again and made sure he arrived early to get a few beers in first. After three quick pints, he was much more relaxed and felt good in his only dark suit with his matching blue patterned shirt and tie. When she walked into the bar, her eyes searched for him. As soon as she spotted him, her face broke into a beautiful open smile. He stood up. Jesus, she looked amazing. The barman couldn't help but notice either and questioned how someone like that lanky nervous eejit could pull such a stunning blonde. He sighed at the unfairness of it all and turned away to wash another load of dirty glasses.

She walked over to Val and immediately noticed that one of his hands had been bandaged up. She took hold of the damaged hand and asked him with concern,

"You alright?"

He shook off her question and answered casually.

"Ah, this? It's nothing. You look lovely."

She enjoyed the appreciative look in his eyes as he kissed her cheek lightly and added a little breathlessly, "Really amazing."

She studied his hand again. It didn't look like nothing.

"Does it hurt?"

"No, I'm good! Forget it. I've been looking forward to this all week."

He gulped down the remainder of his beer and asked, "If you're ready for some scran, shall we go straight to the table?"

She nodded, thinking about the word scran, likely he meant food. She was hungry and even more keen to have a glass of wine. Although Kieran had talked through their plan many times, she was still nervous.

"Yes, please. I could eat a horse!"

Val waved to the apron-clad waiter, who took her coat and hung it up. He then led the couple to an intimate corner booth where he presented them with two black leather-bound menus and offered them aperitifs. Instead, they decided to go straight to wine.

The restaurant was impressive. She'd never been in such a beautiful setting. Exposed red-brick walls were supported by thick, dark, time-warped beams above a grey flagstone floor. She remembered hearing the place had been a mill at one time. There were candles burning on every table. It was dreamy. She was going to make the most of this, she decided, and eagerly picked up a menu.

To her surprise, she hardly recognised the names of any of the dishes. Val immediately noticed her frown. He chortled, touched her hand and whispered conspiratorially, "Don't worry, flower. Leave this to me."

She laughed with relief. Once again, he'd surprised her. He was sweet.

Val, in turn, was thrilled to have an opportunity to impress her and blessed his spell washing dishes in a fancy Newcastle restaurant before he'd joined up.

The waiter returned, and she watched her date confidently order their food. She was particularly impressed when the waiter added, "Good choice, sir." They giggled together when he'd gone, and Val raised his glass in a toast. He beamed as she clinked her glass with his.

"To us!" he cried.

"To us!" she answered brightly.

The evening was fun and the food delicious – he'd chosen well. They both ate sole accompanied by the tastiest vegetables she'd ever had. She loved it all and realised she liked him. He was a nice guy. As quickly as the thought came into her head, she dismissed it. Kieran had told her incessantly that this man and others like him were "denying Ireland her Nationhood and Unity". She had to keep that thought at the forefront of her mind.

Two bottles of wine later plus a few brandies (mostly drunk by Val) the novelty of the evening was beginning to wear thin. She wondered whether he'd had a few drinks before she'd arrived. He was now undoubtedly intoxicated and rather loud as he talked incessantly about his family. He told her more about his best friend, Robbie, who was like a brother to him. Earlier in the evening, he'd asked her lots of questions, but she'd always cleverly turned the conversation back to him.

He finally asked for the bill and paid in cash. Thank God. It was time. She leaned across the table and whispered seductively, "Would you like to come back with me for a drink?"

*He sat back in the booth and raised his eyes. Shit, yes, he would. He was thrilled by the prospect. In fact, he'd hoped she'd ask him tonight! It'd been a very long time since he'd been with a woman – a very long time. His face was literally aglow as he slurred, "Why, yes, pet. I would **very** much like to go back with you for a drink. Just a small one, mind!"*

She clapped her hands in joy. She was nearly there and just wanted to go home. She was now feeling weary of the pretence of it all, especially since he was so clearly smashed.

"Grand! Give me a minute. I'll scoot to the Ladies and order a taxi. Won't be long." She kissed him on the cheek and left.

Val lifted his arms and rested them along the sides of the booth. He leaned his head back, closed his eyes and waited with keen anticipation for the night ahead. He was on a promise!

As instructed, she stopped at the public payphone adjacent to the toilets and made a call. Two words were all she said before she hung up.

"Five minutes."

In the Ladies, she stood still and stared at the mirror whilst taking deep breaths to control herself. She couldn't stop shaking and had to work hard to calm herself down before making her way back to the booth. She was so unbelievably nervous she didn't notice most of the male diners gawking at her, much to the annoyance of their female companions.

She smiled as Val drunkenly watched her approach. He smiled languidly and mumbled, "You really are very beautiful, you know."

She was relieved to see that he'd finished his last glass of brandy into which she had slipped the powder given to her by Kieran. She had to get him out of here. With all the alcohol he'd already drunk, he'd be out cold soon. She stood and offered her hand to help him up. In a concerned tone of voice, she told him, "Val, there's a cab outside. The waiter said someone's just been dropped off."

He felt relief at her words as he suddenly didn't feel too good and struggled to stand. He swayed to and fro and knew he was going to fall so grabbed her and pulled her back down into the booth. The other diners were definitely not amused and whispered and frowned at such a commotion.

The waiter promptly arrived to help. Val draped his heavy arm around her shoulders.

"I have had the most b-e-a-u-t-i-f-u-l evening!" he slurred.

She didn't answer but struggled as she and the waiter virtually carried Val across the dining room. She collected her coat from the attendant and apologised to the waiter, who proved to be a true professional and responded courteously.

Outside a blast of cold air greeted them. She saw the taxi with its light on at the other side of the car park and strode towards it, trying to keep Val steady and awake.

"Val – come on, please. I'm freezing!"

The taxi drove towards them. It stopped, and the driver's window was wound down. Kieran sat inside. He looked at her and barked angrily, "Don't say a fucking word. Just get in!"

She froze. What on earth was going on? She had no time to think as he roared at her impatiently.

"I said, get the fuck in the car!"

As if in a trance, she struggled to get Val into the back seat. Kieran made no effort to help. As soon as she'd got Val inside the cab, he was out cold. She climbed in and closed the door. They took off with alarming speed. She shouted out, confused and scared.

"What the hell is going on, Kieran? Where are the others?"

He ignored her and continued to drive, almost incoherent with rage. He'd set it all up for the Boys and was sick to the core at the failure of his scheme. When she'd trapped the first Brit, they hadn't kept their word: they hadn't killed him like they'd promised. They'd wasted a golden opportunity by only giving the bastard a good hiding.

And now this! They hadn't even bothered to show up. Well, he'd finish it himself this time – the proper way. He continued to drive, oblivious to the girl's angry screams from the back of the car. Stupid bitch. Did she seriously think he'd be interested in the likes of her except as a means to an end? He smirked as he thought of the way he'd set her up and admitted to himself it'd been a first-class performance. She'd been putty in his hands.

Half an hour later, he turned into a country lane and switched the car lights off. In the darkness, he carefully drove up to a disused barn that stood high on a hill a mile or so from the border. The farmer was sympathetic to the Cause, and the site had been used for such purposes as this on a few previous occasions.

Kieran, still blinded by fury, switched the car engine off. The girl hadn't said a word for the last few miles. He caught her eye in the driver's mirror and told her scathingly, "Get out and give me a hand with him."

She didn't move but instead stared back at him defiantly. Eventually, she pointed to Val and asked incredulously, "YOU want ME to move him? No way. I'm not touching him!"

He lurched towards her through the gap between the front seats. She shuddered as through clenched teeth he hissed: "You think? Well, I'm telling you **NOW** to get off that fat arse of yours and help!"

He tried to hit her but missed. Wisely she jumped out of the car as fast as she could. He followed, slamming the car door behind and slowly walked towards her. His face now just inches from hers, he studied her from top to toe with an expression she'd never seen before. Pure contempt. The change she'd seen in him devastated her and full of fear she realised she didn't know this man at all. He was dangerous, and she knew she'd no choice but to help him. He simply nodded in the direction of the car and so tottering on her high heels, she helped him roughly pull Val out of the cab and on to the stony ground. Kieran swore.

"Jesus, I don't want to kill him – not yet anyway. Get his clothes off."

She was truly terrified and instinctively found herself backing away quickly as she cried. *"I told you! I'm not going near him!"*

His silence acted on her like a weapon. She knew she was in trouble when he ran and stood directly in front of her, head on one side, and began to smile – a vicious smile. Without any warning, he callously hit the side of her head with his fist and spat out his words.

"You will do exactly what I fucking tell you! Do you hear me? I've no time for this shit!"

Her head was reeling. She couldn't believe what was happening. Dear Jesus, what had she done? She knew then he'd likely kill her too – he was a nutter. A complete nutter!

He screamed impatiently at her again, *"I said, get his fucking clothes off!"*

Shaking with terror, she kneeled beside Val and slowly unlaced his shoes and rolled off his socks. She noticed sadly that his bare feet were long and thin, the skin milky pale. She deliberately took her time.

Meanwhile, Kieran searched Val's pockets. Apart from a few loose coins, he found a black leather wallet. It was old and well worn. He smiled as he rifled through it and retrieved two five-pound notes and raised them triumphantly in the air. *"Happy days!"*

She made no comment as he put the cash in his own pocket and searched some more. He found a few receipts that he read and quickly stuffed back into the wallet.

Next, he pulled out a small black-and-white photograph and passed it to her to take a look. It was a couple at some sort of formal event. They looked happy. Val stood between them, looking proud and beaming for the camera. He wore his military dress uniform. Kieran laughed and kicked the soldier's ribs as he lay on the ground.

"Sweet! It's his Mammy and Daddy. Shame they won't recognise him next when they see him again."

He tore the photo into small pieces and stuffed the remnants back into the wallet.

She walked a few steps away and watched him remove Val's jacket, shirt and tie. The unconscious man stirred a little but then lay still. Kieran looked at her and yelled, "Jesus, woman, where are you going?! Come here, help me with these!"

He pointed to Val's trousers and ordered, "I'll hold him up; you pull them down!"

Kieran put his arms under Val and pulled him into a semi-seated position. Val's head hung low. Kieran unbuckled his belt and opened his zip. He lifted his head, telling her she had to take the trousers off.

Sweet Jesus. One leg at a time, she eased them off and sighed when she'd finished. She looked nervously at Kieran, who shrieked in frustration.

"Fuck it, Honey! Are you stupid? Underpants as well!"

She felt overwhelmed with guilt. This was awful! How could she have been so naïve as to believe that Kieran cared for her? Her face burned with shame. He'd played her like a violin.

She grimaced as she removed Val's white Y-fronts and tried her best to ignore his nakedness. As soon as the pants were off, Kieran – who smirked as he watched her embarrassment – quickly grabbed them from her hand and gathered Val's remaining clothes and personal effects. As if contaminated, he bundled them hastily into a black plastic bag and tied it.

He then walked across the cobbled farmyard to a barrel that stood next to a milk bottle half-filled with yellow liquid. He put the bag along with a splash of the liquid into the barrel, struck a match and threw it on top. The petrol caught light and there followed an almighty whoosh. Seconds later, brilliant flames rose from the container. Kieran leapt backwards and stood as if in a trance until the flames died down. Once satisfied everything had been destroyed, he returned to her side.

She looked away. She felt uncomfortable, standing beside the naked man. Kieran laughed inwardly, enjoying her continued humiliation. He nudged her hard on the arm, sucked in a breath and chuckled. Pointing to Val's lower regions, he asked her, "What do you think, love? I'd only give him six out of ten for that!"

She stared at him and knew he wasn't just mad; he was evil.

Kieran clapped his hands and cried, "Love it! Now go and get me that box and other stuff from the car boot."

Too crushed to resist, she walked slowly to the car and opened the boot. Inside lay an open brown cardboard box filled with tape, some black and white plastic bags next to a large reel of rope. A handgun half-wrapped in green cloth was tucked into the corner of the box which she took and held under her arm as she closed the boot. She knew then what was going to happen.

She walked to where he stood and heard him asking where the rope was. Her body full of fear chose not to move or respond as she stood frozen in shock. Kieran watched her scornfully. She was pathetic! He cursed under his breath as he quickly ran back to the car to retrieve the reel of rope, then rushed to the barn where he threw it in the middle of the barn next to a single chair.

He marched back to her, took her chin in one hand and squeezed it tight, hissing out his words.

"Fuck this, Honey. Pull yourself together and help me get him inside, do you hear me?!"

By now she was so scared she could only stare back at him in complete incomprehension.

Shit! He realised he'd overdone it. Better try a different tack. He took her cold hands and rubbed them between his. In a soothing voice, he asked, "Can you do this for me, Honey? I'm sorry for losing it, but we weren't supposed to be doing it ourselves. I didn't want you involved in any of this – none of this part anyway. Word of honour. Honest."

He pointed at Val and imploringly asked her as he held her two arms. "Look, we need to get this one inside. Please try, just for me. Okay?"

She stared at him as he continued to pacify her until she began to understand what he was saying and was overwhelmed with relief to hear him speak in his usual kind voice. It was all a mistake! He hadn't wanted her to be here. He'd been let down. It wasn't his fault. Her Kieran was back.

He hugged her and kissed her tenderly on the forehead. She sighed with relief, exhaled nervously and nodded okay.

Soon they were dragging Val's body across the short yard and into the barn although Kieran bore most of the man's weight. Kieran smiled at her once again. He'd won her over. God, he was good at this!

"Well done, Honey. You're doing great. Well done. Thank you."

His praise delighted her, and she began to relax a little. It was going to be okay.

Sweat poured and glistened on Kieran's face as he groped around looking for the light switch. The small barn was lit by a single bare bulb that hung from a length of electrical cable attached to a wooden beam.

Grunting with effort, he lifted Val onto the chair that stood in the middle of the floor just below the light. He grabbed the coil of rope and carefully tied Val's legs to the chair first, then his torso and finally his hands. He knotted the rope tightly as Val's bloodied head hung low against his chest.

Time passed. She watched Kieran grab a handful of Val's hair and raise his head roughly so as to cover his mouth with tape. He wrapped the tape twice around Val's mouth before finally ripping the roll free. Next, he added a blindfold.

By this time, Kieran was exhausted but pleased and stood back to take in his handiwork. He nodded to her triumphantly. Val began to stir and mumble incoherently.

Kieran was delighted. He rubbed his hands together. Perfect timing. He walked back to her and whispered, "I think lover boy's going to wake up soon, Honey. Christ, I'm sweating! I need a drink. Want one?"

She nodded eagerly. Anything to help her feel better.

"Sure."

He smiled and kissed her. It was a cruel kiss, deep and unforgiving. He forced his tongue down her throat until she couldn't breathe. The more she tried to pull away, the deeper he probed. Eventually, he stopped, let her go and laughed heartily as he disappeared to the car. She felt sick, needed air.

Once outside she looked back into the barn and hastily closed the door to hide its pathetic scene. Hurriedly she looked around the yard, trying to work out some means to escape. She couldn't drive and had no idea where she was. It was useless.

Kieran returned and showed off his find as he raised his arm triumphantly, holding a bottle.

"Look what I've got! The finest Jameson's. We'll have it while we wait for our guest to wake up properly!"

She'd never seen him drink before and watched as he put the green bottle to his lips and drank greedily, followed by a belch. He offered the bottle to her, and she took a long swallow – fuck it. She embraced the sensation of alcohol flowing through her and immediately felt it work its magic. Kieran howled with laughter and slugged more of the liquid from the bottle.

She needed another so grabbed it back and drank insatiably. One, two, three, four swallows and soon she felt light-headed. She'd do anything to block out what was happening.

Meanwhile, Val awoke feeling disorientated and confused. He tried to move but couldn't. What the hell! Where was he? He felt like shit. He racked his brain until he remembered. The girl – treacherous slut! Fuck, Robbie, was right…

He couldn't see a thing, and his mouth was covered. He felt like he was going to suffocate and struggled for breath, drawing it in through his gaping nostrils. He strained to get free but instead fell over onto the solid floor, and his bandaged hand painfully struck the ground. Christ! His whole body convulsed in fear and pain as he tried to control his panic and use the few senses he had left. He listened hard but could only hear a man laughing in the distance. Jesus, he needed to get out of here. In vain, he screamed for help through his taped mouth.

The couple heard him, and the girl ran straight to the car to hide whilst Kieran drunkenly made his way back to the barn.

A wave of bitter-cold air flowed around Val as the door was pulled back. He fought and shook in fury at being tied up like an animal to the slaughter. He heard footsteps and cried out more for help. His chair was levered up off the floor, followed by silence. He struggled to call out, but there was no answer until eventually, he felt a drawn-out flow of ice-cold water being poured slowly and deliberately over his bare head and unprotected body. The Arctic flow was excruciating; it was so cold. He thought it would never stop. It did but was soon followed by a pain that roared through his left knee from a brutal kick. He heard the cartilage crunch as his restricted body started to twist in shock and pain. He squealed like an animal.

"Aaaaggghhhhh! Jesus, noooo!"

His body filled with pain as he fought to get free. Suddenly his blindfold was pulled away. He blinked as a bright light penetrated his eyes, and he tried to work out where he was.

He saw it was an old barn, and whoever had been with him just a few short seconds ago had gone. Pain and fear threatened to overwhelm him as he realised, "he was a dead man walking." Given that they'd taken the blindfold off, he'd be able to identify them. He wasn't getting out of here alive.

Well, he wasn't going to go easy and once again he fought against the ropes. Until he heard a voice coming from behind him. It was cruel and pitiless as it told him,

"Well, well, well. Welcome back to the land of the living! I'm glad you're here. We can start the party now!"

The tape around Val's mouth was pulled off so viciously it made his eyes water. The pain was searing against his scalp and lips. He tried to turn around to see his captor but couldn't, grunting in anger and frustration.

"Fuck you, you sick bastard!"

Kieran was thrilled. God, yes! He was going to have fun with this one. Val's head moved frantically from left to right, trying to locate the owner of the voice whispering in his ear.

"That's just lovely, Valentine. So much for your fucking la-di-da English upbringing. I must say, Mother and Father wouldn't be pleased by such language used to a complete stranger, now would they?"

His captor stepped forward into view. Oddly, Val's initial reaction was one of disappointment. He'd half expected a brutish thug, but instead, it was a lad just a few years younger than he was. There was nothing brutish about him – not a thing. He was good-looking, in fact, and dressed like any other kid his age in a pair of turned up jeans with dark Chelsea boots and a brown duffle coat. There was something weird about him, though; he wasn't like any of the usual PIRA suspects. The young man moved closer. Val stared into a pair of dead cold eyes and knew he wouldn't survive the night bar a miracle. He exhaled and stared back as he decided again that he wasn't going to make it easy for his kidnapper.

He spat at Kieran and retorted angrily, "What the fuck do you want?"

Kieran smirked and told him, "Nothing with you as such. This isn't personal – any of it." He swung his hand as he spoke, indicating the barn and the preparations he'd made. "You're the lowest of the low – a British squaddie – that's all. Disposable and easy to replace. I'm just going to use you to convey a wee message to your top brass. The big guns. A message from me. That's it."

Val hadn't a clue what he was on about.

"What the fuck do you mean, a message, you cowardly bastard?"

Unfazed, his captor came closer and crooned, "It's simple, Valentine. Or can I call you Val? Yeah, I think I will. I mean, Valentine... That's quite a name – bit too gay for my liking!" He laughed heartily at his own joke. "I'll call you Val. More manly." He stopped and thought. "Anyway about this message; it's very simple, really..."

The young man's rant continued – the usual barrage of hatred against the British – but with an added element that was deeply unsettling. It was clear, whatever he said, that this was more than just a means to an end for Val's tormentor. He was blatantly crazy and enjoying himself – until he abruptly stopped talking and walked off. He was out of Val's line of sight but could be heard shuffling and muttering just a few feet away. Val fought desperately against the ropes and tried to think of an escape plan, but they remained tight and fixed.

His feet were in a pool of freezing water, and he shivered uncontrollably. He was no longer afraid; he was terrified, with his heart drumming wildly in his chest. His assailant's footsteps grew louder as he returned and stood facing him. Val gawked in terror at the sight before him.

Kieran was naked apart from a pair of immaculate white underpants and black hob-nailed boots. He smiled knowingly at Val as he watched his fear grow. Val couldn't believe it. The lad looked almost ridiculous but sinister as hell. He appeared oblivious to the cold, his naked torso taut and unflinching. He didn't move an inch, but his cold eyes roamed over Val, assessing him for something. He was holding what looked like a girl's hockey stick in his right hand. Val couldn't see what was in the other.

Kieran raised the stick high up in the air and leaned it against his shoulder and chest for Val to see. He gasped as he saw a number of long, thick nails embedded in the brown-stained head. He dimly remembered then – a hurley stick...

At Val's reaction, his assailant smiled as he placed the stick on the floor. He shook open a white plastic bag he held in his other hand and produced a white plastic apron that he put on and tied around himself. **What the fuck***!*

Val screamed out for help and fought against his restraints. Defeated, he began to plead with his silent and motionless captor.

"Jesus, man, what are you going to do with that? I'm a British soldier! You can't do this! They'll catch you! I'm just following orders! It's a fucking job, mate, that's all! Just a fucking job! Christ, I'm not even that much older than you!"

Kieran was amused by Val's words. He'd heard them so many times before. He hefted the homemade weapon.

"Just following orders, eh? Isn't that what the Nazis said?"

Without warning, the hurley stick was smashed down across Val's thighs. Screams of agony filled the barn.

The nails were rooted deep in Val's thighs, but Kieran pulled and twisted until the stick came away. Spontaneously, blood spurted out of the gaping wounds.

Kieran sneered at Val. His face glistened with sweat as adrenalin flooded through him. He was feeling this! Loving it! He felt himself harden slightly – yes!

He circled the chair and spoke to his writhing victim.

"Let me tell you something, Private Valentine Holmes. I imagine you think I'm a fucking nutter – ranting at you about my country, my people and the Brits. I doubt you know anything about Irish history, do you?"

Val couldn't answer. The pain had paralysed him.

*"No, I didn't think so! You Brits have done nothing but torture and kill for your glorious British Empire! Well, Val, me man, I bet you're not feeling much **GLORY NOW!**"*

With that, the hurley stick struck him again on the same spot. He reeled from side to side in torment and wailed as the nails pierced deeper into the broken skin. Blood sprayed erratically from the puncture wounds and painted his chest and legs red. Kieran struck another blow and then another, each time fighting to free the stick and shouting with glee. Finally, Val's body gave in, and he lost consciousness.

Kieran was glad to stop. He was exhausted and needed to pee. He opened his underpants and used Val's body as he would a wall to pee against. He laughed aloud as he tucked himself back in. Nice touch. He looked down and saw Val's blood splattered on his plastic apron and was pleased. Another nice touch, less mess.

Meanwhile, his reluctant accomplice lay still in the car, half sloshed, until she couldn't ignore the screams any longer. Christ, what was he doing?! She staggered to the barn door and stood half-hidden on the threshold. Kieran was busy and didn't see her as she watched him. What he was doing to Val was unspeakable – terrifying in its inhumanity. She ran, crying, back to the warmth and safety of the car where she curled up and closed her eyes as tightly as she could. She prayed and tried her best not to think about the acts she'd just witnessed.

Inside the barn, Val had regained consciousness and was trying his best to control the overwhelming pain. He breathed slowly in and out through his nose as mucus hung stubbornly from the end. He sniffed and watched Kieran swig from a bottle of whiskey. He saw Val staring at him and saluted, using the bottle. Val saw Kieran's apron, face and body were sprayed with blood. The hurley stick lay abandoned on the ground.

Kieran searched for his cigarettes. He remembered where he'd put them and with a nod disappeared from sight. Moments later, he returned and opened the pack to pull a lone cigarette halfway out. He offered the pack to Val who didn't smoke – unlike many of his friends.

"Want a puff?" Kieran asked.

Val ignored the offer and grunted.

His response pissed Kieran off. "Suit yourself!" He pulled the cigarette out and lit it up. He inhaled slowly and played with the smoke, making circles in the air, one after the other. He looked at Val and confided, "My wee plan for tonight hasn't exactly gone the way I hoped. You see, I wasn't planning to do this all on my own like. And sadly – for me – this means our time together is therefore limited."

He took another puff and bent down closer to Val. He exhaled smoke that swirled into Val's face and whispered grimly: "It's like this. Sad to say, the Professionals aren't here. I've found myself limited for tools and have had to use my imagination to come up with the worst possible way to kill you. Your murder will be my message to the British Government – get-the-fuck out."

Kieran stubbed out the cigarette on the side of Val's face. His cheek pulsated in pain as Kieran spat and screamed at him. Using the back of his hand, Kieran smacked Val's burning cheek.

"That's for those people you killers murdered on Bloody Sunday including that poor photographer you threatened to shoot the very same morning! You got him in the end anyway!"

Kieran struck out again across Val's head and face.

"And that's for those children you cowardly pricks keep shooting with rubber bullets!"

177

By now the pain had ravaged every nerve ending in Val's body. He could feel his body shutting down.

Once again, Kieran picked up the hurley stick and smashed it down, this time onto Val's lower legs. He struggled as he tried to remove it and cried out, visibly frustrated.

"And that's for the kids you fuckers keep stopping and searching on their way to school every day! They're just children!"

On a roll, he punched Val straight on his nose. It broke, and blood squirted out.

"And that's for that wee girl you British pigs ran over and killed in your Saracen when she was just out playing in the street!"

Val's broken body had surrendered although his heart still raced. He could almost hear its determined beat and thought it likely to implode – soon.

Kieran stopped, and through his anguish, Val watched him as he rubbed his bruised hand. He hoped it hurt the bastard like hell. Apparently not, as Kieran casually lit up another cigarette and asked calmly, "You sure you don't want a puff? No. Don't smoke? Well, let's try again. How about this? This might get you started."

The newly lit cigarette was pushed deep and hard into the soft flesh of Val's other cheek. Kieran repeated his actions and counted up the blisters, one, two, three, four, until the cigarette was out.

By this stage, Val was gone. His mind had protectively sent him somewhere else.

Kieran was disappointed and stamped the cigarette out but laughed heartily as he looked over his broken, blood-splashed victim.

"Fags not for you then, eh? Shame. Maybe you're a cigar man instead?

Val was finished. But not Kieran. He wasn't ready to give up. One last blow and the hurley stick hit Val squarely on the chest. His body rocked under the impact and fell still. Kevin screamed at the unconscious man.

"And that was for lifting poor Patrick McLaughlin out of his bed, beating the shit out of him, and now the poor bugger's stone dead!"

Val lost control and emptied his bladder and bowels. Deep down in his darkened safe state, he realised what he'd done. Dear God, no. The hot yellow bloodied fluid stung his wounds as it ran down his cut thighs and legs, turned redder and redder and merging with the pool of crimson water at his feet.

Kieran tutted and giggled.

"Oh, dear me. Mother won't be pleased! I'll tell you what, Val. Let's keep this one to ourselves, shall we? Man to man and all."

Val was crushed and humiliated. Kieran knew he needed to move on. He looked at the doorway to see if she was still there. He'd thought she'd been there earlier but wasn't so sure anymore.

"You can come in now!"

He waited. Nothing. She must be in the car. He ran out, found her half asleep and roughly shook her awake.

Val couldn't see well, but through his clouded vision, he saw the girl walk reluctantly into the barn. She looked a mess. Nothing like she had earlier that evening – a lifetime ago. She'd been crying. Strange, but for a brief moment he almost felt sorry for her.

On the way to the barn, Kieran had asked if she'd like to play a game. She'd told him she wouldn't like to, but he'd laughed anyway and headed back to the car. She wanted to go home. Now.

As soon as she was inside the barn, she widened her eyes and shook her head as she tried to focus on Val. His face and neck were covered in red sore marks. Blood had coagulated around his nose and his face and a series of prominent holes on his thighs and legs. She could smell burning and a stinking, putrid smell. Sweet Jesus.

She walked over to him and gave him a watery smile as she put out her hand to touch his arm, but he used every last ounce of energy he could muster and spat back at her. His bloodied, thick saliva landed on her face and in her hair. As harshly as possible, he hissed, "Go to fuck, you murdering bitch!"

179

She recoiled and cried out as she hysterically wiped his spit off with her hands.

Kieran had re-entered the barn and yelled angrily.

"What the fuck is going on here!"

He soothed the girl and asked her tenderly, "You okay, Honey? What happened?"

The girl sniffled. She couldn't tell him. She was too ashamed. It was her fault, all her fault. If it hadn't been for her, Val wouldn't be here, and none of this would have happened.

"It was nothing. Nothing. I'm fine."

She met Val's eyes and said no more. Kieran knew something was up. He told her reassuringly, "Don't worry, Honey; I'm finished with him now. It's almost over. He's going nowhere."

Val watched as Kieran displayed the pistol proudly and loaded it with just a single bullet. He knew immediately what the nutter was going to do. Christ, no!

In desperation, he attempted frenziedly to free himself one last time. The girl was horrified and stood back.

Kieran sighed and spoke to Val.

"Okay, Val. I'm sure you know how this little game works. Six chambers, one bullet. This lovely young lady and I are going to play a game. And the gentleman that I am, it's ladies first."

He offered her the pistol, but she shook her head manically – openly petrified by the enormity of what he was asking her to do.

"No. No way! I'm not doing that! That's no game! That's sick. I can't!"

He'd never expected her to do it. He'd just wanted to scare the shit out of her. He laughed inwardly and placed his hand on her shoulder – he'd keep it going for a bit longer.

"Honey, it's really easy. Just aim for the side of his head and pull the trigger. That's all you have to do."

Full of fear, she screamed, "No, I can't; you do it!" She ran out into the darkness and left them alone. "Okay, Val. Looks like it's just you and me. Tell you what; I'll go first. Let's see if it's number one!"

Kieran placed the pistol to the side of Val's motionless head. Tears flowed down the prisoner's bloodied face. He closed his eyes as Kieran began to count.

"One, two, three…"

In the stillness of the barn, the only sound was the pistol's chamber rolling and then a single click. Not this time. Kieran was almost disappointed.

Val pleaded with him.

"Please, mate, don't! Please…"

"Sorry, **MATE**. Needs must," Kieran answered coldly as he pulled the trigger one more time. The impact of the shot threw him back a little as a mass of blood, bone and brains enveloped him.

"That's that then," Kieran muttered as he watched the soldier's body twitch for the last time. He removed the plastic apron and tidied himself up as best he could, using some water from a tap in the barn to wash away the blood and gore. He dressed himself. They needed to get a move on, and she was going to play her part in this at least. That would keep her on her toes and her mouth shut! He ran out and half-hauled her from the car and back to the barn.

Inside he pointed to Val, who lay slumped on the chair.

"See what you've done? This is your fault too. You made me do this! You're in this as much as I am!"

She couldn't believe what she saw and was promptly sick. Oh, dear God! He was right… What had she done? She finished vomiting and wiped her mouth with the back of her hand. She looked at the soldier's battered and burned body. What was left of his head hung sideways on his shoulder. His face was almost gone. The air in the barn was filled with a combination of rancid smells as Kieran put his arms around her and whispered menacingly into her hair. She shuddered as she heard what he had to say.

"Take it easy, Honey. I know it's been hard, but it'll be better next time, I promise. Help me get rid of him. I know what to do. Then we'll get you cleaned up too. Trust me."

He lowered her to the cold floor. She sat still and watched him put on another plastic apron. He opened a black plastic bag and placed some cigarette butts and other pieces of rubbish into it. Once more, he burned the evidence in the oil barrel.

As soon as he was ready, he untied Val's body and laid it out flat with a surprising touch of tenderness. He placed individual black plastic bags over Val's head, arms and legs. Then he split the remaining bags and wrapped the plastic carefully around the body, reinforcing it with tape until the last of the young soldier disappeared from sight.

Chapter Twenty-two

Robert was dreaming of Tracey, and the last time they'd been together. They'd been camping in the Peak District with some close friends. After a heavy night of drinking and singing like idiots around a campfire, they'd got carried away and ended up making love for the first time in the back of his father's green Ford Escort. It wasn't the most romantic or indeed comfortable place for lovemaking but, God, how they'd laughed! It had been a blissful sunny weekend, and since then he'd reminisced endlessly about her gorgeous svelte body. Now that he'd had a taste of her, he missed her even more.

He was woken by a hand that shook him roughly by the shoulder followed by a voice in his ear, whispering urgently.

"Sallis, quick, wake up!" Robert slumped back until he was shaken again.

"Sallis! Up… Now!" He opened his eyes and found his Captain standing next to his bunk. The officer was deathly white and the expression on his face spooked Robert. Again he was ordered to get up.

"Get dressed! Private Holmes has gone AWOL. I need you in my office, pronto!"

The Captain walked off as Robert rubbed his eyes groggily and sat up. It was still dark. He turned his reading light on and dangled his legs over the side of his bunk still half-asleep. Even in his thermals, he shivered with cold. He opened his locker and grabbed his black sweatshirt, tracksuit bottoms and red tartan slippers. Finally dressed, he looked at his watch. 4.10 a.m. He needed a piss and ran quickly to the toilet before speeding off towards the Captain's office.

His head was spinning because he knew Val had seen the girl last night. No disrespect to his friend, but she'd sounded too good to be true. Given Val was so happy, Robert hadn't wanted to hurt his feelings and was careful what he'd said about her. He'd warned Val to be careful, though. They all knew about the honey traps devised by the PIRA to entice younger soldiers into danger. Even with the warnings, one of the lads had recently been led into an ambush and had the shit beaten out of him. Fortunately, he'd survived but was sent back to the mainland to recover from his injuries. He desperately hoped Val's girl had nothing to do with his disappearance, though instinct told him otherwise. *He should have gone with his friend and kept an eye out for him!*

As he arrived at the Captain's office, he was ushered in along with two male civilians. Neither of them spoke or acknowledged his presence but stood there in silence. Robert looked around the room. He'd never been in it before. He'd heard it had once served as the Head Librarian's office and it really was quite beautiful. Its oak-panelled walls and high-corniced ceiling were impressive. In the middle of the room stood a pair of leather-upholstered Chesterfield sofas that faced each other at right angles to an ornate stone fireplace. The floor was mostly covered by a well-worn Turkish rug.

Behind a walnut desk hung a large, coloured photograph of the Queen. Robert and the men had been offered a seat by the Captain, but they'd refused. From the visitors' demeanour, Robert thought it was likely they were RUC Special Branch.

Unusually, his Captain appeared agitated and nervous as he enquired,

"Sallis, do you know where Private Holmes went last night?"

Robert paused. *Shit – it was the girl!*

"Yes, sir. He had a date. There's not much more to tell you, sir, only that he'd met her recently. He told me she'd been security cleared and had worked as a receptionist in Belfast but recently returned to Londonderry."

"Hmmm." The Captain thought for a moment and nodded to his guests in confirmation. "It appears she used false ID. Did Holmes describe her at all?"

"No. Not really, sir. All he said was that she was a looker. Blonde. Nothing more than that really." Robert wasn't going to share Val's additional comments.

The two men whispered to each other until the Captain, annoyed by the interruption, coughed loudly. He glared at them stonily and turned back to Robert.

"Sallis, we have a very worrying situation here. Did he say where they were meeting?"

Robert tried to think. His mind was reeling.

The Captain stood and paced nervously up and down the room while he listened for Robert's answer.

"I didn't see him leave, sir. I was in the games room. I do remember he told me they were going somewhere expensive for dinner in the Waterside. Apparently, the restaurant used to be an old mill, sir, but I can't remember its name. Sorry, sir."

"Right. Okay, Sallis. If you remember *anything* else, please come straight back to me. Dismissed."

Robert saluted and left the room. He quickly made his way back to his bunk. He was so weary. They'd been back to Blighs Lane on numerous occasions, and it'd been the same thing every day. They got a complete hammering each time as the unending barrage of missiles smashed into their paint-splattered Pigs. The compound sentries had retaliated angrily again and again as they fired numerous rounds of rubber bullets and CS gas canisters in their attempts to disperse the mobs.

Robert didn't think he could take much more – he was so fed up. When they'd heard about a young lad who'd got trapped inside a burning Pig, it really got him thinking. The sad bastard tried to put the fire out with an extinguisher but instead inhaled the chemicals that eventually killed him. It was unreal.

And now Val was missing. Shit, Val! He questioned why it was that the good guys always got hurt or killed? Why couldn't it have been that prick Morris? He had been a lucky bastard at the weekend when he'd missed a bomb blast by seconds. He'd lost a couple of front teeth that made him – if possible – even uglier.

Robert climbed onto his bunk and laid his head down. He was mentally exhausted and wouldn't be able to sleep but closed his tired eyes anyway. This wasn't what he and Val had signed up for. Not this. Not to fight and die in the UK.

He'd heard about another city curfew that was planned. Every road, bar one, that led into the Nationalist Bogside would be closed to traffic, including emergency vehicles, from 8 p.m. to 6 a.m. Robert thought it was ridiculous and likely they'd only get even more abuse and trouble at the single checkpoint.

They'd been told the idea was deliberately to cut the Bogside population off from the city centre and other parts of Londonderry. It was supposed to make the city safer, but inevitably, it fuelled the tension and made things ten times worse. The rioting had become better co-ordinated and even more sophisticated. The mob didn't have anything else to do or anywhere to go. All the social functions in the area had been cancelled, and even the Catholic Church had changed their Mass times. He didn't believe it made sense to isolate these people, but then who was he to say?

If those men in the Captain's office *were* Special Branch, he knew Val was in deep trouble. He'd heard the stories about the dark, seedy side of SB, including their infamous interrogation and informa-tion-gathering skills. Robert couldn't care less. That was their business. He wanted to be kept out of that kind of stuff and focus on getting home to Tracey. He'd enough on his plate with her recent moods and now Val going AWOL.

He tossed and turned in his narrow bunk as he attempted to get comfortable. His body hadn't fully recovered from the recent battering at the compound. He reflected on the last week, especially the girl who'd discovered him in that unkempt garden. How lucky was he that she hadn't screamed? He wondered why she hadn't. He'd been hiding in that godforsaken hedge, soaked to the skin, for hours. A suspect had recently visited the address, but Robert hadn't seen or heard anything suspicious. Weird. His memory also took him back to the tarred and feathered girl but soon he erased the brutal images, which allowed him to doze lightly for a while until he became restless. With false hope, he looked down and into the immaculately made bunk below but found no sign of life. His watch told him it was 06.00 hours. He'd had enough time to think and so leapt out of bed, grabbed his toilet bag and headed to the unwelcoming makeshift shower rooms.

After a pitifully quick shower, Robert dressed and made his way towards the canteen for breakfast. He noticed Morris approach him with a fake look of concern on his bruiser's face. The Irishman raised his eyebrows.

"All right, Robert?"

He was immediately on the alert. Morris never used his first name. He looked at the toothless man quizzically and replied, "Why wouldn't I be?"

Morris frowned and answered, too quickly, "Oh, man, I thought you'd be the first to know. Your friend Val… Bad fucking stuff that, really bad." He smiled knowingly. The stupid Geordie git evidently hadn't heard.

Robert shook his head in confusion.

"What the fuck are you on about?!"

Without a thought for discipline, Robert used both hands and grabbed Morris by the scruff of the neck. He pushed him brutally against a wall as anger overwhelmed him and gave him unaccustomed strength. Morris couldn't move as Robert raged and spluttered.

"Tell me, you slimy Irish bastard! You think it's funny, winding me up like that? Do you, eh?!"

He deliberately aimed a punch at the man's prominent nose and relished the sound of the loud cry Morris gave. Robert pulled back, and they both took aim to strike again before a loud commanding voice intervened.

"*Attention!*"

Both men froze at the order. The Captain walked purposefully along the corridor towards them as Morris touched his nose. It was broken. Shit! On top of losing three teeth – just fucking perfect! He stared balefully at Robert, who glowered back.

The Captain reached the two men and sensed their anger. In a fearsome voice, he yelled at Morris first.

"Morris, get out of my sight and clean yourself up!" He then pointed at Robert angrily and instructed him to follow. "Sallis, with me!"

Neither of the men wanted to move.

The Captain had had enough. It had already been a disastrous night and today was going to get much worse, so in a deafening roar, he repeated his orders.

"*NOW! MORRIS! MOVE! SALLIS, WITH ME!*"

Morris nodded but made no attempt to wipe away the blood that flowed freely from his nose. The Captain stared at Robert and turned to walk to his office oblivious to Morris, who sniggered, shook his head and raised a single finger at his superior.

Robert hated the Irish bastard but had no choice. He followed his Captain in silence. They reached the office where Robert stood to attention and placed his hands behind his back. His Captain sat down wearily. Robert wasn't ready to hear what the Captain was about to say. He knew what was coming.

His superior looked up and tutted as he regarded the blood on Robert's shirt. He sighed.

"At ease, Sallis. You're lucky I'm going to ignore that mishap in the corridor with Morris. A very unlikeable fellow, I have to say. However, under the circumstances... At ease."

"Thank you, sir."

The Captain ordered Robert to sit. The older man coughed and looked gravely across the desk at the young soldier. There was no easy way to tell him this so he'd just have to spit it out.

"Sallis, I need you to prepare yourself."

Val wasn't coming back. He remained controlled as he half-listened to the Captain, who, in a distinctly unsteady voice, told him more.

"This morning in the early hours, the RUC received an anonymous tip-off that a British soldier had been tortured and executed. They were told the location of the body. It took a while to recover it as they were concerned it could be booby-trapped. Or what was left of it, that is."

The Captain adjusted himself in his seat and inhaled sharply.

"I've just received a call to confirm that the body is that of Private Holmes."

Robert gasped and looked down. He just stopped himself from losing it as his body swayed alarmingly.

"Do you want some water, Sallis?"

"No, sir. Thank you." He pulled himself together and stood to attention. The Captain rose too and waited for him to speak.

"How, sir… How…did it happen?"

The Captain gave it to him straight.

"We don't have all the details yet, only that it was a cold, cruel execution. A single bullet to the head. From what we gather, Holmes was led to an unknown location – most likely by this young woman. He was stripped and, from the marks on his wrists and legs, tied up. It appears he was tortured and then shot. His body was wrapped in plastic bags and strategically placed in the middle of a country road. Unfortunately, by the time the RUC arrived, it had been significantly damaged by a Heavy Goods Vehicle. The driver is still being questioned."

Robert gasped. "I can't believe it, sir. I told him to be careful. We were warned, all of us!"

The officer nodded and added quietly, "I know. My condolences, Sallis. An obvious error on Private Holmes's part. However, we have a job to do. We need to find these monsters. There will, of course, be a full investigation and I will keep you informed. Now, if you'll excuse me, I have to call Holmes's family. Again, my condolences, Sallis. Dismissed."

Robert saluted and made his way out of the office. He closed the door and stepped into the corridor where he leaned against the wall and began to sob.

Chapter Twenty-three

James sat in his Uncle's study at Melrose. He'd needed the privacy and peace of the house as he worked through some sensitive documents and prepared his proposal for the future of the factory. He felt relaxed and comfortable in his black corduroy trousers, white shirt and soft black cashmere V-neck.

As promised, he'd taken Marleen to the beach the day after the unfortunate episode with Jones. They'd travelled to Buncrana first, stopping at the border security checkpoint then through Customs and onwards into the Irish Republic. He'd chosen a beautiful stretch of beach at Lisfannon only thirty or so minutes from the city. As always from the wide bend at Fahan, the first view of Lough Swilly was stunning. It helped that the weather had been kind. As they'd walked the air was crisp and fresh, and the sun shone warmly on the sand. The Lough was still and peaceful as the waves quietly lapped the shore. It all felt so peaceful and far away from the Troubles back in Londonderry.

Over breakfast in the morning, he'd read the papers as usual and found them particularly depressing. The situation was definitely getting worse. In addition to the huge bomb on Saturday, it'd been reported that the young British soldier who had apparently been executed by the PIRA, had his body unceremoniously dumped in the middle of a country road. James sighed as he thought about the tragedy.

Charles Jones's behaviour that Saturday evening had cast a shadow over the following day and James would now avoid Jones as much as possible. As he and Marleen walked together on the beach, James tried his very best to explain to her what was happening in Ireland. She'd apologised for sparking off Jones's diatribe and was distinctly embarrassed that she'd ignored James's request for her to wait until they were alone before they discussed politics. He wasn't angry with her. He loved her to bits but had a feeling she wouldn't be visiting again any time soon. He'd waved her and his other friends off last night, wondering where and when they'd next meet.

He gazed across the rose garden as he placed a call to the factory. Surprisingly he heard Mrs Parkes answer the phone.

"Good morning, Mr Henderson's office."

"Ah... Morning, Mrs Parkes. Is Caitlin there, please?"

He heard her gasp at the other end of the line before she cried down the phone excitedly, plainly desperate to get the words out, "Oh, my, Mr Henderson, I was just about to call you! I've just heard meself! I mean, poor Caitlin. If it's not one thing, it's another with that girl!"

James couldn't grasp what the woman was saying. In exasperation, he asked her to repeat herself.

"What? What is it, Mrs Parkes? Slow down and tell me, please."

Naturally, James couldn't see how agitated and upset Mrs Parkes had become.

"Well, I've just heard from one of the girls in stock and dispatch. Caitlin and her friend – Anne, I think her name is – well… They were in town when that bomb went off on Saturday! They were just across the street from it. Poor mites."

Mrs Parkes couldn't believe it when she'd heard. She knew she could be tough on Caitlin but deep down she was fond of her. She was a good girl.

James's heart took an almighty leap. Jesus! He closed his eyes for a moment. Almost afraid to hear the answer, he asked her quietly, "Is she okay?"

Mrs Parkes, in spite of everything, smiled and nodded furiously into the phone.

"Oh, Mr Henderson – she is! She's incredibly lucky, that girl! Just a few cuts and bruises. But her poor friend lost part of her leg. So sad. But then, I suppose she's alive. There were quite a few killed. I've heard there were body parts all over the place. Can you imagine it?"

James sighed with relief and nodded solemnly. No. He couldn't. He said casually, "I'm glad Caitlin's okay, Mrs Parkes, and no, I can't imagine what it'd be like to witness something like that. I don't suppose you have a telephone number for her?"

Mrs Parkes thought for a moment. "Why, Mr Henderson, I don't think Caitlin has a phone. I've heard her say they sometimes use the next-door neighbour's phone, but I've no idea what the number is."

This was far from ideal. James was concerned about her. She was his secretary after all. He heard a voice at the back of his head but chose to ignore it. *Sure, Henderson. This is all purely professional. Dream on!*

"Ah, I see. How about an address?"

He could almost feel the woman's shock vibrate down the line and imagined her sitting with her mouth open. He smiled inwardly.

"You want an address *for Caitlin! Caitlin!* You're going to see her at home?"

He answered the woman, firmly and quickly.

"Yes, Mrs Parkes, I am going to visit Caitlin at home." Moments passed while he waited to take down the address.

Across the city, Mrs Parkes sat at her desk, feeling totally stumped. There were unwritten rules, and this young man was crossing the line. She'd have to speak to his Uncle. Her thoughts were interrupted as James yelled down the line, and she shuddered at the urgency of his voice.

"Mrs Parkes! Are you there? I need Caitlin's address. Now, please."

She didn't know what to do. He could get seriously hurt if he went there!

"Oh, dear! I don't know. Are you sure? I really don't think that's a good idea, Mr Henderson. You don't understand where you'd be going!" She waited for him to respond, but he remained quiet. She gave up, placed the receiver down and muttered to herself as she sought out Caitlin's address. She returned to the phone, peeved but composed, and warned him in a terse voice,

"Mr Henderson, your Uncle is not going to be happy with me for giving you this address. I have to warn you, Caitlin lives in a very Republican area, and I really don't think you should go there. It might not be safe for you to visit such a place. But if that's what you want… You have given me no choice."

For a split-second, James almost felt sorry for her and answered her kindly. "It's fine, Mrs Parkes. I'll be fine. The address, please."

The woman reluctantly gave it to him, and he scribbled it down in a notebook. He thanked her, said goodbye and replaced the receiver. He quickly tore the page from his notebook and prepared to leave.

As he drove towards the city, he was met by the normal security checkpoints. However, as he reached the perimeter of the Bogside, he started to feel unsure of his mission. There appeared to be large numbers of people gathered on either side of the street. He drove on urgently in the direction of Blamfield Street the opposite end of the Bogside.

When he arrived, he approached the street slowly and looked for number thirty. He stopped the car and looked across at Caitlin's home. It was an unattractive, pebble-dashed semi-detached house with a red front door. The small garden was fenced in places but had many gaps where the wood had been forcibly removed – probably by rioters. There wasn't a single flower in the garden, just a sad dishevelled hedge and a patch of threadbare grass. Rubbish appeared to have been blown into the garden, adding to the impression of chaos.

He looked around the street and saw some young children playing. Some of them stopped their game when they saw the black Jaguar and ran towards it, laughing and screaming – a car like this was a wonderful sight!

A small dirty-looking boy, who wore a black and white diamond-patterned tank top over a murky-white collarless shirt, and short patched trousers, confidently cycled on his battered Chopper towards James and yelled, "Oi, Mister, what kind of car is that then?"

"An expensive one!" James answered and laughed as he suggested, "What if I give you ten pence – will you look after it for me until I get back?"

The boy cycled closer, and James noticed a thick lethal-looking stick attached to the back of the Chopper. In addition, a small grey mutt ran alongside the boy. The dog was filthy, its face, body and paws covered in mud, but looked up loyally at its young master and wagged its tail. James smiled and watched as the boy with the dirty face and long messy hair answered him with a twinkle in his eye.

"Can do. Ten pence is no problem but only for fifteen minutes, mind. It'll be twenty after that!"

Cheeky! James laughed out loud and patted the boy on his matted hair as he agreed to the entrepreneurial offer. He walked slowly towards the house and looked up as he attempted to open the latched gate. He noticed a white net curtain in the front room being twitched back into place. After a few attempts, the beleaguered gate opened, and he strode up the short path to the front door. As he drew closer, he saw the door had been damaged but semi-repaired. There was no bell or door knocker, so he improvised by hammering the flap of the letterbox loudly.

He waited and looked back protectively at the Jaguar. The little urchin and his mutt were cycling and running dutifully and protectively around the car. Almost as a warning to any trespassers, the boy held his stick defensively in one hand and used the other to steer the Chopper. James shook his head and smiled widely at him. The lad was watching him and saw his smile. He stopped cycling and gave James the thumbs up. James reciprocated.

He turned his head away as he heard footsteps in the house, and the red door was opened just a fraction. A young girl's face peeked out. "Yes?"

"Oh, hi. I'm looking for Caitlin."

She opened the door a little more and deliberately ran her eyes over him. He raised his eyebrows questioningly, thinking it rather rude of her to stare. She stretched her neck and looked out into the street. She noticed the Jag and asked abruptly,

"Who 're you then?"

"I'm James. James Henderson, from Caitlin's work. I heard she was hurt on Saturday. I wanted to see if she was okay. Is she in, please?"

"Hmm. Maybe. I'll go and see." With that, the girl slammed the door shut, and James was left standing on the doorstep feeling like a fool. *This was a bad idea.* He decided to leave and began to walk down the path.

The door was suddenly opened but this time by Caitlin, who stared at the departing figure in disbelief. She shouted to him and urged him to return with a beckoning hand.

"James, come back! But what in God's name are you doing here?"

He laughed nervously – unsure himself — and walked towards her.

"Sorry. As I tried to explain to the young lady, Mrs Parkes said you didn't have a phone, and I just wanted to see if you were okay. She told me what happened. Are you? I mean, do you need anything?" He rattled his words out rather too quickly. *Christ!*

Caitlin laughed softly.

"The young lady? You mean, Tina, my sister! She can be funny sometimes. Sorry about that. I'm fine, James, thank you. I was lucky. Although I don't feel too lucky today – I can hardly move!"

James looked closely at the cuts on her face, neck and hands. More worryingly, her hands shook continually as she held the door open. She followed his gaze and smiled as he added, rather quickly, "I-I'm glad you're okay but sorry to hear about your friend – Anne, is it? How is she?"

Caitlin sighed and crossed her arms. Since the explosion, she hadn't been able to stop herself from shaking.

"Awe, she's sad, really sad, and in a lot of pain. I know she's alive, but she's lost a good part of her leg. She's badly cut and bruised and lost an awful lot of blood. It's going to take her a long time to get over it – if ever."

196

They both stood awkwardly on the doorstep and tried to think of something to say until Caitlin realised she was being extremely rude. She pulled the door back, and James saw a narrow hallway leading to a kitchen. He noticed Tina, who sat at a table beside an older woman – presumably Caitlin's mother. They stared back at him with interest until the moment was broken when Caitlin gestured for him to enter.

"We're just having tea. Would you like some?"

He smiled and stepped into the hallway.

"Tea would be lovely. Thank you."

She led him shyly into the first room they came to and pointed for him to sit down on a chair under a large double-paned window.

"I'll get some for you. Won't be a minute."

From the kitchen, he could hear the faint noise of cupboard doors being opened and closed and the clattering of crockery all mixed in with muffled voices. He sat and looked around the living room. It was a big room wallpapered in some sort of orange and brown hexagon design. A few framed photographs were placed neatly on the mantelpiece above an open fireplace. He looked at them but could only recognise Caitlin as a young girl in white – likely her First Communion. The fire was set but not lit, so the room was cold. Long feather-like dried flowers that almost touched the ceiling were displayed in a vase standing next to a brown corduroy-covered sofa. On a narrow wall next to the window was a framed image of Jesus with his hands open and heart exposed. Below that hung a small wooden crucifix. A teak-effect TV with cream push down buttons stood on the sideboard that faced the couch.

He couldn't explain why, but the room felt sad to him. It wasn't homely, too sparsely furnished for that, but it was spotlessly clean with its polished surfaces, vacuumed shaggy rug and stark white net curtains. A small teak table stood in the centre of the floor, with old newspapers arranged in neat piles upon it.

Out of the blue, he heard footsteps pounding up the staircase. They were soon followed by blasting music. Most likely, this was Tina, and without a doubt, she was angry or unhappy.

A short time later, Caitlin entered the room carrying a tray. James got up quickly to help her and held the door open while she placed the tray carefully on the small table. A blue and white Weeping Willow pattern teapot stood on the tray next to two cups, saucers and spoons. The milk had already been poured into the cups. Caitlin poured the tea and passed a cup to James. He looked for sugar but couldn't see it. She knew he liked sugar, but she hadn't offered him any, so he didn't ask. Caitlin closed the door, took her tea and sat down on the sofa opposite him. She smiled weakly.

"Thank you for coming, James, but you shouldn't have. I told Mrs Parkes I needed a few days off, that's all. With Daddy's death and now this; it's just been one thing after another. I'm sorry. I feel so bad for missing work."

James nodded sympathetically and replied. "That's alright. Take as long as you need."

Caitlin sighed and told him, "Mrs Parkes will be relishing this. I know she'll want rid of me now!"

James laughed and put down his cup as he smiled at her reassuringly.

"Don't be silly! If anything, the old bat seemed genuinely concerned! We're all concerned. So much has happened to you lately. I thought the Irish were supposed to be lucky!"

She smiled slightly and dropped her eyes.

"I know it's awkward, given that you work for me, but I would like to help if I can," he said delicately.

Caitlin shook her head. "I don't think so, James. I can't believe you even took the risk of coming here. Do you know what the police and the army call this place?"

He hadn't a clue, so sat back and laughed. "No, tell me."

Caitlin didn't find it funny and in a serious tone told him, "The Reservation. You know – like in the Wild West."

James couldn't help but laugh again at this piece of information. He stood and pulled the net curtain back.

"I didn't know that, so I suppose I have a well-paid papoose watching my car!"

Caitlin had to get up then and look for herself. She'd no idea what James meant. Soon enough, she saw the boy on the Chopper along with a mucky dog, circling and protecting what was obviously James's beautiful car parked across the street. Typical of Liam!

"Why, that's Liam McFadden! I'm not surprised! He's a cheeky thing, but I can guarantee you nobody will get near your car, especially with Lassie on guard too!"

She smiled and without asking topped up his cup. They sat down next to each other on the sofa. He gazed at her and winced in sympathy for the cuts on her face. He could see how tired and jaded she'd become. There was no real damage to her physically given that the cuts would heal relatively quickly. However, he was concerned for her well-being. She'd had more than her fair share of heartache, and once again he felt a wave of protectiveness for her.

Her hair was damp and tied neatly back into a ponytail by a red and white checked scarf that draped elegantly over her long neck. She wore no makeup, but James found her breathtakingly beautiful. Disconcertingly, when she moved, he couldn't help but notice she was braless as her nipples jutted through the white cotton t-shirt she wore with her dark flared jeans. Her feet were bare but for some soft pink nail polish on her toes. He knew he was staring but couldn't stop himself. He wasn't completely sure but thought he felt sexual tension in the air. *Pull yourself together, man,* he chided himself.

He regained his composure and asked her hurriedly to break the atmosphere, "When do you think you'll get back to me... I mean to work?"

She'd felt something in the air too. He'd been watching her with a strange look in his eyes or had she imagined it? She must have, surely.

"I should be back Wednesday or Thursday at the latest. I'm still shaky, and the doctor insisted I take a few days."

He watched her in silence and could see her growing upset. Tears fell as she told him guiltily, "It's all my fault, James! If I hadn't asked Anne to come into town, this wouldn't have happened! I feel awful!"

Her cheeks reddened with embarrassment after her outburst. James wiped the tears from her face with his thumb. He spoke so softly and kindly to her that she cried even harder.

"It's not your fault! My Uncle's warned me so many times about the Troubles, telling me I have to be careful, but I've never really understood why until these past few weeks. I thought it would all blow over. But not now, not anymore."

He passed her a white handkerchief and watched as she dried her tears properly. He looked at her with a twinge of sadness.

"These bombings and killings are crazy." He lifted her chin up, held her gaze and told her determinedly, "But listen to me, young lady. I am telling you now. *It-is-not* your fault what happened to Anne. Sadly, you were both in the wrong place at the wrong time."

His eyes lingered on her for a fraction longer than necessary, and then he smiled the most dazzling smile. He was lovely. Through her tears, she stared at him with sadness and a furtive longing, too choked to respond.

He couldn't resist her fragility, and the next thing he knew, she was in his arms. He could smell coconut or something similar as he stroked her hair and whispered lovingly into the side of her head, "Ah, Caitlin. What am I going to do with you?"

She sighed quietly and breathed in his wonderful smell. She felt safe. Her lips trembled a little, and more tears gathered as she thought of her daddy and how he too, had made her feel safe. They sat and held each other until, with a twinge of sadness, Caitlin pulled away.

She looked deeply into his eyes. No, she hadn't imagined that he felt something for her; it was plain to see. She groaned as he kissed the tip of her nose and added small kisses around her cut, tear-stained face and finally her lips. She smiled at him, about to answer his question when she heard a tentative knock on the door.

Majella semi-opened it and peeked her head around before cautiously entering the room. James could see how emaciated she was from the way her purple dress hung off her thin body. As if reading his thoughts, she smiled self-consciously and looked at Caitlin, who had obviously been crying. Her face was red and flushed. She addressed her daughter and said, "Sorry love, but there's trouble going on at the end of the road. I think it's time for the young gentleman to leave." Caitlin stood up immediately and introduced them.

"Oh, right, sorry. Mammy, this is James. James Henderson from the factory. James, this is my mother."

James offered his hand and told Majella solemnly, "Mrs McLaughlin, I was very sorry to hear about your husband. My condolences. And now this with Caitlin. You've all had a really tough time."

Majella nodded as she watched the young man talk. She remembered him. Up to now, she'd never told Caitlin how she knew him. *Jesus, he looked so like his father.*

"I just called to tell Caitlin to take as much time as she needs before coming back to work, and to see if there is anything I can do?"

Majella answered him politely before she left the room.

"Thank you, Mr Henderson, but we're fine. Nice to meet you but you'd better be off now."

"You too," James called after her, but she'd disappeared.

Caitlin closed the door quickly. They stood in the middle of the room. He kissed her once more, with more intensity and passion. He soon realised he had to control himself and broke away. They both gasped. He closed his eyes, shook his head and smiled.

Caitlin blushed at once as she remembered the way her body had responded to his kiss. She could still feel the blood pumping in her ears. She was ecstatic for a second until the reality of their situation hit home. She felt confused and afraid. He seemed both eager and relieved as he held her damaged face between his hands. He smiled and told her ruefully, "I'm sorry, Miss McLaughlin, but I had to do that."

Her face coloured again as Majella shouted impatiently from the kitchen,

"Caitlin! It's time for Mr Henderson to go!"

"Your mother's right. I have to go. What's the phone number for next door?" Mechanically Caitlin recited the number. "263141."

James found a pen in his pocket and wrote the number down on a scrap of paper. Again Majella shouted impatiently from the kitchen. Caitlin was mortified and cried back, "Okay, Mammy! He's going!"

James boldly stole another long kiss before she literally pushed him out and through the front door. He held up his hands in surrender and reversed away down the path, laughing.

"Okay, I'm going. I'm going!" Caitlin looked at him, walked after him and put her hand on his arm to pull him back. In a low voice, she asked, "Are you sure about this, James? All hell would break loose if anyone found out about what just happened."

He nodded.

"At one time, I would have asked why it would cause a fuss. But I get it. Trust me. I'll see you *very* soon."

She watched him retreat down the path. As he turned and waved to her from the gate, she couldn't believe how handsome he was. She smiled and gently closed the door.

The car was miraculously in one piece as James paid out the promised fee and thanked its grubby protector. As he switched on the engine, his emotions were a mix of elation and fear. He knew that kissing Caitlin had been crazy and dangerous. He'd overstepped the mark

– but she did something to him, and he couldn't help himself. He must tread very carefully and slowly with her.

Determined to get home as quickly as possible, he took off.

Within a short time, he sensed a change in the atmosphere. Mrs McLaughlin was right. He'd hoped to avoid the no-go areas but failed. There was trouble brewing. The earlier crowd had increased tenfold, and he saw plumes of black smoke rising in the distance. He continued as fast as he could and tried his best not to draw attention to himself until he had no choice but to stop at a T-junction with traffic lights.

He waited nervously for the lights to change. Then without any warning, the driver's door was flung open, and James was grabbed roughly by the collar and pulled out of the car like a sack of potatoes. The pain in his head was excruciating as his hair was grasped in an enormous hand that pushed him over to face the rear passenger door. His arms were forced up onto the car roof, and his legs unceremoniously kicked apart. As hands began to search him, a brutish voice snarled, "Who the fuck are you and what the fuck are you doing here, you flashy git?"

James was terrified. He didn't get a chance to answer before the voice screamed right into his ear: "I said, who the fuck are you? I hope to fuck for your sake you're not a member of our beloved Security Services, 'cos that's what you look like, you prick, eh?"

The hijacker slapped James brutally across the back of the head. His coat was forcibly removed and discarded on the filthy ground. James looked across the car roof and saw another man, who wore a black balaclava with slits for his dark eyes that stared fixedly back. In his hand, he held a Browning pistol that he aimed at James's face.

The hands emptied James's pockets and removed his licence, wallet and cash. He was then jerked around to face the hateful voice. This man held a pistol too. Along with his black balaclava he was dressed in a green hooded jacket, faded jeans and scruffy black Doc Marten laced boots. He was a big man – at least six foot five. As he examined James's licence, he shouted out the details mockingly to a gathering crowd.

"Why, it's Mr James Henderson from Glasgow! A Scottish fucking Proddy with a name like that! Well, Mr Henderson, given you're a visitor to this wee town of ours, and especially as we don't see many cars like yours too often, we'd like to borrow it! We do hope that doesn't cause you any inconvenience!"

The crowd roared with laughter until there was a sudden commotion. A small, round, elderly woman burst her way through to the front and determinedly ran over to the Jaguar, lethally armed with a handbag and umbrella. James recognised her immediately as one of the cooks from the factory. She showed no fear as she approached the giant gunman first and shouted and waved her umbrella in his face. For such a small woman she had some vocals on her.

"You leave that young man alone, you big eejit, do you hear me! Do you know who that wee boy is? If it wasn't for his kind, most of us women – including your own mother – wouldn't have a job!"

She turned and pointed the umbrella directly at the other stunned gunman and continued speaking in a fury.

"He's a Henderson from the factory. So don't you dare touch him! I know who you are, you big goofs, and I'll be straight on to your mas if you don't let him go!" The crowd watched in admiration as she took on the two gunmen. Most of them wouldn't!

It was almost comical, and under different circumstances, James might have laughed too. However, he watched in silence, as the gunmen looked at each other in confusion. They said nothing for a few seconds until finally, they nodded and reluctantly let him go.

The green-coated hijacker smirked as he passed James back his licence. He emptied the wallet of cash that he kept for himself and whispered threateningly, "You're blessed today, Mr Henderson. I suggest…" he pushed James back against the car "…that you get the fuck out of here now and never come back. You're a wanker to be driving around here in the first place. So before we change our minds – jobs or no jobs – get the fuck away with ye!"

James bent down to pick up his dirtied raincoat and was simultaneously kicked in the ribs by a huge hobnailed boot. He fell to the ground, completely winded. He exhaled sharply and struggled to stand up as his rescuer's voice cried out again in rage.

"You feckin' leave him alone! I'm telling ya! I swear, I'll be in both your houses no sooner than!"

The giant man laughed and told her, "Sure it's all right, Mrs McConnolly. We hear ye; we're just having a wee bit of fun. That's all!"

James eventually managed to stand and held his ribs for a moment. He took a final look at the gunman, who menacingly returned his stare through his ominous slit hood and reminded him: "Remember what I said, Mr Henderson; don't ever fucking come near here again!"

James nodded and climbed painfully into the Jag. His hands shook and almost caused the car to stall every time he attempted to change gear. He'd never been so frightened in his life. *Dear God, if it hadn't been for that brave woman, they could've killed him!*

He drove on carefully until he reached the Craigavon Bridge checkpoint where the car stalled as it joined the queue. Uncontrollable sweat dripped down the sides of his face. He shook and shivered. Just in the nick of time he opened his driver door and threw up. His ribs contracted, and the pain was insufferable.

He finished and spat out whatever was left onto the ground. His head and body remained hanging over the sill of the car until he noticed a pair of black army boots below his face. A concerned English voice asked, "You all right, sir?"

James looked up to see a soldier and croaked, "I was hijacked. I'm okay. Just a bit shaky." He proceeded to dry retch. Christ, the pain!

The soldier walked quickly towards the checkpoint, waved and cried out,

"Lads, quick! Bring some water over here."

Soon he returned to James, who still hung over the side of the car. The drivers in their cars behind waited patiently and watched as the soldier asked in interest,

"Where and when did this happen, sir?"

James wasn't exactly sure where but tried to tell him. "Just by those big flats in Rossville Street, I think. A few minutes ago."

"Sir, with respect, why would you be so naive to drive a car like this through the Bogside day *or* night?" James knew the soldier was right and slowly nodded his head.

"I know. But there was something I had to do there."

The young soldier grabbed a water canteen and passed it to James, who drank the cold liquid greedily. It hurt him to drink, but he didn't care as he rinsed his mouth and spat it out.

It was a moment until he was able to sit up, and the soldier helped him out of the car. Another man climbed in and drove the Jaguar to the side of the bridge, to allow the waiting traffic to move on.

James walked over the railing of the blue-and-white iron bridge and relished the fresh air. He held his ribs protectively as the soldier commented dryly, "Well, sir, I hope whatever you had to do was worth it. It looks like they've had a good go at you. But tell me, how did you manage to keep the car? I can't believe they let that go."

"Don't ask. It's a long story," James replied weakly. The soldier shook his head.

"Fair enough, but I'll need your ID, sir."

James nodded and passed his licence to the bemused soldier, who thought: *What a complete dickhead! If I'd a motor like that, I'd not be seen dead driving it through the Reservation!*

Chapter Twenty-four

Caitlin couldn't believe it. James Henderson had kissed her and, God, so lovingly.

Early that morning she'd thought she'd never get out of bed and face the world; she'd been so depressed. Her body ached, and her hands continually shook. She hadn't slept a wink since the bombing. She found the wee hours so long and lonely as her mind recalled the last few seconds before the blast and images of the many broken and torn bodies after. She even saw Anne's discarded bloodied shoe. She didn't think she'd ever sleep properly again.

But now, after James's surprise visit, she wasn't sure how she felt about anything. She was bewildered by it all; her emotions were a mixture of fear and elation. She walked into the kitchen and found her mother sitting alone at the table with a cup of tea. She looked worried but smiled weakly when she saw Caitlin enter.

Tina had taken a huff and gone to her room after Caitlin had joined them in the kitchen to make James his tea. She'd only asked her sister to help out a bit more but no sooner had she spoken than Tina had disappeared upstairs in a fury. Moody cow.

"What's going on, love?" Majella addressed her daughter as she closed the kitchen door tight. "Why on earth was someone like him visiting us here?"

"I don't know. Really. I was as surprised as you." Caitlin began to fidget with her hands and looked down at them as she faltered, "Ah, Mammy, it's such a mess. I don't know what's going on. I really don't. First Daddy then Anne and now this… James, I mean."

Majella gawped at her daughter. James? What about him? *Shit*! Her mothering instinct told her everything. She went ballistic.

"Ah, feck, Caitlin! Where's your thinking! For Christ's sake, you've just met the man! You know our Martin will murder you if you get involved with the likes of him. I mean, it's bad enough he's a Proddy, but he's not just your typical Proddy. He lives in a different world from us, love!"

Caitlin was stunned by her mother's outburst and turned angrily on her.

"Don't you think I know that?" She sighed in frustration – *where the fuck had that all come from?* – and Majella yelled at her again.

"Caitlin, you've only just started working for him. He's taking advantage, love. That's what he's doing. He just thinks he can take what he wants. You're so naive! He's fucking taking advantage!"

Majella was livid and banged her fist down on the tabletop. The cups shook. She stood up and walked over to the kitchen window so she could look at something other than her daughter's stricken face. Her eyes welled up. She couldn't believe this.

Caitlin had never seen her mother so angry, and it scared the living daylights out of her. But still, she tried to explain the unexplainable.

"No, he's not like that! It was a few kisses, that was all. I swear I won't tell anyone! But don't you think I deserve some happiness?" Majella stared round blankly at her daughter's flashing eyes and red-cheeked face as she added fiercely: "Our Martin's locked up! Me Daddy's dead. And you, Mammy? You're in fucking cloud cuckoo land whether you're up or not! As for our Tina... None of us has a clue what's going on in that stubborn head of hers! Don't *I* deserve a life of my own and a chance for some happiness!"

A cold silence filled the kitchen. Finally, Caitlin said, in a calmer voice, "If anyone understands love, Mammy, it should be you."

Majella sighed heavily, shook her head sadly and tutted.

"Hmmm. I didn't realise you were so angry with life, Caitlin, but it was different for me. Your Daddy and I knew each other for some time before we got together *and* we were from the same side!"

Caitlin wouldn't accept this denial and grabbed her mother's arm.

"Think about it! Granny was furious with you for seeing Daddy, and you gave her up so you could be with him. You must understand after that!"

Majella wasn't going to take any more of this shit and pushed her daughter away. She shrieked at Caitlin, "Jesus Christ, will you grow up! Don't you fucking get it? He's not Catholic! I'm warning you; this-will-end-badly – very badly. As for Martin, he might be out sooner than we thought. That's even *more* reason for you not to get involved with the likes of your boss. Remember, our Martin doesn't miss a trick!"

The kitchen door was thrown open, and Tina walked in, sullen faced. She wore a red scarf and a long red woollen coat Caitlin hadn't seen before. It clashed with her hair.

Tina ignored her sister completely and asked Majella contemptuously: "What's going on? I could hear you upstairs even with me music on. And what does our Martin not miss?"

"Nothing. It's nothing, love," Majella replied, with a shrug.

"Then why was the kitchen door closed? We never close it. And what was that man in that posh car doing here?" Tina asked, finally deigning to glance at Caitlin.

"He was just seeing how I was," she muttered.

Tina appeared unconvinced and said dryly, "Bit snobby even for you. He's got a nerve, coming around here in a car like that. Strange though, him coming here." She mulled over it for a moment and then grinned uncontrollably.

"Aaaahhhhh, there is something! It's him, isn't it? You and him!"

Caitlin lost her temper then – which was the worst thing she could have done – and cried, "It's nothing, Tina, okay? Just mind your own fucking business!"

The girl snorted derisively. "Yeah, right. Nothing to do with me. Anyway, I'm off out." She scurried from the kitchen with Majella crying after her: "Where are you off to now? You can't go out! There's rioting! Jesus, get back here now… I mean it!"

As usual, her daughter's response was to bang the door shut behind her. Majella sighed wearily. She needed a drink or at the very least the chance to close her eyes and sleep. She spoke as she yawned tiredly.

"I don't know what's got into her lately – always biting my head off."

Caitlin felt sorry for Tina. She couldn't be right. None of them could be after their bereavement.

"She's upset about Daddy. It's going to take time. Now sit with me, please. We need to sort this out. We've *never* argued like this. I hate it."

Majella didn't trust herself to talk. She couldn't cope with bad feeling between them either. The radio played softly in the background. Neither of the women spoke. Instead, Caitlin made more tea and poured it into mugs. They each took their turn to add some powdered milk. Caitlin had given James the last drops of real milk, but to her embarrassment, they'd run out of sugar, and she couldn't offer him any. She knew he hated tea without sugar, but he'd said nothing and politely drunk it. He was sweet himself.

Caitlin made sure she kept calm as she attempted to placate her mother.

"I'm not sure how I feel about anything, so please try and understand. I don't know where this is all going. Believe me, him turning up here was a shock to me too. I don't want us to hide anything from each other, Mammy – we've never had secrets."

Majella shook her head. She wasn't having this. Caitlin had no idea what she was getting into. It wasn't right. She'd get hurt – and badly. Majella knew James Henderson's type.

She had to take control and end this now for her daughter's sake.

"I'm frightened for you, love. I know we've never kept secrets, but this time it's different. Dangerous. No more, Caitlin. I'm sorry, but it's got to stop."

A big hole seemed to open up in Caitlin's chest. The suffocating sadness she'd felt earlier returned worse than ever. She'd never before gone against her mother's wishes. And so Caitlin had no choice but to lie.

"Okay, I'll stop it," she said in a forlorn voice. "I'll stop it for you. You're right."

Majella's eyes narrowed: it couldn't have been that easy surely? She was slightly relieved but knew she'd have to keep an eye on her elder daughter. She'd stop drinking from tomorrow and wouldn't take any more pills – or at least not as many.

In an effort to move on and change the subject, Caitlin asked, "Have you heard anything from the solicitor about Daddy?"

The family had formally insisted on a public inquiry into Patrick's death. Their solicitor, Brendan Hegarty, had requested copies of the paperwork and witness statements from the army and Security Services. So far, they'd got nothing back. Majella sighed miserably.

"Nothing. It'll take years for that to happen, if ever. At the end of the day it's not going to bring your Daddy back, is it?"

"No, I suppose not. Although knowing Brendan, he'll not let it go. He's a human Rottweiler!"

Majella smiled sadly at Caitlin's attempt to cheer her up.

"Yeah, I know. He's had some sorry cases to deal with this past while. Bless him."

Caitlin stood and gathered the empty mugs so she could wash them.

"Listen, I need to go and see Anne this afternoon," she said, her back to her mother "I'm dreading the journey, but I have to see how she's doing."

Majella shook her head vehemently. "No way, love. I'm not letting you out of my sight. Ask Mrs McFadden to use the phone and call the hospital. There's likely to be trouble out there now. You're shaking like a jelly still so leave it 'til tomorrow or the day after."

Caitlin knew she should see Anne, but she was feeling so emotional and tired. Her mother was right about the trouble on the streets, and the last thing Caitlin wanted was to upset her again.

"Okay, I'll go and call them."

Caitlin walked to the staircase cupboard and removed her mother's coat; her own having been ruined by the blast. Majella's coat was much too short, but she had little choice and anyway she'd order a new one from Mrs McFadden's Littlewoods catalogue.

She knocked on the McFaddens' door and gazed around the street as she waited. She noticed plumes of black smoke in the distance and two minuscule helicopters that were likely monitoring the riots from the safety of the sky. Caitlin prayed James would get home safely.

The door was soon opened by Charlie. The TV volume was so high that Caitlin heard it from the doorstep as a sports presenter excitedly announced his pick for the next horse race. Charlie stood at the door in a soiled string vest, his thick neck adorned with a gold chain and crucifix. His black pyjama bottoms were creased and stained. He obviously hadn't shaved and held a can of beer in one hand, addressing her past the roll-up that dangled from his lips.

"Alright, Caitlin? Come in, come in."

"Grand Charlie. Just wondered if I could use the phone to ring the hospital and see how Anne was doing. Okay?"

"Aye, no bother." He waved her along a hallway identical to Caitlin's home but much better decorated than theirs. Mrs McFadden worked hard.

Caitlin waited while Charlie searched for the key to the flat-roofed shed that housed the phone. As he hunted for it, he asked,

"Who was that then that owned the posh Jag parked opposite yours earlier? Bit flash, ain't it? Our Liam says he got twenty pence for minding it. Told me some man with a weird accent asked him to."

He found the key and displayed it in his hand. Before he handed it to her, he waited for her response.

"Oh, that. He's just my boss from the factory. Wanted to see how I was doing."

Charlie nodded.

"Hmm. That's nice. He needs to be careful, though, driving a car like that around here. He'll be lucky if he's not hijacked!" He laughed and passed over the key.

212

"Here you go. I doubt they'll let you talk to Anne at that place but if you do, tell her we were asking for her."

"Will do Charlie, thanks."

Caitlin walked through Mrs McFadden's spotless modern kitchen and out of the back door. The phone call was a waste of two pence. They wouldn't let her talk to Anne. The patient was asleep, it seemed. Caitlin asked if they could tell her friend she'd called and they all sent their love. She doubted they'd pass the message on but at least she'd tried.

She locked up and returned to her neighbour's house. The sky was getting dark and angry. It looked like a storm was coming in. She made her way back to Big Charlie, who lay spreadeagled on the sofa, eagerly watching the TV. The room stank of cigarette smoke. She handed over the key and thanked him. As she made her way out, he called her back. *What now?*

She sighed and re-entered the smoke-filled room. Charlie looked a real mess, but he'd been good to her family, and she was very fond of him, so she made an effort to be polite.

"Bet they wouldn't let you talk to her," he said smugly.

"Yep, but they're going to pass on a message."

He shuffled his huge body around and faced her. He looked at her properly for the first time and was immediately concerned.

"You sure you're all right, love? You look sick. You've been through more than most, you know?"

"Just tired, Charlie; that's all. Didn't sleep too well."

"Aye, well, no wonder. How about a drink, love; that might help you?" He kindly offered her a can of lager, and she smiled back graciously.

"I don't think so, but thanks anyway. I'll be off then."

As if he didn't want her to leave, he exclaimed, "Ah, Caitlin, wait a wee minute! Just a second! I have to tell you this one! This'll cheer you up... You remember that critter your Uncle Tommy told you about.

You know, the wee fella who'd been asked to wait for that 'special' car? Well, you won't believe this one. It's even better!"

It took all of Caitlin's will-power to appear interested as Charlie paused to take another slug of lager from the can. It dribbled down the sides of his mouth, and she noticed he was pretty smashed. Poor Mrs McFadden. She listened patiently while he told her the story in a muddle of slurred words and laughter.

"Apparently, Stephen's not speaking to anyone! So… he was manning an IRA checkpoint, right? Can you just imagine him in his black balaclava and all decked up to the eyes in IRA gear!" Charlie laughed heartily and drank some more.

"Anyway, so he's stopping the drivers and asking questions and the like and then telling them to move on. Well, they all can't help but burst out laughin' and shoutin' out as they drive away: '*Thanks, Stephen!*' The eejit gave them a serious bollocking and was livid – he couldn't understand how they knew it was him! Him with his balaclava and everything on… I mean, Jesus, Mary and Joseph, Caitlin, he's a feckin' dwarf – the only dwarf in Derry – of course, everyone knew who he was!"

"Poor Stephen. You lot are awful! That's cruel that is, I'll see you later."

Caitlin got in just as the rain started to pelt down. She went straight into the living room and thought about James again as she picked up the tray that held their empty cups. In the kitchen, she found her mother hadn't moved from her chair. She looked up as Caitlin came in.

"Any luck?"

"They wouldn't let me talk to her."

"Aye, well, I'm not surprised. Maybe tomorrow."

"Hope so. I saw smoke. Looks like you were right – rioting."

Majella sucked the last of her cigarette and stubbed it out in a yellow Double Diamond ashtray. She stood up. "I don't think it'll last. There's a bad storm coming. I just heard it on the radio. They'll not want to get soaked. I'm going to kill Tina when she gets back." Caitlin studied her and had an idea.

"Stop worrying; you know what Tina's like. Our Martin's the same. Two peas in a pod. Come into the living room. I'll light the fire, and we'll watch some TV together."

The living room was cold, and the women shivered as Majella turned on the TV and waited for it to warm up. It would take some time for them to get the benefit of the fire that Caitlin had started, so she quickly ran to the linen cupboard and brought back some flannel blankets.

Caitlin shivered and jumped on the sofa next to her mother, who she covered with a blanket. She wrapped one around her own shoulders as they cuddled together and whispered, "Better?"

"Aye, love, that's better.

Eventually, the TV screen lit up, and black-and-white images began to form.

Majella sighed as she told Caitlin her latest news.

"Guess what? I got a letter from the undertaker this morning. Chasing payment for the funeral. I don't know what we're going to do. I'll have to talk to Tommy." Caitlin knew they'd no money to pay for the funeral and hoped her Uncle could come up with a solution. She tucked the blankets tighter around them.

"I told you to stop worrying. Leave it to me. Now let's just try and forget everything while we watch this."

Chapter Twenty-five

"How long have you known?" Robert asked quietly down the phone.

"A while."

A heavy silence hung in the air as he tried to control his anger. "And when were you gannin' to tell me?"

Tracey sighed. "I was waiting while you got leave. But after what happened to Val, your mam insisted I tell you now. I didn't want you to worry."

Robert couldn't believe she'd kept such news from him.

"I think I should've known first off, Trace – after all, I am the Dad! I mean, I've been worried sick about you. You haven't sounded yourself for ages, and there's me thinking you were about to call the wedding off! I love you, Trace, and I'm sorry if I don't sound over the moon like, but with all the shit that's going down here, I'm just a bit shocked. This was the last thing I expected to hear."

Tracey had originally wanted to tell him, but Robert's mam had demanded she wait. Seemed she couldn't do right for doing wrong.

"I know, Robbie," the girl sighed. "And I'm sorry. I just didn't think it was fair to tell you by phone. Aren't you pleased just a little bit?"

"'Course I'm pleased. I am really. Just saying, it's a bit of a shock. What about the wedding… and honeymoon? I hope we're still on for that?"

Tracey breathed in with relief at the change in his tone and told him encouragingly, "Don't fret. Leave it to your mam and me. It's not that long now 'til your home, and we can celebrate properly… And for your twenty-first as well. Mind, the bairn means I'll have to give up the drink and fags. Shit!" She laughed merrily.

A few moments passed before she asked him delicately, "And how are you, with Val and all? Have they caught anyone yet?"

He could still barely bring himself to mention it.

"Trace, I just can't understand this country. They've got no one, and the girl who led him on seems to have disappeared off the face of the earth. You don't want to know what they did – especially now, in your condition. I spoke to his Dad. Will you go to Val's funeral for me? I can't get away from here."

Tracey didn't want to go; she hated funerals but knew she had to. She was always afraid it would be Rob next.

"'Course I'll go."

Robert was nudged by another private, who stood close by impatient to use the phone. He pointed to his wristwatch.

"I have to go now, Trace. I'll call you soon. Look after yourself and don't worry about me. Love you to bits… Both of you."

It hadn't been the most exciting of calls and Tracey was hurt Robert couldn't talk for longer.

"Oh, right. Okay then. Love you too. Bye now." The line was cut and Robert, feeling depressed, was about to put the handset down when it was grabbed off him by the impatient soldier.

"Sorry, mate, didn't mean to rush you but time is precious!"

"No problem," he replied, half smiling as he looked at the eager young squaddie. Little did he know what he was getting himself into. Robert hoped he was better prepared for this tour than he and Val had been.

Robert then made his way back to his quarters and tried hard to digest the news. A Dad. He was going to be a Dad! Of course, he was pleased… Well, *sort of.* He'd wanted children but at the right time. Must have happened on their camping trip. Shit, they should've been more careful. They'd never given it a thought – mind you, they were pissed! His first impulse had been to tell Val then go for a few bevvies to celebrate. Funny how his mind still occasionally blanked out the fact that his best friend had gone for good. Now it hit him like a train.

He walked into the barracks and saw that Val's bunk had already been stripped. The thin mattress had been rolled up, and the bunk looked empty and forlorn. All his personal belongings had been gathered up and sent home along with Val's broken remains. Robert groaned and climbed up to his bed. He gazed up at the familiar cracked ceiling and thought about the conversation he'd had earlier that day with the Captain in his office.

"Sallis. At ease. Take a seat."

Robert sat on a visitor's chair and stared solemnly at the serious-faced officer, who'd talked to him quietly and sympathetically. For a Rupert, he wasn't a bad sort.

"Sallis, I appreciate the past few days have been particularly difficult for you. I understand you have also been in contact with Private Holmes's family."

"Yes, sir. I spoke to Val's father yesterday."

"Good. Good. I did too. Sometimes one really can't find the words… A tragedy, Sallis. Just awful. However, as I always say, we have a job to do, and ultimately, we are aware of the risks.

"So, to you, Sallis. I've heard good reports about you. I'm told you have shown calm and composure under extreme pressure – apart from your skirmish with Morris, about which I'm prepared to offer you some latitude. Now I'd like to give you an opportunity to use those competencies in a new initiative we are planning."

The Captain paused to sip some coffee before he continued.

"Our presence in Northern Ireland has changed substantially, and we've begun to realise we need to evolve into a more covert operation. The Government has agreed that to win this 'War' – as it's referred to by our Nationalist friends – we need to play them at their own game. To date, our intelligence has been lacking and, quite frankly, has frequently caused us more trouble than it was worth. We need to obtain much more sound and reliable material."

Robert wasn't sure where this was going but continued to listen with an expression of polite interest on his face.

"So far, a number of brave men and women have applied for this new initiative, which requires them to work undercover. They come from all sorts of backgrounds, with different experience, and to date, we have only accepted sixteen of them for training. The induction process is deliberately harsh and demanding, so the failure rate is quite high. The candidates learn new skills, including breaking and entering, specialist hand-to-hand combat, the local dialect, and firearms. I understand you're a cracking shot, Sallis, and indeed have won several inter-regiment awards."

The Captain had Robert's full attention now. *What the heck!*

"This will be highly dangerous work – highly dangerous. We need to identify the real enemy, confront and destroy them as necessary. Consequently, off the record and under exceptional circumstances, the Yellow Card or Rules of Engagement may not necessarily apply. This unit will be crucial in identifying people, such as those who tortured and murdered Private Holmes. It has already been proved that one successful undercover operative can equate to the efficacy of a company of one hundred and twenty on the ground."

The Captain looked at the young soldier, hoping for some sort of reaction, but Robert sat quietly and gave nothing away. Good.

"Cutting to the chase, Sallis; I believe you have the necessary mindset, skills and abilities to join this unit and so I am recommending you apply. It's your decision."

Robert didn't move an inch. It was likely the Captain was playing on his emotions by referring to Val's murder and, fuck, yes, he was angry! He was furious now that he knew the real story of what the bastards had done to his mate. He wanted revenge… But to apply for something like this? Him? It'd had never crossed his mind to go undercover. He just wanted to do his job and pay his bills. He asked the Captain cautiously, "Sir, I do have a few questions."

"Good man."

"Well, sir. You say the failure rate is high. So why do you think I can get through something like this when I've done nothing like it before? I'm pissed off… Angry. No, it's more than that. I can't explain to you how I feel. Val was like a brother to me. I would have died for him."

The Captain answered this outburst objectively.

"Don't you see, it's really quite simple? You're a professional soldier. It's time to either turn this justified anger of yours around and use it positively and effectively or keep allowing your anger to fester and eat you up from the inside. Holmes's death was calculated and pitiless. If anyone has good reason to catch and stop these bastards, Sallis; it's you. Now you have the opportunity to achieve that."

Robert knew his Captain was right but still wasn't sure undercover work was for him. He'd never wanted to be a hero.

"Sir. Would I have to go back to the mainland – and what would I tell my family?"

The Captain rose from his chair and looked out of the window over Brooke Park with its ancient oak trees. He was struck by the paradox of such a beautiful place stuck in the middle of hell.

"No, Sallis; you'd be trained here in Northern Ireland at an undisclosed location. The first phase of the process takes up to six weeks. If you are successful after that, you will be sent out on a medium-risk surveillance operation. Intermittent training in specialist skills would continue thereafter. We'd instruct you on exactly what to tell your family."

The Captain felt tired and disillusioned. He hadn't slept all night and had hoped by now to be finished here in Northern Ireland. This was his third and hopefully final tour. He sighed heavily and turned to face Robert.

"Sallis, I'd like to give you more time to decide, but my hands are tied. I must have your decision by 18.00 hours."

Robert had no idea what to think. Christ! He suddenly thought of something else – the most important reason not to agree.

"One final thing, sir. I'm due leave at Christmas. It's my twenty-first, and I've just found out I'm going to be a Dad. If I apply, would my leave be cancelled?"

The Captain offered his hand, and enthusiastically shook Robert's, smiling.

"Congratulations, Sallis. A Dad, eh?"

Nonetheless, his smile quickly disappeared, and his hand was lowered as he added, "Ah! Ah…right, yes. I see. I'm afraid your leave would have to be cancelled, yes."

At this, Robert felt despondent but thanked the Captain anyway.

"In that case, sir, I'll have a good think. And thank you, sir. For everything." Both men knew what Robert meant.

Now he found himself staring at the ceiling. His mind was in turmoil as he ran through his options. Talk about shit timing! Could he take such a risk, especially now that Tracey was pregnant? She'd never forgive him if she found out. He knew he couldn't tell her anything about it, only that he was not coming home.

And then he thought about himself. Was he up to it? Could he do it? He wasn't sure about anything anymore although he felt flattered that the Captain had recommended him.

He listened as a pair of loud footsteps clomped into the room and stopped by the bottom of his bunk. Someone coughed and asked, "'Scuse me. Are you Sallis?"

Robert sat up and found an unbelievably young-looking private standing awkwardly by the bed. He was tall, around six foot two, excruciatingly thin with cropped jet-black hair and a face that was smothered with teenage acne scars. He couldn't have been any more than eighteen years old.

Robert moaned. Sweet Jesus, they were getting younger and younger. The lanky lad looked at Robert and repeated himself.

"Scuse me. Are you Sallis?"

Robert nodded. "Yeah, I'm Sallis. Who are you?"

A wave of relief passed over the youngster's face. Good, he was in the right place.

"Ah, that's great. I'm Fraser… Anthony Fraser. Call me Tony. I've been told this is me bunk." He indicated Val's old berth before he added tactfully, "Is that awright wiv you? I 'eard about your mate. Sorry. Bad deal."

"Aye, it was," Robert answered and lay down again to avoid any further conversation.

He listened while the youth unpacked his gear and made up the lower bed. As soon as he'd finished, silence weighed on them both. Tony sat on the edge of the bed and waited. He wasn't sure what he was waiting for, but he waited.

Minutes passed like this, and soon enough, Robert began to feel guilty. Poor bugger. He knew he should make an effort and jumped off the top bunk.

"Okay, Tony. You're from London, I assume? Hungry?"

The young man stood up so enthusiastically he nearly took the head off his body as he hit the top tier of the bunk. He rubbed his head and cried, "Jesus, yeah! I'm an East Ender, Befnal Green, me! And I ain't eaten anyfink since this morning. Been travellin' all day. I'd kill for a Rosie Lee!"

"Rosie Lee?" Robert asked, bewildered.

"Oh, sorry, mate. Cup of char… Tea, like!"

Robert laughed and slapped him playfully on the shoulder. "Come on then. Let's get you a cup of your Rosie Lee!"

The two men talked about football on the way to the canteen. It was too early for dinner, so it was relatively quiet with just a few people scattered around. They found a long rectangular table next to a window at one end of the room. Outside, a serious storm was brewing. The sky was dark and angry, and the rain fell fast and furious, rattling against the windows. Robert watched Tony as he gobbled up his doorstep sandwich in no time. Robert wasn't hungry so just drank a cup of strong coffee. He looked at the boy thoughtfully and asked, "What made you join up?"

Through a mouthful of bread, he mumbled, "Had to like."

Robert wasn't sure what that meant. "How do you mean?"

Tony stopped eating and looked at Robert, baffled.

"Runs in the family, don't it? Me old man, his old man, and his old man before that... And then me bruv, see?"

Robert understood. "No pressure then."

"Nah, not much there ain't!" Tony laughed. "It's awright. Although, meself, well, I never had the call like. I wanted to play for Arsenal but I 'ad to join up, din't I?"

Robert was interested in where the conversation was leading. "Why then?" he asked.

He noticed sadness creep into the boy's open face and a glassy look to his small dark eyes as he said steadily, "Well, for me old man really. Yer see, my bruvver 'Arry... muppet only got himself shot in the head in Belfast, din't he? Sniper from Devis Flats. Poor bugger, he never knew what hit him – thank fuck! Anyway, the old man's gutted like – 'ates the Irish he does. I felt I 'ad to do somefink, you know, to try and sort it out like? I mean, we're all part of the same country, ain't we? UK. I don't get it. We shouldn't be fighting each other. I joined up and pissed the old lady off big time. She's 'ardly spoke to me or me old man since!"

Robert whistled. "Whoah! So, Tony, you're telling me you joined the British Army to sort out the Irish, did you? Well, I hate to tell you this, bonny lad, but no chance! No power on earth can sort these people out." He drank more coffee, saddened by the youth's naivety.

Tony, however, wasn't going to be put off so easily.

"I hear you, mate. But someone's got to try, don't they? They can't keep goin' round and killin' us off one by one – that ain't right. I mean, what about your mate? That was really bad shit. They're shafting us all, ain't they? Blowing kiddies up too! A right fuckin' mess!"

A stillness came over the two men as Tony waited eagerly for some reassurance. And a light bulb seemed to go on for Robert. It suddenly made sense. Of course, it did!

"You're right, Tony," he said slowly. "It's a godawful mess. And, yes, we do need to do something."

His mind was made up, he discovered. He would do this for Val.

"You keep yourself safe, mate. I'm likely leaving tonight," he said. "Keep that head of yours down; do you hear me? I'll find someone to keep an eye out for you. You're all right."

The boy didn't understand what he had said to produce such a reaction and looked at Robert with a face full of surprise. With his mug of tea still raised in the air, he cried out: "Wha'd I say? Why you leaving? Fuck, I just got here! 'Ave you 'ad enough of me already?"

Robert laughed, and suddenly everything felt right.

"You've done nothing wrong, mate. In fact, you've done me a favour. I have to go. Promise I'll see you before I leave!"

There was a new lightness in Robert's step as he hurried to tell the Captain of his decision.

Chapter Twenty-six

RUC Chief Constable George Shalham sat opposite James as they ate supper with Roger later that evening. Surprisingly, James Snr had been invited to stay with Charles Jones in Belfast and had not yet returned. Much to James's distaste and dismay, his father seemed to be getting remarkably close to Jones. The Chief Constable had been on duty when he'd received a call about James's near-hijack. He was still dressed in his uniform with its dark green tunic and trousers worn with a silver belt. His rank was evident from his epaulettes with their silver and red buttons and RUC insignia, while his red-trimmed lapels were bordered by six small green and gold shamrocks. It was a uniform with elements of comic opera to it, but there was nothing funny about the Shalham's rage when he challenged James about his earlier behaviour.

"It was downright stupid of you! What on God's earth were you doing in the middle of the Bogside at that time of day... And in the Jag too? Man – you'd have stood out like a sore thumb, *and* you nearly gave Roger here a heart attack!"

James understood Shalham's anger. He'd had to arrange for a police constable to drive the Jag home followed by an RUC Hotspur Land Rover giving a lift to James. He had felt embarrassed and ashamed by the special treatment being given to him, thanks to his Uncle's connections. The constable hadn't spoken a word to him, and James could only mouth a weak "*thank you*" after the policeman had dropped him off and climbed back into the jeep. He'd heard laughter as the Land Rover drove away. No doubt at his expense.

When James walked into Melrose, Roger had already heard from Shalham and called out Dr Harris, who stood waiting in the hallway. He'd checked James over, strapped up his ribs rather roughly, and departed without a smile or a pleasantry. None were broken, but three were badly bruised. He couldn't believe the pain and had to move with great care. As he held his sides sheepishly and occasionally winced, he attempted to tone things down at the table. He deserved a good blasting, yes, but he was getting annoyed now. He just wanted to eat his supper and climb into a hot bath.

"All right, George. I feel a perfect fool, but I had an important meeting, and my normal route was closed. Unfortunately, I found myself in the middle of a disturbance. It was a stupid mistake, and I assure you it won't happen again. It was... "

Before James could explain, Roger rudely shouted angrily at his nephew.

"Important meeting, my bollocks!" He looked askance at his influential friend. "I don't understand this young idiot, George! I've warned him so many times!"

George ignored him and instead turned to the injured man. He wasn't finished with him yet.

"No, James, it *can't* happen again! You must remember, these are very dangerous times. The Nationalists won't tolerate Unionists coming into their areas. Droves of Unionists are moving out of the city and Belfast to the South or the mainland."

James knew of the Unionist exodus but made no comment as Shalham – whose uniform seemed to add gravitas to his words – finished his sermon.

"You must be more sensible, James. And, Roger... most – if not all – of your management team are Unionists. It's increasingly likely they won't be able to work at the factory and remain safe. You need to think about improving your security or else relocating."

Roger wiped his mouth with a napkin and looked with concern at his friend.

"It's a coincidence you should mention the factory, George. I've been doing a lot of number crunching and, unsurprisingly, relocating would cost us a small fortune. Money, we don't have, regrettably. If we were to try to sell, I can guarantee you no one would touch the factory with a bargepole given its proximity to Blighs Lane compound. So none of these options are viable."

George and James weren't surprised but listened attentively as Roger told them more.

"If we closed now, we couldn't even pay redundancy money. The only option is to sit tight and stay put. Our order book is relatively healthy – at the moment. Most importantly, we have to consider the workforce. Rocola is responsible for the livelihood of nearly three thousand people – most of them women. So, yes, security is a priority if we want to stay open."

George groaned. "That many, Roger? I hadn't realised it was so many."

He nodded. "Yes. We're one of the last big factories left. The women are predominantly Catholic and live in and around the Bogside and Creggan. Another reason for us not to relocate is that they couldn't afford to travel far and we can't afford to lose their skills."

The men shared some bread from a basket offered by the housekeeper, who left quietly. As soon as she'd disappeared, Roger spoke up again.

"A few of our managers are already complaining about intimidation. They're naturally frightened, and we've had some resignations. I've tasked James with thinking of ways in which we can raise capital and improve security. The safety of our employees is paramount, but we must find additional capital in order to survive. Quite a task, I'm afraid, James."

The young man sighed and raised himself in his chair. He growled as a sharp pain seared through his side. It hurt, but he was more relieved that the two men's tirade was over, and hopefully, the subject was closed.

"It is," he replied. "Mind you; I have an idea that we can work on straight away. I thought we could hold a series of one-day meetings with the city's most established businessmen from the Chamber of Commerce, the City Council and senior members of **both** Churches. I want to see if, *together*, we can come up with ideas on how to raise investment and, as George says, improve security for everyone. After all, it's in the interest of Londonderry's wider economy that Rocola remains open."

The older men knew James was right. It would be an unmitigated disaster for the city if the factory closed.

James sucked in his breath. "Thousands of jobs being lost in such a poor area would be catastrophic. If it means getting these people in a room together – no matter what religion or background – we just have to make it happen somehow. Even if it means I lock them in there myself!"

Roger and George smiled as they listened. They'd seen a glimmer of light at the end of the tunnel. James saw he had their full attention.

"George, this is where we need your experience, especially were security's concerned. Your presence at these meetings would add impetus, and your reputation would help to allay any fears."

George was flattered but warned them that not everyone would welcome his presence.

"Though I think it's a novel approach, James. A brave one too. Keep going."

"I'm glad you think so. It won't be easy, I know that but we have to try, and quite frankly I can't think of any other options yet."

George was impressed by the young man's passion.

"I agree in principle," the Chief Constable told him. "But I'd like to approve the invitation list. You'd be amazed at the complicated personalities in this city, and I know who the real trouble-makers are from both sides."

He stood up and walked over to the fireplace, where he warmed his hands and thought for a moment. He turned back and spoke to them candidly.

"For this plan to succeed, gentlemen, we need to ensure there's a fair balance of representatives from both communities. Last month a chunk of Catholics withdrew from public bodies in protest at internment, and anti-Unionist Councillors walked out across the Province. There's too much at stake to lose more people like them. The right people *must* attend. However, it's going to take some persuasion. Provided I can approve the guest list; I'd be happy to help."

James, who was delighted, added, "Of course. Thank you. We hope to make the first meeting happen within six weeks, at least, in the City Hotel. My secretary will be arranging the logistics, and I've already drawn up a draft invitee list. We can go through it together."

George nodded, but as an afterthought, James asked him hesitantly.

"Actually, given what you've said, I assume we should invite a top dog from the British Army too?"

The Chief Constable scoffed. He wasn't so sure. Relations with his British Army counterpart were strained and highly unlikely to improve.

"Hmm, that might be difficult, but I suppose we should. I'll see what I can do."

The three men continued eating and talking through the plan until they naturally moved on to lighter topics. The Troubles and Rocola were temporarily forgotten as the wine flowed freely and any tension dissipated.

George Shalham finished a small glass of port then announced it was time for him to leave. Referring to his personal protection bodyguards, he said, "Well, gentlemen, I must go. My carriage awaits, and it's unfair of me to keep these young men out too late and away from their families."

George himself was top of the IRA's assassination list. Up to now, James hadn't thought about the personal risk to the Chief Constable and found himself admiring the man more than ever.

As they were leaving through the back door, George pulled James aside out of earshot of his Uncle.

"James, I know where you were today," the Chief Constable said quietly. "Don't ask how, but I know. For everyone's sake, keep away from there and don't get involved in something you'll likely regret. Trust me. Good night."

Perplexed, James leaned against the kitchen door and watched the bulletproof car's rear lights fade down the drive. He locked up and walked back through the kitchen into the square hallway. Roger was there waiting for him, cigarette in hand. He offered the pack to James, who declined and instead asked, "Nightcap, Uncle?"

"No, thanks. Bit tired now."

Referring to his unfinished cigarette, he added, "I'll head up once I've finished this. But have a drink yourself if you wish. You're obviously still in pain."

The men walked into the dining room together until out of the blue, his uncle retorted. "Why can't you be honest and tell me the **real** reason you ended up in the Bogside today?"

James stood still and silent as Roger took another drag on his cigarette. His nephew's stubbornness made him noticeably angry.

"Just so that we are clear, young man, I know exactly where you were, though I'd hoped you would be gentleman enough to tell me yourself! Mrs Parkes rang me in hysterics two hours after you called the factory. She'd heard there was trouble near the Bogside and wanted to know if you'd returned home. It's not often I agree with that woman, but on this occasion she was right. She told me she tried to warn you not to go."

James was angry beyond measure. Did he have no privacy? George Shalham first and now his Uncle and that bloody woman! The silence between the two men became deafening. But he had to defend himself and announced coolly,

"She did, and I didn't listen. How many times do I have to apologise?"

"You really are, at times, James, naïve when it comes to the Troubles in this country. And to visit your *secretary* in the middle of a Catholic ghetto is just ridiculous and foolish. You could have been killed!"

230

Roger stubbed out his cigarette angrily. He exhaled, shook his head and looked in open disappointment at his nephew.

"James, I pray to God that 'secretary' is all that young girl is to you. Just a secretary. Because if I find out otherwise, I assure you, your father will be the first to hear, and he'll have you in the army so fast your feet won't touch the ground! Don't tempt fate. Don't do something very stupid – not just for your sake, but for hers and all your family's too!"

Roger was exasperated and disappointed in his nephew, whom he loved like the son he never had. He couldn't remember the last time he'd been so angry, and James suddenly began to feel nervous. In an attempt to lighten his uncle's mood, he smiled back reassuringly and told him, "Och, Uncle, Mrs Parkes loves to dramatize – you know that! Did she not tell you I asked for a phone number first? I bet she didn't! I'd no intention of going anywhere. I only went because Caitlin doesn't have a phone." Silence hung in the air until James added quietly and genuinely.

"My visit was intended to show due concern for a valued employee. She's been a tremendous help to me so far, and her father died recently, remember. On top of all that, she was hurt in that bomb explosion on Shipquay Street. Her best friend was with her and lost half a leg. I just felt it was the right thing to do, to check how she was. Elsewhere it wouldn't give rise to any comment. Believe me, Uncle, she means nothing to me."

Roger shook his head in despair and said sadly, "The trouble is, I *don't* believe you, James. I only wish I could." He bade his nephew a brusque goodnight and walked out of the room.

James, alone at last, poured himself a large Glenfiddich. He added a few pieces of ice and sat down in a deep red leather-upholstered reading chair. He drank his whisky and stared into the dying fire. He'd blatantly lied to his Uncle and felt bad about it. For the first time in forever, he thought about his mother. Her love affair and subsequent rejection of her family commitments still had a knock-on effect to this day, especially with James's father, who had evidently never recovered from her desertion of them.

His thoughts began to drift, and he found himself wondering how he and Caitlin could get away from all those prying eyes. And how had George Shalham known he was at Caitlin's house today? They'd have to be extremely careful.

He sighed as he enjoyed the warm sensation the whisky gave him. He finished it off. He knew he shouldn't have another given the painkillers he'd taken but what the hell!

Defiantly he topped up his glass and greedily gulped down the deep golden liquid. As a punishment for his defiance, he choked and coughed. His ribs contracted painfully as he pressed both hands against his sides and swore. Jesus Christ. What a day!

Chapter Twenty-seven

"Are you feckin' serious? I mean, do you have any idea what you're doing? Does your Mammy know?!" Anne folded her arms across her chest, clearly unimpressed by what her best friend had just confided in her. She looked at Caitlin perched on the bottom of the hospital bed. Caitlin watched her friend's face darken in fury. She'd been on the ward for weeks and was due home within a matter of days.

Her lower body was obscured by a green cotton bedcover. Caitlin scanned the outline of her friend's upper legs until they reached the lower right limb, which was noticeably missing. She'd visited Anne as much as she could but with the new job and having had to take a few days off work; it hadn't been easy. James had kindly made sure she wouldn't lose pay for the missed days, which was something.

Majella's good intentions had relapsed soon after their cosy afternoon together, and she was now even worse. She seemed to have lost interest in anyone else in her perpetual diazepam haze. Caitlin hadn't even seen Tommy. He hadn't been around much. Tina had just done her own thing as usual. Their home felt soulless and empty.

Until now she hadn't told Anne about James, but Anne being Anne, knew Caitlin was up to something and continually pestered her to tell her until Caitlin had no choice. Boy, was she sorry now!

"How long has this been going on then?" her friend snapped.

"Since after this," Caitlin nodded, observing her friend's missing limb once more and cringing inwardly.

"It wasn't an *accident*, Caitlin! It was a feckin' bomb those UVF bastards planted!" Anne wailed.

"I know, I know. God, I'm so sorry. It's my fault!"

Anne suddenly felt a knife-like pain shooting up her right thigh and gasped loudly, screwing up her eyes in pain.

"Jesus!" She waited a few seconds until the pain subsided. Feeling suddenly tired and guilty for being off with her friend, she yawned, took Caitlin's hand and apologised.

"No, it's my fault. I'm biting the head off everyone! Come on. I'm listening, and this time I'll keep my gob shut!"

Caitlin smiled in relief.

"There's nothing really. As soon as I got the job, we just hit it off. He's tough to work for, Anne, but he's really committed to what he does. He's kind and funny. I mean, a bit of a snob, to be honest, but I really like him. That old bat Mrs Parkes told him about the bomb, and he came straight to our house. Imagine! I've never given Mrs Parkes the McFaddens' phone number, and he couldn't call me, so he got in his Jag and drove right over.

"So there he is, turning up in his big flashy car. He came in, and we were in the living room on our own, having a cup of tea, and it just happened! The next thing I know; we're kissing! I've seen him at work every day, but we're hardly ever on our own. There's always someone about, and Mrs Parkes is *everywhere*. I told Mammy, but she went ballistic and warned me to keep away from him, so I haven't mentioned a word since. Anyway, she's away with the birdies again these days and wouldn't even notice if I was dead or alive, the state she's in."

Anne looked at her with a stony expression on her face.

"Don't, Caitlin. Remember she's just lost her husband. You can't blame her for taking those tablets. Remember, most of the women in Derry are high as kites. It's the only way they survive all this shit!"

But Caitlin wasn't having it. "Anne, for fuck's sake; she's in a world of her own, doped up to her eyebrows. She's not capable of noticing anything!"

She sighed and pulled her hand away, sliding off the bed and over to the window. She felt miserable and misunderstood as she looked out over the nearby housing estate that surrounded the hospital with open fields beyond. Anne was right about the women of Derry. It was common for them to be on pills. Many of them couldn't cope other-wise with the unending jail visits, the house raids in the wee hours and the poverty they endured with no husband at home to support them.

She'd really hoped Anne would be a bit more understanding and was bitterly disappointed in her friend. Angry clouds outside made the ward darker, and Caitlin could make out her reflection in the glass. She'd sewn up some clothes from fabric she'd bought with her pay rise and wore a home-made short black-and-white floral skirt with a chunky cream-coloured woollen jumper. She'd bought thick tights and wore them along with a pair of clumpy black platform-soled shoes. Her hair was parted in the middle and tied in twin bunches that lay against her shoulders. She didn't take any joy in the new outfit – it didn't matter anymore.

She turned back to her friend and sought some kind of under-standing. Anne had lost so much weight. Her body was pathetically thin and frail, her face almost lost against her once healthy mass of hair that needed washing, badly. Very obviously depressed, Anne had made no effort to tidy herself up. With each visit, Caitlin had found her friend's mood slipping deeper and deeper into a dark depression. It was as if her desire to live had been stolen from her. That wonderful light and energy that had made her Anne had disappeared.

Caitlin walked to the bed and clutched her friend's hands. She wanted the old Anne back. She needed the old Anne back. So in an effort to be bright and breezy, she talked excitedly.

"Listen, let's not mention him anymore. Let's plan something for us to look forward to – just you and me. What do you think? I'd do anything for you. You know that."

Anne knew. She'd been so miserable and found it such a struggle to keep positive but knew she shouldn't take it out on her friend. "I know. And, yip, we'll do something. It's just that I'm so cross. I mean, why us? We were just going for a cup of tea! Jesus, they chose Saturday afternoon when the town was packed. And look at this!" Anne pointed to her leg.

"Fuck it! There go me lovely stilettos. And who the hell is going to want me with half a leg missing?" She seemed unsure whether to laugh or cry, but the tears won out. Caitlin hugged her friend like a mother with a child and kissed the top of her head. She murmured words of re-assurance and told her everything would be okay. A few minutes passed until Anne looked up as Caitlin apologised.

"I'm so sorry. If it weren't for me, you wouldn't have been there. It's my fault." Caitlin's eyes welled up until she too cried. The two young women remained quiet and held onto each other for dear life. There were no words that could ease their sorrow.

They stayed like that for some time until Caitlin was nudged by a nurse and gently asked to leave as visiting time was over. Caitlin quick-ly grabbed some tissues from the box and passed a handful to Anne, who wiped her face and spoke in between wipes.

"Listen, this isn't your fault, so I don't want to hear more of that talk. You say you'd do anything for me? Then, for my sake, stop seeing this guy. It'll end badly for all the reasons you know. You're going to get really hurt."

Caitlin answered tolerantly. "We'll see. More importantly; just get better, please. It'll be good for you to be home in your own bed. That should cheer you up. This place is so depressing."

The nurse re-entered the ward with raised eyebrows that carried a clear message. Time to leave.

"I have to go, Anne. I'll see you soon, promise."

She put on her mother's coat and found it too small to button up. Her mother had always been a slip of a thing, but nowadays the coat was huge on her. Caitlin had ordered a new coat from Littlewoods, but it had yet to arrive. Anne looked on and commented, "Nice coat."

"Don't," Caitlin answered with a smile and kissed her friend good-bye.

"Bye, you."

"Bye," Anne replied in a small voice.

The journey back took forever as the Craigavon checkpoint caused its daily mayhem. Inside the bus, the smell of cigarette smoke was overwhelming and Caitlin knew she'd stink by the time she got home. She rested her head against the window and thought about her afternoon with Anne. When she'd had the chance to talk to James alone, he'd warned her that her friend couldn't be her old self after suffering such a shock and it was understandable for her to be feeling so miserable. But Caitlin felt helpless, wanting to make things better for her when it seemed like nothing could cheer her friend up. Before the bomb, she would never have snapped at Caitlin. Never. She'd tried to talk to the nurses about her concerns, but they'd only talk to Anne's family. Frustratingly Anne's mother, now heavily pregnant again, couldn't make the journey and her siblings were either working or at school. In the end, Anne had very few visitors – which didn't help her mood. Caitlin knew she'd have to stay close to her when she got out of hospital.

James and Caitlin had been racking their brains to come up with a plan for how they could get together. She wanted to be able to talk to him properly. She wanted him to hold her again.

She'd been deliberately avoiding Father McGuire who'd attempted, unsuccessfully, to check in on her mother. Caitlin hadn't been to Mass since the funeral, so he most likely knew something was wrong. As a family, they'd never missed Mass before now. It was a sin.

She reached her house, unclicked her handbag and searched for her keys. Annoyingly, she found them at the very bottom of her bag. As she turned the key, the door was already being opened, and a man's smiling face appeared before her.

"Hello, Sis."

"Martin! When did you get here?" Caitlin exclaimed as she pushed the door wide.

She dropped her handbag on the hallway floor. He hugged her to him and held her for much longer than normal. He'd never hugged her like that before, and Caitlin was surprised by such a show of feeling.

She was almost glad to see him. Maybe he could help her sort out their mother. Majella always listened to Martin, her eldest, her only boy.

He closed the door, picked up her bag and dragged her by the arm into the living room. Another surprise. Uncle Tommy was sitting on the sofa dressed in a smart, black suit, white shirt and black tie. He quickly got to his feet and gave her a peck on the cheek. The smell of alcohol and cigarette smoke mixed with the familiar aftershave she remembered her father using, Old Spice, was momentarily overwhelming.

"Hello, love. How are you?" he said.

"I'm okay, Tommy, thanks. Haven't seen you for a while. I've just been to visit Anne in hospital. She's in bad form. I'm worried about her."

She took off her coat and threw it over the back of the sofa before she sat down. Martin sat opposite, and she looked at him properly for the first time. She thought with a twinge of sadness that he'd lost weight and needed a haircut. His cheekbones jutted from a hatchet face, and three of his teeth were missing. He hadn't shaved so looked unkempt and dirty in his stained suit trousers and a black jumper that badly needed washing. He wore no socks, just his bare feet in a pair of plastic slip-on shoes. She felt for him. It looked like he'd been through the mill.

"I can't say you're looking your best, Martin," she told him. "How long have you been here? Has Mammy seen you yet?"

Martin knew he looked like shit. He felt like shit. All his strength had gone. The interrogations had gone on and on, and psychologically he was shattered. He stumbled over his words.

"No, no... She's in bed asleep... I think. I... We weren't expecting me to be out so soon. 'Cos of Daddy, I suppose. It's good to be back, mind."

Caitlin pointed to the teapot on the small table.

"Any left?" Tommy sat up and looked into the pot.

"Might be just enough in it."

Caitlin ran to the kitchen and returned to the living room with a mug. As Martin poured the tea into it for her, his hands shook uncontrollably, and Tommy and Caitlin looked silently at each other. Martin saw but ignored them and passed the shaking mug to his sister. She watched with a mixture of pity and concern.

"We've no sugar." he said.

"We never have sugar." Caitlin took the tea gratefully. It was tepid, but it didn't matter.

Her brother looked out the window and asked, "Where's Tina?"

Caitlin didn't know. "No idea. I've been working late. I've hardly seen her."

He smiled through broken teeth and joked, "Ah, yes. Heard you got yourself some fancy job! Good on you."

The room was quiet for a short while until Martin sniffed his shirt and weakly laughed. "I'm minging. The water should be hot by now. You want me to leave it in for you?"

Caitlin answered brightly, "Nah, you're all right!"

She hoped her brother's return might take the pressure off. But, deep down, she knew it was likely he'd put further strain on the household.

Martin stood up and thanked Tommy for the ride home. He went upstairs for his bath. Tommy and Caitlin remained in the living room.

"He's not good," Caitlin commented.

"No, love, and no wonder. He won't say what went on in there. It'll probably come out over time what the bastards did, but it's added years to him."

Caitlin shook her head and asked in despair, "Tommy, what's happening to us?"

"I don't know, pet. I really don't. I'm struggling as well. If it's not one thing, it's another. Have you seen the state of your mother?" he replied unhappily.

Caitlin shook her head. Not today.

She commented on his dark clothing. "Were you at a funeral?"

Tommy hadn't heard her, so she touched his hand gently and repeated her question.

"Tommy, were you at a funeral?"

"Sorry, yeah. Really bad. Youngster killed by the SAS. Turns out his father rang the police to tell them the lad had found a cache of weapons in a graveyard. They never called him back, and the following morning the wee lad went to see if they were still there. Fucking SAS were waiting. They believed he was the PIRA and shot him outright. No warning and him only sixteen too. Enormous funeral. The father's devastated – poor man thought he was doing the right thing. Just shows ye, doesn't it?"

Caitlin shuddered. "Jesus, Tommy, that's awful. I hadn't heard. God love him."

"I know." Tommy shook his head and said steadily, "They'll never get anyone for it, you mark my words. They'll do nothing."

Tommy looked lost in his thoughts, so Caitlin started to collect the used mugs. The noise seemed to bring him round, and he told her, "I've been meaning to let you know, love – I've managed to get the money for your Da's funeral. I know Majella won't be happy, but I don't think we've much choice in the matter. The Boys have paid it so now we've one less thing to worry about." Forgetting the tea was likely to be cold, he took a mouthful and immediately spat it out.

"Shit, that's freezing!"

"Want a fresh one?" Caitlin couldn't help but grin. Tommy hauled himself up.

"Nah. Thanks, I need to get moving. Do me a favour will ye, don't tell anyone the Boys paid the bill. Just tell your Ma the community pulled together. She doesn't need to know, not yet anyway."

Caitlin nodded reflectively. "Thanks, Tommy. I'd no idea how we were going to pay it, but I'm more worried about Mammy. She's away in cuckoo land half the time. Maybe now that Martin's here, things might get better."

Tommy looked sceptical. He put on his black waterproof coat, and they walked to the front door.

"I'm sure it will – for as long as he keeps out of trouble."

Chapter Twenty-eight

"That's fine. Thank you, Mr Holmes… I'm truly sorry I didn't make it… Yes, yes, I know. You too… Thank you now. Bye."

Robert sighed as he hung up the payphone. Val's funeral had taken place some weeks previously. It had even made the BBC News. As Robert had expected, he hadn't been able to attend. This afternoon, for the first time in ages, he'd been allowed to make contact with the outside world. He'd spoken to Trace earlier. She hadn't said much. When he'd told her he might not be home for his twenty-first and Christmas, she'd gone crazy. He'd half hoped she'd understand that it wasn't easy for him either, but she hadn't. Tracey's worst trait was her inability to see anything from a different perspective to her own.

In a way, he was glad he hadn't been able to contact her until today. It meant he could focus on his training. To her credit, she'd done what he'd asked and gone to Val's funeral. From their brief and frosty conversation, he'd gathered it was a sad affair, and that Val's family were heartbroken. Robert wished he could have been there.

He caught sight of himself in the mirror. One of the first orders they'd been given was to let their hair and facial hair grow. He wasn't used to growing a beard – he'd never liked them. His skin felt dirty and itchy as he touched the newly appeared spots tenderly, a result of the beard growth, and noticed that his hair had started to curl slightly. It certainly wasn't long enough yet, but as the days passed, he looked less and less like a soldier.

After listening to the young Londoner in the barracks, Robert had gone straight to his Captain and accepted his offer. Since then, his life had become a roller-coaster ride of constant briefings and training – some of it exhilarating, some frankly terrifying. He and five other candidates had been inundated with facts about undercover tactics, surveillance procedures and interrogation techniques. Photography was another vital skill. At first, they learned the basics then moved onto advanced night-time infra-red photography, including how to conceal still and video cameras in their clothes and cars. They memorised the geography of the Nationalist areas in and around Londonderry, and were taught how to manage contacts, bug phones and track weapons and vehicles using tracking devices. They'd discussed in depth their options should their cover be broken. That was the nightmare scenario.

He recollected the mission statements and warnings drummed into the small team, day after day.

> *ALWAYS assume your enemy has a weapon.*
> *REMEMBER to maintain your self-control at all costs.*
> *The (P)IRA MUST be weeded out.*
> *We MUST minimise their activities.*
> *We MUST act like a terror group and play them at their own game.*
> *Let's sort them out and finish them off!*

At first, the physical side of training had been excruciating. The assault course left every muscle and sinew of his body sore and burning. As time passed, it had become slightly easier. In hindsight, the assault course had been a breeze compared with the "real-life" forty-eight-hour interrogation sessions. He'd been locked in a dark cell, stripped, blindfolded and sporadically washed down with ice-cold water fired from a high-pressure hose. For those endless minutes of sluicing, kicks and verbal assaults, he'd curled himself into a ball as his body sought what little protection it could in the corner of the cell. Throughout the ordeal he was frozen, his body trembled from the cold and shock. He had nothing to cover himself with and soon became confused and disorientated as he lost all sense of time.

Periodically he would fall asleep – curled up like a puppy – only to be savagely woken by brutal kicks to his body so as to undergo further interrogation by his many unseen assailants. The whole exercise had been unbearable, but he understood why. Should he be exposed, he'd have to be prepared for the torture and beatings that would undoubtedly come. Lives were at stake. He would have to keep his mouth shut at any cost. With the help of psychological tactics they'd been taught, he'd learned to switch off both mentally and physically. He thought of nothing, felt nothing. Ironically, he welcomed this feeling. It allowed him to block out the memory of Tracey's disappointment and his concern for her and the bairn as well as the loss of Val.

He'd particularly enjoyed the advanced driving skills course including high-speed driving, using the vehicle as a weapon, controlled crashes, skid recovery and anti-ambush skills – it'd been brilliant. Val would have loved it.

When he'd arrived, Robert wasn't sure where their training camp was. No one would tell him. They were placed in a cordoned-off area of Nissen huts. He thought it likely they were close to Bessbrook Mill – the largest helicopter airbase in Europe – given the distant noise of numerous heavy craft that took off and landed all day and night. It was only the applicants and their trainers who worked and slept in these huts. They never saw any other regular soldiers or civilian staff. Food was prepared and laid out in advance for every meal. There was absolutely no contact with the outside world. At times, Robert heard the incessant sound of automatic rifles. If they were at Bessbrook, then it was likely the PIRA were shooting at them from the nearby Republic. The army couldn't give chase across the border, so the PIRA were one up.

He finished washing his bruised body and cleaned his teeth quickly before he climbed stiffly into a hard, single bed. Of the six trainees, four were men and two were women. He shared this small hut with the men.

Only one candidate would be successful. They'd done physical and written assessment tests over the past two days, and he knew he'd performed well. The results would be out in a few days and, if successful, he'd be in the middle of it all within days. He was both terrified and excited by the prospect. He'd never have thought he had something like this in him and was pleased to find that he did. The whole experience had changed him. He felt more confident and self-reliant. Mentally he felt good. Physically his bruised body ached like hell, and he was exhausted, but they'd prepared him for anything. He was ready to become an undercover operative in a perilous new world. He was doing it for Val. Finally, and with relief, Robert had given up trying to understand these people and their godforsaken country.

Chapter Twenty-nine

Unusually, the weather was similar to an English autumn day, and Robert felt nostalgic as he walked through the thin early-morning sunshine to the main hut.

It was decision time. He and his casually dressed fellow applicants quietly took their seats. Someone had set out six chairs in a semi-circle directly in front of a wooden desk with a single chair tucked in underneath.

From the moment they'd arrived for training, each applicant had been instructed not to share any personal information with his/her peers. Absolutely nothing. As a result, they had not become friends and mostly kept themselves to themselves. They'd also been given code names. Robert's was "Kentucky".

There was nothing particularly special about the group. They looked like the sorts you'd see any day in a queue of ordinary people at a bus stop.

One of the women was a young girl with long brown feather-cut hair. Her code name was "Iowa". Today she wore a white-collared, brown floral shirt dress that hung well below her knees. For some reason, underneath the dress, she wore a pair of checked bell-bottom trousers. Unmistakeably, fashion wasn't her forte. She noticed Robert watching her from the other end of the row of seats and stared back at him contemptuously.

He hadn't liked her from the moment they'd met. She appeared permanently edgy and angry. Likely she was one of those women, the competitive type, who hated to fail. She'd a giant chip on her shoulder, and so far, he'd avoided her at all costs.

The man who sat next to her was well-built with mid-length greasy brown hair and had the advantage over Robert of having long thick sideburns. He wore a heavy woollen fisherman's jumper and jeans. He simply stared at the floor and ignored everyone. Somehow Robert had a feeling he'd done something similar to this before.

The hut door was opened loudly as the Training Co-ordinator strode into the cold room. He was dressed in one of his unending supply of immaculate white cotton tee-shirts, black training bottoms and plimsolls. He referred to himself as "TC", confirmed by a chained security pass that hung long around his neck. TC – Training Co-ordinator. They knew little about him other than that from his accent he was Welsh. He was a wiry, bald man but unmistakably fit. He reminded Robert of a typical Sergeant Major from an American war film – minus the American drawl. He was supremely confident with a charismatic presence that filled the room. Robert had grown to respect and like him. He was tough but fair.

TC slowly pulled out his chair and sat down at the desk. He coughed and looked around at his silent audience.

"Good morning, ladies and gentlemen. I'd like to thank each of you for your dedication and commitment to these trials over the past weeks. This was never going to be an easy experience. However, our training may well save your life in the future, and so we make no apology for taking you to hell and back."

He retrieved a single piece of A4 paper from a file, studied the group with renewed interest and told them: "It has been officially noted that the quality of this intake has been exceptionally high and you have *all* performed extremely well. Unusually, because of this, we have decided to approve two applicants for our new unit instead of the customary one."

This surprising news was met by an almost inaudible but definite intake of breath from various candidates.

"The British Army in Northern Ireland has been viewed by many as 'the meat in a sectarian sandwich'. We must change this view and prove that we can and will end this bloody war. For the two successful candidates, the purpose of this unit will become clear over the coming months. Remember, ladies and gentlemen, if you are caught, you will be killed and most likely tortured first. We are in one of the most dangerous countries in the world, and this is war! Undercover means undercover."

TC pointed outside and said in a harsh voice, "There is evil abroad, ladies and gentlemen, and you must remain vigilant even if you do not make the cut."

He took another sip of water before he made his announcement.

"Okay. First things first. Those of you who have *not* been accepted are Ohio, Kansas, Arizona and Washington. Despite sterling efforts by you all, you have on this occasion been unsuccessful. May I please ask you to leave the room, gather your belongings and be at the meeting point at 13.00 hours. Each of you will be taken back to your respective barracks. Thank you, and good luck."

The four unsuccessful candidates shook TC's hand and left quietly.

Meanwhile, Robert's heart leapt with joy. Fuck, he was in! It'd been agonising, but he'd done it! He struggled to contain his emotions. No. *We did it, Val.*

Iowa remained silent and still, sitting four empty chairs away from Robert. TC congratulated them.

"Iowa, Kentucky, congratulations and well done. My orders are to put you together as a team. You will be the first male and female operatives in this unit, acting like a couple. Accommodation has already been arranged for you in Londonderry. You will be going straight there tonight. However, I'd like to see you back here at noon so we can talk through your assignment in detail, your new identities and other necessary logistics. We will also discuss how and what you can communicate to your families."

Robert thanked TC, who responded with a small smile and left. Iowa made no attempt to thank him. She was livid. This wasn't what she'd signed up for! She wanted to go it alone, not with some green twat who plainly had done nothing like this before. She'd already applied once and failed to get in. She wanted this so badly, but she wanted it on her own!

Robert stood awkwardly and waited for Iowa to speak, but instead, there was nothing but hostility. He shrugged, smiled ruefully and made to leave – he'd had enough of this shit.

"I wanted to do this alone!" she announced to his retreating back. "This was the last thing I wanted – *a couple?* Really!"

Robert challenged her back. "Well, I wasn't expecting to work with anyone either, especially with a stroppy cow like you, but you don't see me shouting the odds, do you?"

She tried to stare him down, but he wasn't interested and left to return to his room, where he packed what few possessions he had and randomly threw his army gear into a large, clear plastic, labelled bag. His civvies were placed in a battered suitcase that had been left ready on his bed. He carefully removed his dog tags and placed them in a small red velvet box shared with his only pair of initialled white gold cufflinks – a present from his parents for his eighteenth. He carefully added the box to the plastic bag.

As ordered, Iowa and Robert returned to the meeting room at noon. TC was already seated at his desk. The furniture had been rearranged, and two empty chairs sat before the desk with a large brown cardboard box beside each of them. TC gestured for the new recruits to sit down.

"Iowa, Kentucky, I assume you've packed all your gear and personal items into the bags and cases provided. For your own benefit and safety, you are not to keep any personal possessions that link you to the British Army or your family."

He looked at them questioningly, and they nodded to acknowledge the order.

"Good. I have arranged a car for you to use when you arrive in Londonderry. However, you must only use this vehicle when strictly necessary. Walk or use public transport whenever possible. Your tout is a local man. He's the disgruntled owner of a mobile laundry company in Londonderry, who has agreed to work with us. Ironically, he's well known and trusted within the community. At first, you may find him a little sharp and evasive, but like many other sources – as soon as he gets used to taking our money, he'll be more forthcoming."

TC took a breath before he continued.

"Your first operation will start tomorrow, last four weeks, and if successful, perhaps longer. You will accompany your tout as he operates in and around the Creggan housing estate. He will pick up and deliver laundry using his company van. Iowa, you look less conspicuous and will therefore drive the vehicle. There will be very little interaction with the locals. Kentucky, you will photograph and video any suspects or suspicious goings-on from the back of the van. It is imperative you get to know Creggan and its residents inside out."

Robert listened intently.

"Any laundry that is picked up from a suspect's house will be sent to Forensics and quickly analysed for traces of explosives, gun residue, etc. For a quick turnaround, we have erected a makeshift laboratory attached to the laundry company's warehouse just outside the city. Based on any new evidence we find, we will carry out the necessary searches and arrests."

Iowa was livid: she didn't want to drive. She'd rather have taken the photographs. Fuck it! Just when she'd thought her day couldn't get worse. She sat there in disbelief as TC told them, "We've arranged accommodation for you in a local bed and breakfast. The proprietor will ask no questions. We've used her before. Everything you need, including money, clothes, and identification documents, are in these boxes. We will make contact with you when we need to. You will not under any circumstances, contact us. Included in your box is a written brief containing additional information. I'd like you to read it carefully and memorise it. The brief must then be returned to me, and we can cover any final questions."

Robert and Iowa took a box each and spent the next hour discussing the finer points of the operation. Importantly, TC told them how to break the news to their families. It was simple, really. They were to say they were going overseas on an advanced training programme that could ultimately lead to promotion. This meant the families wouldn't have to worry. The "trainees" would be safe but unfortunately, out of contact for some time, and no, they wouldn't know how long.

As soon as TC left, Robert ignored Iowa and returned to his hut. He began to write some letters. The first was to Tracey, telling her how much he loved her and how sorry he was for disappointing her. He wrote about his excitement over the baby and how he looked forward to them all being a proper family. He also wrote a difficult letter to his parents. As he wrote the words, he knew if he were killed, they'd be able to take some solace and comfort from his last letter. Job done, he placed the letters into the plastic bag and tied it up securely.

As TC walked away from the hut, he thought about the new operatives and knew he'd made the right choice. They looked just like any normal couple – unhappy and pissed off.

Chapter Thirty

Caitlin had finally returned to work after the bomb blast, and James was thrilled to have her back. He'd almost forgotten how lovely she was. Her wounds had practically healed, and she wore an outfit he hadn't seen before. Her shining hair was tied back in a loose sexy bun. She looked very professional in her short black skirt, white blouse and matching black jacket. He was proud of her. As he'd said good morning to her, secretive smiles passed between them.

James had found that time passed too slowly when she wasn't around, and this new feeling was strange. He could sense his Uncle watching him. Roger's threat to tell his father about his visit to Caitlin worried James. Uncle Roger knew that for years James Snr had wanted his son to join the army and follow in his footsteps, so the threat was real.

In Caitlin's absence, James had worked late into the night on the talks proposal.

George Shalham had spent considerable time with him, going through the draft invitee list and, after much debate, agreeing to the final list. The invitations had been posted, and any necessary follow-up phone calls had been made, to explain in more detail what they were trying to achieve. The RSVPs were trickling back including one from Charles Jones. James was disappointed Jones had been asked. He hadn't wanted to invite him, but Roger had been insistent. They'd almost fallen out because of it. James knew Jones wouldn't contribute positively and would likely stir things up intentionally. He was a bigoted bastard.

Like a bee to honey, Mrs Parkes continually snooped around James's office. She was there when Caitlin arrived and hovered around pretending to search for something but instead paying close attention to James and Caitlin.

Eventually, James had had enough and got to his feet. He stared coldly at her before closing the door in her prying face. Hateful woman! Mrs Parkes was far from amused and scampered back to her own office.

James was able to smile at Caitlin properly now.

"How are you? Are you feeling better? You look amazing!" he told her, gesturing for her to sit in one of his leather visitors' chairs.

"Thank you. I've been busy sewing. I'm glad you like it," she said, genuinely thrilled by the compliment.

He was impressed. "Really? You made the whole outfit yourself, clever girl?!"

She looked at him sideways and said, "My mother was supposed to help, but she's not been very well."

She was nervous then and felt her face redden before she asked, "James, this thing… I mean, me and you… What happened between us was the last thing I ever expected. Yet it's the only thing that's keeping me sane. Why?"

He knew this wasn't the right time for them to talk and quickly explained how Mrs Parkes had told his Uncle about his visit and the decisive way Roger had reacted.

That was that then, she thought. James couldn't lose his work and his home. It was over. She waited fearfully for his next words. She was likely out of a job now.

But instead, he leaned closer across his desk and spoke tenderly to her.

"Caitlin, no one was more surprised than I was when I kissed you. But I had to."

He laughed and added, "My imagination has been running wild ever since!"

"James, I understand why your uncle is so concerned. When you get to know this place better, you'll understand too. Think about it.

You and I are from two worlds that don't mix, never have and never will. It's the way it is, and it'll not change."

James couldn't understand her restraint. "I don't care. Where you come from means nothing to me. It's you I want, just you."

He stood up too fast and flinched.

"Are you okay? What happened!" she asked immediately.

"Oh, I'm fine; I guess I overdid it with the running."

They noticed Mrs Parkes's silhouette once again outside the door. Caitlin got up. In a low voice, she said, "Let's take this one day at a time. I love being here so at least we'll have that for the time being. I have to get on now; the old bat is hovering again."

James was unconvinced. He needed more than just being with her in the office.

"That's not enough. I need to see you on your own. But we can't talk now. Later. We'll talk later. Okay?"

"Okay," she agreed and smiled radiantly.

James abruptly opened the office door, much to Mrs Parkes's surprise, who almost fell through it.

"What is it this time, Mrs Parkes?"

"Oh… nothing. It's nothing, Mr Henderson," she replied nervously, and hurried away. James smiled and mockingly cried in an authoritative voice: "Caitlin, diary, now!"

Caitlin sniggered and walked to her desk, positioned just outside the office door. She picked up the red leather desk diary, a spiral notebook and pencil, and walked back to join him. This time they deliberately left the office door wide open.

Time passed too quickly while they discussed the plan to safeguard the factory. The City Hotel had confirmed the availability of rooms and accommodation for the meeting. James discussed the idea of having an informal dinner afterwards, and they both agreed it would be a good way of getting the guests to relax, but special attention would need to be given to the seating plan.

Already, a decent quantity of prominent businessmen and women from all areas of the community had committed to attend. These included the weary traders of William Street – who fought hard to keep their businesses open again and again amidst the worst riots – as well as city councillors, bankers and politicians. At first, the army had been reluctant to get involved but eventually promised someone would attend. To his uncle's delight, representatives from both the Catholic Church and the Free Derry Presbyterian Church had also agreed to join in – it was a most unusual occurrence to find them under the same roof.

James and Roger were keenly aware that they'd need capital investment and very soon. They were under extreme pressure from their Glaswegian clients, who were far from happy about their many delayed deliveries thanks to the riots. James had spent hours on the phone, convincing them not to cancel.

Even with all the difficulties he'd already encountered, he was secretly pleased with their progress.

Caitlin and James continued to work until there was nothing left to do but separate and get on with their own tasks. As Caitlin picked up James's diary, she asked, "Can I get you a cup of tea or anything? I think there might even be some biscuits?"

He patted his stomach and tutted. "No, I'm fine, thanks. I haven't been running for a few days, and I can feel it!"

With a twinkle in her eye, she closed the door gently behind her. So he had been lying about running too much. She'd thought as much and made a point to find out more.

The phone rang at James's desk. "Good morning, James Henderson."

He instantly recognised the caller's voice and sank comfortably back in his chair. He swung it around to face the window while he took the call. He never grew tired of watching the factory at work.

An eight-foot-high steel fence surrounded the three-quarter-acre site. There was only one gated entrance next to a security guardhouse.

The employees' car park was hidden behind a single-storey red-brick building with a weather-boarded white apex roof. This modern building housed quality control. Roger had added it to the factory site, which had originally been developed in the Victorian era and bought derelict by him fifteen years ago. It was an ornate building with large white ferrous-framed windows set in a stone and polychrome brick façade.

Goods In and Goods Out were on the ground floor. The first floor held the cutting department; the second was filled with bench after bench of sewing machines. On the third and fourth floor, hundreds of workers were employed to make the collars, fronts and cuffs for shirts and other garments. Not only did Rocola produce shirts, but they also made underwear and nightwear for a number of Scottish and international clients.

"Hello? Hello, James. Are you there?"

James made himself concentrate on the call again.

"Yes, Father, I'm here. Well, yes of course, if you insist, I'll be back in time for dinner with Harris... Yes, I know, he's not the easiest... Okay. Right, see you at home at seven... No, I won't be late. Bye now."

James slowly replaced the receiver. The last thing he needed was another boring men-only dinner. He'd never liked Dr Harris. Once, whilst visiting as a child, James had come down with chickenpox and Harris had attended him. He gave James the creeps then, and as he grew up, he still thought of Harris as nothing but a maladjusted loner with unfortunate political views. Surprisingly for a doctor, Harris was virtually emaciated and his appearance often shambolic. He had a nervous habit of picking and scratching at his dry diabetic skin rash. He was a thoroughly unprepossessing man, and James couldn't understand why his father and uncle entertained him.

At lunchtime, lost in thought, James heard a knock on his open door. Caitlin stood half in and half out of his office. She appeared flushed and excited as she asked, "Can I have a quick word?"

James was intrigued. "Sure, what is it? Come in. Close the door."

Caitlin walked gracefully into the room and stood impatiently before his desk. She'd removed her black jacket enabling him to see the curves of her breasts through her sheer blouse. He could see the outline of her lace bra and his eyes moved slowly downwards to appreciate the slimness of her tiny waist and boyish hips.

"Mr Henderson, please!" she said, noticing. "Look, this is important; I've had an idea."

"Okay. I'm listening." James clasped his hands behind his head, lay back on the chair and waited.

"Well, I've just been invited to a twenty-first birthday party on Saturday week at the Malin Hotel. I've said I could make it but... I thought I could use it as an excuse for us to spend the day together instead. What do you think?"

James remained silent and pretended to look shocked by her request.

She frowned in despair. Had she gone too far?

Eventually, he couldn't suppress it any longer, and his face broke into a cheeky grin.

"Fooled you!"

Caitlin narrowed her eyes briefly and muttered crossly at him, "That's not funny, James. I mean it."

At her words, he laughed even more. It was a wonderful idea, though.

"It's brilliant. I can tell my uncle and father that I'm meeting a friend somewhere. If you tell your mother you're at this birthday bash, it could work out beautifully. What date was it again?"

Caitlin told him as Mrs Parkes strode boldly into the office, this time without knocking. She had a quizzical expression on her face as soon as she noticed Caitlin's flushed cheeks. There was a palpable air of excitement in the room.

"Excuse me. Mr Henderson, I need your signature on these invoices." She acknowledged Caitlin by lifting her chin. In silence, James signed the invoices, and Mrs Parkes left without further comment.

James found it hard to concentrate for the remainder of the afternoon. His mind reeled at the thought of being alone with Caitlin. Mrs Parkes had undoubtedly sensed something earlier. He had to get rid of her somehow and soon.

He thought about Caitlin's idea and wondered whether he could push her a little further and ask her to stay with him overnight. Perhaps in Donegal Town? It was far enough away from the city. No one would know them there. He'd think about it. He needed to be sensitive about how he suggested it.

Chapter Thirty-one

It was a perfect plan. She'd try and mention the birthday invitation casually to her mother first, so she'd get used to the idea – that was if she even took in what Caitlin was telling her. The thought of being alone with James both terrified and excited the girl.

That evening she'd finished on time. Mrs Parkes had left early, so she and James said goodnight openly in front of the other girls and he'd sneaked her a cheeky wink. He was going home to dinner with his family. They'd a guest tonight: Dr Harris. This reminder of the man whose negligence or indifference had led to her father's death took Caitlin aback. She told James of the doctor's involvement and was surprised and hurt when he told her there was no getting out of it. He couldn't stand Harris either, but he had no choice. He was under the microscope as it was and couldn't afford to upset his father or uncle again.

She believed him and his words made her feel a little better until he completely stunned her when – out of the blue and rather abruptly – he asked if she'd spend the weekend with him.

"Caitlin, you know that twenty-first party of yours... What if we were to make a weekend out of it?"

She was stunned.

James knew immediately that he'd made a complete hash of it. He'd seen how upset she was to be reminded of Harris and had thought the offer of a weekend away might make her feel better. The look of horror on her face told him it did not.

Caitlin was stiff with fury. What kind of a girl did he think she was? She left his office without answering.

The walk home these days felt long and lonely without Anne. The dark nights had arrived, and she desperately missed her friend's humour and energy. She wanted to tell her everything, especially James's proposal, but sadly for the first time ever, she couldn't do so.

She reached her house and was still fishing for her key when the door was yanked open by Martin. He stood there dressed in his Army & Navy coat over a heavy grey turtleneck jumper that had seen better days. His trousers, also grey, were loose on him and had formed several folds on top of his filthy unpolished boots.

Surprised to see her as he'd opened the door, he cried, "This house is killing me. I can't listen to me Ma anymore, Caitlin, she's lost it! Keeps calling me fuckin' Patrick. She's off her rocker – I have to get out of here!"

Without another word, he pushed her aside, and she struck her arm against the wall. She saw him march down the path and slam their pathetic wooden gate behind. It rattled back and forth but remained intact – just. Caitlin cried after him,

"What's happened, Martin?" He raised his hand to the air waving her calls away, ignoring her as he walked on.

"Nice," she said to herself as she entered the house. Cold air surrounded her, and instinctively she tightened her coat and mumbled, "Jesus. It's freezing in here."

She ran up to her mother's bedroom. As she entered, she noticed the curtains were still tightly closed, and the room depressingly dark and cold.

"Mammy? Are you awake? It's me."

She sat on the edge of the bed and switched on a small shadeless light. The dim bulb helped but not a lot. She pulled back the bedcovers gently to expose the top of a curled, skeletal body. Her mother had refused to eat, and they'd been forced to call in a doctor. He'd been due to visit that morning and Martin had agreed to be here. Caitlin had hoped he'd refer Majella to a psychiatrist, but she wouldn't find out now, given that Martin had done a runner. Majella pulled the bedclothes back over her head tightly as Caitlin gently shook her.

"Mammy, please, are you awake?"

She heard moaning and muttering coming from under the blankets.

"Leave me be, pppplllllleeeaaaaasssssseee. I just want to sleep, Patrick. Patrick, I'll get up in a while."

Caitlin heaved a tired sigh and tucked the blankets in over the emaciated body. She noticed the sheets were stained and slightly wet in places. Gloomily, she switched off the bedside light and made her way out of the bedroom, closing the door behind her.

In her own room, she sighed, feeling suddenly exhausted as she removed her new black overcoat and suit jacket. She wiped the last of her tears away carelessly with her blouse sleeve and threw the jacket and coat onto her bed. She returned to the landing and took a set of fresh sheets from the linen cupboard.

After great difficulty, Caitlin managed to change the bed and freshen her mother up a little. She kissed her and closed the bedroom door.

Downstairs in the kitchen, she looked around. It was a pit. She'd been greeted by a collection of dirty dinner plates, glasses, cups and several overflowing ashtrays. The smell of old food was repugnant. Sadly, her mother's once immaculate worktops were now stained with cup rings, spilt beer and other unidentifiable fluids. Evidently, Martin had invited his so-called friends over for a party.

"For fuck's sake!" Caitlin cried.

Any happiness she'd felt that morning had long since gone. Even when she thought about James, it didn't make her feel any better. He'd hurt and insulted her. Never before had she felt so lost. She sat down on her chair and closed her eyes. Her weary head nodded, and she drifted off to sleep, to dream of her home when it was a safe and happy place.

Much later, Caitlin jumped as a hand gently nudged her shoulder. Shit, she was still in the kitchen! She'd fallen asleep. Tina stood next to her and was looking worried.

"Caitlin, Jesus. What are you doing sleeping in the kitchen? You all right?"

Caitlin wasn't quite sure.

"Aw, Tina, where have you been?"

"I've been next door. I was waiting for you to come home. I take it Mammy's still in bed?"

She removed her coat and hung it under the stairs.

"Yeah. Zombied. Our Martin's a bastard, Tina. He stormed out as soon as I put the key in the door. Did the doctor come?"

Tina returned to the kitchen and tutted despairingly as she saw the mess.

"Huh! Our Martin is all over the place, Caitlin. Sure he wouldn't let me in when all those eejits were here earlier, that's why I had to go next door. And sorry, I don't know if the doctor's been."

As ever, Tina defended their brother while Caitlin tried to explain what he'd done.

"He stormed right past me, Tina, ranting and raving, nearly took the gate off its hinges and completely ignored me. Then I walk in here, Mammy's a mess, you're not here, and the kitchen's a fucking pigsty!"

"Do you know what, Caitlin?" Tina said suddenly in a monotone. "Leave Martin to me. You and I, well, we're just going to have to deal with it. Let's tidy the kitchen first and get us all, including Mammy, something to eat. I don't know about you, but I'll go crazy if we just sit here. I'm close to breaking point – and from what I'm seeing, you are too. We've no other choice so let's get this place sorted."

Caitlin grinned half-heartedly. Tina was right. They had no choice. Who else was going to do it?

The two young women took in the scene of devastation and looked at each other. Two small but visible smiles emerged. They could do this. Tina reached for the old tape recorder and pressed the stiff 'play' button. Music that she'd taped from Radio 1's count-down show engulfed the room. The sisters laughed as Tina turned the volume up to its highest, and they attacked the kitchen until it was spotless.

Lost in the music, they imitated the singers using wooden spoons as microphones. They challenged each other with their dance moves.

God, they needed this! They needed a laugh! They needed anything that could bring back a taste of the carefree days before Martin, before Daddy, before the bomb and before their mother's breakdown.

Later that night, after futile attempts to feed her mother, Caitlin walked into the living room. Tina was sprawled lazily on the sofa in front of the TV. The fire was low, but the room was relatively warm. Caitlin could hear Eddie Waring presenting *It's a Knockout* – Tina's favourite. Her sister raised her eyes and asked, "Did she eat anything?"

Caitlin sighed and threw herself down next to her sister.

"Not a bite. She's taken too many of those pills. Her mouth is dry and coated in white stuff. I don't know what to do."

Tina didn't know what to say. She'd tried to cheer Caitlin up earlier. Tried so hard. She wanted to watch TV. Forget about everything.

"Leave her for tonight. It's probably better to let her sleep them off. We'll keep an eye on her."

Caitlin was glad her sister was with her.

"Do you think so? I'm at a loss, Tina, I really—"

She didn't get a chance to finish as the front door was thrown violently open. Martin was back!

He stood at the living-room door, swaying slightly, and looked with disdain at the two women. He grunted and walked towards the kitchen. Both of them immediately got up and followed him. He switched the light on, and they watched him. He was sloshed. He took off his Army & Navy coat and hurled it angrily across the back of his chair.

"What the fuck are you two staring at? Buzz off and leave me alone!"

Next, he placed a brown paper bag on the table and removed a bottle of white lemonade followed by a 40-ounce bottle of vodka. He drunkenly placed them dead centre of the table. The women stood and watched. He laughed, loudly and for all the wrong reasons. Finally, he gestured for them to join him.

"Pay no attention to me! Would you like a drink, ladies?"

Caitlin looked at him with disgust. He was hammered and, God, he reeked. She'd been leaving for work early in the mornings and getting home late and had hardly seen him. Now she noticed his greasy, limp hair and unshaven face. His pullover was stained with something egg-like alongside other stains.

She didn't recognise her brother anymore as he theatrically declaimed, "Ock, me darlins, aren't you going to join your hero for a jar? I've some friends coming over. Sure we'll have a wee party, all of us!"

Christ almighty! Caitlin couldn't believe he seriously thought he was going to party in the kitchen they'd just spent forever cleaning.

"Martin, you're fucking hammered! For Christ's sake, that's all we need!"

Caitlin looked to Tina for support. Instead, her sister snapped,

"Ah, Caitlin, leave him. He's just winding you up, and you're falling for it. Come on." For the second time that day, Caitlin was mortified. Tina smiled at Martin and said merrily, "I'll have a wee jar with you, Martin, since you're offering."

Caitlin was horrified. "You will not, Martina McLaughlin – over my dead body!"

Tina needed something, anything, to help her switch off, and now Caitlin was getting on her tits – *big time.*

"Jesus, Caitlin, get a life, will you? You're doing my head in! Martin, throw us a drink."

Tina was glad Caitlin wouldn't join them. She'd have their brother to herself. Martin squinted his eyes and tried to focus on Caitlin. His head swayed from side to side as he considered her. He didn't like his snooty sister very much. She was too big for her boots and thought she was above everybody else. Now, Tina – she was a different matter, he'd all the time in the world for Tina.

"You're some girl, Tina McLaughlin! You're a real trooper, so you are. Get the glasses. You're not like that stuck-up bitch over there! Her and her posh job... Miss Goody Two-shoes. You're a puke, Caitlin McLaughlin, that's what you are... A stuck- up fucking prissy puke!"

His words were venomous and cruel. She was deeply hurt. She watched, dumbfounded, as her younger sister poured the cheap vodka into two tumblers and confidently topped them up with a minuscule measure of lemonade. The drinkers cried in collusion: "*Sláinte!*" The near shots were gulped down fast, and together they shook their heads and cried: "Yes!"

Caitlin's life had become a roller-coaster. She was up one minute and the next hurtling to a new low. Her chest heaved with the effort not to cry. She watched them take another shot and said quietly, "Fuck the both of you. Be it on your own heads."

She went to bed and put her pillow over her head in an effort to keep out the noise and commotion of the drunken party. But it only grew louder and louder as the front door was continually opened and more guests were invited in. She'd never forgive Martin for this, nor Tina for that matter. Unsurprisingly, sleep eluded her.

Chapter Thirty-two

It hadn't turned out exactly the way he would have liked although he felt the Boys would be pleased by the publicity. By fuck, he'd learned from the experience. Always be prepared for the unexpected. The soldier's murder had been given pretty good TV coverage, but in true BBC style, they never gave the whole story other than to blame the Republicans. He'd guarantee most Brits on the mainland didn't know the reasons they were fighting this war. They probably didn't care.

Bigotry, gerrymandering, internment and murders on Bloody Sunday, to name but a few reasons among many, were why they were fighting. But it was all one-fucking-sided. It suited the British Broadcasting Corporation to ignore the murders and interrogations happening on their very own doorstep. They'd be ashamed if they knew the truth, but truth would prevail. It always did – eventually.

He hadn't slept since the night of the murder. His mind raced for days afterwards, and he'd been delighted with his own performance. He'd loved every single fucking moment of it. She'd done all right but just all right. He hadn't really seen her since and wasn't bothered or surprised. He'd scared the bejesus out of her as he'd taken her home. He remembered his own pitiless words.

"If you breathe so much as a fucking word about what happened tonight, or any other night, I will kill you! I will kill you first, and then the Boys and I will kill your family. You'll be responsible for the soldier's death and the beating the other one got. Just you. No one else. And remember, it was you who set them bastards up. If I'm caught, I'll tell them it was your idea. They can't link me to anything. Do you hear me?"

She'd nodded, hating him and knowing she had no choice.

After they'd dumped the body, in a deceptively friendly tone, he'd apologised.

*"I'm sorry you got so involved in this, but I will need you again, so when I ask for your help – **you will not refuse me**. Otherwise, you leave me with no choice. Do you understand, Honey?"*

She'd nodded numbly and got out of the car. She couldn't believe how quickly he could change. One minute he was loving, the next pure evil. What the fuck was wrong with him?

Kieran lay bare-chested on top of his bed and relished the last of his spliff. The air was heavy with perfume from the weed, and the room was hot. He could feel sweat roll down the valley of his torso and onto his stomach. He laughed gently as a long-fingered hand appeared and gently wiped the moisture away. His eyes followed its graceful fingers as they were slid into a full-lipped mouth and sucked teasingly. They stayed there until a suggestive smile broke out over the most beautiful face Kieran had ever seen. He giggled as he jumped onto the equally perfect body and whispered seductively, "I can think of other ways of putting those fingers to good use!"

Kieran was in heaven when he heard a voice answer wickedly,

"I bet you could. Of that, I have absolutely no doubt, my love. However, I have to get to work! I have a whole load of stuff to finish."

The couple kissed passionately before Kieran was left alone in bed. He lay back, finished his joint and watched as his lover showered and dressed in elegance and grace. He loved to watch this beauty. An airborne kiss goodbye, and he was abandoned.

Kieran sighed and relived their loving from the previous night and morning. He smiled. The minutes passed until it was time for him to get up. He jumped off the bed and took a quick peek out to check the weather. Hmm, not bad.

An hour later, as he was reading the local paper, *The Derry Journal*, and finishing a mug of coffee in a local café, he sensed somebody lingering nearby. He looked up to see who it was and saw Martin McLaughlin staring coldly back at him. Kieran had never met him face to face though he knew him from a distance. McLaughlin was high up with the Boys, but he looked like shit. Kieran had heard rumours he'd hit the bottle hard as soon *as he'd got out and they were right. McLaughlin already had the look of a drunk with his red-veined cheeks and nose and those heavy, watery eyes. The aroma of stale alcohol was the clincher. Most likely he'd been sleeping in his pathetic second-hand military gear too. He looked and smelled like a hobo.*

Kieran – who was fanatical about his own personal hygiene – drank more coffee as he tried to evade the smell that oozed from McLaughlin, who sat down uninvited from him across the booth. He looked pathetic as he asked in his husky hung-over voice, "How's it hangin'?"

"Good," Kieran answered as he folded up his newspaper and placed it to the side of the table next to the ketchup and HP sauce.

Martin took a look around the café until he caught the eye of the elderly white-haired waitress. She immediately walked over. She knew who he was and that he warranted quick service.

"Yes, Martin. What would you like?"

He answered the woman with a smile and pointed to Kieran.

"I'll have a full Irish breakfast and a strong black coffee, please, Siobhan, and he's paying."

Kieran nodded and ordered another coffee. McLaughlin slumped across the plastic tablecloth closer to Kieran, who instinctively shrank back. Christ, the man hummed.

Martin laughed and sat back. He knew he smelled. This was nothing to how he had been in prison, though, day after day. He took a single John Player's Special cigarette from Kieran's half-empty pack lying on the table. It was his first of the day and, fuck, he needed it. Kieran offered him a light. Martin inhaled deeply and deliberately encouraged the smoke to stream into Kieran's face.

"I heard your assignment didn't go quite to plan the other week although I understand you made up for it. Good work! Although we think you might have got a bit carried away, all in all – we dig it. I've been asked to pass on our thanks and apologies. Our lads were lifted on their way to you. These things happen, Mr Kelly – or can I call you Kieran?"

He nodded as McLaughlin continued to drag on the cigarette.

*"Right, well, Kieran, it's a bit like this. You're a lightweight as far as I'm concerned. You're just a weasel. However, there's one thing the Boys don't know about you – **yet**. You see, it's been brought to my attention that you've been a naughty boy and this concerns me a great fucking deal. I don't suppose you know what I'm on about, do you?"*

Martin waited for an answer. He couldn't stand this obnoxious skinny fucker with his posh and perfect clothes! Well, he was onto him. He'd been given some very useful and gratifying information.

Kieran's answer was delayed as Siobhan brought two mugs of coffee and placed them down. She immediately sensed the atmosphere and, in her haste to get away, spilt some onto the plastic table cover. Normally she would have made a fuss and wiped it off, but this time she scurried off.

Both men carefully sipped the coffee. Kieran had been extra careful about who he'd told about Honey and what. He'd practically given nothing about her away. In turn, they weren't that bothered. They'd trusted him and just wanted the soldiers.

He knew exactly what else the reeking bastard was on about but shrugged his shoulders and instead played the naivety card.

"I don't know what you're on about, Mr McLaughlin. Your guess is as good as mine."

Martin wasn't surprised by Kelly's response. It was exactly as he'd expected.

"You're a fuck-face liar, Kelly. You know what I'm on about. You've been playing a very dangerous game. And unless you stop playing, you moron, I will take you from your playground and finish off your game along with your other players. Dig it?"

Kieran wasn't stupid but pretended to be.

"Honestly, Mr McLaughlin, I don't know what you're on about. You're not making any sense!"

Martin reached out and grabbed Kieran by the collar.

"*Listen, your sleazy piece of shite; you want me to spell it out here and now in the middle of this wee café managed by the lovely Siobhan over there? It'll be around this town in fifteen minutes! So deal with it before I really lose my temper!*"

Kieran felt a flicker of fear as he saw madness in McLaughlin's eyes. He'd seen that look before – in his own reflection.

Martin hoped the geek wouldn't listen to his warning. It'd give him a chance to deal with him personally. He'd beat the shite out of him and enjoy it.

Anyway, he was hungry. He looked up in search of Siobhan and remembered something. Ah, shit, yeah.

"*By the way, Kelly, we'll need to pick up our gear. Where is it?*"

Kieran had hidden weapons and explosives for the Boys on a few occasions. However, he wasn't parting with the latest stash now or any time soon. In their dreams.

"*It's well hidden.*"

Martin was satisfied. "*Good. I'll be in touch. Now pay for me fuckin' breakfast and fuck away off out of me sight!*"

Outside Kieran lit a cigarette and inhaled deeply. He looked through the café window to see McLaughlin scoffing his breakfast down and laughing with Siobhan.

Anger and hatred for him and the Boys permeated Kieran. Why the fuck should they have the power to threaten him like that?

He stormed off towards the unemployment office and joined an excruciatingly long queue to sign-on.

Afterwards, he walked back to his flat. A gentle mist of rain came down, and he swore as he pulled his light jacket around him. Anyone watching would have seen a handsome, well-dressed young man who looked worried. Well, they'd have been wrong. He wasn't worried or frightened. He was livid, and he'd been betrayed by the people for whom he'd given up so much. He thought of his beautiful cancer-riddled mother who'd adored him. She'd warned him not to get involved, and he hadn't listened. He'd hurt her badly, and she'd never forgiven him. He didn't even see her before she died. And now they were threatening him! Well, fuck them! Wasn't he the one who knew where the stash was? He'd think of some way to use it and get the bastards back!

He was about to open the main door to the flats when a hand grasped his arm, and he jumped back in fright.

"Fuck!"

It was Honey. Christ! She was **NOT** *what he needed right now.*

"What the fuck are you doing here?" he snarled.

She immediately regretted she'd come. But she had to tell him. She couldn't live with herself and had been dying inside for days. She couldn't sleep, and her head was full of the soldier's screams and blood – there'd been so much blood! She had to do something. She had to make it stop! She started to cry hysterically and shrilled, "I need to talk to you. You have to listen to me! I've made a decision. This is over. It's finished!"

"You too, eh? You'd betray me too? I don't think so, Honey! It's not finished until I fucking say so! You've seen what I can do. Now come here!"

He grabbed her hair and pulled her through the open door. She fought as he pulled her up the stairs to the first floor. Her screams became louder as he roughly pushed his hand between her legs and shouted crazily, "You want some, do you? Well, you've not given me a moment's peace, so I'd better give you some!" He continued to hold her hair with one hand while he retrieved his key from his jeans. He unlocked the door and used his foot to kick it open.

"Get the fuck in there now!"

She landed painfully on her knees. Terrified, she watched him slam the door closed and lock it securely. What was he going to do to her? He threw his keys angrily into a bowl and took off his dampened jacket before placing it carefully on the back of a chair.

"Okay, Honey, you've got my attention."

She tried to rise, but he stopped her.

"Take your clothes off."

She couldn't! Relishing her fear and because being rough turned him on, he repeated himself, slowly and deliberately. "I said, take your clothes off." He was confident no one could hear them given the other pads were always empty during the day. She'd picked the wrong time for a surprise visit!

Honey shook her head and gazed at Kieran's twisted face, appalled. She couldn't comprehend what was happening. He pushed her down flat on the floor. He pulled off her blouse and tore away her bra. He then pulled down her skirt and pants. Somehow, he'd managed to hold her hands together high above her head. He was so strong. She froze. Dear God, no! Not like this! How could she ever have thought that this was what she wanted?

He laughed as he felt her go limp. Dispassionately, he noticed her breasts were young with full large red nipples. There was a birthmark half-way down her left breast.

Suddenly he stopped what he was doing. He didn't have the time or the inclination for this. He'd made his point and regained his composure. He got down beside her and spoke softly into her hair.

"Relax, Honey. Take it easy. I'm not going to hurt you. I was just showing you that you can't mess with me."

His change of mind and tone took her by surprise. What was he up to? Was it a trick? She didn't know how to respond. To her amazement, he released her and stood up. She stayed on the floor and watched him walk around the room. He quickly tucked in his shirt as he said lightly, "Go on. Use the bathroom to tidy up."

She crawled over the floor and retrieved her clothes, sobbing in shame as she shuffled into the small bathroom where she innocently locked the door.

Kieran removed his trousers and shirt and picked up his jacket to hang it up. He swapped them for a grey tracksuit. The few clothes he had were hung neatly on wooden hangers in the colour-coordinated wardrobe.

What the fuck was she doing in the bathroom? He called out. He was hungry since earlier McLaughlin hadn't given him the chance to order his breakfast, but there wasn't much left in the fridge. Nevertheless, he grabbed two beers, opened the cans and watched the froth overflow.

At last, the bathroom door opened and she stood there, dishevelled and evidently in shock. He'd enjoyed their little adventure, and from the condition of her, she'd got the message. He smiled encouragingly.

"Honey. Have a beer?"

"No."

He sniggered. "Ah, come on now, come over here and relax. It could have been a lot worse. Come on now. I miss you." He patted the cushion next to him. "Please, sit down beside me."

He revelled in the power he had over her and decided he wouldn't get rid of her quite yet.

"I'm begging you, Honey. Please come here."

After a pause, she walked over and sat down meekly beside him. She flinched as he took her hand and apologised.

"I'm sorry, Honey. It wasn't supposed to happen that way. Sure I was just playing with you. Sometimes men do that when they play – didn't you know? I thought you did. Take my hand, please, talk to me."

She refused to hold his hand but accepted the beer – she needed something to calm her – and thirstily drank from the can. He rubbed her leg up and down gently with his fingertips.

"Now isn't that better? I didn't mean to lose my temper. Next time we'll take it much, much slower, I promise. You're beautiful, Honey, and you're mine. You're so beautiful. I think I'm falling in love with you. Please, trust me."

She gazed at him and melted. He was the beautiful one, not her. She was evil. She'd done horrible things. She looked at Kieran and saw the old one was back, the Kieran who told her he loved her. She sighed deeply and contentedly as he stroked her hair and put his arm around her protectively.

He laughed to himself. He'd done a good job on her. She was easy pickings. He only needed her this last time, and then he'd gladly and quickly get rid of her.

Chapter Thirty-three

Robert was already bored, claustrophobic and feeling downright miserable, and they'd only been at it for a few days. He'd recalled the fury and disappointment in Tracey's voice when he'd told her about his *potential promotion*. Their call had upset him. He hadn't wanted to think so much, but this operation gave him no choice.

It was the same thing, day in, day out. Iowa drove the van whilst the fat, sweating, crazed up laundry owner trudged up and down the many neglected garden paths and knocked the household doors. He'd wait patiently to collect or return their weekly laundry. A few lucky ones on the estate owned their own washing machines but most didn't.

You couldn't like their tout, Thomas Deeney. He was a huge man, bald as a coot and morbidly obese. There was something slimy about him, and Robert had already learned that he was a tight, mean bastard. On more than one occasion, they'd listen to him rant on about why he was helping them, totally forgetting that he was getting paid and paid well. His language was vile too.

From their briefing, and Deeney himself, they'd learned he had been born in Londonderry. His mother had raised him by herself in a condemned two-up, two-down terraced house just off Cable Street – one of the worst slums in the Bogside. When she couldn't cope with him, which was regularly, he was put in the local Nazareth House orphanage.

He'd never known his father – only that he was part of the old IRA and he'd had to get out of Ireland and go to America. His mother never forgave him and brought Deeney up to hate not only his father but the Cause that had stolen her husband away. She became a recluse and never left their home until recently when she fell down their stairs, died in hospital and subsequently occupied a pitiful grave alone.

Deeney rarely met women socially and so had never married. "Lux Laundry" was his only family, his only pride and joy. But the business was in financial trouble and working for the Brits proved to be a stroke of luck. He didn't have to think twice about what he was doing. It was for the money, pure and simple.

Their day was ending, and Robert watched through one of the two rear windows as Deeney's portly frame accosted another unsuspecting customer. No doubt he'd return soon and in his foul language tell them everything about the householder. Unbelievably, Deeney could list the names of who lived in which house, who they were related to, who they were shagging, and who – most pathetically – went to Mass regularly! For some unexplained reason, people trusted Deeney and told him everything. Much as Robert disliked him, he'd proved very capable in his capacity of mole and informer. They'd already gathered good solid information and were able to update their suspects' mugshots.

They were in the heart of Creggan or "Stony Place" the translation from Irish of Creggan. It was a massive but poor council development. Most of the men couldn't find jobs and so spent the long depressing days either in the local bar or at home looking after their many children. The air around the estate was filled with grey smoke from the coal fires that often produced an inert low cloud that shrouded the hillside. Robert had grown used to it and liked the smell – it reminded him of home.

It was highly probable that there were other undercover operatives and look-outs spread amongst the estate's inhabitants. They were likely disguised as council road sweepers, phone engineers or even meths drinkers who clustered on the street corners. Robert knew there was a good chance that somewhere out there were the fuckers who'd murdered Val.

Working with Iowa had been particularly depressing. She'd spoken very little, especially to him. Their pad turned out to be a shabby bedsit. He couldn't understand how the military had come to trust their ancient, near-blind landlady. On the rare occasions they'd meet, she'd squint her weak eyes to focus. She'd sometimes get too close to him, and he'd almost taste the rancid breath that emanated from her rotten teeth and infected gums. She was horrid.

The four-storey townhouse was filthy and permanently dark. It was eerie with Catholic relics, pictures and statues displayed on the walls and hallways. She had cats. Robert hated cats. They were everywhere, and the smell of cat piss and shit got into every room, including theirs. The house was rotten, and he despised it. He was convinced they were the only tenants and if so, knew why.

On the day they'd arrived, as they'd walked up the stairs, Robert whispered humorously to Iowa that the place was like something from a horror film, but she'd ignored him.

The old woman had led them slowly up the stairs to an L-shaped bedsit on the third floor. At once they noticed just one small double bed. Fortunately for Robert, a shabby sofa stood in one corner. His relief at not having to share the bed was overwhelming. A small kitchen was half-hidden around the angle of the room. It appeared unwelcoming and dirty. Robert couldn't find any mod cons, certainly not a TV and on closer inspection not even a radio.

His mind returned to Deeney as Robert watched him struggling to carry a large, labelled cotton sack back to the van. Deeney took a good look around before he swiftly opened the rear door of the van. He carelessly hefted the sack into the back of it and hit Robert full in the face. He closed the door firmly after him and waddled back to the front passenger seat, sweating and panting as he climbed in. Robert cried furiously at him, "Christ, can't you take it easy when you throw that stuff in? That's the fourth time you've hit me today!"

Deeney laughed at him. "Ach, don't be such a fucking pussy. The orders were, you fuckin' eejit, to get the stuff in and out as fast as possible. Come on. Let's move on to the next!"

Robert wasn't quite sure what Deeney had said. The man had the strongest Londonderry accent he'd ever heard. He understood some – something about getting the stuff in and out as fast as possible. He's got to be joking!

Robert snapped. "Get the stuff in and out fast! Are you kidding me! For fuck's sake man, you stand there talking for hours to these people while we're stuck waiting in here. Don't you realise how exposed and vulnerable we are? We'd get through so much more if you kept your trap shut!"

Deeney could only manage to turn his vast body halfway round to face Robert. Iowa stared straight ahead as Deeney spoke in his nasty, aggressive voice.

"Listen to me, you English fucker. I'm doing my bit here. If I don't talk to these people, one, it will look strange. They know me; they've known me for years. They EXPECT me to talk.

"Two – and fucking more importantly – you bastards want me to find out information, don't ya… don't ya? So if I don't talk, they don't talk! Stop giving off to me about fucking taking too long. I'm doing what the British Army asked me to do and let's face it, *mate*, you don't like me, and I certainly don't fuckin' like you since all you've fucking done is fucking complain! Your woman there, she's all right, doesn't say a fucking word!"

Deeney turned to face the front and whispered to himself under his breath. Robert hated him more now but knew he was right. The laundryman was doing what they'd asked.

Deeney picked up a list from his lap and ordered as you would to a posh chauffeur,

"Okay, James, Blamfield Street. Straight ahead and second right."

Iowa started the van and they took off. Robert settled himself down at the back and picked up his Leica 35mm camera with its telephoto lens. He raised himself to look out of the side window. He noticed a crowd of hoods had gathered around Stones Corner.

He was excited, put the camera to his eye and focussed the lens in preparation for some close-ups. He shouted into the front, "Slow down a bit, will you? I'll get some good shots here."

The van slowed down, and Robert took numerous images one after the other. Suddenly the van stopped completely, and he cried out angrily. They shouldn't stop here. It was too dangerous. Christ!

"Why are we stopping?"

Up ahead Iowa spotted two RUC jeeps and a Saracen. They'd halted the traffic. In a controlled voice, she told them, "It's a checkpoint up ahead. Sit back."

Deeney mumbled under his breath, "I hope to fuck these guys know who you are. Otherwise, this could be fucking it."

The van moved forward until it had no choice but to stop. Iowa was right, it was a police checkpoint, which couldn't have been worse. Very little, if any, information about operatives was shared between the army and police.

Iowa wound down the driver's window. Robert couldn't see what was happening but heard a man's voice.

"Morning, missus. Can I have your driving licence, please?" The policeman bent down to look across to the passenger seat and laughed heartily.

"Is that you in there, Deeney? You don't normally do the rounds yourself. Where's wee Rob?"

Deeney responded nervously and babbled.

"Who… Rob? Sure did you not hear, got himself involved. He's on the run; sure I thought you'd know that! Business was bad enough without all this shite going on. I'm just trying to make a living. You know what it's like. I mean, we all have to work, right?"

He continued on and on about how unfair and difficult life was. The policeman couldn't get him to stop talking and soon grew bored. He looked questioningly at Iowa. Deeney picked up on it.

"This is me niece over from England. Bless her wee heart, her Mammy came up with the idea of sending her over – wanted to keep her away from boys – you know what I mean?" He winked at the policeman who nodded knowingly, having two daughters himself.

"Poor wee girl's never been nowhere and doesn't say very much, mind, but then she probably doesn't get a chance to get a word in with me. You know what I'm like. I'm dead pleased, though… I mean, you can't trust anyone these days, sir – at least she's family, eh? You can trust family. I'm a fucking lucky man!"

Robert closed his eyes and clenched his fists and wished to fuck Deeney would shut up.

Iowa passed her licence to the policeman, who paid little attention to it but commented solemnly, "You are that, Deeney, a lucky man. Family is what it's all about. Thanks, missus. Can you just open the back of the van for me, please, 'til I take a quick look? You never know what you could be up to, Deeney!"

Adrenalin screamed through Robert. His heart rate hit the top of the scale, and time stood still. He was sure they were finished. He could almost hear his watch ticking.

Deeney nearly died on the spot but coughed in an effort to regain some composure. Suddenly there was an almighty thud on the roof of the van, and the policeman hollered: "Deeney, get yourself out of here, quick! Christ, man, they're at us. Get that wee girl out of here now!"

Robert cautiously peered through the window. It was like the Cavalry – literally! He never thought he'd be as glad to see a sea of rioters with masks and handkerchiefs over their faces attack a police Land Rover.

The policeman ran like wildfire towards the jeep. Robert roared at the top of his voice, "Iowa, *MOVE NOW. MOVE!*"

The van was already moving – fast – as she drove away from the riot and into the safety of Blamfield Street.

All three of them were flung about as Iowa braked hard and stopped the van. Deeney breathed in hard and fast and then slowly began to laugh. It grew louder and louder as he lost control. His fat Buddha frame was such a sight as it shook uncontrollably that Robert couldn't help but laugh himself. Iowa was her usual self, but Robert saw the merest hint of a smile on the side of her face.

Deeney wiped his eyes with his sleeve and cried, "Fuck me! That was close! Fuck me! Brilliant!"

They sat for a few minutes and allowed themselves to calm down. Deeney looked around to work out where they were, studied his list, then opened the van door. He stepped down and waddled to the nearest house. Robert's heart slowed and soon returned to its normal rate. He whispered to Iowa,

"Good work."

No response. Fifteen minutes passed in silence as they waited for Deeney, who stood chatting to a young, bearded, military-clad man. The man disappeared and returned with a load of laundry. They attempted to get it all into a single sack, with no luck. Robert took numerous wide-angle and close-up shots. He remembered the house and recognised Martin McLaughlin from his mugshot.

In frustration, Deeney grabbed the leftover laundry from McLaughlin and tucked it under his arm. He then held onto the other heavy sack. Deeney nodded at McLaughlin, who waved him goodbye. With the weight of the bag and extra laundry, Deeney truly struggled to make his way to the back of the van, where he dropped the sack and loose laundry onto the ground. He opened one half of the double doors, leaving Robert semi-exposed. The laundryman was exhausted and struggled to breathe. Suddenly the house's red door opened again, and McLaughlin cried out urgently with more laundry in his hand.

"Hold it, Deeney, there's a bit more! Here. Me ma's all fucked up over me da. If I don't give you all the washin' our Caitlin will kill me!"

Deeney stood breathless and shocked as McLaughlin cranked open the door some more. As the men continued to talk outside, Robert frantically picked up the camera and radio and shrank to the farthest point from the open van door, burying himself deeply in the stinking laundry sacks they'd collected that morning.

Thinking on his feet, Deeney quickly grabbed the laundry out of Martin's arms and told him, "Ah, sure, don't you worry, I've got it. I'll label it up later when I get back. Give it here."

Deeney calmly piled the laundry on top of some bags in the van and closed the open door. Robert heard him mumble, "Right, Martin. Right. Sorry again about your Da and now your Ma. Look after yourself."

As Iowa started the engine and the van moved on, Deeney sighed. Robert looked at him and grew worried. He looked awful. Sweat poured down the sides of his fat red face, and his lips were purple.

"You okay, Deeney?" Robert asked. The man couldn't be that bad – he'd just saved their bacon.

"Didn't need that on top of everything else today, did I? I just feel a bit funny, that's all. Fuck it! See that fucking young lad there... You need to keep an eye on that one. One angry man is that Martin McLaughlin. It was his da who got fucking beat up and died in custody there a while back. Fuckin' massive funeral, there's a lot of people still angry about it. A good man too. Never involved in anything, kept himself to himself. Fuckin' Martin was inside when it happened. They let him out to 'calm things down'. Fuck me, that was the worst thing they could have done, let him out. They said he murdered a cop but couldn't prove it."

Robert made a mental note of Deeney's tip. Training had taught them not to write anything down but to keep tabs in their head.

Finally, they returned to the launderette where all three of them removed the soiled laundry quickly from the back of the van and took it through into the makeshift forensic lab. Deeney grabbed a new sack and added McLaughlin's extra laundry to it, labelling it neatly.

"That's it," he announced. "I'm off. Too much fucking action for me in one day. I'll leave you to it. Night now."

Robert looked at him as he walked away. "Are you sure you're okay, mate?"

Deeney raised his right arm wearily and disappeared.

Iowa looked at Robert and shrugged her shoulders. He still couldn't get over her dress sense. Today she looked like a mannequin from a charity shop window. It seemed she deliberately wanted to make herself as unattractive and unpresentable as possible.

One of two white-coated lab technicians approached. In the time they'd been working with Deeney neither of them had spoken a word to him or Iowa. Geeks.

The woman surprised Robert by telling him in a monotone, "We've found substantial traces of gelignite on a number of the male items you guys brought in two days ago. Here you go. Good job."

That was it. The white coats said nothing more but handed Robert and Iowa their report. Robert was pleased at this news and looking forward to his evening with foxy Iowa…

Yeah, right.

Chapter Thirty-four

Once again, James sat at the dinner table. He'd messed up badly today with Caitlin and dreaded the evening ahead. The diners sat at one end of the table. James watched in disgust as Harris chomped his guinea fowl like it was his last meal on earth. Between guzzling his wine and chewing his food, he vented his rage about the McLaughlin "incident".

"I was only doing my duty, you know. No one told me the man had a bad heart! You've no idea the pressure they've put me under! No idea. They take me to check out these people and put me on the spot there and then. Sign there, they say. They never give me a chance to do a proper medical. It's like a production line. Tell me, what am I supposed to do?!"

James turned his eyes up and looked at his father in desperation. This was what he'd been afraid of. He didn't want to hear Harris's tirade since he didn't believe a word of it, and loyalty to Caitlin made him view the man with renewed disgust. He remained silent and listened as Roger answered him forcefully.

"I understand, Harris. However, I've said it before and I'll say it again: internment has been an unmitigated disaster. George Shalham is my friend, I know, but it appears the intel the RUC gave the Brits for the first bout of arrests was so outdated it included the names of dead men, for Christ's sake! And now the Government has asked Faulkner to add known UVF terrorists to their lists and he won't. I'm ashamed. This whole thing is shameful."

James sighed and thought. *Here we go again* whilst Harris paid no attention. He'd heard this shit so many times.

Roger was infuriated. "Not one Unionist has been arrested, and we **know** they're committing atrocities too. It's just ridiculous, bloody stupid! Then Bloody Sunday, fourteen dead, and Bloody Friday,

283

twenty-two bombs in Belfast in *one day*! And what are we left with?! An angry divided Province! Our beautiful country is now one of the most dangerous places in the world."

Harris watched Roger for a moment. He couldn't listen to this anymore. His head and heart hurt. Special Branch had him between a rock and a hard place. They'd told him he'd no choice but to do what he was told and no comebacks. They had "info" on him. Harris knew exactly what they had on him, and he was scared.

But Roger wasn't finished. "Harris, it turns out that man you're talking about, Patrick McLaughlin, well, he'd no history of involvement with any group. He was just another innocent. Internment has backfired; it's a catastrophe. Always has been, always will be, and after Bloody Sunday it seems to me it's the Provisionals who are benefitting the most from it in terms of attracting world attention."

Roger read avidly and listened in depth to the BBC News. It always depressed him, and he could see no hope for the future here. He was feeling old, tired and broken. Alcohol seemed to be the only thing that helped him relax these days. As for Rocola, he couldn't even think about what was happening there, not tonight anyway. He prayed James's proposal would work.

James Snr had returned from staying with Charles Jones in Belfast and was hyped up. He'd listened to Jones and begun to really understand his viewpoint on Northern Ireland. It all made sense to him now. He'd thoroughly enjoyed the visit and, to top it all, even managed a few wins at Blackjack. Jones had proved to be an exceptionally generous host.

He felt he understood the doctor's frustration and announced angrily to the table:

"They should be shot – all of them! If I had my way, I'd take them out and shoot each one of them through the head! It's a disgrace what's happening to Ulster, a bloody disgrace! Look what they've started – fuck their civil rights!"

Roger looked at his brother in surprise. What had happened to him recently? He was barely recognisable. He'd obviously fallen for Jones's bigoted rhetoric. Disappointed in such a foolish statement, he looked at his younger brother and answered him reproachfully.

"I'm disappointed in you. That's probably one of the most stupid things I've ever heard you say."

James Snr grunted angrily but otherwise remained quiet as Harris stopped eating and stared blankly back at his host. The doctor shook his head in frustration and slowly put down his knife and fork. He bit the inside of his lip and embraced the pain – at least it assured him he was still alive. In a low voice he said, "Well, Roger, tonight has certainly let me know whose side you're on. Tell me, how long have we been friends?" Harris waited for an answer that wasn't forthcoming before he continued speaking.

"Twenty-five years, Roger. And I came to your home tonight for moral support... But what do I get? You on your soapbox lecturing me. Get real, Roger! You're trying to tell *me* what's happening in this Province?

"Well, let me tell *you* something: I know exactly what's going on here. And why? Because I'm in the fucking middle of it, day after day! Don't you understand? I've been threatened, man. Told to get out or I'll be assassinated – I mean, shot! I love this country, and I'm the one being told to get out!"

As Harris spoke, James watched his anger mounting. They'd no idea he'd been threatened, and James could almost feel sorry for the unsavoury little man at that moment. Roger sat motionless and dumbstruck. Someone had to say something, so James attempted to appease their guest.

"Dr Harris... we had no idea. No idea at all. How can we help... What can we do?"

But Harris wasn't having any of it. It was too late, and he'd said enough. He dismissed the young man's concern.

"You can't do anything. Thank you."

Dinner was quiet and difficult after that, and soon Harris complained of fatigue. He desperately wanted to leave. He thanked Roger for dinner and took his leave under a very dark cloud.

Uncle and nephew escorted Harris to the front door and his car. They returned to the table, both feeling depressed, and fell into their respective seats in silence. James Snr watched and shrugged. James refilled their glasses and complained, "That was an unmitigated disaster."

Roger nodded. He was still slightly bewildered by the evening's events, especially his own brother's outburst.

"'fraid so," he sighed.

The young man scrutinised his uncle, who didn't look well. His face was grey, and his eyes watery. He looked tired and much older than his years.

"Are you alright?" asked James, since it seemed his father wasn't going to express any such concern.

Roger nodded and took a sip of wine. He was feeling quite drunk. Thank God.

Almost surprised at himself, he suddenly revealed to the table.

"You know what?" he told them both. "I'm a little bewildered as to why but somehow I feel relieved that Harris has gone. I mean, he was a good doctor to your Aunt Jocelyn when she was dying, and I've always been loyal to him because of that." He thought to himself before continuing. "To tell you the honest truth, I've never liked the little prick. He gives me the creeps!"

The two brothers laughed knowingly. James couldn't believe what he'd just heard. As soon as the older men calmed down Roger stared into a candle flame and observed,

"Serious stuff, mind, about the death threat. I don't know what we can do about that. Poor old bugger."

"I don't think we can do anything," James replied. His father made no comment until Roger soulfully answered.

"Anyway, let's see how it goes, shall we? I'm sure he'll sort something out – do a deal of some kind. He'll most likely be back."

James hoped he wouldn't see the doctor again too soon and, in an effort to change the subject, told Roger, "Well, Uncle, we're nearly there with our final list of attendees for the first meeting. Thirty-seven, I think it is. We've got some top dogs just as we wanted. George convinced the army to attend. It's obvious you're very highly thought of in this city. Credit to you. As soon as I mention your name, it's easy after that!"

Roger tried not to take the compliment and brushed it away with a wave of his hand.

"Don't be silly, James. You've done all the hard work. Don't flatter me."

The young man smiled. It was true. Roger was highly thought of – he'd been told many times how much his uncle was respected.

James Snr abruptly stood up and muttered goodnight before he disappeared to his room. Perplexed, Roger and James shook their heads.

"I'm not sure what's going on with Father. I'll try and talk to him tomorrow. Leave him to me," said James.

Roger shook his head and sighed. Everything was going wrong lately, and he wasn't sure what to do next. Christ, he was tired. If only his beautiful Jocelyn were still here. She'd know what to do – she always had. He half-listened as James continued.

"Going back to Rocola, Uncle, you've said it yourself. None of the political parties is prepared to talk about peace, but somehow we've managed to get them into one room for a whole day. I mean, all of them! It's a giant step forward. I know we're ostensibly meeting them to find a way to protect the factory, but it's bigger than that now. This could be the way ahead for Northern Ireland's whole future."

Roger recognised this was true and for the first time, acknowledged the scale of his nephew's undertaking. It was right what they said, he reflected: ignorance was bliss.

"It's quite an achievement, son. But please, believe me, there have been so many summits and meetings already and promises made... in the end for nothing! Be careful. You could be bitterly disappointed. We must stick to our agenda: where can we source additional investment, and how do we improve security? That's it. Politics and religious affiliations must not under any circumstances be mentioned, though, believe me; they'll tinge every breath of air in that room."

James nodded vehemently. He understood. "Security for the meeting has been thought through very carefully by George. He's taken a personal interest in making sure it'll all run smoothly and safely."

Roger was relieved. "That's good to hear. You've brought up some very valid points in what I've seen so far: the security of the workforce, the need to outsource locally, apprenticeships, cross-border trading and so on. I admire you, James, and I'm proud of you. These people are a tricky lot to deal with, but let's keep working at it. Perhaps, old man that I am, I need to dig deeper and have more faith, eh? Enough of that for tonight; now how about one for the road?"

James slept badly. He had upsetting dreams about Caitlin, the factory, his near carjacking and finally Harris.

Morning came, and he got out of bed slowly and ran his hands through his hair. He needed to talk to Caitlin. He needed to explain.

Chapter Thirty-five

The day after James asked her to spend the weekend with him, Caitlin noticed how tired and – unusually – unkempt he looked. He'd stayed in his office the whole day, not even taking a break for lunch as his meetings ran back to back.

She too felt exhausted after Martin's party had run into the very early hours and kept her awake most of the night. Fortunately, Big Charlie eventually came to her rescue by knocking angrily on the door and telling Michael and his friends to pipe down, or he'd punch their lights out! They weren't stupid enough to take on Charlie while they were drunker than he was. Caitlin didn't go downstairs but remained tucked up in bed, wide awake. There wasn't a sound from her mother's room.

Since their argument, she'd kept herself to herself. James spent the rest of the week on the road, and any communication between them had been strictly professional. Each night she'd check on her mother and make sure she was clean and fed. She'd only seen Tina briefly and still hadn't forgiven her for siding with Martin. She was pissed off with everyone and had been in a foul mood all week. She'd even snapped at an astonished Mrs Parkes!

It was late on Friday evening and time to go home and face a lonely weekend. It'd been over a month since the bomb yet it felt like yesterday and still no one had been charged.

She'd thought about James's suggestion all week. One minute she was furious. How dare he assume such a thing! The next minute, she'd feel like a prude. It was 1972 after all, not 1872. She didn't know what to think.

As she picked up her bag to leave on Friday, she was startled to see James appear in the doorway. He wasn't due to come back to the office that day.

He looked around. They were alone. She looked as down as he felt.

It had been a very long and shitty week – there was no other way to describe it. He hadn't stopped working and couldn't find the right time to talk to her and explain. He'd lifted the phone so many times but each time put it back down without calling her. He already knew what she thought of him.

"Caitlin," he acknowledged her.

"Mr Henderson," she replied coolly.

"Everyone gone?"

Caitlin looked around and was suddenly nervous. "Yeah. I'm just about to go myself. I'll see you on Monday."

She buttoned her coat up and put her bag over her shoulder. James didn't move from the doorway. He stared intently at her, daring her to look at him. He wouldn't let her through. She dropped her eyes and spoke softly.

"James. Please. I have to go."

She tried to leave again, but he stopped her and touched her hand. It felt as if someone had set fire to it. His voice was full of remorse when he started to explain.

"Ah, Caitlin, you've got me so wrong. When I suggested… you know. Well, it all came out wrong, and I am very sorry. I would never take advantage. I didn't mean to ask if you would come away with me – together – I mean. Jesus! I'm not explaining this very well, am I?"

He was nervous and making a total arse of it again! He sighed and placed his briefcase on the ground. He held her by the arms, but lightly so that she knew she could shrug him off if she wanted to.

"What I meant was that we could use the party as an excuse to be to-gether, but obviously in separate rooms. I never meant for us – you know – to be together, together. Believe it or not, I really am a gentleman!"

Her face reddened. Shit. She'd got it wrong. *She* was the one who'd assumed the worst and hadn't given him a chance to explain. What a stupid waste of time and indignation.

"It was more the way you asked me – just out of the blue – and your tone. You were quite abrupt."

He shrugged. He couldn't deny it.

"I know, Caitlin. I know. I just thought since you were so upset over Harris, I'd try to cheer you up. Boy, did that backfire!"

She was feeling horribly guilty, but in spite of everything smiled and added impishly, "I must admit, it wasn't the most romantic way to ask for a first date."

He smiled with relief. "Can I try again then, please?"

She couldn't say no. "Fine."

James double-checked to ensure no one else was around. He threw his arms open and formally requested, "Miss McLaughlin. Would you like to go to Donegal Town with me for dinner and to stay the night – in separate rooms, of course!"

She gave him a stern look as she pretended to think about it but soon broke into a smile.

"Mr Henderson, I'd be delighted to go for dinner with you in Donegal Town and to stay the night – in separate rooms, of course!"

He whooped loudly and hugged her quickly before anyone saw them. She nearly wept with joy.

Chapter Thirty-six

James always loved Fridays, but this one was particularly special. They'd planned everything with great care and tonight would drive away for their weekend together.

James wasn't too sure his Uncle believed him when he'd said he was meeting some English friends, who were touring Ireland and staying in Donegal Town. James Snr only snorted and made little comment when James told him he'd be gone for a few days. His father had been in a nasty mood for a while now, and James had no idea what was going on with him. The way he himself was feeling, he didn't particularly care.

The drive to the factory that morning had thankfully been uneventful, but the news was much grimmer than usual. That week alone five people died in separate incidents and Jack Lynch, the Irish Prime Minister, had closed down the Sinn Fein office in Dublin. It was depressing, but James couldn't remember the last time he'd felt so energised.

When he arrived in the office, Caitlin was already there working at her desk. Mrs Parkes had been ill for a few days, and with her absence, it felt like the whole building took a deep breath and sighed with relief. The atmosphere was much more relaxed as the team continued to work hard without her baleful presence overshadowing things. He had to suppress a smile when he saw Caitlin. She looked lovely. Her eyes were bright, her wounds healed, and a new and positive attitude radiated from her.

"Morning, Caitlin."

"Morning, James."

"I have a feeling this is going to be a good day," he told her as he walked through to his office.

"That it is, Mr Henderson. I'll bring you in a cup of tea in a second."

"No hurry. Thank you."

Once again, James spent most of his day in his office. He worked on his presentation and a storyboard for the first meeting and rarely saw Caitlin. When he did catch her, he noticed she seemed a bit edgy. She wasn't the only one; he was anxious too and focussed on his work to help control his nerves. By the end of the day, he'd produced a great set of numbers to present to the meeting.

Unusually, he heard the girls laughing in the outer office in their excitement at the forthcoming birthday party. It was good to hear them happy. Something needed to be done about Mrs Parkes.

He stood next to Caitlin's desk as the two young women giggled together and said their goodbyes. When they'd gone, he told her, "Hey off you go. I'll see you at Pennyburn Church. I've hired a car, so we're less obvious. I'll meet you at seven by the gate. Off you go before I take advantage of you. You're driving me crazy. Go, go, go!"

"I'm going! I'm going!"

Caitlin tidied her desk with hands that were suddenly clumsy and placed everything in a locked drawer. James snatched her coat from the stand and held it open for her. He caressed her shoulders as he tidied her collar. She shivered at his touch, and goosebumps crept up her back. She shot him a warning look and whispered mischievously, "I'll see you soon, Mr Henderson."

"Soon," he agreed happily.

Chapter Thirty-seven

Caitlin had attempted many times to see Anne as soon as she got out of hospital, but her mother told her the girl was too depressed to see anyone. She'd tried to insist but the poor woman, cradling a very young crying baby, could only apologise and close the door. Caitlin was left, forlorn and disappointed on the doorstep.

As predicted, Majella remained in bed oblivious to her surroundings. It was impossible for Caitlin to explain to her about the party. She'd been riddled with guilt – although that wasn't enough to stop her from going!

Tommy had called in earlier in the week. He'd said he was worried about his sister and felt they'd no choice but to ask his mother for help. He'd also confided that Martin was deeply involved with the Boys again. Caitlin wasn't surprised. She told him she'd be going to a party at the weekend and her Uncle had said he'd call in to see her before she left.

As soon as she'd left Rocola and walked home on Friday night, she opened the front door to be met by loud shouting. Without taking her coat off, she walked straight through to the kitchen and found herself in the middle of a raucous exchange between Tommy and her grandmother. Her uncle's face was puce with rage and frustration.

"…because I had no other choice, Ma, who else was going to pay?!"

Her grandmother raised one hand and pointed at him dramatically. "Tommy, have you any idea what you've done? It means we're committed to them now. Don't you understand – she's likely to kill you when she finds out!"

Caitlin's grandmother sat in her daughter's usual chair. She wore a floral crossover pinafore dress wrapped tightly around her scrawny body. Her long grey hair had been pinned up in a bun off her long face. She looked much older than the last time she'd visited the house.

Caitlin looked at her, questioningly.

"Who'll kill you, Tommy? What's going on?"

He stood next to the dish-filled sink, still in his flat black cap and long raincoat. Red-faced and fuming, he jabbed one finger at his mother and explained heatedly:

"She's giving out to me because the Boys paid for your Da's funeral and I haven't told Majella. I mean, who else was going to pay for it, eh? You've just enough money in this house to put the fucking electric on! And tell me this, Ma, where were *you* when Patrick died? You've got a few bob yet you didn't offer to help. You didn't even turn up! So don't you go all righteous with me and come in here and tell me what I've done right or wrong. I'm away to fuck out of here!"

Clearly infuriated by Tommy's harsh tone, his mother retorted, "Don't you dare use that language with me, Tommy O'Reilly! Do you hear?"

He'd had enough of the self-righteous old cow. He threw his cup into the sink, readjusted his cap, looked at Caitlin and said, "I'm off. I'm not listening to any more of this shite. Hope you enjoy the party, love. You're the only one who deserves a break around here, keeping this fucking mad-house together!"

With that, he left, and the two women were alone together. They weren't easy in each other's company. Caitlin's grandmother wore a sullen frown.

"So you're off for the weekend, are you? No one told me! You expect me to manage all of this on me own then?" Caitlin looked around the kitchen – the place was a real mess. But she didn't need to justify herself to her grandmother. She intended to get away as fast as she could.

"Granny, it's a twenty-first party. Everyone's going. I tried to tell Mammy, but she's gaga."

The older woman didn't respond directly. Instead, she stood up and walked over to the sink with its piled-high dirty dishes. She turned on the taps and muttered under her breath, "Do whatever the hell you like."

Caitlin ran to her bedroom. She'd already packed a few warm jumpers, a pair of jeans and a new red dress plus her best shoes. This time she hadn't forgotten tights. James had told her they'd go somewhere special for dinner tomorrow night. She couldn't wait!

As soon as she'd finished freshening up, she changed into her favourite jeans and pulled on a soft pink V-neck jumper. Her toiletries and best underwear were added to her small suitcase.

Before she went back downstairs, she popped in to check on her mother. Her grandmother's handiwork was evident. Caitlin saw that her mother lay in a fresh bed and wore a clean nightie. Her hair had been brushed and carefully plaited. Her face, however, was puffy and pale.

Caitlin nudged her gently on the arm. Her mother's grey eyes opened and focussed on her.

"Hello, love. You okay?" Caitlin was thrilled to hear her voice.

"I'm fine, Mammy. How are you?"

"Grand. The old battle-axe is here. Made me eat and won't give me any more tablets. Tommy tells me you're away for a birthday thing this weekend with the girlies. That's good, love. I'll be better when you come back, I promise."

Her eyes closed again.

"Love you."

"Love you too, sunshine."

A huge wave of guilt hit Caitlin as she rushed to her bedroom where she put her coat back on and grabbed her suitcase before speeding down the stairs. There wasn't any point in saying goodbye to her grandmother, so she opened the front door and found Martin standing there with his key in the air, about to come in.

He looked flushed and asked in a scornful voice, "You away then?"

She nodded and looked him over. "Yeah."

He still looked like a hobo, but worse. He hadn't shaved in days, and his long hair was greasy and unwashed. He reeked of booze and cigarettes, so she quickly turned her head and started to walk on, but he seized her arm to prevent her and forcefully pulled her back.

"Well, you have a *nice* time, Missy. Don't you be worrying about us round here. We're all fine and dandy!"

She pulled her arm free with difficulty. He smirked at her then staggered into the living room and slammed the door so hard it shook in its frame. Within seconds he'd switched on the TV and turned up the volume so loud that noise filled the house.

Having heard the commotion, Caitlin's grandmother came out of the kitchen, wiping her hands on a tea towel, and asked irritably, "Is that your Martin?"

Caitlin nodded and watched as she opened the living-room door and entered. Caitlin followed her. Her brother, still in his coat, lay sprawled out on the sofa. He stared sullenly at the older woman as she snapped the tea towel at his legs.

"Martin McLaughlin, you take those big filthy boots off that sofa *now!* Who do you think you are? You might have those out on the street afraid of you, but I'm not! So no jacking about… Feet off!"

Granny was able for him, Caitlin could see. With a muttered good-bye, she picked up her case and left for the bus stop. As she approached, the bus stood waiting, so she ran like crazy, grimacing as her case hit her legs. Fortunately, the driver saw her and waited. She climbed in, thanked him and walked to the back where she threw herself and her case onto an empty seat. She'd done it! She was out!

She was nervous about spending time in close proximity to James. She knew he was a gentleman, but whatever he'd said about not wanting to take advantage, it was inevitable that their thoughts would turn to sex when they were alone together. She knew hers already had! She was naturally nervous, given that she didn't know much about it – not really. She'd nearly done it with Seamus, but it hadn't felt right, and she'd pushed him away. Anne had taken a different attitude alto-gether; she was much more experienced and at times had talked about nothing else! She loved sex and described – in great detail – certain acts she'd performed on her lovers. They'd laughed together about the "extras" barbers would discreetly offer her older brothers after a haircut or shave, particularly extras for the weekend! Anne knew a lot more about men and how they thought and acted than Caitlin.

After a few stops, she watched a young couple get on. The girl looked scruffy and miserable. She was hauling a small suitcase and a plastic carrier full of books. Apart from her dress sense, Caitlin could see she was rather pretty. Shame she seemed so sad and obviously not interested in how she looked.

She assumed the guy with the girl was her boyfriend and looked at him more closely. There was something about him. She knew him… She was sure of it… But from where? He half-smiled as he caught her stare, sat down beside the sad girl and placed a suitcase of his own on his lap.

The bus drove on, and Caitlin forgot about the couple as she switched her thoughts to the weekend ahead. Finally, it was her stop. Feeling as excited as a schoolgirl, she jumped off after the young couple, who quickly disappeared in the opposite direction.

She looked around and spotted a black Cortina parked beside the iron gates of the church. James sat in the driver's seat.

She carefully crossed the busy road, pausing for a moment behind the car to open the rear door and toss her case carelessly onto the seat. She slammed the door shut and climbed in beside James.

He laughed as the car vibrated. "Are you sure it's closed?" he asked jokingly.

"Oh, God! Sorry, I always do that!"

Caitlin glowed with happiness. They were finally together on their own.

After a few miles, they approached the army border checkpoint. Not surprisingly, there was a long queue. It was always busy on a Friday evening. Those lucky few who had caravans or holiday homes over the border liked to get away to the safety of the Republic at the weekend.

From the little she could remember from school, Caitlin told James the history of Grianan of Aileach, a sixth-century stone ring fort that stood proudly on a hill as they drove past. The drive was pleasant and easy, both sharing stories from their childhood. They spoke of their dreams too, especially Caitlin's desire to travel and see the world. She loved Ireland but desperately wanted to see what else was out there.

James was fascinated to hear this – he'd never have guessed her wanting to be a wanderer. It was great to have the time and chance to find out more about her. Caitlin was incredible! There were a few moments when common sense would raise its ugly head and tell him this whole thing was dangerous. But he dismissed them. This girl was gloriously different from anyone he'd ever met. As he listened to her talk freely, he found her funny, intelligent and caring. It helped that she was very beautiful too.

Soon darkness fell, and they couldn't see any of the mountainous countryside, but James assured Caitlin it was stunning and she'd see it properly in the morning.

They arrived at a quaint upmarket hotel that had once been a grand manor house. The entrance hall blazed with light. A burnt orange terracotta tiled floor led to tall, black double doors with a young female receptionist in the hall on the other side, seated at a Georgian writing table.

They used fake names. How they'd laughed as they made them up: Jack Pointer and Siobhan White. James confidently completed the two registration cards, and soon a porter escorted them to their rooms. He took them to Caitlin's first and smiled as he opened the door. He knew any young lady would love this room, and he was right.

Instantly, Caitlin was taken to Wonderland. The room was like something from a dream; she'd never seen anything like it. A magnificent, red-draped four-poster bed took pride of place in the centre of the bare oak floor. The room's other eye-catching feature was a stained-glass window in glowing jewel colours. An open fire burned brightly in an iron grate set inside a carved wooden fire surround. She clapped her hands in delight when she looked around.

She saw another door and quickly wondered whether it led to James's room. She opened it warily and discovered a magnificent roll-top bath with big brass taps. The floor that surrounded it was tiled chessboard black and white. *It was perfect*, she thought but was surprised when for a second she felt a tinge of disappointment that it didn't lead to James's room.

The smiling porter placed her case on a luggage stand and passed her the key. He and James proceeded down the corridor. Finding herself alone, Caitlin screamed with pleasure and dived on top of the soft, yielding mattress. Sweet heaven but this was a big bed for just one person!

Chapter Thirty-eight

He was well aware that Auntie Kay didn't like him much and didn't give a fuck about him. Most of the time, he didn't like her either. She was a hypocrite. She'd be all holy holy and pretend to be a good Catholic, when he was sure every time that poor priest came into her house, she'd get wet between the legs! She looked nothing like his elegant mother, her sister. Kay was everything unattractive in a woman: short, obese, ugly, flat-chested and a royal pain in the arse. No surprise that she never married.

But Kieran was her only living relative and, pain that it was, he'd deliberately kept in with her. The house had to be worth something by now, and that antique crap she'd hoarded would be worth a bit one day. He hated to ask her outright for money but needs must.

Tonight they sat in her large kitchen and ate the dinner she'd prepared. He half-listened to her whining voice as she attempted to tell him what to do. He'd heard it all before. Nag, nag, nag...

"Do you know what you need, Kieran? You need a job. I've got three now – what about that, eh? Three!"

Auntie Kay used her fingers to emphasise her point. "There's the canteen at Rocola's, lunchtime, then cleaning St Peter's after school... and now the City Hotel. Hmmm, what is it they say? 'Without hard work, nothing grows but weeds.' That's it! That's right! Without hard work, nothing grows but weeds!" That's what you are, Kieran Kelly, a weed!"

She laughed heartily at her own joke and looked around lovingly at her sparkling, well laid out kitchen. Kieran watched her. A weed, eh! He had to admit that was funny, and fair play to her she did work hard. But he laughed at her inwardly as he allowed her to make her joke at his expense. Keep working hard, Aunty Kay, 'cos one day this will all be mine without me needing to work a stroke!

In an exaggerated fashion, and to stop her from nagging, he pretended to take a real interest in job number three.

"So what's the job at the City Hotel then?"

She seemed excited by the thought of it. "Well, it's only for a few days to start with. They've overbooked themselves for some top-secret thingy and two big posh weddings the week after next and need some extra help. Mrs McFadden says the hotel can't afford to turn down the business. It's just cleaning, mind, nothing important."

By now, she had Kieran's full attention.

"How do you mean – a top-secret thingy?"

She'd been warned not to say a word about the meeting and instantly regretted her loose tongue.

"I really can't tell you, love. Mrs McFadden said I had to keep me gob shut about it."

Auntie Kay topped up his tea and walked around the kitchen in the hope he'd not ask her more. She should have kept quiet, but she'd been so excited. The extra work meant she'd get those new curtains she desperately wanted for her bedroom.

Kieran had to know more. There could be something in this for him. He told her to sit down and said, laughingly, "Sure, Mrs McFadden's got the biggest gob this side of Derry. It'll be on the front page of the Journal next. Go on, Auntie Kay, tell me more." He blessed himself and said in his most sincere voice: "Cross me heart; I won't say a word."

She slapped his hand and giggled.

"Honest to God, love, I can't say anymore. Sure I'd be fired before I even started!"

Kieran picked at his food and put on a show of disappointment. "Ah, right then. I get it."

She knew precisely what he was about, and most of the time, she didn't really like her nephew. He was a real pain in the arse – always asking her to lend him money that she never saw again. It was rare she'd find a good thing to say about him, but he was her only blood relative. When he was off gallivanting and doing whatever he did, she'd only Father McGuire for company. Bless his soul. He regularly called in for a cup of tea and a bit of cake. He was a decent man. Someone who always listened to her.

She watched Kieran's pathetic play-acting. Poor soul. She felt she should try to exercise more Christian compassion towards her sister's only child. She knew that he expected her to leave everything to him in her will. Well, he was in for a surprise. It was Father McGuire's.

She shook her head to dismiss her bad thoughts and said a quick Act of Contrition. Kieran sat in silence and continued to pick at his plate. Sure it couldn't do any harm to tell him. He was hardly likely to gossip since the little gobshite never had any friends! Kay huffed and wriggled a bit in her chair.

"All right, ye eejit, I'll tell you. Mind, you mustn't say a word, Kieran!"

He put on a big childish grin and looked suitably gratified. Bingo!

She told him all she knew. It wasn't a lot.

"There's some posh hob-nob meeting with loads of business-people from Derry and the like. That young Scottish fella from the big factory Rocola… Well, he's asked the police, the army and some Church people to meet him and these business types. That's all I know."

Kay wasn't very good at keeping secrets. She sighed and drank from a cup that – unbeknown to her nephew – held a good dollop of Jameson's along with her tea.

Kieran thought fast. This was exactly what he'd been waiting for. He remained calm and poker-faced.

"That's it? Jesus, Kay, you'd me dead excited there for a minute. Who cares about some old factory? It's all bullshit."

Kay was disappointed by her nephew's response. Selfish young git.

"Ah, Kieran, what about all those poor people if they lost their jobs? Most of the women in Creggan work at that factory. If those jobs go, half the town will go down with it and then what?"

She probably had a point, but he couldn't care less. However, to keep her sweet, he answered apologetically.

"Ah, well, I suppose when you put it like that – you might be right. Anyway, that dinner was lovely. Thanks."

As they ate dessert, Kieran listened to her with half an ear whilst she gossiped about the Parish.

His heart beat fiercely as a plan formed in his head. He'd heard nothing from McLaughlin since their encounter in the café some time back. He wondered if he could stay at Kay's for a while… Work on his new plan in peace.

At the end of their dinner, Kay was feeling merry, having drunk a substantial amount of "tea"! She'd convinced herself that she'd "sort of" enjoyed her nephew's company that night and – astoundingly – asked him: "Why don't you stay here for the weekend? I've been asked to go on a retreat. Mrs McFadden is going, and Father McGuire says Mrs Boyle cancelled at the last minute. She's not well. Don't say anything, but she's got a problem with the old alcohol."

Kay hiccupped and quickly continued: "I've got food in, and it'd be a sin for it to go to waste."

Kieran was flabbergasted. There was a God!

"Jesus, Kay, I was about to ask if I could stay a few days. My landlord's painting our building over the weekend and there's decorators everywhere – noisy gits!"

She realised what she'd just let herself in for and groaned inwardly. She always did stupid things when she drank. Kieran in her house, poking about in her things… She needed another. With her back to him, she slyly topped up her tea with the whiskey hidden behind the kitchen curtain. She cringed even more when she heard his next words.

"I don't suppose there's any chance you could ask Mrs McFadden for me if there's any work going?"

It never stopped with him, did it? But she reluctantly said she'd help him. After all, they were family.

Chapter Thirty-nine

The following morning, Kay – deliberately ignoring the fact she'd had too much to drink and was now feeling it but instead convincing herself she'd eaten something dodgy – left for the bus stop with Kieran walking alongside her. He carried her case for her, inwardly mortified to be seen out with such an apparition.

She looked ridiculous in a black lace scarf that hung veil-like over her head and covered her face. She was a big lump of walking black and reminded him of a Mafioso widow at an Italian funeral. She'd dressed herself in the scarf plus black coat, black tights, black shoes – and for what? To make a good impression on fusty old Father McGuire. He'd been right all along. She was a hypocrite. All the Holy Joes were.

She climbed onto the bus and walked down the aisle in search of an empty seat. Outside, Kieran mirrored her. As she sat, he shouted at the top of his voice through the glass window to her.

"Auntie Kay! Don't forget to say a prayer for me soul. Loads of them! You have a ball now and behave yourself… I've heard what happens at those retreats!"

She waved him off angrily and turned her cherry-red face away. Dear me, she didn't feel well, she didn't feel well at all. It must have been the pork.

Kieran couldn't stop laughing as he walked back to her house and made a phone call. He waited for an eternity until a voice finally answered. He asked for Honey and was told to wait. Jesus! He hung on and on until he heard her voice.

"Hello?"

"What took you so fuckin' long?"

Her heart hit the floor. She wouldn't have gone near the phone if she'd known it was him. As if reading her mind, before she could say a word or hang up on him, he spoke to her menacingly.

"Don't even think about it, Honey – do you hear me! Don't you fucking think about putting that phone down! Remember what I said 'cos if you hang up on me now, I fucking swear, I'll do it! I'll do you and the rest of your lot today! I AM SO READY!" She felt she had no choice. It was out of her hands now. He was in control, and she was lost, too tired to fight him anymore.

"Okay," she said reluctantly.

She was back.

"Good girl. Listen, Honey, I'm at my Auntie Kay's house, and I need you to come over."

He gave her the address. She hadn't known he had an Aunt, but then she hadn't known him at all. If she had, she'd never have set foot in this nightmare.

She told him reluctantly she'd get there as soon as she could and hung up.

By now Kieran had convinced himself Kay would get him into the City Hotel. She'd known Mrs MacFadden for centuries! He laughed as he recollected her embarrassment on the bus. Serves her right.

By lunchtime, Honey and Kieran sat together in Kay's kitchen. It hadn't taken long for Kieran to make his mark – the house was already a mess. He'd made a shopping list and passed it to Honey, who limply accepted it.

Fuck. He'd better make an effort with her. He needed her help this last time.

"You all right, Honey? You don't look the happiest."

She shrugged and said nothing.

He had to cheer her up. Raising his arms and waving them around, he said jokingly,

*"Did you know, me Auntie is going to leave this place to me? One day it'll **aaallllll** be mine! Would you like a kitchen like this, Honey?"*

Not with him, she wouldn't. She hated him so much, yet part of her acknowledged he looked so good in his tight blue denim shirt and jeans.

She watched him haul a black sports bag onto the table and care-fully open the zip. She immediately recognised the handgun when he placed it on the tabletop, followed by an automatic rifle. It brought back troubling memories of Val's tortured screams. Images of flowing blood and broken bone filled her head. She screamed and pointed at the weapons.

"For fuck's sake, Kieran! What the hell are you doing with those?!"

He placed his hand on her arm, but she jerked away from him.

"Relax, Honey. Those eejits that didn't turn up the night we did the Brit in, well, they haven't picked up this stuff yet, that's all. I've had it stashed away for them."

He took out some soft cloths and a few bottles and expertly took apart and cleaned the guns.

She peeped into the bag. Rounds and rounds of boxed ammunition lay at the bottom along with a clear plastic-covered packet of putty stuff.

She guessed what that was.

"Kieran, what the fuck are you doing? I'm really scared now!"

*Christ! Did she never give up? He worked hard at keeping himself calm otherwise he'd be forced to kill her right here and now. He composed himself and said quietly, "Chill, baby, and trust me. Will you **please** just sit there for a minute and give me some peace?"*

She sat and glanced around the room for a while, taking in the pho-tographs of Kieran as a boy with a tall, fine-boned woman – obviously his mother – and a short fat dumpy one, who must be Auntie Kay. There were other pictures of Kay too: in her garden… at a social in what looked like the church hall… in St Peter's Square… gathered around a country shrine with a group of neighbours and their priest. Honey's eyes dwelled on him the longest. She knew him.

Kieran's beautiful hands stroked and rubbed the gun components until they were pristine and gleaming. He slowly and meticulously repositioned each piece of the handgun one at a time until it was reassembled. Then he cleaned the automatic rifle and carefully wrapped both weapons in a soft cloth. Finally, he put them back in the bag and closed the fastener. Satisfied with his work, he looked at her and said confidently, "Honey, I have a great plan, and you're going to help me."

She sat quiet as a mouse as he told her what he wanted from her while inwardly she prayed for deliverance.

Chapter Forty

It happened so suddenly, but in hindsight, Robert hadn't been surprised. It was evident the laundryman's enormous body couldn't handle the physical side of the job let alone the mental pressure – especially after yesterday.

Early last night Deeney had suffered a fatal heart attack while he ate his dinner and watched TV. An office girl from the laundry found him. The poor girl needed to talk to him about the accounts and, unusually for Deeney; he hadn't phoned her like he did first thing every morning. She'd eventually given up and visited his home where she peered through the front window after he failed to answer the door. And there he was, sprawled on the living-room floor, his body smeared with spilt food and beer. The sight scared the living daylights out of her, so she ran and knocked hard at a neighbour's door. She'd eventually persuaded him to break a window and climb in to open Deeney's door.

It was a major setback for the undercover operation. They'd had communication the previous night that briefly raised their spirits and confirmed what the lab technician had said earlier. Their drudgery had paid off. A number of arrests were being planned.

Their current orders were to remain indoors until further notice. Robert thought he'd take the opportunity to catch up on some sleep, but sadly he couldn't while confined to the lumpy sofa. You could have cut the atmosphere between them with a knife as he gazed reproachfully at Iowa, sitting silent and comfortable on the double bed surrounded by her books. She wore what looked like a pair of men's striped pyjamas that engulfed her tiny frame.

He'd slept badly again last night, not because of the uncomfortable sofa but because of Iowa. She snored like a pig. He knew he couldn't say anything, though, or he'd have to live with the fall-out. He decided to make a hot drink so filled the black kettle from a single cold tap, lit the gas ring and placed it on top. He reached for a mug and asked politely, "D'you want tea?"

"Yes," she mumbled. He noticed she'd forgotten the other word.

"Yes, what?"

"Yes, *please*."

"Right." Good. Definitely progress. He made tea and added sugar to hers. She liked lots of sugar which – given her size – astounded him.

He placed her cup on top of a worn pine bedside table next to her. She seemed to be permanently surrounded by books. He wasn't even sure where she'd got them, but six or seven thick novels lay piled on the floor by the bedside table.

She looked up at him and enunciated sarcastically, "Thank you."

"You're welcome!" he retorted. Christ, he was sick of her attitude! He snatched her book from her hand, but she angrily grasped it back and looked at him as though she hated him.

"Listen, Kentucky. Just because you made me a cup of tea, it doesn't change the way I feel about you. Why don't you mind your own fucking business and leave me be!" she yelled at him.

Robert grimaced. He'd had enough of her nasty temper and, if she'd been a man, wouldn't have thought twice about lashing out. But she wasn't, and so he stopped himself. Instead, he spat angrily at her, "Fuck you, Iowa! What *is* your fucken problem anyway? Jesus, we're supposed to be in this together – a team, you know? You should have my back, but I don't see it happening! ***THAT IS NOT GOOD!***"

She hadn't expected such a display of anger. He looked at her with open contempt and said, "Is it 'cos I'm a man, Iowa? Are you a man-hater? Because, you know, if you prefer women that would explain everything. I mean, let's face it, you dress like a dyke!"

She flinched at his cruel words, placed a bookmark at her page and slowly closed the book. She put it down on the bedside table next to her untouched tea and studied him.

Kentucky was a good-looking guy, but he irritated the shit out of her. She'd taken an intense dislike to him as soon as she'd met him, and when she'd been assigned to partner him, she'd been beside herself. She didn't want to be responsible for *anyone's* back. That was why she'd wanted to join the covert branch. She wanted obscurity and purposely wore her pathetic clothes because she didn't want to be noticed. She felt empty and soulless, and that suited her. She had one purpose and one purpose only: to kill as many of those terrorist fuckers as she could, and **nothing** was going to stop her.

She'd been relieved when this assignment had been terminated by Deeney's death. It'd been torture for her, sitting close to his stinking lard body day after day. She hoped now to be sent somewhere else – preferably Belfast, and definitely on her own.

"Typical man's behaviour," she said snootily in answer to her partner's comment. "If you don't understand something, pin a label on it 'til you do."

Robert stood back, feeling a bit ashamed of himself, as Iowa swung her legs over the side of the bed, looked down at the floor and added pointedly, "Listen. I made it clear from day one I wanted to work on my own. I haven't got the energy or the time to sit and listen to your petty tantrums. For now, we are stuck in this godforsaken place together, so… please… stop huffing and puffing like a child and get out of my face!"

It was the longest she'd spoken to him since they'd met and every word was to the point. He felt like an ignorant fool. She'd got to him, and he'd lost it. If she wanted to be on her own, so be it. He'd brooded over her attitude for days, and now she'd made herself very clear. He searched for his coat, found it and put it on. Then he looked at her and said, "Okay, I'm gone!"

She couldn't let him leave. She grabbed his arm and yelled, "I didn't mean for you to walk out, you fool! We've been ordered to stay put. Jesus, man, don't be such a wanker!"

Robert glowered at her and snarled, "What? You think I'm going to sit here looking at that miserable face of yours for the rest of the day?" He pointed at the window and sneered, "I'd rather take my chances out there!"

They stared at each other. He knew she was right about not walking out, but her negativity and the dingy claustrophobic room were killing him. He shook his head wearily and slumped down on the sofa. He buried his face in his hands then ran them through his hair and in exasperation said, "Iowa... Please. What really is your prob—"

But suddenly there was a loud knock on the door, and the two soldiers raced for their weapons. As they'd been taught, they stood either side of the doorway with their handguns at the ready. Robert placed his face against the door panel and cried out loudly, "Hello."

Silence. He tried again. "Hello."

They heard movement from the other side of the door, and soon enough, a voice quavered, "Ah, hello. It's Mrs Mulligan here. I have an envelope for you. I'd slip it under the door, but I can't because of me back, you see. It nearly killed me climbing those stairs. I did shout up, but you two were screaming the house down!"

Robert nodded at Iowa and opened the door slowly. He hid his weapon as the old woman passed the envelope through the semi-open door. She muttered something incomprehensible and carefully made her way down the stairs, holding on for dear life to the rail. He knew he should make some effort to help her but couldn't be bothered. He locked the door and quickly read the contents of the envelope.

Abandon ship.
Pier F1. Black Sabre. 19.15 hours.

They were to abandon their base and the car and return to Pier F1, a code name for Fort George at the bottom of Pennyburn on the other side of Londonderry. The passwords were Black Sabre, and they had to be there at 7.15 pm this evening.

To pass the time, they spent the next few hours cleaning the bedsit until it was unrecognisable. It probably hadn't looked as good in years, and anyway, they couldn't leave any sign of having been there. They then cooked in silence, ate in silence, washed the dishes in silence and waited – in silence – until it was time to leave.

It would take at least thirty minutes to get to Pennyburn. For Robert, it'd been the longest afternoon of his life. For Iowa, his brooding silence had been a godsend.

A little after six-thirty, they left the townhouse and immediately linked arms like any other couple on their way to the bus stop. They each carried their suitcase and Iowa her precious books.

When they arrived at the stop, an old man and woman acknowledged them with a smile. The bus arrived quickly, so Robert stepped on board first to pay the driver, who looked as pissed off as Robert felt. Iowa followed him along the aisle towards some empty seats. From habit, they studied the passengers carefully as they passed. Surprisingly, Robert recognised a beautiful young woman who sat alone next to a window. She felt his stare and looked at him, seeming puzzled. He remembered that face well and suppressed a small smile as he sat down and placed his case on his knees. His heart raced. He knew she was likely trying to figure out who he was. There wasn't a chance in hell she'd remember – she couldn't, it was pretty dark with his black painted face.

A while later Robert nudged Iowa. It was their stop. He pressed the bell and waited while the bus slowed. The young woman got up too and glanced at him again. Robert quickly looked away. As they climbed

313

down, he grabbed Iowa's arm roughly and dragged her in the direction of Fort George near Pennyburn. After a few strides, he looked back to see the girl from the bus crossing the road in the opposite direction. He sighed and relaxed.

Iowa knew something was going on and asked him, "What's the matter? Who was that?"

"Just some girl," he muttered in response.

She wasn't happy with his explanation so stopped walking and whispered harshly,

"Just some girl? What girl?!"

"I've seen her before. That's all. I thought she might know me."

Iowa couldn't believe him. "That's all! Jesus, are you serious?"

Robert hissed, "She wasn't sure it was me… and don't raise your voice."

"I'm **NOT** raising my voice. Don't you realise, this could jeopardise everything?"

Of course, he knew that and only half-listened while Iowa continued to rage until they reached the Fort's gate. Robert gave the passwords. They were immediately ordered in and led to a small meeting room where they were told to wait.

While she still had the chance before anyone else came in, Iowa told him in a threatening tone, "You've a choice here, Kentucky, you either tell me who that girl is or I'll report you."

Robert didn't like her tone, not one bit, but deliberately appeared unbothered.

"Take it easy! I was holed up in her garden doing surveillance in Creggan a while back when she caught me but didn't squeal. There's no way she'd recognise me. I mean, the light was shit that morning, and I was camouflaged up. So will you fucking let it go, *please?* You're really beginning to get on my nerves."

His complacency infuriated her, and she was on the verge of losing it when the meeting room door swung open, and a man dressed in civvies entered. Neither of them had ever seen him before.

He was in his late fifties, medium height with thin greying hair. He was dressed in a navy three-piece suit and a white shirt. A red tie hung loosely around his neck. He was smoking a cigarette that dangled from one corner of his mouth. He looked tense and dishevelled and reminded Iowa of the way her father had looked when he'd come through their front door after a tough day at the office.

The tired man barely acknowledged them, but he did introduce himself as their handler. They'd already sensed he was high up in the chain of command. In a strong Belfast accent, he told them, "I understand you've done some good work in your first operation. It was only disappointing that lump of shite cut it short, dying on us." The handler stood up, walked around the room and finally flicked some cigarette ash onto the floor.

"We've got some sound intel and updated mug-shots from your stint there. Anyway, you'll hear more about it tomorrow morning at your formal debriefing here at 09.30 hours. Most likely you'll continue with the next phase of your training and remain together as a unit since—"

"But sir!" Iowa broke in. She rose from her seat so fast it fell back onto the ash-strewn concrete floor. Its steel frame made an almighty crashing noise as it fell.

With a stare as sharp as a razor, the man looked at her. He was clearly insulted and not used to being interrupted.

Iowa knew she'd cocked up and slowly righted the chair. She stared at him and nodded an apology. Robert watched but felt no pity for her.

The man spoke coldly and directly at Iowa.

"As I said... before I was interrupted." He paused while he stubbed out his cigarette. "You will remain together as a unit since it appears you have done remarkably well in such a short time in Londonderry. So, 09.30 hours debriefing. Goodnight."

He left them then, off to conduct another long night of interrogations.

Chapter Forty-one

James was thrilled Caitlin was so pleased with her hotel room. It hadn't been cheap, but her reaction had been worth every penny. He'd learned so much more about her on the journey here, and finally, they had a whole weekend to spend together.

It was clear she loved her family. She talked about the tragedy of losing her father and the effect it had on her heartbroken mother. It was especially sad when she told him how Martin had changed from a fun-loving young lad into an angry and bitter man. His experiences in prison changed him beyond recognition, and she found him hard to tolerate now. Even worse, she blamed him for her father's death. James just listened and made no comment. She laughed when she told him stories about Anne and their long friendship. Her eyes welled up when she talked about the explosion and how her friend's injury had broken her spirit.

So many young men and women like Caitlin had suffered here. He learned that a lot of them had left the city to find work overseas and, to his surprise, that she wanted to do the same thing. She was adamant about wanting to travel, though the thought of her leaving came as a shock to him.

They ate together in the bar since it was getting late and the dining room was closing. After supper, they sat in the snug by the fire. The smell of burning turf was strong and comforting. They drank hot whiskies and stared contently into the flames. There was no awkwardness in their silence; they were comfortable together, each lost in thought.

James studied Caitlin from the corner of his eye. She looked flushed but appeared relaxed. Good. He wanted her to forget the pain and trauma she had suffered recently. She caught his eye and smiled lazily at him.

"I do believe, Mr Henderson, that I'm a little bit tipsy!"

He couldn't understand how. She'd only had two glasses of wine with supper and had hardly touched her whiskey.

"Well, Miss McLaughlin, evidently it doesn't take a lot to get you tipsy."

She hiccupped. "I told you, I'm not used to drinking – especially at this time of night!"

Pointing to her unfinished drink, he whispered, "Why don't you leave that and we'll get to bed? I've got a full day planned tomorrow, and we're out in the evening, so it's likely we'll be late."

She suddenly sat upright, placed her hand on her chest and said loudly,

"Mr Henderson, are you propositioning me?"

He wasn't sure if she was serious or not until she shrieked with laughter and pointed at him.

"You should have seen the look on your face. I'm joking! I think you may be right about going to bed, though. It's just this place is so beautiful I want to make the most of it. I never thought I'd ever feel like this or be in a place like this – it's just amazing!"

James smiled with relief and finished his drink. He offered his hand to help her up, and she smiled and swayed towards him until their faces almost touched. She said shyly, "James, I can't thank you enough. Thank you."

She leaned forward and kissed him gently on the lips. He looked at her for a few seconds then took her hand.

"You're very welcome, Caitlin. Let's just enjoy this weekend and forget about the rest of the world."

He led her to her room, where it took every ounce of self-control for her to remember what he'd promised and act like a perfect gentleman. He reluctantly kissed her goodnight and walked back to his own room.

The following morning he found her at the breakfast table waiting for him. The sun shone so they decided to take a long walk around Lough Eske. It turned out to be a magnificent day.

For lunch, they'd sat on a park bench and basked in the autumn warmth, eating fish and chips from a newspaper. Dinner couldn't have been more different. They dressed up and ate at a beautiful fish restaurant in Castle Eske just outside Donegal Town. The flavours of the food and its presentation stunned Caitlin. She'd devoured every morsel.

Afterwards, they'd been invited to join a wedding party where they listened to traditional Irish music, danced and got quite merry.

When they got back to the hotel, they staggered along the corridor towards Caitlin's room. James had had an incredible day but felt it had gone too fast. It seemed only minutes ago that they were having breakfast, and now the day was almost over. Caitlin looked radiant tonight. Her hair was loose, and she wore little makeup and a simple red dress with black shoes. She had no pretensions and talked freely to everyone and laughed with them light-heartedly. He'd loved the way she was so friendly. She made him feel alive and carefree.

He laughed when she attempted to open the door but missed the lock. After a few attempts, he took the key off her and opened the door. He wasn't quite sure what to do next and suddenly felt completely sober. Christ! This was painful. The last thing he wanted to do was spoil the night, so he stood in silence and waited by the threshold of her room. He couldn't believe it when she said tentatively, "Do you want to come in?"

His body screamed yes, but he didn't want to risk upsetting her.

"I don't think so, Caitlin. I'd love to, but I did promise to be a gentleman."

She felt warm, fuzzy and truly happy. She knew she'd had too much to drink but didn't care. Today had been the happiest day of her life.

"I know you did, and I trust you. I don't want the day to end. Please, James. Come inside."

Caitlin wanted him desperately. Alcohol had drowned most of her inhibitions, but she was still slightly nervous. James tried to refuse again, but she insisted, and soon he followed her into the room.

Almost afraid of not being able to handle himself, he ordered a bottle of Chianti Classico from room service as a diversion. His plan was that they'd sit together for a while, have a nightcap and talk. Nothing more.

He put the phone down on its cradle and looked at her. While he watched, she stood up and turned off the main lights. Bugger. Within seconds she was standing in front of him, close enough to touch. His fingers lightly brushed one of the small round imitation pearl earrings she always wore. He looked deep into azure eyes that sparkled back at him, full of trust. He froze for a moment, reluctant to do anything to shatter the mood of the moment, and she sensed this. She assured him with a smile: *It's okay, I'm ready.*

He understood and kissed her pouting lips. It was an undemanding kiss at first, but soon he became much more eager. He struggled to control himself.

"You are so beautiful, Caitlin. But we have to take this slowly, difficult as it is for me. And trust me – *it-is-difficult!* Give me just a minute, okay? Why don't you take a lazy soak in that amazing bath in there? I'll call you when the wine arrives."

Caitlin was disappointed. She knew he'd been trying to be kind, but she wanted him to know she was very much aware of what she was doing. She didn't want him to think she was inexperienced because she wasn't – well, not really. School had been useless. The poor nuns spoke so clinically about sex that their pupils squirmed in their chairs with embarrassment and some with revulsion. It was obvious they were teaching something they'd never experienced themselves nor ever would – the lessons were horribly awkward, and none of the pupils dared to ask any questions.

At home, sex was a taboo subject, so Anne had been Caitlin's chief adviser. With James, everything felt different from the way it had with Seamus. She wanted to do everything... wanted to please him. She decided to take control. She grabbed James's hand and whispered, "My bath can wait."

She started to kiss him. Without warning, he felt her fingers fumbling at his belt. He was astonished when she unbuckled it and obviously wasn't going to stop. He'd certainly not expected this! She continued to whisper reassuringly in his ear. He was intrigued to see where this would lead.

"What are you up to?" he murmured.

Caitlin wasn't quite sure herself, but she'd remembered some of Anne's tips.

"Trust me. Please. Relax."

He wasn't going to stop her. She seemed to know what she was doing as she pulled his trousers and underpants down. He awkwardly kicked them off and tossed them aside. Caitlin placed her hands around his waist and trailed them down to cup his buttocks. She pulled him against her for a while, but soon her hands moved around to the front where she grasped him.

James couldn't help but respond to the touch of her fingers. He shivered and was soon fully aroused as they continued to kiss deeply. Caitlin led him to the bed where she sat him on the edge. Her eyes were full of desire as she looked at him intently. Her hair half-covered her face and made her look stunningly sexy. He knew then what she was intending to do. *Jesus, no way!*

As if she'd read his mind, she smiled mischievously and disappeared between his legs where she took him fully in her mouth. Delicious! He groaned and leaned back on one arm while gently caressing the top of her head with his free hand. His head fell back in ecstasy. Every nerve ending in his body was on alert, the exquisite sensations heightened by the pounding of his blood. She tasted and tormented him with her tongue until he lost himself on an unstoppable wave of desire.

He moaned deeply, lifted his head slightly and found her creeping up from the floor.

Caitlin knew now that Anne was right: *it* was lovely, but only with the right person. She'd enjoyed seeing him so powerless and vulnerable;

it had turned her on. She tingled at the thought and cried gleefully, "Time for that bath!"

James nodded, breathed deeply and grinned as Caitlin vanished into the bathroom, leaving the door ajar. He sank down on the bed with a racing heart and listened while she drew the bath. He was surprised when she began to sing and instantly recognised the song – Patsy Cline's "Crazy".

His emotions were in turmoil. Where on earth had she learned to do *that*? Unbelievable. He shook his head and chuckled as she sang. She hadn't a note in her head!

Minutes passed while the bath filled. James jumped off the bed and took down a white towelling bathrobe from the wardrobe. Without thinking, he found himself looking into the bathroom at Caitlin.

She hadn't noticed him as he watched her undress. He stared as she stripped off her dress to reveal a black lacy bra and simple black panties. She had the most glorious lean body he'd ever seen – like a ballet dancer's. She took off her underwear and naked, she finally turned to find him watching her.

"That's a bit sneaky!" she protested.

He laughed. He was in heaven – pure and simple.

"A lovely sight. Okay, I admit it, I'm a perv. But more importantly, where on earth did you learn to do *that*!"

"Learn to do *what*?" she asked with apparent innocence.

She felt amazing and not in the least shy in her nakedness. She appreciated that he was both surprised and noticeably pleased.

"*That*!" he laughed, pointing to the bedroom again.

"Ah, *that*! You wouldn't believe me. I'll tell you later; it's quite funny!"

Anne had told her about it. She'd seen some pictures in a porn magazine ages ago that some girl had found next to the Gents in the factory. A group of them had brought it into the Ladies' toilets, or "parlour" as they called it, and giggled together as they'd gawked at the images.

Anne had tried it herself on a couple of her then boyfriends. At first, she wasn't too sure, said some of the guys stank of wee, but with her last boyfriend it'd been different, and she liked it.

James couldn't imagine how Caitlin knew of such things, but frankly, he didn't care. It hadn't happened to him very often, and he certainly wasn't complaining.

"Caitlin McLaughlin, you are something else! However, you'd better turn that bath off, or we'll be in real trouble, it's about to overflow."

Caitlin looked at the bath, which was now filled to the brim with water and bubbles. "Jesus, I've put too much bubble bath in! Help me, James!"

She tried frantically to close the antiquated taps, but the bubbles kept rising, and they both laughed hysterically. James grabbed the tap and with difficulty closed off the flowing water. Wet and covered in bubbles, they sat down exhausted on the saturated floor and howled with laughter.

There was a loud knock on the bedroom door. James got up quickly and answered it to find a night porter with a tray looking worried.

"Room Service, sir. Everything all right?"

James grinned at him.

"Ah, yes, we're great! Sorry. We had a problem with the bathroom taps. All sorted now, thank you."

The waiter needed to be reassured. His guest stood soaked and covered in bubbles, even with his bathrobe on. What in God's name were they doing in there! At least he had something to write in his logbook. Not much happened in this neck of the woods, and he was normally bored stiff. He'd definitely heard a scream and made a move to enter the bedroom as he said, "Sir, I'm sure I heard a woman crying out."

James put out his hand and stopped the night porter in his tracks. "Ah, no. Not at all! We just had a mishap with the bath. We're good now. Thank you." With that, he smiled, took the tray and closed the door.

Caitlin laughed to herself as she closed the bathroom door. Good thing the waiter hadn't insisted on coming any further! She tied up her hair and descended slowly into the deliciously hot water. Sheer luxury so far away from the cold bathroom and water at home. Her body tingled as goosebumps from the heat engulfed her. She rested her head back, inhaled deeply and closed her eyes in thought.

She knew she'd surprised him. Jesus, she'd surprised herself! Her Catholic guilt struggled to be heard for a while, but she ignored it. She hummed a tune to keep it at bay. She wasn't going to let anyone or anything spoil her mood.

Moments later, James came into the bathroom. He could just see her under the vast volume of bubbles.

"Are you alive in there? Is it good?"

"Honestly, James, I don't think I've ever had a bath like this. We always run out of water at home and our bathroom's freezing! This is heaven. It's so lovely and hot."

She raised her hands and waved them around like a conductor as she sang:

"Oh Mary, this London's a wonderful sight...where the people are working by day and by night..."

He loved this side to her. She was relaxed and confident but, dear God, she couldn't sing for love nor money! He cringed as she hit a high note and asked mockingly.

"Tell me, Caitlin McLaughlin, where'd you learn to sing like that?"

She knew she couldn't hold a note but was so happy and carefree that she didn't care. She was happy, so she was singing.

"I'm told I'm a natural. Do you think I've got potential?"

James shook his head and smiled. He looked at this beautiful Caitlin and, for a laugh, suggested, "Can I join you in heaven?"

She blushed. He'd caught her off guard. A bath – the two of them together in a bath! She sat up and asked in surprise, "Really? Both of us in here!"

"Yip, but you'd better let some water out first otherwise we'll be in real trouble!"

Any self-consciousness they'd had left was soon wiped out as he watched Caitlin move to release the bath plug. Bubbles stuck to her back and slid down the sides of her small, firm breasts with their perky brown nipples. His body began to respond. He quickly walked back to the bedroom and shouted, "Don't let out too much water! I'll be there in a second!"

He switched the radio on and soon found the warm, velvety tones of Ella Fitzgerald. He smiled with relief when Caitlin stopped singing. He poured two glasses of red wine and carried them into the bathroom. Caitlin chuckled when she saw them and took one from him.

James placed his carefully on a stool by the bath and removed his robe. Caitlin noticed his bruised ribs and saw him flinch when he bent over. She reached out a soapy hand and touched the spot tenderly.

"What happened?"

He wasn't going to tell her about his near hijacking.

"Oh, it's nothing. I'm fine. I told you; it happened at the gym. I got carried away, boxing and sparring."

She accepted his response – although she didn't believe him – and told him to be more careful next time. She sipped her wine and savoured its taste. Before this weekend, she'd never drunk red wine and discovered she liked it – a lot. She watched James step carefully into the bath. He was gorgeous and with such an erection! How weird life was. It could be so cruel and unfair on the one hand yet so amazing and fantastic on the other, and all within such a short time.

James knew he looked good. He worked hard to keep in shape. He saw desire in her eyes and relished it. This night was miraculous. He retrieved his glass and descended deeper into the suds. Caitlin was right: this was heaven, albeit as hot as hell. He raised his glass in a toast.

"To the weekend."

"The weekend," she replied merrily.

They sipped their wine and carefully placed their glasses on the floor next to the bath. Top to tail they lay back and savoured their intimacy. James played with Caitlin's toes. In silence, he teased each of them with his fingers.

Next, he moved his hands upwards and massaged her calves. Their eyes locked as his caressing hands crept higher to her thighs, waist and back.

He slid her body easily along the bath to face him more closely. She laughed timidly but instinctively wrapped her legs around his torso. His fingers stroked her back and moved around to her breasts. She moaned as he played with her foam-covered nipples and gently cupped them whilst he kissed her deeply. In time, he took a nipple in his mouth, licked it at first and then with great care teased it with his teeth.

Their intimate touching carried on until they were lost in their discovery of each other. His hands moved slowly down to her inner thigh where he delicately stroked between her legs. She found herself breathless as his momentum increased, and her heart raced wildly. What on God's earth was he doing! She wanted him to stop but at the same time needed him to continue; it was luscious! He toyed and teased her as he whispered soothingly in her hair.

"Relax, my love. Just enjoy it."

In rapture at his roaming and probing fingers, she found herself on the edge of a precipice, and soon a vast wave of intense pleasure conquered her. She cried out in liberated joy. She'd never felt anything like it! James smiled knowingly.

Caitlin shook her head, dazed.

"Mr Henderson. Where on earth did you learn to do *that?*"

He laughed. "Ah, now, that would be telling! You have to tell me your story first."

They kissed again until an almighty gurgling noise erupted from the tub.

"The plug's come out," he chortled. "Quickly, let's get out!"

He lurched from the hot bath and grabbed one of the warm towels from the rail. Caitlin rose and waited while he lovingly wrapped it around her. He kissed her shoulders and neck as he dried her off and slowly savoured her beauty. Like a young child, she turned around, and he dried her back and behind. He noticed a small round birthmark on her lower hip and kissed it. She smiled.

The bath soon emptied, and the couple picked up their glasses and walked into the bedroom. James pulled back one of two soft chairs before the fireplace. He topped up her glass.

"Madame! More wine?"

She nodded in acknowledgement and gave him her glass. She looked at the clock on the mantelpiece, which read 1.30 a.m. What a day! James sat on the chair, and Caitlin sat on his knee where they cuddled and chatted.

The wine was soon finished. While fused coals glowed warmly in the hearth, James took Caitlin's hand and pulled her down onto the sheepskin rug that lay before the fire. He'd never wanted anyone so badly. Earlier, as he'd tidied his clothes, he'd secretively retrieved a small silver packet from his wallet and placed it ready for use under the edge of the rug. He knew it was a sly move, but they had to be sensible.

They lay down together. James removed Caitlin's towel, threw it aside and looked longingly at her as he took in her perfect body. But for her birthmark, there wasn't a blemish on her. Her skin was milky white and smooth. She looked like a doll.

There was no need for further words. They both knew Caitlin wanted it as much as he did. They kissed, the energy between them intense. They lost themselves in uncontrolled passion with her taking him in her mouth again. But there was emotion there too. Their lovemaking was absolute.

Hours later, James lay still and awake on the rug. The room was cold since the fire had long gone out. Caitlin lay asleep next to him.

He was afraid to move in case he woke her. He'd never experienced lovemaking like that. His emotions had strayed into unknown territory. Caitlin continued to surprise him. She possessed such a natural and loving manner, thought only of pleasing him; he was both elated and terrified. *Oh, shit,* he thought. *Am I ready for this? Is this love?*

Chapter Forty-two

Caitlin woke and for a split second wasn't sure where she was. Christ, her head hurt! Her face clouded as memory took her back to the previous evening. *Sweet Jesus!*

In the cold light of day, she groaned and turned to see James looking at her sideways and smiling mischievously at her. "Morning, you."

She realised she was naked but refused to appear bothered by it. "Morning."

He seemed remarkably unfazed and laughed when he asked, "How's the head?"

She'd a hangover! *Oh, God! Make me disappear!* She groaned and answered quietly, "Not the best. How much wine did I drink?"

James had tried to tell her to slow down, but she hadn't listened.

"I did tell you. You drank half the bottle of red rather quickly last thing – on top of what you had at dinner."

She didn't trust herself to talk, so he told her comfortingly, "Young lady, you were amazing. You finally fell asleep on the rug, and I carried you to bed although you'd left me exhausted!"

She was mortified and said apologetically, "I'm sorry."

"Don't be silly! I had a fantastic time. I don't know about you?" he added. She hit him softly on the arm, and he squeezed her, relieved that she was okay with what had happened between them.

Caitlin swung herself around and faced him properly. She stretched like a cat and looked at him. He looked amazing in the morning light and very content indeed. They had spent a beautiful evening together and still had the day ahead to look forward to.

"Do we really have to get up? I mean, *right* now?"

She attempted to look contrite, but instead, it made her look even more desirable.

He grabbed and tickled her. "If you mean, do we have to get out of bed, no! I'm not letting you out of my sight, young lady!"

Their morning together was exceptional. They ate breakfast in bed, played and giggled like children under the sheets, and made love again. Reluctantly they had to get up for a late checkout and then ate a carbohydrate-laden carvery lunch. Soon it was time to leave. Caitlin was expected back home by teatime and didn't want to be late.

Thunder and rain accompanied them on their journey back. Unlike their trip on Friday evening, they were both quiet and thoughtful. James concentrated on driving, and Caitlin looked out of the window at the beautiful scenery. A nasty feeling of heaviness and melancholy threatened her newfound contentment, but she pushed it aside and sought comfort in watching James. He looked as sad as she felt so she tried to cheer him up.

"Well, Mr Henderson, that was quite an interview. I do believe I'll take the job!"

He smiled at her efforts, and they began to chat as normal, at least until they reached the border. Then a black cloud of reality washed over them.

As they waited in the queue, James felt miserable and told her sadly, "I don't want to go back."

She nodded in understanding. "I know. Neither do I."

The customs and border checkpoint were relatively quiet, and they were quickly through. As the car took them closer to the city, their hearts grew heavier. Caitlin felt as if hers would break, but after all James's kindness and loving, she didn't want him to see her upset so bit her lip and tried her best not to get emotional.

As they reached Pennyburn, he steered the car into a lay-by next to her bus stop. Concerned at the continuing heavy rain, he asked, "Are you sure you're okay getting the bus, my love? It's pouring. You'll get soaked. I can drive you home if you like."

She shook her head, vigorously. "I don't think so, James. We can't take the risk."

He grasped both her hands and squeezed them tight. Her stomach lurched painfully as she told him, quietly and sincerely, "I'm not going to kiss you now, James, for obvious reasons. I'm going to get out before I break down. I'll see you tomorrow. 'Bye and thank you for a truly wonderful weekend."

His heart dropped as he replied sadly, "Bye Caitlin. It was perfect, wasn't it? Night now."

She opened the car door and stepped out. Once again, she closed the door very hard and opened the boot for her suitcase. She lifted the case as he whispered,

"Missing you already."

"You too, James, you too." She shut the rear door.

Bang! James smiled as the car shook again. He watched her blow him a discreet kiss as she stood motionless in the rain. He drove away, and once he'd gone she sighed heavily and ran towards the bus stop. Given it was Sunday, she knew it'd be a slow service, and she'd have to change buses.

Sitting under the decrepit shelter, she reflected on the weekend and blushed several times as she relived everything. It had been perfect apart from her morning-after headache! She felt like a different person from the young woman she'd been on Friday. She knew she was no longer a naïve and innocent girl; James had made her a woman.

The bus arrived sooner than she'd expected, but the journey proved to be slow and depressing as the route took them along the abandoned WWII warehouses of the quayside and River Foyle towards the Guild-hall. The city always looked drab in the rain, and this impression was not helped by the many blown-out relics of once-proud Victorian buildings and warehouses.

Numerous army checkpoints slowed the journey. Caitlin pretended to be asleep as the caped soldiers walked up and down the aisle, mostly questioning the men and occasionally searching the women's handbags. Fortunately for Caitlin, she wasn't disturbed.

She arrived home and opened the front gate. A huge wave of depression hit her as she looked up at the house. She didn't mean to be ungrateful; she knew this was her home, but she'd grown to hate it with a vengeance – more so since her stay in Donegal. This was a house of pain. She thought of the luxurious bedroom and bathroom in the hotel and yearned to go back. It wasn't that she needed luxury all the time; she just wanted some sort of normality. Not having to worry about whether the electricity meter would run out, or if there was enough food on the table or indeed hot water for a bath, would have been luxury enough.

She hated the weather-worn, pebble-dashed front of the house. She hated its unkempt garden and even the pillar-box red door her father had painted last summer along with the matching, red-trimmed window frames. She couldn't survive here. She had to get out. But to where, and how?

She opened the door with her key and was greeted with the overwhelming smell of cabbage and bacon. She remembered the amazing aroma of the food she'd eaten over the weekend and felt even more disheartened. She placed her suitcase at the bottom of the stairs and took off her wet coat to hang up.

Before she entered the kitchen, Caitlin took a deep breath to pull herself together. She wiped herself down and tidied her hair. Inside she was greeted by Tommy, who sat beside her grandmother at the kitchen table.

Granny O'Reilly saw Caitlin and grunted, "How was it then?"

"Fine," she replied quietly. "It was good."

She made some fresh tea and offered them a cup. Tommy nodded. He appeared stressed and told her, "Listen, love. All hell broke loose on Saturday night. Your Martin's been lifted again. They found him in Mailey's bar having a pint. Something about traces of explosives on his clothes. Turns out that fat prick Deeney's been working for the Brits and their forensics people test everyone's laundry. Just as well the fucker's dead. Dropped like a boulder with a heart attack. Too good for him! Anyway, looks like Martin's away for the long term now."

As soon as she'd heard the news, Caitlin was amazed by her instinctive reaction. Relief! Martin hadn't been home long, but he'd been a nightmare and had made her life miserable. Fortunately, her relief didn't last long, nor did it show, and soon she felt guilty as hell. He was her brother, after all.

"Christ. Does Mammy know?"

Tommy yawned before he answered. "Nah, she's none the wiser. We've told her nothing. Your Granny's worked miracles here, so we don't want her to know yet. Majella's ate more in the last two days than she has in the past two weeks. Fair play to you, Mammy."

Tommy raised his cup to his mother, who waved away the compliment with her hand. Caitlin watched her fold a newly ironed blouse. The old woman looked at her son and told him haughtily, "Well, she's me daughter, isn't she? I'm not going to let her lie up there and starve 'til they take her out of this house in a box!"

Tommy winked at Caitlin and secretly pulled a face behind his mother's back. He smiled at her and answered dutifully, "No, Mother, you're not."

Caitlin grinned at his antics and stood up to leave. "I'm just going to check on her."

Her grandmother stopped folding the laundered clothes before her in a basket, looked at her and replied coldly, "Suit yourself."

Caitlin decided to ignore her and walked wearily out of the kitchen. Tommy cried out after her, "See you later. I'm glad you'd a good weekend. You deserved it, love!"

Caitlin reddened as a little voice inside her answered: *Bless you, Tommy. Little do you know!*

This house drained her of energy. Before going to see her mother, she knocked at Tina's bedroom door and waited. Nothing. She sighed at the lack of response, stepped away and entered her parents' bedroom where she smelled fresh bedlinen.

Majella was pleased to see her daughter and smiled at her lovingly. She tried to hug her but slumped down in the bed as she was still too weak.

"Ah, Caitlin. Did you have a good time, love?"

"I did, Mammy. It was great. Bit tired, though. How are you doing?"

Majella smiled. She was drying out and felt like shit but couldn't let anyone know. She'd the shivers and couldn't stop shaking. As for eating – it'd been a nightmare. However, she answered brightly, "I'm fine, love. Much better. I admit the old bat has tortured me to eat! She's even washed my hair. I might try and get up tomorrow. Start of a new week and all."

Caitlin was relieved. She'd thought her mother looked better but noticed her tremors still hadn't stopped.

"That's good, Mammy. You're shaking."

"Just cold. That's all," Majella muttered.

Caitlin tucked the blankets up and around her and fixed the pillows to make her warmer and more comfortable. She sat on the edge of the bed as her mother held her hand and asked feebly, "Where's Martin or Tina? I haven't seen them."

Caitlin wasn't going to tell her so answered, "Don't know! I haven't seen them either. Tommy's downstairs with Granny. I think he's trying to get back into her good books – he lost it with her on Friday night!"

Majella nodded. Her brother had visited her earlier.

"Ah, right, he told me. How's work, Caitlin? I know I've been zoned out, but I have been thinking about you. No more thoughts of young Mr Henderson, I hope?"

Caitlin lied blatantly.

"It's been really busy. And, no, I promised, didn't I? No more thoughts about Mr Henderson."

Majella was hugely relieved. She laid her head back and sighed. "Right. Good to know. I love you."

"Love you too, Mammy."

Caitlin walked to her bedroom and closed the door on the world. She didn't want to talk to anyone so got undressed and climbed into the cold bed. She covered herself up with heavy blankets to get warm as fast as she could. Memories of the weekend overcame all her other thoughts, and soon she was warmed up and relaxed. She relived every moment of it and felt both elated and terrified. Finally, she thought, *is this love?*

Chapter Forty-three

Kieran had enjoyed staying at Kay's. The fridge was full, and the house welcoming and warm. What little he'd seen of Honey irritated the shit out of him – she'd been withdrawn and miserable. Thank fuck she'd be out of his face soon!

Kay returned from her retreat in a frosty mood. However, he soon wooed her over, and she eventually gave in to his relentless good humour. She told him she'd got him an interview at the hotel and that, along with McLaughlin's re-arrest, convinced him life was sweet.

He'd returned to his flat last night but hadn't slept well. His head spun as he thought through his plan and sat eating cornflakes and drinking tea. Although tired, he felt good.

He'd deliberately kept away from alcohol to keep his head clear and to work through his idea. He'd already made a number of decisions. Honey would know nothing about his plan; she'd just help him get the gear on site. He'd rid himself of her immediately after the operation – she was too immature and innocent sexually and was becoming a liability. Her death would hurt her family badly, he knew. All to the good.

He finished his tea and threw himself onto the sofa. Kay had told him if he got the job, he'd need to provide his own clothes. That suited him. He'd prefer to wear his own stuff instead of some cheap uniform. He looked appreciatively at his open wardrobe, noting the few beautifully ironed shirts and trousers that hung perfectly on individual wooden hangers. He loved his clothes. When he'd left home at fifteen, he'd sworn he'd only buy and wear the very best. As a result, he didn't have many items but what he had was quality bought from the profits of unethical activities.

He had to find out more about this "secret" meeting. Kay remained vague, but he knew he was onto something big. He imagined the place full of police and soldiers or even, if he was lucky, some of those Proddy fuckers who controlled the city. What if he were to wipe them all out! He'd go it alone so there'd be no risk or need to rely on the Boys since they'd fucked him over with the soldier. He imagined the headliner in the Derry Journal, *"Wipe Out at City Hotel!"*

He was wound up and excited as he considered his options, but soon the notions were interrupted by a soft tap on the door. It was way too early for visitors. He ran to the bottom of the wardrobe and carefully removed the revolver from the sports bag. He added ammunition and heard another knock — this time much louder and impatient.

He walked to the door warily, and called, "Who is it?"

"It's me."

He smiled. How he loved that voice! He opened the door but kept the revolver in his hand. Alex saw the gun straight away and jumped back in fright. Kieran couldn't help himself; he laughed heartily as Alex cried, "That's not funny! You scared the living daylights out of me!"

The look on Alex's face made Kieran realise he'd gone too far.

"I'm sorry! I was only joking! God love you – you're white as a ghost!"

Alex wasn't pleased and walked past him stiff-backed as Kieran closed the door behind them. He expertly emptied the barrel of the revolver and placed it and the ammunition back in the sports bag. He offered to put the kettle on, but Alex didn't want anything.

"No, thanks. What the hell are you doing with a gun, Kieran?

"Precautions."

"What type of precautions?

Kieran shrugged. Alex knew he had been up to all sorts of shenanigans over the past few weeks, though details had been sparse.

"What's going on? Tell me. Please."

Kieran smiled back as he said gaily, "Listen, I've had a good weekend, and I missed you! I was at Kay's. And… I've got a job interview later this morning!"

At last some good news! "Wonderful! Where?"

"City Hotel."

Alex congratulated him. "Let's celebrate. Give me a big wet kiss then!"
The couple laughed as they kissed and fell down on the bed. The noise of their fall and laughter was followed by an angry knocking on the wall by the neighbour, which only made them laugh harder.

Kieran looked at his lover. "McLaughlin's been lifted. We're in the clear."

Alex was relieved. "So I heard, but I don't want to talk about him. Forget him now. Work is manic. Everyone's hyped up about some big meeting. Funnily enough, it's at the City Hotel. What's the interview for?"

Kieran couldn't believe his luck. He sat up, ignored Alex's question and asked innocently, "What meeting is that then?"

Alex couldn't really talk about it. "I can't say much although I bet half of Derry already know more than me!"

Kieran laughed at the coincidence and told him, "I've heard about it too!" He was amused to see Alex's shocked expression

"Tell me you're joking? What'd you hear?"

"Just that there was some big knob meeting being organised by that Scottish git from Rocola's, with all sorts of VIPs expected. That's all."

Alex's arms rose in exasperation.

"See what I mean? That's exactly my point! Who told you?"

"Only my wonderful benefactor, Auntie Kay."

Alex was really worried. The meeting's agenda and attendees justified complete secrecy.

"Jesus, that's not good, Kieran, if people know. I need to warn them. I won't be there meself, I'm just helping with some arrangements, but this could screw the whole thing up."

At these words, Kieran was even more intrigued.

"Why? What's the big deal?"

Alex daren't say anymore and answered nervously, "Nothing. It's nothing. Come here!"

But Kieran's internal antennae were bristling. He was right! This meeting was bigger than he'd thought.

They kissed and slowly undressed. Their lovemaking was harsh and brutal – exactly the way they liked it. For a split-second, Kieran thought about Honey and how he'd scared her. She'd never be able to turn him on like Alex. In comparison, she was too prim and innocent for his liking. He liked a bit of rough.

Their trembling bodies intertwined, sweat ran down their backs and legs. They whispered sexual taunts to each other about what they needed and were going to do. Intermittently, various sex toys were shared, further adding to their intense pleasure. Pain was a vital ingredient for both of them. The room was filled with moans and grunts as each sought fulfilment from the other.

They no longer heard the knocking on the wall from their disgruntled neighbour. They were in the zone. Their natural habitat.

After a while, too exhausted to continue, they lay in each other's arms in the crumpled bed, both extremely satisfied.

Kieran's tightly muscled stomach was tenderly stroked by Alex as he enjoyed a cigarette. Soon an idea floated into his head. As soon as he got this job over, why didn't they go away – just the two of them? He asked excitedly, "How about us taking a wee holiday somewhere? America maybe?"

Alex was doubtful. "I can't, Kieran. Not yet, anyway. I've only been here a few months, and I'd find it hard to come up with an excuse to get away."

But he was determined. He'd have to ask Kay for another loan, but if he got that and some more work over the next few weeks, he could pay for a great trip.

"We don't have to go straight away. It'd just give us something to look forward to. What about Miami? Think of all that sunshine. I'll get the money!"

Alex answered unhappily, "I can't, Kieran. I'm sorry. It's too soon."

At this, Kieran jumped out of bed. He violently squashed out his cigarette and cried in fury, "For fuck's sake, Alex, I've just asked you to come to Miami with me. Most people would jump at the chance!"

"Don't lose it with me, Kieran. It's not my fault. You know that. Come here." Alex patted the bed. "Come and lie next to me. Please."

Kieran sniffed and lay down reluctantly. Alex lovingly stroked his dark hair, and soon Kieran fell into a light sleep. There'd been subtle changes in his behaviour over the past few months and in particular the last weeks. Alex's pretence of not noticing the small items of women's clothing that lay around the flat and the faint smell of perfume hadn't been too hard to maintain. Their relationship was too strong to be rocked by a minor irritant such as that. Anyway, no one else could please and satisfy Kieran so much given the way they made love.

Alex trusted him implicitly and knew that without this continued trust, they'd never be together. Allowances had been made. They knew they were in dangerous waters and if they were found out – it didn't warrant thinking about!

A short time later, breaking free from Kieran as he slept, it was time for Alex to leave.

Not long after, Kieran woke to find the other side of the bed empty. Ah, fuck. He'd messed up. He rubbed his hands lazily through his hair and sighed as he searched for his watch. It lay next to their used sex toys, which he grabbed angrily and threw one after the other under the bed. In the harsh daylight, a sudden surge of anger engulfed him. He was bitterly ashamed and gutted that he couldn't show off Alex to the world. He felt disgusted with himself, and guilt encompassed him, but he couldn't help himself. He was too much in love.

Time to get up. Soon he was in the bathroom where he washed and shaved in preparation for his interview. Finally, he nodded approvingly at his appearance and left the flat.

Outside, he looked up at the blue sky and smiled. It was a beautiful morning. The hotel was only a short walk away. He enjoyed being out and about on days like this. Every step he took away from the flat improved his mood.

He waited in the queue for the first checkpoint at Butcher Gate – one of the seven gates of the walled city. When it was his turn, he raised his arms and spread his legs apart as he was searched by an unsmiling soldier then rapidly turned around. The soldier searched under his collar and literally patted Kieran's body down from head to toe.

All the time he studied the group of squaddies and wondered if any of them had known Val. He laughed inwardly and watched as they searched the men sullenly and feebly attempted to converse with the waiting women and children. None of the people responded or acknowledged them – they daren't.

He was waved off and walked away. He passed the shattered remnants of the War Memorial in The Diamond and saw for the first time the bombed-out Austins store and bank. The street looked like a war zone now. Most of its mature trees had been destroyed. He reached another checkpoint at Shipquay Gate and was once again searched.

Eventually, he got to Foyle Street and stepped up into the City Hotel. At reception, Kieran took an instant dislike to a fair-haired man in a tight grey suit, who asked him, in a musical voice, "Can I help you, sir?"

Clearly a raving queer, thought Kieran, before answering abruptly: "Mrs McFadden."

The receptionist hesitated and studied Kieran before he asked reproachfully,

"Do you have an appointment?"

He nodded. "Yes. Kieran Kelly."

The receptionist didn't like the look of him either and immediately sensed his loathing. He'd experienced contempt so many times in this small-minded hellhole of a city that it didn't bother him so much anymore. Not long now. He'd almost got enough saved to get the fuck off to London and then onwards to San Francisco.

"In relation to what, sir?"

"In relation to minding your own fucking business!" Kieran whispered venomously so no bystanders would hear. This guy pissed him off with all his questions.

The receptionist didn't react but stood unmoving and unperturbed. They stared at each other for a moment until he pointed to an empty chair by the revolving entrance door.

"Take a seat."

Kieran thought about saying something back to the twat but didn't. Normally he would have given him a good hiding for his attitude, but he couldn't fuck up this interview. He needed to get in. Meanwhile, he took a seat and coldly watched the poof meet and greet new guests.

Mrs McFadden soon arrived and shook Kieran's hand. She asked him to follow her. He took a final look at the receptionist who, to his annoyance, smiled back and waved at him. Kieran gave him the finger unbeknown to Mrs McFadden, who told him cheerfully, "Thanks for coming in, Kieran. I had a good weekend with your Auntie Kay. Has she recovered yet? I think I'm prayed out!"

She laughed as they walked through a door marked "Staff Only" that led into a noisy canteen. Several hotel employees, in various uniforms, sat at long bench tables and ate their breakfast and talked. Some looked up as the new arrivals entered but most paid little attention.

Mrs McFadden found the end of a quiet table in a far corner of the room and asked kindly, "Do you want a drink, Kieran?"

He shook his head. "No, I'm fine, Mrs McFadden. Thank you."

She told him to sit while she went and poured herself some hot water from a large catering urn and added a teabag. After a few seconds, she threw the teabag away and carefully carried the cup back to the table and sat down. In a cagey voice, she told him, "Now, Kieran, I'm not promising you much, but Kay said you needed work. Well, this is where I'm at. I need muscle to help with an event we're having here next week. We've booked two weddings and a huge business meeting all on the same day. Four hundred people. Jesus wept! Anyway, we need to turn the rooms around fast, and that's where I'd need you. We'll have to clear chairs and tables for the dance floors and such like. You'll be just working on the weddings, not the meeting. That's completely separate and organised already."

341

Kieran's heart dropped like a stone.

Mrs McFadden drank some tea before she added, "You'll have plenty to do before and at the weddings, believe me. Now the thing to remember is, security will be tighter than normal. You'll be given an ID badge that you'll have to wear all day. Other than that, that's really about it. If you do well, I'll try and sort you out something more permanent afterwards."

Deliberately flirting with her, Kieran answered, "You're an absolute star, Mrs McFadden, that's brilliant. But what's with all this extra security? Is the Prime Minister visiting or what?"

Mrs McFadden laughed heartily. "Ach, Jesus! It's nothing like that!" For a moment, she looked a little unsure. "At least I don't think so anyway. You'll get three pounds cash in hand a day. How does that sound?"

"Sounds perfect, Mrs McFadden. Thank you very much. You've made my day!"

He gave her his best smile. He knew he'd got the job, but he'd found out nothing else and was feeling pissed off. Mrs McFadden stood up to leave.

"Good stuff. All right then, six a.m. next Wednesday. By the way, Kay said you'd no problem getting a white shirt, black trousers and tie."

"All sorted, Mrs McFadden."

She liked him. He was nothing like his Auntie in the looks department, which was lucky for the lad. With a twinkle in her eye, she murmured, "'Course you are, Kieran. I'll see you then. Be good!"

Chapter Forty-four

After leaving Caitlin, James dropped off the hired car, returned to his own and decided he'd go to the factory. He wasn't ready to face his father or indeed his uncle and needed time to set his mind straight. Beating rain poured mercilessly onto the Jag.

As soon as he reached the factory gate, one of the four security men – an ex-professional boxer – stopped him and stood next to the car. James rolled down the window and attempted a smile.

The security guard had recognised the car instantly and was surprised – it was unusual for the young fella to visit the site at the weekend, especially on a Sunday. Rain drove into his face as he observed, "Mr Henderson, not like you to be here at the weekend. They've got you working on Sundays now, have they?"

James smiled and half-heartedly said, "Lots to do, Neil. All okay here?"

It'd been an uneventful day but the night before had been something else.

"Grand today, but mad and rowdy last night. Now the rain is on; it'll keep them rioters away. I'd put money on it, there'll be no trouble tonight with the bad weather, and there's some footie on the TV. Anyway, I'm here 'til the morning if you need me." James rolled the car window up and answered gratefully, "Thanks, Neil. See you later."

He waited patiently as the man opened the tall metal gates. James parked the Jag and climbed out quickly, running for cover under the partially covered entrance to the block. He fumbled for his keys and opened the double locks. As soon as he was inside, he took off his wringing wet coat and shook it as he walked along the corridor.

On Sundays, the factory felt like another place. The quietness of the huge open space was weird after the normal sounds of machines, shrilling voices and shouts to be heard over strategically placed radios in the workrooms. He loved those noises and suddenly felt very alone.

The lift – finally working – took him to the fifth floor and soon he entered his office where he opened a teak sideboard and pulled out a half-empty bottle of Jameson's, pouring himself a stiff measure into a crystal tumbler. He drank the whiskey quickly, savouring its flavour and warmth. Almost instantly, he felt better. He threw himself heavily into his chair and mused over the past forty-eight hours with Caitlin.

Christ, she'd been everything he'd dreamed of and more. She'd been loving, sexy and great fun. He'd found her clever and a wonderful listener. She'd made him feel fully alive and carefree for the first time ever.

Sadly, the feeling didn't last long. Fear slithered into his thoughts. Its cruel negative voice attacked his newfound peace.

What would his uncle do if he found out about Caitlin – after he'd been so generous and he warned him not to get involved? His father too would go ballistic! They were Protestant and she Roman Catholic. It couldn't be! She was right; they were from different worlds.

These thoughts raged round his head until he had no choice but to make them stop and angrily slapped his hand down on the desk. The empty tumbler jumped as he called out: "Enough!"

His hand shook as he poured himself another huge slug of whiskey, and this time murmured despairingly, "Enough… please."

He shuddered, feeling desperate, put his face in his hands and closed his eyes. He could hear his inner voice, this time posing the other side of the argument.

I have a beautiful, trusting lover who unmistakeably adores me. She is loving, giving, helps me in my work and makes me laugh. I must be out of my mind to feel worried or depressed with Caitlin in my life. She's just made me happier than I've ever been. I can't give up on her. To hell with everyone else!

James felt slightly tipsy and in exasperation slammed the desk again and swore. This time the tumbler admitted defeat and fell to the tiled floor where it smashed into slivers of glass that scattered everywhere.

A soft knock sounded on the glass panel of James's semi-open office door. He kept his head low and didn't look up.

Paddy, another of the security guards, stood by the door and took in the broken tumbler, the near-empty whiskey bottle and James. He was worried by such a sorry sight and asked in concern, "Mr Henderson, are you okay?"

James looked at the guard, feeling utterly deflated. He studied him for a few seconds, telling the man he was fine, but when he tried to stand, he drunkenly slipped and fell clumsily on the floor, where his hands barely missed contact with the sharp pieces of glass. Paddy ran to help and steered him back onto his chair.

Both men were embarrassed as James attempted to sit upright and tidy his clothes. He pushed the guard away gently and said, "I'm sorry, Paddy. Sorry for that. I'm fine, honestly. I'd little lunch and drank on an empty stomach. Hit me a bit harder than I realised. I'll just sit here for a while. I'll be fine. You go on."

Paddy looked at James with genuine concern. He liked this young man. Unlike most of the other managers, James never missed an opportunity to say hello and ask after him and his family. Paddy didn't want to leave like this.

"Are your hands okay, Mr Henderson? I can make you some strong coffee if you like?"

James looked at the broken glass and depleted bottle and answered, "No, Paddy, I'll be fine. Off you go now. I'll most likely be gone when you come back. There is one thing, though. Could you do me a favour – not a word to anyone about this, please."

Paddy nodded and answered man to man, "Of course not, Mr Henderson. That goes without saying. You know where I am now. Take care of yourself."

James nodded his appreciation.

"Will do, Paddy. Goodnight now... and thank you."

"No bother," Paddy sighed, and closed the door. He was going to make the lad coffee whether he wanted it or not – it was a real bummer to see him like that.

Meanwhile, James's thoughts were in chaos. He was sure he was in love with Caitlin but didn't know what to do about it.

He replaced the top on the whiskey bottle and returned it to the cupboard. He opened a window to allow some air in, but large droplets of rain ran onto the sill and splashed inside. He shook his head in bewilderment and muttered at the mess he'd made.

As he picked up pieces of broken glass, his ribs ached. *Christ, what a couple of weeks.*

He carefully placed the glass in a tissue and deposited it in the bottom of the round stainless-steel bin next to his desk.

Eventually, he felt the benefit of the fresh air and breathed in deeply. He remained standing by the window until he recovered himself.

Paddy brought him a large jug of coffee and watched as James drank it, cup after cup. Satisfied that he'd recovered enough, Paddy bade him goodnight again and left. James unlocked a drawer to remove a thick brown lever-arch file. His inner voices were soon drowned out by the contents of the folder – it was his proposal to save Rocola.

Wired from drinking the whiskey and coffee, James arrived home later that evening. He snatched his overnight bag from the boot of the car and entered Melrose. Literally, as his foot touched the threshold, his uncle cried out urgently from the dining room.

"James! Is that you?!"

He sighed despairingly, placed his bag at the foot of the staircase and unsteadily entered the brightly lit room. Roger encouraged him to enter.

"Come in! Come in! Good to see you, boy – by God, you look tired! Heavy weekend, was it?"

He laughed and winked at James, who felt a huge wave of guilt envelop him as he replied meekly, "You could say that, Uncle."

He quickly glanced at his uncle's guests. **Fuck!** Jones again. He was the last person James wanted to see! Fortunately – and with much relief – he noticed that George Shalham was present also and quickly went to shake his hand.

Shalham had never thought for a second that Henderson Jr could manage such a coup as getting the different communities to meet, but by God, he'd pulled it off! It was nothing short of a miracle, and Shalham had to admire the young man's tenacity. Roger was lucky to have him.

Jones remained seated and stony-faced, sullenly nodding at James.

Roger noted Jones's rudeness but suggested James should join them for a late dinner.

"Won't you have a bite with us, James? Mrs Moore's made her Irish roast beef and is about to serve up. We'll just add another plate."

The idea of sitting within sight of Jones made James squirm, but hunger prevailed, and so he agreed. Roger was pleased.

"Great stuff. Sit! I'll go and get Mrs Moore to set another place."

Roger was relieved beyond words to see his nephew. His brother had recently borrowed what little money he could afford and jetted off to the South of France – no doubt to the gambling tables of Monte Carlo. Roger had no idea when he'd see him again and had told James that his father had gone to an army reunion on the mainland.

The atmosphere between Jones and Shalham had been excruciating all evening. If James could help to alleviate it, Roger would be more than grateful. In the dining room, James deliberately sat down next to Shalham, who asked him attentively,

"So where exactly have you been? Your uncle said Galway."

He shook his head. "Not exactly… Donegal Town. I had some friends over from London. They're doing a tour of the Republic."

George smiled affably and, in an effort, to embroider the lie, James added, rather too eagerly, "I tried to coax them to come up here, but

I'm afraid they're all rather nervous. It appears no one wants to come near the Province. It's too dangerous. Sad, really."

Jones chose that moment to interrupt. "Sad my arse!"

James gaped at the fat, unyielding face and thought, *I hate this man.* Jones was drunk again – Roger did seem to be unstintingly generous in his hospitality towards the boor. James refused to rise to the comment, and after that, Jones blatantly ignored him.

Shalham and James shared a glance of mutual understanding as Roger returned from the kitchen.

"All sorted; dinner will be with us shortly!" He immediately noted the tension in the room. He needed to do something so asked his nephew nervously, "Other than partying too much, did you have a good time?"

James could see how rattled his Uncle was and answered merrily, "I did, Uncle Roger. Thank you! I was just explaining how my friends didn't want to come near the North." He found repeating the lie a second time slightly easier.

Poor Roger – unaware of his own faux-pas – answered gloomily, "Wise of them, I suppose. Sad really."

By now Jones's face was creased with irritation. He snorted, drunkenly pushed back his chair and stood up to propose a toast.

"To the Henderson's and to Rocola!"

The other diners remained seated and didn't clink glasses with him but acknowledged his toast with polite nods. Jones fell clumsily back into his chair and, looking directly at James, said belligerently, "I'm a keynote speaker at the First Derry Presbyterian Church later in the week. It's our second big rally hereabouts, why don't you come? I've got everyone riled up. It'll give you an idea of what people really think of that lot of Pope-loving swine you employ!"

Silence enveloped the others seated around the table after his xenophobic words. The only sounds came from the mantelpiece clock that seemed to tick reluctantly and the flames of the fire that appeared to spit in disgust.

Out of respect for Roger, neither James nor Shalham responded to this provocation. James declined Jones's invitation to the rally, without saying exactly where he could stick it.

The meal was a nightmare after that. All the diners except Jones lost their appetite.

Coffee was soon served, and the evening drew to a close.

Jones staggered as he stood and attempted to push his chair under the table. Surprisingly, a huge stocky man appeared from the kitchen and made his way over to help. James watched and thought the man looked like a hoodlum, dressed all in black with a black leather jacket on top. He noticed the man had a tattoo on his lower arm.

The "heavy" helped Jones on with his coat without any acknowledgement from the man himself, who then turned to the others and said with a curl of his lip,

"Gentlemen. A delight as ever."

He snapped his fingers at his henchman and said, "Morris." With that, the two men disappeared into the night.

The remaining diners waited until the pair were well out of earshot.

It was Shalham who spoke first, through clenched teeth. "I-really-cannot-stand-that-man!"

"Nor I!" replied James and Roger in unison.

Roger topped up their drinks. He'd something very important to tell his friend and nephew and had been dreading this moment for weeks. He coughed and said forcefully, "Strongly as we feel about our friend there, we have to remember we need him. For two reasons. First, he has overwhelming influence with the unions all over the place – his word alone or just one snap of those fat little fingers could get them all out on strike. They run the utility companies, the local councils and have the power to stop the cogs of this Province's machinery within minutes. They could cripple what's left of an extremely fragile economy."

Shalham and James knew he spoke the truth. Roger took a deep breath as if he were preparing for a fistfight.

"Secondly, gentlemen, and here I have to be straight with you, I find myself in the unfortunate position of owing our friend a *great* deal of money. That is why I have no choice but to entertain Jones and insist he attend your meeting, James. You have to understand; he could call in my debt at any time. Simply put – he has me by the balls!"

Shalham and James sat gobsmacked, unable to come up with a reply to this unwelcome announcement.

Roger had tried to tell them so many times, but there never seemed to be the right moment. He knew he was a coward. His eyes pleaded for their support and understanding.

"You must see my position! I *had* to keep Rocola from sinking, and once the bank refused to extend my loans, I had no other choice. Somehow Jones knew about it all and offered to help. I was desperate!"

Shalham gulped down his brandy. Visibly perturbed, he walked across to the fireplace where he leaned his head wearily on the mantel. Almost afraid of the answer, he asked: "How much, Roger? How much do you owe him?"

"He has a charge of forty per cent over the company. If I don't pay him back two million plus interest within three months, he can acquire another eleven – giving him control. The bank wouldn't even talk to me, George! What else was I to do!"

George Shalham looked infinitely weary as he responded to this.

"I wish you'd told me, Roger. I really do. This piece of news changes everything. Don't you see? Even if we come up with an idea to keep Rocola open, the final decision could be Jones's. I mean, for the love of God, anyone but him! He's not interested in the workforce. He doesn't give a shit! He hates *all* Roman Catholics. He'd love to close that site, no matter what the hit to him personally, and we all know he could afford it. This is a catastrophe!"

The three men remained silent and deep in thought. Mrs Moore entered the room and quickly noticed their expressions. She decided to turn back to the safety of her kitchen.

Watched by James and Roger, the Chief Constable wandered around the dining room deep in thought. The minutes passed until, in a resolute voice, he declared, "Okay, listen. James, Roger, this meeting of yours... You've achieved something that I and many others thought was impossible. It's a huge accolade to you both – especially you, Roger."

He could barely acknowledge the compliment after his difficult confession but smiled tiredly.

As George Shalham continued, his voice grew stronger.

"Confidentially, I've been liaising with the Secretary of State about this meeting. And he's very impressed. He even suggested he attend, though I managed to dissuade him! This meeting is not about politics. It's about keeping the Rocola workforce and the city alive.

"Gentlemen, forgive me, but I thought for a while there we were quite literally fucked. However, I've got an idea! What if we..."

Chapter Forty-five

"I can't get the hang of this! It's crazy, man!" Robert screamed in frustration at the sky.

They were into their third day of voice coaching, and it was late in the afternoon. He was tired and annoyed. Iowa had taken to the lessons naturally and seemed to have "*got it*". Her attempts at the local Londonderry accent, albeit far from perfect, were admirable. However, it pissed Robert off – badly. The elderly voice coach, who spoke with a cultured BBC accent when he was not speaking the broadest Derry dialect, placed his hand on Robert's shoulder and told him reassuringly, "Listen, my boy. The more you think about it, the more difficult it is. I've told you to close your eyes, relax and listen carefully. Listen to the tone of the words and how they link. It's simply like learning to sing a song. Note the timbre. Come on, young chap – you can do it."

He held a cassette tape in his hand, waved it in the air and suggested to Robert,

"Take this over to that quiet corner and do what I've told you. Tone and timbre Robert. Go slowly. And remember, we're not expecting you to recite the Declaration of Independence in a Londonderry accent! Work on the tone. It's all about listening."

Robert laughed, took the tape from the old man's hand and walked to the corner. He sat and fed the cassette into a tape recorder, placed the huge earphones on his head and listened carefully. At first, he struggled, but as the tape played and his ear became attuned, he relaxed more and began to understand better. He recognised a few local phrases and, as instructed, repeated them one after the other, over and over.

They'd had a debriefing on Saturday morning. It had gone well. After that, outside of the voice lessons, he hadn't seen much of Iowa. Astonishingly, even in class, she'd continued to give him the cold shoulder. He was relieved that she hadn't reported him about the girl. He knew she was within her rights and could have put him in the shit.

For their next operation, they'd been tasked to infiltrate a political party led by a North Antrim man, Charles Jones. The dossier stated he was an ardent Unionist, who over the past few months had been speaking at numerous Orange Order and Unionist rallies. A fervent bigot, he was stirring up hatred. They were certain he was involved – at a very senior level – with the staunch anti-Catholic Ulster Volunteer Force or UVF. Normally they'd leave well alone, but British Intelligence considered him a political threat. He'd talked about bringing the Government down and was adamant there'd been a lack of control in their governance of Northern Ireland. Jones was violently against any initiative by the Government to discuss power-sharing and especially any consultation with the Irish Government in Dublin.

The dossier contained lists of his associates including family, friends and business contacts as well as detailing his regular haunts. His financial portfolio was substantial and proved he was an incredibly wealthy man in his own right. He was well in with not just various high-level political associates and unions in Ulster but, more worryingly, in conversation with a number of notorious right-wing parties on the mainland. It was rumoured he'd pinpointed several innocent Catholic men who were then assassinated, coldly and clinically.

Robert's and Iowa's task was to observe and gather as much information as they could on him. Nothing more. It was early days, and at this stage, it was to be only a monitoring exercise until they gathered more evidence. They'd seen his calendar for the next few weeks, and he was due to attend numerous rallies and meetings.

What drew Robert's attention, in particular, was a forthcoming meeting at a local hotel hosted by James Henderson, nephew to the owner of one of the last factories in the city, namely Rocola. Rocola was sited between Stones Corner and Blighs Lane army compound and employed over three thousand men and women. The dossier told him a large number of their delivery lorries were being hijacked and burned by rioters and that many of the Protestant management team had been verbally and physically abused by the locals. Security at the factory was a huge issue, and the factory was bleeding money. It was highly likely it would have to close if something wasn't done and soon.

Miraculously the nephew had managed to get a number of the city's prominent businessmen and women, as well as top Nationalists, Unionists and Church representatives, to meet to discuss the factory's future. He'd also included security personnel from both the RUC and army in the hope that working together, they'd find a way to improve security, keep Rocola open and even raise extra capital.

Robert had read the dossier with great interest, along with an overview of the Orange Order and Unionism in Ireland. It'd been fascinating and, the more he read, the better he understood. It also caused him a great deal of concern. He'd read the pages of the Protestant *Telegraph*, which was packed with pronouncements such as, *"Romanism breeds poverty, ignorance, Priest-craft and superstition"*, and, *"We will terrorise the IRA terrorists, but better!"* It was clear the Unionists felt betrayed by the British Government as they reiterated, *"We will not be bargained over by ANYONE!" "Never, never, never… No surrender." "We will not be sold out!"*

The cassette recorder clicked as it came to the end of a tape and Robert switched it off. He'd had enough for one day. He turned to see Iowa and the vocal coach laughing together. He'd never seen her laugh like that, so carefree and openly. He was taken aback by the transformation in her. She could really be quite pretty. Her eyes were alight as she spoke to the coach, complemented by a beautiful, radiant smile. He removed the tape and walked over to them.

As he approached, the atmosphere changed instantaneously. He saw the light in her eyes, and her dazzling smile disappear. She thanked their coach and walked out of the room.

Robert sighed and gathered up his papers. The teacher felt sorry for the young man and asked him hopefully, "Was that any better?"

Robert nodded and said with relief, "Yes, it was, thank you. I guess I just have to keep practising."

The coach knew it wouldn't be easy. The army expected so much of these undercover johnnies. Trying to pick up such a difficult accent in a matter of days was a truly daunting task. It should be the work of weeks, at least.

"It's never easy at first with this type of accent. There's a bit of a Yankee tone in there somewhere – not easy for a Geordie lad like you, I know. Practise, practise, practise."

He smiled and added, "Iowa is doing well, fortunately. She's a clever girl, that one."

"Hmmm," Robert replied.

The teacher had already sensed the lack of empathy between the two. The atmosphere had proven tense and difficult, especially over the last few days, and probably hadn't helped the young man.

"I take it you two don't get on particularly well."

Robert laughed. *What an understatement.*

"No, not really. Between you and me, she's a pain in the arse! Sorry, excuse my language."

The coach said lightly, "Don't worry. I agree she can be difficult at times... but she'll come through."

Robert was surprised by his comment. He'd had no idea the man knew Iowa, though it explained why she'd looked so comfortable with him before. Robert quizzed him.

"I'm sorry, I didn't realise you'd met before this."

The coach knew he'd said too much and squirmed. This was rather awkward.

"Well, yes. I've known her for quite some time."

Robert couldn't believe it. "*You have?*"

"Sort of, yes. Or, no... I mean, I don't know her that well. I shouldn't say anymore, I'm sorry. Lessons are over."

The man picked up his belongings hurriedly, but Robert held him back, desperate for some fresh insight into Iowa and her attitude to him.

"Please, tell me, what *is* her problem? She's been at me from the very minute I met her. I mean, her attitude to me is unbelievable. I feel like she doesn't have my back!"

The coach stared at him and suddenly looked very sad.

"Kentucky, you know I can't share *any* personal details with you. There is clearly no synergy in this partnership and, believe me; I've fed this back. Potentially it could be dangerous for you both." Robert knew he was right and listened as the old man said guardedly, "I will tell you one thing because I believe it explains her behaviour towards you. Iowa was engaged to a very young and talented soldier – just like you are. More worryingly, he looked like you too. Alas, he was the first soldier to be murdered in Northern Ireland."

With that, the man smiled sorrowfully and wished Robert goodnight. He was left alone, feeling he'd rushed to sit in judgment on her and was keenly regretting it.

The time came for them to attend their first Orange Order rally. It was watch, listen and learn time.

The rally was to be held in the four-hundred-year-old First Derry Presbyterian Church, the only Presbyterian church within the city. Robert's beard had thickened, and his hair had grown a little more. He no longer looked like a soldier. As for Iowa, he still daren't comment on her calamitous dress sense.

She'd turned up in a long, shapeless black coat buttoned from head to toe. It made it impossible to see what she wore underneath – not that Robert wanted to. He was embarrassed. He didn't see any sense in the way she dressed. If anything, she could draw attention to them, which was the last thing they wanted.

She muttered hello, and they left silently through a small, camouflaged gate at the side of the fort. She immediately linked her arm in Robert's, and they started to walk towards the Strand Road that led straight to the city centre. Her continued silence was killing him. He hated silence. As a child, he was forever using humour to break the deafening silence of his unhappy parents, who – for one trivial reason or another – often wouldn't speak to each other for days on end.

Once the voice coach had told him about Iowa's fiancé, he thought he'd give her another chance. Now he told her humorously, "Love the coat!"

She didn't respond so he repeated himself. "I said, love the coat!"

Iowa stopped suddenly and forcibly broke the contact between them by pulling her arm away.

"I heard you," she said, her voice unamused.

Robert laughed. "Ah, it speaks!"

She hissed at him in fury, "Fuck off, Kentucky. I'm not here to be your friend. We've a job to do so let's just fucking do it!"

She linked her arm back in his and attempted to walk on. Robert shook it off as if he feared contamination. Seething now, he yelled back, "Listen, you! I don't need this – what *is* your problem?"

Iowa shook her head slowly.

"Jesus! How many times do I have to tell you – my problem is *you*! They've paired me with a right twat. Don't you realise how much danger we're in? This is all a game to you, isn't it? Why are you even here, Kentucky? You think you're James fucking Bond, don't you!"

She walked on. Robert shook his head in despair and bit his lip. He thought for a second and walked speedily after her before grabbing her arm and spinning her round to face him.

After making sure they were unobserved, he pointed his finger right into her face.

"Listen, you fucked up bitch, I'll tell you why I'm here! I'm here to get those fuckers who tortured and killed my best friend – *all right*? They fucken tortured him, cut him, burned him, used a stick studded with nails on it and hit him over and over! They hit him everywhere – and I mean *everywhere*! And finally, when the fun was over, they assassinated him – a bullet through the brain. They *even pissed* on him!"

Robert felt his eyes well up as he imagined the scene. His heart boomed, almost ready to explode, as he added passionately, "And what was left of him was put into black bin bags and left in the middle of a road, to be hit by lorry after fucking lorry! So that's why I'm here, Iowa. I'm here to find those fuckers who did that to my best friend and *kill them*!"

A soft drizzle began to fall. Robert almost welcomed it. It cooled him down, distracted him from the urge to let her know how much he despised and resented her treatment of him. Instead, he walked around in circles to try and calm himself.

A number of people walked past them and pretended to ignore their heated argument. At the same time, they were intrigued by what was happening.

Iowa was blown away by what she'd heard. She understood exactly how he felt, and his story filled her with raw sorrow. She'd heard about Val's murder but hadn't known Kentucky was so close to him.

She moved to take his hand, but he shook her off. Instead, she attempted to apologise.

"I didn't know, Kentucky. I'm sorry."

Robert walked away, deflated and miserable. She walked a steady two paces behind.

"How the fuck would you know? We don't know *anything* about each other. Just give me a fucking break and act like you're supposed to, will you?"

He stopped walking and crooked his arm. She came level with him, slid her arm through but took his hand, which she never had before. They remained silent but were easier together, more accepting of each other's frailties – her lack of trust, his tendency to fly off the handle – as well as the personal loss motivating both of them.

When they arrived at the church, they looked around carefully and paid particular attention to the faces in the swelling crowd. Before they'd left, they'd studied a series of mugshots of known activists. There were hundreds of people of all ages at the meeting, holding large black-and-white placards adorned in Union Jacks and screaming in unison: "No surrender! No surrender! No surrender! No surrender!"

The pair quickly found a corner on some steps that allowed them to look down on the crowd. The street was well lit. They instantly recognised a few faces and mentally took note of them for the debriefing later.

Soon a pair of car headlights appeared in the distance. The car manoeuvred down the narrow-cobbled street and made its way through the sea of bodies. The chassis and roof were pounded on by the baying crowd, who shrieked wildly,

"No Pope here, Charlie! You tell them, Charlie! No surrender!"

The car stopped, and two burly men climbed out as quickly as their overdeveloped frames allowed. They were dressed in black trousers, shirts and leather jackets, each embellished with the infamous Red Hand of Ulster on the back. Robert was stunned and took a double look at one of the men. This was completely crazy – Morris was one of Jones's hoods. Fucking Morris! Why on God's earth was he here?

Morris and his companion pushed the crowd back as the rear door of the black Rover opened, and Charles Jones stepped out. He waited a while and then raised both hands in the air, playing the crowd. He ceremoniously closed his right hand to form a fist. The crowd loved it and screamed back in delight. From what Robert could see, Jones wore a beautifully cut black suit along with an orange tie and white shirt.

He walked slowly and deliberately up the steps into the pillared church, obviously relishing the adoration and shaking the sea of hands extended to him as he was ushered on and protected by his minders. Soon he disappeared from view. The crowd swarmed together in a desperate bid to get inside after him.

Robert grabbed Iowa frantically, and together they jumped down the steps.

The couple pushed their way forcefully through the crowd. A few of the spectators tutted at their determination, and some were far from happy at being pushed aside. In exasperation, a teenager yelled, "Oi! We're all trying to get in. Leave off!"

Iowa looked at him, and suddenly her whole face was transformed. She broke into a wonderful smile and beamed at the young lad. In a near-perfect local accent, she told him, "Sorry. We're dead excited, that's all!"

The young boy blushed and was immediately smitten. He smiled back and laughed apologetically.

"Sure that's all right, miss. Isn't he brilliant? Our Charlie – he's our man!"

Iowa nodded enthusiastically. The blushing boy stepped quickly aside and let them pass. A smile still lurked on Iowa's face as she looked sidelong at Robert, who winked at her. *Clever girl.*

Somehow, they managed to find a space at the very back of the church, but their view was hindered by one of the many wooden pillars. They could, however, hear everything as the speeches began.

The first speaker was boring beyond words and talked incessantly about Protestant reformation along with his own fundamentalist beliefs. Robert hadn't a clue what he was going on about so looked out over the crowd. It was obvious that neither did they. Most of them yawned with boredom or sat with their heads lowered, picking at their nails, praying that his speech would soon end and Charlie would get up there. Twenty minutes passed until the speaker ended their pain. A few loyal listeners clapped and the remaining, but relieved, congregation dutifully joined in.

It was time for Jones to step up to the pulpit. As he took his place, the congregation went wild. They cheered, wolf-whistled and applauded. *This was why they were here! This was their man, their future! He'd the balls to say what they all thought! He wasn't afraid of anyone, not their Charlie!*

Jones nodded and used his hands to indicate he needed calm and quiet. He fiddled with the microphone until it suited his height and gently tapped the top. It responded, and he coughed. He lowered his head in thought until finally he looked up and in silence, stared into the crowd.

He purposely focussed on a few individuals at the front until they began to feel uncomfortable under his stare and squirmed visibly. Then he began speaking.

"Good evening, all of you. Thank you for being here tonight. I am privileged to be talking to you in such beautiful surroundings. We are so lucky to have this amazing church in which to congregate, but more importantly within *our city and our walls!*"

The crowd roared and howled their approval as Jones attempted to speak over their outburst.

"We *must…* we must remember the many fights we have fought to be here together tonight. We *must* remember the Siege that proves us as Ulster men and women, if we have to starve again to save this city and Union, then starve *we will!* We will *never* give up! We will *never* give in to those Catholics who breed like rabbits and multiply like vermin. This is *our* city, *our* Ulster! Our fathers and forefathers fought at the Somme for democracy and freedom for us, our Queen and our Empire! We *MUST NOT* fail them! We *WILL NEVER* fail them!"

The mob applauded and stamped their feet in response. They relished each and every word of Jones's message.

Robert took Iowa's hand again and tried to move in closer. He smiled at those who good-naturedly moved aside and allowed them through. Fortunately, they managed to get halfway up the church and had a much better view of the pulpit and Jones.

His speech continued, hands and arms moving in unison to reinforce his tirade of emotive statements.

"I tell you this: the IRA is the military wing of the Catholic Church! Their Pope-hugging priests claim to be holy men, but no, they are *not!* They're the terrorists too! They are men in frocks who hide guns and bombs and, even worse, hand them out! Their churches are treated as havens for those murderers who plant bombs that kill our innocent Protestant men, women and children. Get them out of *our city, our LONDONderry.* Am I right? Out! Out! Out!"

In unison, the frantic crowd shrieked. *"Out, out, out!"*

Hatred flooded the church like a rising tide. Jones spoke on as sweat beaded his face from his exertions and the heat of the lights.

"We must keep the thoroughfares open for our Protestant faith and our Protestant heritage! Ulster is **ours**!"

Once more the crowd roared in agreement, but this time he waited for them to calm. *This is what he was made for! Look at them – they loved him! He was finally telling them what needed to be said!*

He started up again, vilifying Catholics and their faith, exhorting his own loyal followers to ever greater efforts to keep the Papists in their place. By the time he'd finished, sweat was soaking his collar. Robert felt sick as he listened to Jones's vile words.

"The dog will return to his vomit; the sow will return to wallow in the mire, but by God's grace, **we will not return to Popery again – no Pope here**!"

The crowd went absolutely wild, and the noise of their screaming and clapping bounced off the high ceiling and intensified. Jones's face was crimson, and his thin hair plastered his forehead.

It reminded Robert of the old Pathé newsreels of Hitler's rallies where he'd spat out similar words of hatred against the Jews. *Jesus, they were right to be concerned – this was one mad bastard!*

Jones pushed his hair back from his face, impatiently. He wasn't finished.

"I'm here to tell you as people of Ulster to think long and hard. Listen carefully as I tell you this. The British Government has failed us! They talk incessantly about power-sharing. **Over my dead body!** They are in collusion with the Catholic Irish Republican Government. But will they talk to us? By God, they won't! **US,** who have fought in so many wars for **OUR** Crown! **US,** who fought and starved four hundred years ago to keep this city under Protestant rule. The British Government is a traitor to us! They are forcing this upon us. I tell you now, as God is my witness, *I will not have it*! **WE WILL NOT HAVE IT**! We will *not* be bargained over by anybody. Ulster will fight, and Ulster will be right! There will be *NO SURRENDER!*"

That was it – he'd finished! With one fist raised high in the air, he began to get down from the pulpit. The crowd screamed and surged forward, desperate to touch him. This was exactly what they wanted to hear. They fought hard against each other in their attempts to get closer. Some slapped Jones on the back or patted it lovingly; others raised their fists and screamed. The air was electric as they cried repeatedly: *"No surrender! No surrender!"*

Chapter Forty-six

Caitlin had been fretful for days. James had been distant with her ever since they'd come back from their weekend away. She'd just woken up and found herself lying on her bed, fully dressed. She'd been so upset the night before that as soon as she'd arrived home, she'd spoken to no one but disappeared to her room where she'd fallen asleep.

Other than for the blue neon hands of a cheap bedside clock, her room was dark. It was 4.30 a.m. She removed her clothing quickly and climbed back into the bed in just her panties, pulling the blankets tightly around her. Her eyes closed, and she wished for sleep, but it eluded her. She tried her absolute best to empty her head of troubling thoughts but instead reflected over the past few days.

She'd been nervous about returning to work on Monday morning and seeing James but decided she'd act as if it was business as usual and take her lead from him.

In the end, though, she'd hardly seen him; he'd been confined to his office with his uncle and the accountant. He'd been in a foul mood with everyone, and she felt he was commanding her when he asked her to fetch him file after file in a snappy tone. She hated him for it – hated too the way Mrs Parkes's beady little eyes noted their every brusque exchange with a trace of malicious pleasure.

By the end of the day, Caitlin had begun to wonder whether the weekend actually happened. He'd obviously got what he wanted – another notch on his headboard. Anne and her mother had been right all along. Caitlin was angry and ashamed. She felt like a naive fool.

Anne's brother had called to the house whilst she'd been away and left a message for her. Anne finally wanted to see her, so after work on Monday evening, Caitlin called in. She desperately wanted to see her friend too but almost immediately regretted her efforts. Anne was a mess. The RUC had identified the bombers but couldn't – or wouldn't – charge them, claiming lack of evidence. Another one of the many injured had died early that morning and for the first hour or so after Caitlin called in her friend had done nothing but sob uncontrollably.

When she'd finished, Caitlin suggested they have some tea and unthinkingly presented Anne with a gift box of toffees she'd bought on the way home from Donegal. Originally, she'd bought them for her mother but thought Anne would enjoy them more since Majella was still barely eating. Anne, tear-stained and wretched, removed the cellophane from the box and was curious as she studied the covering image of a village.

"When were you in Donegal?"

Caitlin screamed inside. *Christ, how stupid!* She lied badly and defensively in response. "Who, me? I haven't been to Donegal in ages."

"Then where'd you get them?" Anne asked, throwing the box down angrily.

Caitlin decided she couldn't lie anymore, especially after James's behaviour that day, and whispered the truth to her remorsefully.

"James and I went away for the weekend."

"Oh, you did, did you? Jesus, Caitlin. You promised! Have you not got any sense? Where did you say you were?"

"I told Mammy I was at Sinead's twenty-first birthday party in Malin."

Anne sighed and picked up a few of the scattered toffees. She was truly pissed off and couldn't believe Caitlin hadn't listened to her. "And she believed you, did she?"

Caitlin shook her head and sadly whispered. "I told you she's been off her head for weeks, but she's a bit better these past few days and knew I was away. I guess she was too tired to ask more. I'm not sure about me Granny; I think she knows I've been up to something."

Anne was struck dumb for a moment and immediately stopped picking up the toffees. "What! What the fuck is your Granny doing in your house? Yous all hate her."

Caitlin began to get flustered as she tried to explain. "We don't exactly hate her, Anne. That's a sin. Let's just say there's no great love there. She's a cold one although she's been a real help, she's doing Mammy the world of good."

Anne quickly blessed herself twice and half laughed. "There is such a thing as a miracle!"

She took Caitlin's hand and looked at her in the old way. She was genuinely worried about her friend, who looked sad and lost, not at all like someone radiant with happiness because she was loved. Anne loved her to bits but believed this thing with the office Adonis had set Caitlin on the road to disaster. Men like that were users – those professional types always were, with their swanky cars and clothes.

Yet she understood why Caitlin could fall so hard for him. Anything other than the poverty, unemployment, and needless arrests they'd experienced daily would seem like a fairy tale – especially to someone innocent like Caitlin. And to be taken to some fancy hotel in Donegal for a weekend with a rich, good looker... Well, that was something else! A bit of Anne couldn't blame her. However, he'd proved himself a smooth one all right, and Anne already hated him for taking advantage of her friend's naivety. She curbed her anger and decided to approach the subject from a different perspective. Rather than telling her off, she decided she'd listen to Caitlin and be supportive. That way she'd find out the truth.

She looked at her friend and calmly asked, "Okay. I know I'm going on and on at you and I'm sorry. I'll say no more. Let's get straight to the point then. How was *IT*?"

For a moment, Caitlin was confused but soon realised what Anne meant.

Anne cried out wickedly as she stuffed a toffee in her mouth: "You know, *IT*! You and him!"

At first, Caitlin was too shy to tell her friend everything, but Anne continued to sweet-talk her, and soon she proceeded to tell it all – with nothing excluded. They began to cheer up visibly as they blushed and giggled sporadically over the tale. Anne squealed in delight at one detail.

"I told you my wee tit-bits from that magazine would come in handy, didn't I?"

It felt like old times as Caitlin replied jokingly, "You did, Anne. You did. I nearly 'blew' his mind away!"

They almost peed themselves with laughter until Anne asked delicately about Caitlin's day at work and how James had been with her.

"I bet he was full of charm and delight after the weekend?" she said leadingly and noticed Caitlin's face drop. *She knew that look!*

Caitlin couldn't speak as embarrassment and sadness consumed her. She saw Anne's loving face fill with concern, and without warning, she burst into tears.

"God, Anne, he's been awful. He's been in a rotten stinking mood all day and hardly looked at me. I feel like a real bike. He didn't even say goodnight. When he did speak, he'd only ask for one file after another. All I've done all day is carry them in and out. He's been locked up in his office with his uncle and the accountant. I feel so stupid, Anne. I've been a fucking eejit!"

Anne knew this realisation was inevitable. However, she said nothing, only that she was sorry, and tried to coax her friend back into her lighter mood.

"I'm so friggin' sorry, love. Maybe that's just the way he is, and he can't help it? You know what users some men are. You have to try and move on. I know you've got it bad but, believe me, it could be worse. At least you're not lying here like Hop-a-long without a leg!" Anne laughed as she struck the injured limb, emphasising her words.

Caitlin sniffled and wiped her running nose with the back of her hand. How incredibly brave Anne was, but she was right; it could've been a lot worst. To Anne's credit, she hadn't given her friend a hard time. However, Caitlin had seen Anne's expression when she'd first told her. It simply said, *"Told you so."*

It didn't matter now anyway, and at least she had Anne back in her life. She smiled, squeezed her friend's hand and vowed to get over it, but would she? Would she ever be the same again?

When she'd got home, her Granny and Tommy were ensconced in the kitchen, both smiling and getting along grand. It seemed Majella had come down briefly that afternoon and eaten half a bowl of porridge before returning to bed. Caitlin had been relieved to hear it and hoped to have the chance to talk to her, but when she'd glanced in on her mother before going early to bed, she was sound asleep.

Tuesday passed in much the same way at work, and once again Caitlin went to bed early, pleading that she had so much on at work with the conference day looming she needed to sleep. Restless all night, in the early hours, she heard someone up already and saw light streaming from under the closed kitchen door. It had to be Tina, who sometimes came down and ate some cereal if she got hungry.

Deciding it was time she caught up with her sister, Caitlin went into the kitchen but instead found her Granny sitting alone at the round table dressed in a blue towelling bathrobe and smoking a cigarette! Caitlin was aghast. She'd never known her to smoke and thought she hated the habit. The old woman jumped up as soon as she saw Caitlin and furiously stubbed out her cigarette, waving her hands frenziedly in a bid to dispel the smoke and smell. Caitlin could only burst out laughing at her efforts, and for a split second, her grandmother looked back at her angrily.

Eventually, however, she stopped flailing her arms about and allowed a grudging smile to creep across her face. She patted her granddaughter's arm and said, "Okay, Caitlin, you've got me! Whatever you do, don't tell your mother or Tommy. I'll never hear the end of it. Let's keep this one between us, love."

Granny O'Reilly was visibly embarrassed. However, Caitlin decided to take advantage and enjoy having the upper hand for once. For a slight moment, she pretended to think about it but quickly assured her,

"Of course I won't tell. I have to admit, though, I can't believe you. I thought you hated smoking!"

In the past the old woman had, but over the last few lonely years, with Majella and Tommy virtually ignoring her, she'd tried it, and now she needed it – desperately. It kept her sane.

"I know. Say no more," she told Caitlin. "This never happened. Now sit down, and I'll make you a cup of tea and a bit of toast."

She looked at her granddaughter properly for the first time in ages. The girl looked tired and sad, so she asked apprehensively, "Why are you up so early anyway, it's only 5 o'clock? You look shattered."

"I couldn't sleep," was all the explanation she received.

Now that the women had a shared secret, they drank their tea and ate toast companionably, talking about Majella's progress. Caitlin thanked her grandmother for the difference she had made to the house. Martin's name and his trailing mess weren't even mentioned.

After a while, Caitlin rose to leave. She felt better and in a rare feeling of emotion, kissed the old woman on the cheek and told her candidly, "Granny, I needed that. Thank you."

The older woman had enjoyed the moment too and unbent enough to admit it. "Aye, love, it was nice. I'll see you tonight. Don't worry about anything here. Go on now; go to work. Someone has to in this house!"

Caitlin smiled and with a heavy sigh, climbed the stairs to dress and collect her things. On her way, she glanced in on Tina and worryingly found her bed had not been slept in.

Later that morning, Caitlin sat at her desk, staring into space. As expected, James was holed up once again in his office with his uncle and the accountant. She was truly worried now – something serious was going on with the factory. From what she'd seen this morning, it looked like they'd been hard at work all night. She bet that was what all the files were for – redundancies. Shit – they were going to close Rocola!

Her racing thoughts were disturbed when James's office door was thrown back, and he appeared, holding tightly onto the handle for support. He looked exhausted but smiled weakly at her for the first time in days. Unusually for him, he hadn't shaved, his hair was dishevelled and his face gaunt with dark, deep circles under swollen eyes. He looked awful.

Her heart hammered when he asked her, "Caitlin, can you come in, please."

This was it. She would be one of the first to go. Dear God. What would they do at home? They needed her money!

She nodded and self-consciously walked into the room where she acknowledged Mr Henderson and the accountant Mr McScott, who both politely bade her good morning. They looked weary and dishevelled too. James gestured for her to sit down in a vacant chair next to his Uncle's.

James sank into his own chair, looked evenly at Caitlin and told her gravely,

"We have a big problem, and we need help."

Her heart skipped a beat and then another, as finally, James told her everything.

Chapter Forty-seven

*The day of the meeting at the hotel finally arrived, and Honey was full of raw fear. She thought about the last time she'd seen Kieran at his aunt's and specifically remembered the moment she'd recognised the black-clad old man in the photograph standing in pride of place on Kay's sideboard. She couldn't understand why she hadn't thought of it before as an idea popped into her head. It was a good one. No – it was more than that – it was perfect. He'd been around her all her life, and she trusted him totally. It meant she could tell him **EVERYTHING** and then maybe he'd help her, tell her what to do to get out of this nightmare. Relief overwhelmed her. He couldn't divulge to anyone what Kieran had made her do – not to a single human being.*

She shuddered as she thought about what Kieran did to her that day. It had been humiliating and had frightened her senseless. Ever since, she'd struggled to sleep as, night after night; she'd suffer the most awful nightmares where he'd murdered her family and cruelly told her time and time again that it was all her fault. At times, she'd been so desperate that the thought of killing herself and ending it all seemed a way out but, in the end, she couldn't – it'd be a sin and anyway she didn't have the guts. She felt a thousand years old.

She was cold and stood out as she sat at the end of a wooden pew in the church amongst a row of silent, patient and weary old men and women. It was a Holy week at St Mary's, and Confession was being held extra early in the mornings. To pass the time, she watched the elderly parishioners take their turn in the confessional and then leave quietly with discreet smiles and nods to those still waiting. Her heart beat so loudly she could almost hear it hammering. She feared his reaction when she told him. She knew he'd be furious, but he had to help her – he must!

After a lifetime, she was next and rose to enter the Confessional when, without warning, she heard loud footsteps stamping down the middle of the long church aisle. She looked around and was surprised to see Father McGuire. Who then was taking Confession? She hesitated to accost him as he strode towards the altar, mumbling loudly. He didn't see her, seeming harassed and far from his usual authoritative self. At the altar, he quickly blessed himself and strode off in a hurry towards the vestry. She started to run after him, alarming him when she wildly called his name.

"Father! Father McGuire!"

The surprised priest turned around. When she drew level with him, she looked into his eyes and noticed they were badly blood-shot; in fact, she thought the priest looked excruciatingly old and tired. Nevertheless, just being in his presence was a huge relief to her.

"Father, I need to talk to you. It's really important," she began.

He held up his hand and shook his head. He couldn't listen to another outpouring of minutely detailed trespasses and self-reproach – not today. For years he'd miraculously managed to control his drinking but to his dismay had failed miserably last night. It was the first time in fifteen years he'd missed the retreat but, remembering the reason, he felt he surely couldn't be blamed for having a drink or three too many. He'd driven a young PIRA man tucked in the boot of his car over the border late last night. The whole experience had taken its toll on him, and he was left riddled with remorse and fear along with a cracking hangover. He didn't have the energy or time for anyone. Not now at least. He put up his hand for her to stop as she pleaded with him.

"It's good to see you, but I'm sorry – I have to go to Magilligan Camp. There's been some serious trouble and a couple of prisoners are in a desperate state. If you'll excuse me?"

He attempted to walk away, but she grabbed his black sleeve manically and squeezed it tight. She felt her eyes well up as she pleaded.

"But Father; you must listen. I have to talk to you; it's important…"

The black-garbed priest attempted to move on.

"You're not hearing me. I can't. I have to go!"

Determined to make the old man listen, she squeezed his sleeve even tighter and dragged him closer to emphasise her point. Through gritted teeth, she told him:

"Father listen to me. You have to. It's about Kieran Kelly… He's made me do bad things, and he wants me to do more."

For the shattered priest, the young woman's tone and her effrontery in touching him were too much. She was annoying him. He roughly pulled his arm free then looked at her properly for the first time and frowned. The skin on her face was red and sore and, added to the look in her wild watering eyes, the sight of her frightened him slightly.

Lately, there'd been onerous demands and heart-wrenching duties coming at the old priest from all directions, and they were beginning to take their toll on his health, both physical and mental. He knew he was neglecting his parish and was angry and frustrated with himself. He gazed at the hysterical and most likely hormonal young woman, crying openly in front of him. He couldn't help her. He just couldn't. He didn't want to hear about her boyfriend troubles. He had to leave and with relief looked to the back of the church to see a dark-haired young priest exit the Confessional box and approach them. Father McGuire urgently signalled for his novice to hurry.

"I'm truly sorry, but I have to go. Father Moore here will help you. Calm down now, please. He'll look after you. He'll hear your Confession."

To his dismay, she screamed like a banshee and grabbed him, determined not to let him go. "But, Father, you don't understand. I trust you. It has to be you! Please, Father; you've got to listen to me. Please!" The confused young priest immediately noticed something was very wrong and began to run to help his mentor.

Father McGuire, by now desperate to get away, gently detached himself from the girl and urgently walked towards the running priest. "Father," he told the novice, "this young lady needs to make her Confession. As you know, I have to be elsewhere. Help the wee mite now, will you? She's very upset, and I have to go, really. I'm already well late."

The young priest nodded solemnly and attempted to take the girl's arm and move her back towards the Confessional boxes. Instead, she furiously pulled herself away from his touch and glared insolently at the priests. This was useless! She took a final enraged look at her lifelong spiritual adviser then spat in his face.

"Forget it… and forget your fucking God! Where is He when I need Him most, eh?"

With that, she left the two stunned men standing before the altar and ran back down the long aisle to burst through the church's double doors and out onto the steps. She sank down on them despite the rain, put her face in her hands and cried. She was appalled to think of what she'd just done. She'd never done anything like it before... And to poor old Father McGuire in his own church! She hoped he'd follow her outside and fetch her back in. She desperately wanted him to, but after a while, when he didn't appear, she knew she was on her own – again.

Inside the church, the young priest attempted to wipe spittle off his mentor's face and jacket with his dirtied handkerchief but his efforts were quickly brushed away by Father McGuire's shaking hand. The long-suffering priest had never dreamed he'd see the young girl behave in such a way. As he thought about what she'd done, the hairs on the back of his neck began to rise. For her to do such a blasphemous thing meant something was indeed very, very wrong.

He fought to remember the name of the man she'd mentioned and hit his head with his hand in frustration. Kevin... Keith... No – Kieran, that was it. Jesus wept, not Kieran Kelly! He knew all about the lad from his Aunt Kay and immediately understood. "Bad things" she'd said. Kieran was making her do bad things. What sort of things? The old priest stood there speculating until Father Moore nudged him and told him he'd better get moving. They'd talk about what had happened when he got back from Magilligan.

A small voice in her head told her no one was going to help her, ever, and she'd no choice but to do what Kieran wanted. He'd warned her if she didn't follow his instructions to the full there'd be fatal consequences. He'd given her the keys to his place and ordered her to put on a school uniform, plait her hair and wear no makeup. She was to become a schoolgirl again and deliver a parcel to him at the City Hotel that he'd left ready for her on his bed. He'd said he'd kill her if she opened it.

She stood up to leave. This would be the end of it. She knew she was too close to breaking point.

Chapter Forty-eight

Early the same morning a few miles away, Robert and Iowa sat outside Charles Jones's Regency red-brick townhouse in their undercover car. Since Kentucky's revelation about Val's murder, Iowa had been more forthcoming, and the atmosphere in the car was alert but devoid of tension. The streets were quiet. Iowa wore a thick red jumper and blue jeans, with her hair tied back in a neat single plait. To Robert's amazement, she looked perfectly respectable, pretty even.

A young man caught Robert's attention as he walked quickly past their car. Dressed in smart black trousers, a white shirt and black coat, he muttered incoherently to himself. Robert felt something was not quite right about him. He saw a name badge under the coat but couldn't read it. On a street patrol with his unit, he'd have stopped him on sight but he couldn't – not today. Robert continued to scrutinise the man until he disappeared around the corner. He was likely being paranoid, and the youngster was simply on his way to an early shift at work.

Iowa nudged him to look at the townhouse. The glass-panelled front door had been opened, and Billy Morris was standing outside, carefully scanning the street. His eyes fixed on their battered Austin Marina, and he raised his hand in salute before he went back inside. Robert felt the knots in his shoulders ratchet up uncontrollably. "Shit!" he yelled.

He had Iowa's full attention now – he'd scared the living daylights out of her. "What is it?" she asked, having assumed the hand gesture was to another of Jones's goons.

"He's seen us." There was nothing they could do.

Iowa was confused at seeing Kentucky so panic-stricken when there was no apparent threat.

"It's just one of Jones's goons doing his best to show the boss how vigilant he is. What's the problem?'"

"He's not just a goon – it's Billy Morris. I know him! He was a soldier, and he's one psychotic bastard. I saw him at the rally the other night too. I checked with Intel after that and turns out Billy's been up to his old tricks. I saw him pull some stunts when we served together – excessive force, shooting before we got the order – everyone knew he was a loose cannon. Turns out he beat a fifteen-year-old lad to death while we were off in training on lockdown. The kid had thrown shit at him while we were on street patrol – Morris always said he'd get even. He should be in military prison, but it seems he had an influential contact… Mr Charles Jones. The army washed their hands of him, dishonourable discharge, but no other sanctions. He's a Loyalist of the worst kind – and I mean the worst!"

Iowa couldn't believe this was the first she'd heard of any of this. She was about to tell him so in no uncertain terms when the door to Jones's mansion was nudged open, and Morris reappeared.

"Look, he's clocked us, he's coming over!" she said.

They waited like sitting ducks while Morris made his way carefully across the street holding two steaming mugs. As he drew closer, he studied the passengers through the windscreen and made for Robert's side, knocking on the driver's window with one elbow. Robert lowered the window reluctantly as Morris bent down to look in.

"Would you like a cup of tea for yourself and the wee lady?" the big man enquired breezily.

Robert tried his best to draw on his vocal training and answered in a very poor Derry accent.

"Naw, thanks."

An alarm seemed to go off in Morris's head. His eyes narrowed suspiciously as he took a closer look at Robert and asked curiously, "I know you from somewhere, don't I?"

Robert shook his head, rubbed his bearded face and mumbled, "Nah. Don't think so."

Morris was pretty sure he did, but he wasn't bothered, he'd too much to do, and he needed to get on. He offered Iowa a hot drink, but she declined. At their slight, he told them contemptuously, "Me and Mr Jones have been watching you two since you got here. We just thought you might want a wee cup of tea to pass the time an' all. Mean to say, that car of yours stands out like a sore thumb – two eejits sitting about in it at this hour. I do believe we've blown your cover!"

With that, Morris straightened up and simultaneously poured the hot tea onto the roof of the car, roaring with laughter as the liquid spilt into the driver's seat through the open window. Robert swore as it burned his legs. He struggled to roll up the glass. Morris laughed heartily and called through the receding space: "Good to see you again, Sallis. Not sure about the beard, mind!"

Robert and Iowa looked at each other in dismay as Morris, with a cold, calculating smile on his plug-ugly face, whistled his way back to the townhouse. Halfway across the road, he stopped suddenly and ran back to the car. He indicated for Robert to open the window again. Reluctantly he complied.

"By the way, Sallis," Morris told him gleefully, "we know who did your mate Holmes in. I suggest you and that spying cunt alongside you there go to fuck, get out of me sight, and leave it to us real professionals to get the Fenian bastards!"

Robert was distraught at this revelation and struggled to convince Morris to tell him more. His pleas were ignored as the ex-soldier laughed contemptuously and returned inside the house.

Shocked beyond belief, Robert switched on the engine and sped away. The wheels screamed in fury as he accelerated. His rage was mounting just as fast.

"Fuck! Fuck! I hate that bastard. He knows who killed Val! Can you believe it, that arrogant dickhead knows who killed Val? Disloyal bastard. I swear I'll kill him!"

The shock and distress he felt were too much to bear. Tears flowed unreservedly down his face. Iowa watched him, rendered speechless for a moment. Not only had he lost it, but their cover had also just been blown, *and* she knew his surname, which was counter to operating procedure. They'd better get back to barracks and their handler – fast! She gazed at his red face, appalled.

"Kentucky, Sallis… whatever your name is… just cool it. You'll draw more attention to us. We need to get back – right now!"

Robert was mortified at breaking down. He slowed the car and pulled into a lay-by where he turned to face her. He was confused by her suggestion and shook his head.

"What do you mean, go back? I'm not going anywhere with my tail between my legs. Didn't you just hear what that bastard said – he knows who killed Val, and I'm going to find out who they are then hunt them down!"

Iowa answered obstinately, "No way, Kentucky! Fuck it all; Morris knows who you are! Don't you understand? You can't risk going any-where near him."

Robert didn't give a damn and cried angrily, "I don't care! I'm going back!"

He was about to drive off again when Iowa grabbed his arm. She nipped his skin with her nails and said calmly, "Stop and think, man. Just slow down and think for a minute. Please."

Robert remained motionless, groaned loudly and put his hands to his face. What a mess, what a fucking mess! Iowa was right; they should go back. Their handler had warned them if their cover was blown, they were to get the hell out. But Robert couldn't go back. He just couldn't. He owed it to Val to find out more.

A plan formed in his mind. Jones was due at the meeting at the City Hotel that day, and where he was, Morris wouldn't be far behind him. If Iowa wanted to go back on her own, that was fine.

He steadied his breathing and told her, "Listen, I'm sorry our cov-er's blown. I really am. You can go back but, remember, we're finished on ops in this city if we tell them what's happened. Or… we can go to that hotel and wait 'til the bastard is alone and then you and me, we make Morris tell us who killed Val. I'm going in any case. It's up to you what you do."

At these words, Iowa knew she'd no choice. She couldn't leave him – not now he had a chance to avenge his mate's death. He was right: if they admitted they'd lost their cover, they'd likely be thrown on the scrap heap. She couldn't allow that to happen until she'd had her pay-back too. "Okay," she told him tersely.

Robert put his foot down, and they made for the City Hotel.

Chapter Forty-nine

Caitlin walked up the steps into the hotel lobby at 7.30 a.m. There was no doubt it was going to be a long, stressful day, but that didn't matter. She felt so much better since James had explained everything. It all made sense to her now, and she understood why they'd been so secretive. She knew about Charles Jones's loan and the consequences for Rocola if it wasn't paid back. Hopefully, if they'd done their preparation properly, a way out was at hand.

There'd be forty-five attendees at the meeting – a terrific turnout. The Catholic Bishop of Derry had suggested a new local parish priest should take the minutes of the meeting. Caitlin was to do the same – that way they'd ensure everyone was absolutely clear on what they had to do and by when. The agenda had already been sent out, and every speaker briefed on what they had to present that morning and how to prepare for the brainstorming session in the afternoon.

Unexpectedly, Caitlin had been invited to James's house the previous night, to run through some last-minute changes. His home had overwhelmed her, and it was there that she'd met George Shalham for the first time.

At first, she found it incredibly difficult to speak to the Chief Constable. He and the uniform he wore represented the enemy. To her surprise, as they were introduced, he'd shaken her hand and spoken sympathetically to her.

"Caitlin… George Shalham. I'm sorry to hear about your father."

She gasped at that but held his gaze defiantly. *How dare he!* She stayed speechless, and he continued, "I was, of course, aware of the tragic incident. After what young James here told me, I've instructed my officers to work closely with Brendan – Brendan Doherty – I believe he's your solicitor? I'll make a point of keeping a close eye on things."

She didn't believe a word he said but knew she had to appear professional so forced a smile and thanked him. James was pleased George had made such an effort and smiled at Caitlin, who stared back stonily.

Together with Roger Henderson, the four of them spent the next few hours running through the next day's schedule with a fine-tooth comb. Every minute of the day had been planned and thought through. This was their golden opportunity, and they had ensured that none of the time would be wasted.

Caitlin studied George Shalham as he talked about his security plan. She hated herself for subconsciously warming to his enthusiasm, but it was clear he too wanted the meeting to be a success. He assured them that the guests in the main hotel and the wedding parties would remain oblivious to their meeting as all the attendees would arrive by the back entrance, at a designated time, using the service lifts. They'd be searched and escorted straight to the conference area, which would be closed off to the general public. Only a few extra security staff and a select number of hotel employees would be allowed access to the main meeting area.

Roger Henderson eyed his nephew's assistant closely throughout the meeting and Caitlin was worried he'd sensed there was something between her and James. All in all, it'd been a strange and stressful evening, though a bittersweet opportunity to be close to James again.

This morning she felt good and was well prepared. She and James would meet and greet the guests as they arrived at the third-floor conference area. Today she wore her favourite black skirt, white blouse and black jacket. Her shoes were flat and sensible. She glowed when she saw James approach her with an admiring look in his expressive green eyes.

Last night, as soon as they'd finished their meeting, he'd arranged for a taxi to take her home. As he led her out to the car, he apologised again for his recent behaviour.

"Caitlin, believe me, I'm sorry for acting like I have the past few days, but when my uncle confessed about the hold Jones has over him, it knocked me for six. Charles Jones is a racist thug – a highly dangerous man, not fit to live in civilised society. My poor uncle only became involved with him because he was desperate. You've probably noticed Uncle Roger continually watching us? So… I had to pretend to be a cold-hearted bastard otherwise he'd guess how I really feel about you, and he doesn't need anything else to worry about at the minute. I know I've been a total pig to you but, believe me; it's been tearing me apart, seeing you so sad."

Caitlin was relieved beyond words by what he'd said and retorted jokingly,

"Well, you did a bloody good job. You deserve an Oscar!"

They both laughed, and she finished, "It's fine. Though I admit, I thought you'd had your bit of stuff, and that was it."

She couldn't have been further from the truth, though he wasn't going to embarrass them both with protestations in front of the taxi driver. He'd felt awful about it but had no choice. If his Uncle found out about them – on top of this disaster with Jones – it could likely kill him as he'd been running himself into the ground lately, worrying how he was going to save his business and the workforce's livelihoods.

"I know. I can't blame you for thinking like that, and I'm sorry. But once this meeting is over, I promise we'll get away again – maybe we'll go to Sligo, eh? I'll make it up to you; I swear."

She couldn't help but grin. "You'd better!" Deep down, she knew it was unlikely they'd be able to see each other again like that, but just the idea of it made her happy.

Back at the reception desk, a young, fair-haired, good-looking man studied Caitlin as he passed her a written telephone message. She was a looker all right, but better still, what about that gorgeous hunk walking towards her with a certain glint in his eye? He thought and sighed. *Dear God – what I could do to him!*

As though he'd been heard, James smiled, and the young man blushed. Evidently embarrassed, he began to tidy up the desk but couldn't help himself and looked up again at the young couple. Then he saw as a meaningful glance passed between them. *Ah-ha*! Something was going on here! He knew that look. *A secret love – How exciting!*

Caitlin and James moved away from the desk towards the revolving doors, ready to walk around to the rear entrance of the hotel. He brushed her fingers with his and whispered, "Morning, gorgeous."

Caitlin smiled. "Morning, you. How are you feeling?"

James felt liberated from worry – he could see all was good with Caitlin again.

"I'm much, much better, Miss McLaughlin. And you?"

"Much, much better, Mr Henderson. Although nervous about today."

James nodded, "Me too. Remember, we've thought of absolutely everything… so let's get this show on the road!"

Billy Morris drove his employer's Rover across Craigavon Bridge towards the City Hotel. He grinned to himself as he remembered the look on Sallis's face. He'd never liked the smarmy Geordie shit. It'd been a class and brilliant wind-up, given Morris had no fucking idea who'd really killed that joker Holmes, but seeing Sallis so desperate had given him a thrill. Perhaps playing with his head was more painful than anything he could inflict with his fists or feet.

Life was a blast now that he was out of the army, and he idolised Jones. If Billy had to, he knew he'd give his life for the wee man. Everything Jones preached hit the perfect note with Billy, and he could listen to his boss talk all day. The British Government had no fucking idea what was going on here, and everything they were doing was wrong! When that little Catholic fucker who threw the shit and piss over him on patrol had walked into Morris a few days later, he'd run like a rabbit. Morris couldn't let him get away again, and despite his Corporal's orders to stay put, he'd run after the lad and got him in a corner. He couldn't help but beat the Tag fucker to a pulp. Within days he was out on his ear... After serving Queen and Country so unselfishly. Well, this was his army now, and he'd had one purpose only for joining it – to kill Catholics. He was loving it – fucking loving all of it!

Last night he'd been over the moon when the wee man had asked him to do something very special and important for him. As he'd listened to the request, he'd been overjoyed and hadn't thought twice about agreeing. His task would also gain him serious credibility within the Order.

Unlike the British Army, there weren't any rules when you worked for Jones – he'd already proved that many times. The boss was going places, and Billy Morris would have his back all the way to the top.

At Mrs McFadden's suggestion, a couple of days previously Kieran had come into the hotel where he'd been shown around and introduced to some of the staff. He now worked relentlessly in the conference rooms as they prepared them for the weddings later that day. With fine-tuned charm, he'd flirted continuously with the waitresses and Mrs McFadden, but cleverly made a deliberate point of keeping in with the male staff too. At first, they hadn't been sure about him but soon accepted him when he willingly volunteered to do the awkward and heavy jobs.

In particular, he'd pursued a petite young waitress who, from the moment he'd arrived at work, had sniffled and cried over a boyfriend who'd recently dumped her. She was perfect for his plan, so he'd fussed over her and listened as she complained again and again about her cheating boyfriend.

She'd grown to like Kieran and quickly rather fancied him. He was a looker all right, and his clothes were spotless, but importantly he'd listened to her rantings and cheered her up no end – unusual for a guy so young.

Fortunately, Kieran's efforts proved fruitful when the young waitress informed him that a select few, herself among them, had been asked to go upstairs and serve at some VIP business meeting. He knew then that he'd stay close to her – maybe she could get him up there to see what the fuss was all about.

Honey arrived at the front steps of the hotel right on time, feeling fool-ish in a moth-eaten school uniform. When the lone but busy security guard saw her walk up the steps, he'd merely smiled and signalled for her to go straight in. She was just a harmless schoolgirl.

As instructed by Kieran, she walked speedily across reception and sat quiet and unseen in the closed hotel bar. To plan, fifteen minutes later, Kieran sought her out and found her waiting discreetly in a corner. He was pleased. His eyes searched around for the satchel, and as he sat beside her, he asked urgently, "Did you bring it?"

She nodded, pulled the satchel out from under her chair and said un-happily, "Aye it's here."

He shifted closer to her.

"Did you look inside?"

She didn't respond, so he grabbed her wrist and squeezed hard. It hurt her so much that she yanked her arm away and cried, "No! No, I didn't – you told me not to!"

"Good girl." He looked around and saw that they were still alone.

Glancing back, he noticed her eyes had filled with tears and decided to leave her alone to her weeping. She was pathetic.

He grabbed the satchel and in a terse tone, asked, "Have you got the keys I gave you?" Her answer – she drearily threw them on the table. Kieran picked the keys up slowly and stared at her thoughtfully before closing the conversation. "Gotta go, Honey, I have to get back to work."

"Right," she answered sullenly. She hated it now when he called her Honey whereas once she'd loved it. She'd believed it made her special.

He offered her a kiss, but she quickly turned her face away and heard him grunt with annoyance before he disappeared out of the bar, holding tightly to the precious satchel.

She didn't want to go anywhere yet. The awful incident with Father McGuire preyed on her mind. There was no point in rushing off; it was nice and peaceful here. She was exhausted after so many sleepless nights and

rested her head back on the soft chair, closing her heavy eyes with relief.
She'd done what Kieran wanted. It was over.

The credentials of the attendees at James's meeting were undoubtedly impressive. They included the Catholic Bishop of Derry, a number
of Pastors and Reverends from the Presbyterian and Anglican Churches plus leaders and representatives from the Chamber of Commerce
and a few minors from the various political parties. George Shalham
represented the RUC, and the British Army had sent an experienced
Captain who knew the Province well.

The meeting room was beautiful. It was a white-painted panelled
room with ornate plasterwork ceilings and antique paintings of bucolic
Irish scenes. Unfortunately, the rarely seen sun had been blocked out
in the room by large white window shutters that – for security reasons
– remained tightly shut.

The previous night at Melrose, the small group had spent a great
deal of time chopping and changing the seating plan as they'd considered the various religious and political sensitivities of the attendees.
It had proved to be an almost impossible task, but somehow, they'd
managed to make the best of it and were as satisfied as they could be.

In a large square hallway outside the meeting room, coffee and
tea were being served by hotel waiting staff to the clusters of attendees who'd been checked through the rear security point and were now
gathered in readiness.

It was time to start, and James exhaled nervously before announc-
ing, "Ladies and gentlemen, please take your seats."

The volume of noise in the room suddenly increased as the attendees topped up their drinks and filed into the meeting room. James
allowed a little time to elapse and when they were all settled, nodded
to his Uncle.

Roger Henderson felt tired and nervous as he stared out uneasily
at the rows of faces all focussed on him. He'd never enjoyed public

speaking. Hated it, in fact, but conveniently remembered some amusing advice he'd been given a long time ago: imagine them naked!

"Good morning, ladies and gentlemen. My name is Roger Henderson, and I am the owner of Rocola Limited. I sincerely thank you all for being here today for the first of what, I hope, will be a series of constructive meetings." He needed to cough now but refrained. *This was crucifying!*

"The purpose of this first meeting is to help convince you of why it is vital – not only for Rocola's employees and their families but for the city as a whole – that we keep our business operating successfully for the foreseeable future."

He drank a little water from a tumbler and added nervously,

"The files we've handed out contain another copy of the agenda and a set of necessary facts and figures you will need as our speakers make their presentations this morning. We have also included some worksheets for our brainstorming sessions later this afternoon. So I will say no more for now, except to formally introduce you to my nephew James Henderson, who will be chairing today's meeting. Thank you."

And so it began.

Downstairs Kieran was getting jittery. He'd deposited the satchel in the staff locker allocated to him before going back to work. He was finding keeping up a pretence of efficiency and joviality tiring, and physically the work had proved much tougher than he'd expected. At first, he'd almost enjoyed it, but now he was fed up. He'd lifted and laid out something like 400 chairs for the wedding guests —the first of whom he'd already heard laughing and drinking from the specially reserved bar.

At last, he was on his first proper break and sat alone in the staff canteen. He saw the pretty young broken-hearted waitress enter. She looked around, and as soon as she noticed him made her way over next to him. He realised something was up but continued to eat his breakfast. She fidgeted in her chair, clearly dying to tell him her news. Nonchalantly, he lifted a sausage off his plate, put it down untouched and casually looked at her instead.

"What's cheered you up all of a sudden?"

"You!" she answered quickly and giggled at her own boldness.

That wasn't all, and he knew it.

"Well, I'm glad I've put a smile on that lovely face. But that's not it. What's really up?"

She'd been overwhelmed when she'd seen who was at the meeting upstairs. She'd never been so close to the Bishop – well, not since her Confirmation anyway – and he'd been so lovely to her as she'd served him tea. She looked around the canteen to see they were practically on their own. She whooped with excitement and clapped her hands as she told him.

"Jesus, Kieran, it's unbelievable, they've got everyone but the fucking Queen in that room!"

"What d'ya mean?" he asked. His heart jumped and raced wildly. He literally sat on his hands to keep control of his excitement and waited patiently for the silly cow to tell him everything. However, at that precise moment she suddenly realised she might have said too much and wailed, "Shit, I wasn't supposed to say anything. Please don't let on I told you!"

Just as he had with Kay, Kieran pretended to lose interest and noisily slurped down his hot tea before answering her rudely.

"Don't worry. I don't give a flying fuck anyway."

She was taken aback by his rapid switch in tone and the silent treatment that followed. She began to feel bad: after all, he'd been so sweet to her, and he was rather dishy. She sidled over and placed a hand on his arm, saying, "You've been a real tonic to me today. I was dreading coming into work, but you've cheered me up no end. Listen, we were all warned not to breathe a word about this meeting but since you've been so nice and I'm really dying to tell you anyway…"

The girl began to list the VIPs she'd seen in the room. Kieran listened carefully and played her along as he would any other gossiping woman. Jackpot!

Fifteen minutes later, he'd retrieved the satchel from the locker and managed to get into a bedroom carelessly left open by a chambermaid. He locked the door behind him, sat on the bed and quickly opened up the satchel. He first took out a handgun and placed it tightly and deeply down the back of the waist of his trousers. Next, he opened a tightly wrapped package and studied the Memo Park Timer that would give him plenty of time to get away. Finally, he carefully removed a white sandwich box he'd stolen from his Auntie Kay who boringly told him she'd bought a load of the stuff from a recent neighbour's Tupperware party. He pulled off its plastic lid and looked inside at two silver foil-wrapped packets. He threw the top, unopened, packet that contained a cheese sandwich into the bin but took out the lower one and placed it slowly on the bed. He pulled it apart from the top, smiling as he looked down at the sandwich filling. The contents looked like an ordinary square of creamy putty, but this was Frangex – a powerful and deadly explosive. He smiled as he rolled up his shirtsleeves and removed some fine electrical wire, he'd discreetly tied high around his upper arm earlier that morning.

In the early days with the Boys, he'd had basic bomb-making training but had never before put it to use. It was simple, really. Just a few easy steps to put the detonator together and… voilà! As he set the timer to noon, his groin fluttered, and he became slightly aroused. He thought of Alex and smiled as he placed the component into a plastic bag. Later.

By now, Charles Jones was bored rigid. The meeting had been going on for over an hour. He didn't give a shite about Rocola but had to be seen to be doing his bit. He looked across the table at Bishop Hegarty, who sat in his ridiculous attire including a violet zucchetto. Hegarty was a smug bastard, he thought, but he was clever and extremely influential. He'd always been a thorn in Jones's side, and the Protestant hated him passionately, both for the Church he represented and personally.

Ironically, as he'd watched Henderson Jr, Jones almost felt sorry for him. The poor lad had obviously worked hard to get this group of reprobates in one room and most likely knew by now that Roger owed Jones a small fortune that was due to be repaid soon. Charles Jones had no doubt Henderson would default on the payment and then, finally, Rocola would belong to him. He'd recently come up with the ingenious idea of ordering a few of his boys to set fire to a number of their container lorries as they'd passed through the Waterside on their way to Belfast Port – it had clearly put an additional squeeze on their already falling profits. Soon it would be his factory, and he could choose to close it whenever he pleased, bringing misery and penury to thousands of Catholic households. He was determined to let no one get in his way so any misplaced mercy mission that was suggested today would be well and truly scotched by his increasingly useful disciple Billy Morris. Jones had waited far too long to let anyone get in the way of his plan now.

As they'd entered the rear of the hotel earlier, the security team insisted Morris was searched. He purposely wasn't carrying and after being patted down was quickly waved through by the operatives, who'd noticed and admired the Red Hand symbol on his jacket. Jones was next in line, but as soon as the two security men approached him for a pat-down, he'd given them a look of contempt and intoned indignantly, "I refuse to be searched – *do you know who I am?*" They knew exactly who he was and once again quickly waved him through without question.

Caitlin was fascinated as she watched and listened eagerly to the presenters. She sensed they'd done well so far from the looks on the faces of the audience. There was one exception, however, who looked bored rigid, though that didn't surprise her as James had pointed him out to her earlier: Charles Jones.

The atmosphere in the room was relaxed and supportive as a young man spoke passionately about his ideas. His enthusiasm spread like a current of electricity around the room, and James was delighted. The speaker was Tim Hines from the SDLP, who was well known and re-spected in the city. Hines was trustworthy and committed to his con-stituents, many of whom worked in the factory. He understood better than most the catastrophic fall out there would be if Rocola were to close. James liked him and badly wanted him and his party on their side.

The night that Roger had told them about owing Jones the money, George Shalham had come up with a lifesaving plan: they should ap-proach the British Government directly for funding. The scheme was a work in progress so far but definitely one that the Secretary of State for Northern Ireland was keen to discuss, although time was short. They'd less than a month to make their case and finalise the funding. It was a daunting task, but one James believed they could achieve. If the SoS agreed, then Roger would produce this ace to Jones, but only at the right time. They had to keep their plan very close to their chests as Jones could be equally Machiavellian if he got wind that they were planning to elude his grasp.

James watched the arrogant little shit, who looked bored and stared lazily and uninterestedly around the room. He caught James's eye and smirked knowingly. *You're wasting your time, son.*

Downstairs, the schoolgirl began to wake up slowly. She realised she'd drooled in her sleep and quickly wiped it away. She'd no idea how long she'd been asleep and looked around in vain for a clock. The bar remained empty and closed. She stretched and tidied herself up before she walked to the reception area to find out the time.

Chapter Fifty

By now, Kieran had pieced everything together. It hadn't taken long, but he was running out of time and needed to get back, or he'd be missed. He picked up his precious treasure in its plastic bag and left the bedroom.

During the morning he'd watched the staff as they'd filled large silver urns with tea and coffee. When they'd finished filling them, they were placed on top of linen-shrouded trollies and taken upstairs to the conference area on level three.

Coincidentally, as Kieran was about to enter the kitchen, its two swinging doors opened out halfway and stuck there as someone attempted – unsuccessfully – to push over the threshold one of the heavy-laden trollies.

He chuckled and pulled back the doors to aid it through. On the other side stood his pretty new best friend, who moaned, "I don't know why they've asked me to push this thing. I mean, look at the size of me! It's a tonne weight and, to top it all, I've a friggin' ladder in me tights! Mrs McFadden's going to have a fit if she sees me!"

The tiny waitress turned her back on Kieran, looked down and sought out the unsightly blemish on her leg, to see if she could twitch it out of sight – and in the process deliberately gave Kieran an eyeful of what could be on offer.

It was the perfect opportunity. Oblivious to the waitress's charms, he pulled up the linen cloth and, in less time than it took him to breathe, tucked the plastic bag deep inside the trolley. Bloody brilliant!

Beaming at her, he pushed the young woman aside, took control of the trolley and effortlessly steered it over the threshold.

She laughed at his gallantry, fluttered her eyelashes and asked sheepishly, "I don't suppose you could give me a hand with it to the lift? I'm running behind, and they should have had their tea ages ago!"

He didn't hesitate. Even better. "Sure, where to?"

She raised her eyebrows, smiled guiltily and whispered, "Third floor. You can help me get it onto the service lift, too, if you don't mind? That should speed things up."

Kieran nodded fervently and pushed the trolley to the lift. She followed behind and studied him appreciatively "You're an angel today, Kieran Kelly. Do you know that!"

She was right; the trolley was heavy and bloody awkward to manoeuvre. Eventually, they arrived at the service lift, and Kieran pressed the call button. The waitress panicked at the stately pace of the lift as it crept back down to the basement. She walked around impatiently and cried, "Jesus, I'm in real trouble now! What the feck is keeping that lift? What time is it, Kieran?"

He looked at his watch and said soothingly, "Five-past eleven. It's here now. Don't worry."

Morris and a few more men sat outside the meeting room and waited for the first break of the day. He looked around, unsure who the others were, but concluded they were likely security – they certainly looked the part.

Unexpectedly he'd heard a wave of laughter, and a round of applause emanate from the meeting room. A few minutes later, the double doors opened, and a huge cloud of cigarette smoke snaked its way into the hallway, followed by a steady stream of men and women leaving the room. Morris could smell a pipe and was immediately reminded of his brutish father, who had lost himself in clouds of evil-smelling fumes in between regular attacks on Billy and his mother.

Jones was one of the first people out and immediately came over to his watchdog. He brushed down his Savile Row suit and hissed, "It fuckin' well stinks in there! That prick of a Bishop is smoking a pipe!"

Morris empathised, moved closer to him and whispered in his ear, "It won't be long now, Sir."

Jones sniggered as he removed a large bulky envelope from his briefcase and carefully passed it over. *No, not long now.* There was no way he was allowing the Henderson's the kudos of arranging a successful meeting for the city's high ups. And this way he'd settle a personal score too, all thanks to the dogged devotion of Billy Morris. Vicious, unprincipled and ultimately expendable though the bodyguard was, Jones couldn't help but feel a slight twinge of remorse. But it would be up to Morris to disappear quickly once the deed was done.

Robert and Iowa arrived at the hotel late after being held up at a busy checkpoint. It also took forever to find a parking space near the full hotel. Robert hurriedly made his way up the entrance steps ahead of her. As he was about to enter the revolving doors, he was stopped by a security guard, who placed a hand on his chest.

"Sir, I need to search you. You can't go in until you've been searched."

The guard was pissed off. He'd been left to manage the front of the hotel alone whilst all the real action was taking place at the back. He waited for the bearded young man to raise his arms obediently.

Robert stood still. *Shit! He'd never expected this, and they were both carrying!*

Iowa immediately copped onto what was happening and quickly stood next to him. Suddenly a large, noisy Luton delivery van sped up and stopped dead in front of the hotel steps. Everyone turned to watch as within a matter of seconds two delivery boys frantically ran to the back of the van, opened it up and grabbed two huge white floral displays. They were so big they partially hid the boys' faces as they ran up the steps and attempted to push past the guard – a security no-no.

He was angered by their intrusion and turned his back on Iowa, who as she'd been trained, furtively and by sleight of hand passed her handgun to Robert. The delivery boys and the security guard were now in the middle of a heated argument as Robert winked at her, slipped past the guard in the commotion and disappeared into the darkness of the foyer.

Once inside he walked hurriedly to the reception desk and asked a fair-haired young man if he knew which conference room Charles

Jones would likely be in. The receptionist had no idea who Robert was talking about – he'd never heard of Charles Jones, and the name wasn't listed, so he answered truthfully.

"I'm sorry, sir, but from my list, we don't have a Charles Jones here today." He smiled and picked up a ringing phone, thereby closing their conversation.

Robert looked through the revolving doors and saw the guard continue to angrily shout at the two distinctly bewildered and sweating delivery boys. He watched as Iowa pushed herself in front of the men and presented her bag to be searched. She said something inaudible and this time the impatient and harassed guard simply waved her through.

As she came to join Robert, he stared accusingly at the receptionist and whispered what he'd been told.

"I suppose it doesn't surprise me he doesn't know anything. They want the meeting kept low-key. We'll just have to take a look ourselves."

Without hesitation, Robert walked over to a display board and searched until he found a wedding brochure. He immediately looked to the back of the booklet and found a list of conference rooms with both a description and a layout plan. He then read the signboard in the foyer, which told him there were two weddings plus a number of training meetings that day. It also listed the rooms these were in.

"Okay. Let's think. The two weddings take out the large conference rooms on the second floor, and the other meetings… We know where they are. So it's likely Morris will be in or around one of the other rooms, but which one?"

He worked out there were only three likely venues left, and fortunately, they were all on the same floor – level three. He grabbed Iowa clumsily by the arm, slid back her gun and stormed off towards the lift.

Inside stood a young honeymoon couple, who had just finished breakfast in the city and were dying to get back to their bedroom. They waited impatiently for the lift door to close, but Robert stopped it with his foot. He smiled at the annoyed couple, who stared coldly back at him. Robert pressed the button for the third floor, and soon the lift moved upwards.

At the back of the building and in the service lift, Kieran also pressed a button for the third floor. He hummed a tune to the pretty waitress as he pretended to tidy the linen cloth over the trolley. He just wanted to make sure the package was secure and well hidden. The young waitress was still fretful about the time, but more worryingly she knew Kieran shouldn't be with her and she'd be in it up to her neck if anyone saw him. She tensed and said decisively, "You don't need to come out with me, I can manage it now. If anyone sees you up here, I'm up shit creek."

He'd no intention of letting the trolley out of his sight – especially now – and he didn't care if she'd be "up shit creek".

"You're not that late. All I'll do is help you get this thing out of the lift. I won't go near the place, I promise."

She wasn't sure, but what he said made sense.

"You'll just help me out with it and go?"

"Pinky promise!" Kieran laughed as the lift stopped.

He pushed the heavy trolley out of the lift and onto the landing and quickly returned to the lift. He held the wait button. He knew she wouldn't be able to push that weight without him but played her along.

The tiny waitress smiled with relief but was soon exasperated as she struggled to push the trolley along the thick partially carpeted floor. She just couldn't do it and looked back imploringly at Kieran, who nodded sympathetically and stepped out of the lift.

Within minutes, they'd entered a large square tiled hallway outside the meeting room, and Kieran placed the trolley neatly in a corner. A number of the attendees had noticed the arrival of the refreshments and eagerly made their way over. Caitlin was one of the first over; she'd been given a bollocking by one of the women guests who clearly hadn't had her morning dose of strong black tea.

Caitlin whispered harshly to Kieran, "What took you so long? This should have been here fifteen minutes ago!"

Kieran rolled his eyes disdainfully. The waitress apologised to Caitlin for their lateness and started to pour drinks and offer biscuits. Caitlin looked again at the young man and made a mental note of his face. She'd speak to Mrs McFadden about him – arrogant git.

Now that the trolley was in such a perfect spot, Kieran quickly made his way to the hallway but was surprised when he was suddenly yanked back. He assumed it was the stuck-up girl and turned angrily, ready to take her on, but instead was flabbergasted when he saw the familiar face of his lover Alex, who looked furious.

Dragging Kieran aside, Alex hissed angrily, "What the heck are you doing here?"

Kieran couldn't think straight. Fuck… Alex! Alex was here! The Bomb, Sweet Jesus!

*"For fuck sake! What are **you** doing here!" Kieran roared.*

"Ssshhh! Be quiet, Kieran! I'm here with the Bishop."

Kieran was suddenly very, very afraid. He looked at Alex and noticed how beautiful he was in his spotless black suit, black shirt and white dog collar. He'd never seen him dressed like that before. Christ, he had to get him out of here! Christ, They both had to get out!

Kieran swiftly looked at his watch – there wasn't much time.

Caitlin watched the confrontation between the waiter and the priest and immediately sensed something was wrong. She'd begun to walk towards them when Bishop Hegarty rushed out of the meeting room, and called out for his envoy, turning around in a full circle until he saw Alex in deep conversation with a waiter at the far side of the room. With his pipe held tightly in his mouth, he cried out almost impatiently,

"Ah, finally, there you are! Father Alex, where's that tea?"

Alex instinctively turned as he heard his superior's cries and smelled the familiar pipe tobacco whose smoke wafted towards him. He began to walk back when the world as he knew it suddenly stopped as a loud "pop" filled the room, and he saw his Bishop fall down hard on the floor losing his old briar pipe that bounced and skidded across the floor to stop next to a wall.

Alex couldn't believe what had just happened and raced over to his fallen Bishop.

Without being seen, Kieran carefully removed his handgun from the waist of his trousers. He looked around to see where the shot had come from and spotted a hulk of a man standing alone and still. Kieran watched the man as he smiled grotesquely, his eyes tracking every move Alex made. Within seconds he'd taken aim.

Morris was ecstatic; there was another one! Far out! He'd wipe out two of the Papists cunts at the same time!

Kieran knew what was next and screamed out a frantic warning to his lover. "Alex! Noooooooooo!"

Alex heard the warning and froze. There was confusion then as Kieran took aim at the gunman and shot not once, but twice, and then a third and final time. The gunman's body shuddered at the impact of each bullet but refused to fall. He remained stubbornly upright. Morris, with his will intact, even as his strength drained away, fired off two more shots.

Kieran felt a swooshing noise close by and a sharp pain, followed by a warm sensation at the side of his head. Nevertheless, he had to protect Alex and was able to fire one more lethal shot that finally caused the massive gunman to crash heavily to the floor.

Kieran's eyes sought Alex and found him. He was okay. A look of love passed between the two men and Kieran smiled tiredly at his lover as he touched the side of his head with his fingertips. He was baffled at first when he saw they were covered in dark, sticky blood – his blood. He collapsed slowly to his knees and then fell face-first onto the floor. He blinked slowly one, two, three times, as he fought to stay alive until only dead eyes stared out in search of his beautiful Alex.

Robert and Iowa had begun to look through the meeting rooms on the third floor when they heard what sounded like a gunshot. Uncertain at first, they looked at each other until they heard it again and knew it was definitely gunfire. They ran towards the sounds and withdrew their guns as they made their way along the corridor. Out of the blue, a surge of screaming men and women ran towards them and pushed them apart. The couple fought their way through in the opposite direction until they reached a large square hallway and walked into a shambolic scene.

A green-clad RUC man stood with a loaded gun pointed at a uniformed waiter, obviously dead on the floor. Blood from a head wound had formed an almost perfect dark red arc around him. The still body of an old Clergyman whose hand appeared to reach out for a lone pipe lay at the far end of the room. They watched as a second policeman and several security men carefully approached another bulky bloodied body slumped in a corner by the hallway door. They couldn't see who it was. The policemen and security guards nodded to each other in confirmation that the fallen men were dead and no longer a threat.

Oblivious to all, at the back of the room, Jones slinked his way out of the hallway before half-walking and half-running down the corridor after the dispersing crowd. Smiling secretly, he was delighted. To him, the day had been a major success, and without doubt, he was sure they couldn't pin anything on him. He'd planned it all so carefully.

One of the security men suddenly noticed Robert and Iowa, armed and ready. He turned and pointed his gun in their direction, screaming wildly at them.

"Put your weapons on the floor *now*! Hands behind your head!"

Robert and Iowa stood absolutely still. Iowa cried, "Okay, keep cool."

They looked intently at the jittery officer and in unison laid their guns slowly and carefully on the floor, after which they raised their hands over their heads.

George Shalham cried out an order to his officers and the security men. "One of you, call downstairs and tell them to shut this building down and gather everyone in Reception. The rest of you get down there and *do not* let anyone leave this building. I want this place shut down **NOW!**" Caitlin watched as one of the policemen nodded frantically and disappeared down the corridor.

Shalham proceeded to walk off as Caitlin sighed and shook her head. There was something familiar about the bearded man, but she needed to see more. She left James and walked over to the young couple, now spreadeagled and facing the wall. She looked carefully at the bearded man and knew right away where she'd seen him before. He was the soldier she'd seen in her garden and then again on the bus last weekend. Close up, and under that bearded face, she'd remember those glinting hazel eyes anywhere.

Honey wandered around the hotel for some time unchallenged. Everyone appeared busy and ignored her – it made her feel almost invisible, but she was okay with that. She'd managed to have a nosy at the bedrooms as they were being cleaned and even peeked into the conference rooms being dressed for the weddings. They were stunning. She dreamed one day she'd have a wedding reception like that with fresh white flowers, beautiful porcelain table settings and shining candelabra. She sighed sadly knowing it highly unlikely so moved on, keeping away from the lifts and using the stairwells instead.

As she reached the third-floor landing, she opened the door and walked straight into a commotion. She heard something pop like gunfire and thought it likely the staff were having a bit of fun by prematurely letting off some of the wedding poppers.

But she wasn't sure and cautiously walked along the long corridor until she was met by a stream of screaming men and women running towards her. Frightened men pushed sobbing females aside as they fought their way out. They pushed her too and knocked her sideways against the wall. She flattened herself protectively as the tide of people thundered past. What the hell was going on?! Then she knew – Kieran – he'd done something bad again!

She waited until their numbers dwindled and then turned a corner leading straight into a square hallway where a uniformed RUC man was bellowing out orders. He pointed at a waiter, who had fallen to the floor by a trolley. She immediately recognised Kieran's long dark hair and realised that something was dreadfully wrong. He was still as a statue and blood lay spilt and crowned around his head. She knew he was dead and released a guttural scream as she ran towards him. She didn't reach him but was quickly pulled back as pairs of hands coming from all directions seized her. She wailed out in anger as they prevented her from getting to him.

"Ah, Kieran, Kieran! What have you done?! Kieran, God, no! What have you done?!"

Caitlin looked across the room in terror as she recognised the girl's voice. Jesus, no! A sob escaped from her as she rushed to the crying girl.

"Tina! What on God's earth are you doing here?!"

Caitlin pulled the restraining hands off her little sister and tried to take her, but instead, Tina rushed to the waiter's body and attempted to pull his bloodied head up and onto her lap.

But it was all too much for Caitlin, who with superhuman strength yanked her sister away from the dead waiter. Almost immediately, a policeman hoisted Tina out of her arms, and Caitlin's voice became more and more hysterical.

"Leave her alone; she's my sister – let me talk to her!"

The policeman was confused and looked straight to Shalham. His boss nodded, and the wailing, blood-soaked schoolgirl was released to her sister. Tina couldn't believe Kieran was dead. She couldn't understand how she could feel ecstatic but at the same time, devastated. She remembered their beginning when he'd been so loving and kind.

Tina released an ear-splitting scream until Caitlin had no choice but to slap her. Taking a moment, she spoke softly into the girl's hair and implored her to listen. "Tina, it's me, it's Caitlin. Please, listen to me."

She took Tina's face in her hands and forced her to look at her.

Robert and Iowa remained spreadeagled against the wall listening carefully to everything that was being said by the two distraught girls.

Tina had slumped onto the floor with tears streaming down her freckled face. Caitlin tenderly held her hands. "Tina, who is he?"

She appeared surprised her sister would ask such a stupid question.

"He was my boyfriend, Caitlin. I loved him!"

The weeks of fear and remorse finally caught up with Tina as she began to recede into a new safe world she'd built in her mind. A world that encouraged her to forget Val's murder, Kieran's seduction and abuse and now his death. Caitlin watched her eyes mist over, and instinctively knew she was losing her. She needed to find out why Tina was here and weirdly dressed in her old school uniform with plaited hair.

"Okay, love, it's okay, but why are you here dressed like that?"

Tina smiled sleepily and remained silent. Caitlin losing it shook her and screeched: "Why are you here, Tina, tell me!"

The schoolgirl's eyes flashed, and she began to laugh hysterically. In between outbursts of laughter, Caitlin heard her mumble something about a schoolbag and asked her despairingly, "What is it, Tina?! What about a schoolbag?!"

By now, Tina just wanted to go home to her mammy and curl up beside her, but Caitlin was stopping her – she kept asking so many questions, and once again, Caitlin cried out impatiently.

"Tina, you have to tell me. What did he ask you to do?! It's important!"

A split second of sanity entered Tina's mind as she looked at her big sister. She felt heartbreakingly alone as guilt and shame crowded in to overwhelm her.

"My schoolbag, Caitlin. There's something in it. He's done really awful things. He made me do things too… Poor Val. He called me Flower."

Caitlin shook her head in confusion. She'd no idea what Tina was going on about.

"What kind of things?! Tell me, Tina, please, and who's Val?"

But Tina's tired and broken mind couldn't cope any more as she slipped into a marshmallow world, where everything was soft, rosy and welcoming.

Robert and Iowa heard them use Val's name, but the rest was mumbling. They craned their necks to hear more. Robert watched the young girl lie down like a broken doll in her sister's lap and thought, *Sweet Jesus, don't tell me she was Val's honey trap? That child helped kill him! It couldn't be; it's impossible!*

Caitlin, still unbelievably confused, shook her head. She locked her sister tightly in her arms and felt the bearded man watching them. She looked back at him for a second until Robert dropped his head sadly and closed his eyes.

Further up the corridor, James had been helping the attendees, including his uncle, to get away. He quickly ran back to the hallway and stared in shock at the dead bloodied bodies. He wanted to vomit until he saw Caitlin rocking a schoolgirl back and forth like a baby. He couldn't hear as she whispered lovingly into the girl's hair. "It's okay, Tina. It's over, love. He's gone. He can't hurt you anymore."

The look on Caitlin's face was too much for James. Her colour and expression scared him beyond belief. He ran across and knelt beside her. Unsure who the plaited-haired schoolgirl was, he pointed and asked bleakly, "Who is that, Caitlin? What's going on?"

Caitlin looked at James's handsome, beloved face and released her sister, who was promptly lifted and carried off by a bulky policeman. She began to sob uncontrollably as she wrestled to find the right words to explain everything.

"James, that was Tina."

He didn't get it until he suddenly remembered.

"Tina. Your sister! Tina?"

Caitlin nodded and pointed at Kieran. "I couldn't understand everything she said, but that guy made Tina bring something in her schoolbag for him here. Into the hotel, James!"

Suddenly, in a moment of sickening realisation, she'd a good idea what Tina meant and looked frantically as George Shalham's eyes met hers. He recognised fear. She looked petrified, and within seconds, he felt the hairs on the back of his neck rise.

"What the hell is it, Caitlin?" He roared impatiently.

Through uncontrollable sobs, she tried to explain.

"M-Mr Shalham. I… I think he's planted a bomb!" She pointed again to Kieran's lifeless body and cried beseechingly, "We have to get everyone out *NOW*!"

Coming Soon

Stones Corner – Darkness

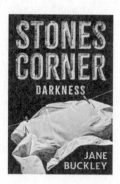

The next instalment from author Jane Buckley; *Stones Corner – Darkness,* captures an era in Derry in the early 70's, considered the **darkest** years of *The Troubles* in Derry.

It reveals the catastrophic fall-out from the doomed Derry City Hotel meeting and how it impacted on the lives of so many; from the rich, vibrant James Henderson to the love-struck factory girl, Caitlin McLaughlin.

Fighting to overcome trauma, grief and poverty in the face of violence and death, once again, the people of Derry continue to portray courage, guts and idealism that prevails through love for family and friends.

Darkness is a brutal, hard-hitting but scrupulously unbiased account of communities on both sides of the sectarian divide struggling to live and love against a background of chaos and carnage.

Pre-order your copy today from www.janebuckleywrites.com.

About the Author

I was born in Derry in the late 60s and, like many young people, I had to leave to find work elsewhere. So, at the naïve age of 17, I moved to London and lived and worked there for over twenty-five years before moving to France. My husband John (born in Cork) and I finally returned home to Derry in 2017. We love living here but had forgotten how unpredictable the weather can be!

I lived predominantly in London throughout the awful time that is known as "*The Troubles.*" It was apparent at the time – and still is today – that not all the facts of the horrific events that took place in Ulster – by both warring factions – were presented in an honest and unbiased way. This was especially true with the media on the UK mainland.

John and I over recent years have recognised that many of the people we've been fortunate enough to meet on our travels around the world, didn't understand why or how the conflict here in the North of Ireland began and continued over a number of decades. I found this particularly frustrating and so decided I'd take it upon myself to perhaps *educate* them and others by writing a historical fiction novel based around the events of this horrific period in our history. I've never written anything substantial before and, me being me, decided I wouldn't write just one novel, but I'd write a series!

It is right for us all to try and move on from "*The Troubles*", but in doing so, it is important to understand how and why they occurred. In any event, we must also take into account the lessons, hardships and sorrows that affected our country, individuals and others so we can continue the healing and reconciliation process.

Please Review

Dear Reader,
If you enjoyed this book, would you kindly post a short review on Goodreads? Your feedback will make all the difference to getting the word out about this book.

Thank you in advance.